T4-ADP-362

MIRKA ANDOLFO

un/sacred

• VOLUME 1 •

Publisher's Cataloging-in-Publication Data

Names: Andolfo, Mirka, author.
Title: Un/Sacred , Vol. 1 / Mirka Andolfo.
Description: Portland, OR: Ablaze Publishing, 2020.
Identifiers: ISBN 978-1-950912-05-6
Subjects: LCSH Angels—Comic books, strips, etc. | Devil—Comic books, strips, etc. | Sex—Comic books, strips, etc. | Fantasy comic books, strips, etc. | Graphic novels. | BISAC COMICS & GRAPHIC NOVELS / General
Classification: LCC PN6728.U56 A53 2020 | DDC 741.5/973—dc23

Un/Sacred, VOLUME 1. First printing. Published by Ablaze Publishing, 11222 SE Main St. #22906 Portland, OR 97269. Sacro/ Profano TM and © 2020 Mirka Andolfo. First published in Italy in 2018. Publication rights for this American edition arranged through Edizioni BD. For the English edition: © 2020 ABLAZE, LLC. All Rights Reserved. Ablaze and its logo TM & © 2020 Ablaze, LLC. All Rights Reserved. All names, characters, events, and locales in this publication are entirely fictional. Any resemblance to actual persons (living or dead), events or places, without satiric intent is coincidental. No portion of this book may be reproduced by any means (digital or print) without the written permission of Ablaze Publishing except for review purposes. Printed in Canada.
For advertising and licensing email: info@ablazepublishing.com

WRITER / ARTIST / COLORIST
MIRKA ANDOLFO

GUEST WRITERS
GIORGIO SALATI, ROBERTO GAGNOR,
MICHELA CANTARELLA, FEDERICO MEMOLA,
DAVIDE G.G. CACI, FRANCESCO ARTIBANI,
MASSIMO SOUMARÉ, DAVIDE LA ROSA,
DANIELE BROLLI, DENTIBLÙ,
VINCE HERNANDEZ, LUCA BLENGINO,
GERO, EMILIANO PAGANI, ELENA ZANZI

LOCALIZATION
MARGUERITE BENNETT

LETTERING
FABIO AMELIA/ARANCIA STUDIO

COVER ARTIST:
MIRKA ANDOLFO

EDITORS
RICH YOUNG & DAVIDE G.G. CACI

DESIGNER
RODOLFO MURAGUCHI

SPECIAL THANKS
MIRKA ANDOLFO
DAVIDE G.G. CACI,
MARCO SCHIAVONE,
FEDERICO SALVAN,
JEFF & BENITA WEBBER

un/sacred

How I met your MOTHER

(That is, the first real meeting of ANGELINA and DAMIANO.)

(And their mothers.)

ANGELINA! SIT LIKE A LADY, NOT LIKE A CHIMPANZEE!
YOU WANT PEOPLE TO THROW BANANAS AT YOU?!
DAMI! DON'T LICK THE CART...
PRENDI 2 PAGHI 10
...OR IF YOU DO, SLATHER ON SOME NUT-HELL-A FIRST, HA HA HA!
PERA SODA
DIABETELLA
YOU ARE SUCH AN EMBARRASSMENT! AS IF IT WEREN'T ENOUGH TO HAVE TO COME HERE LIKE A COMMON PLEBIAN--
I'LL HAVE TO CUT THIS FROM THAT HOUSEKEEPER ASDRUBALE'S SALARY! HEART SURGERY IS NO EXCUSE FOR MAKING ME RUB WINGS WITH--
SAN BIO
VVVH
VVVH
OH FOR SATAN'S SAKE!
WATCH YOURSELF, YOU SNAKESPAWN HARRIDAN!
TUMP
CRAAASH

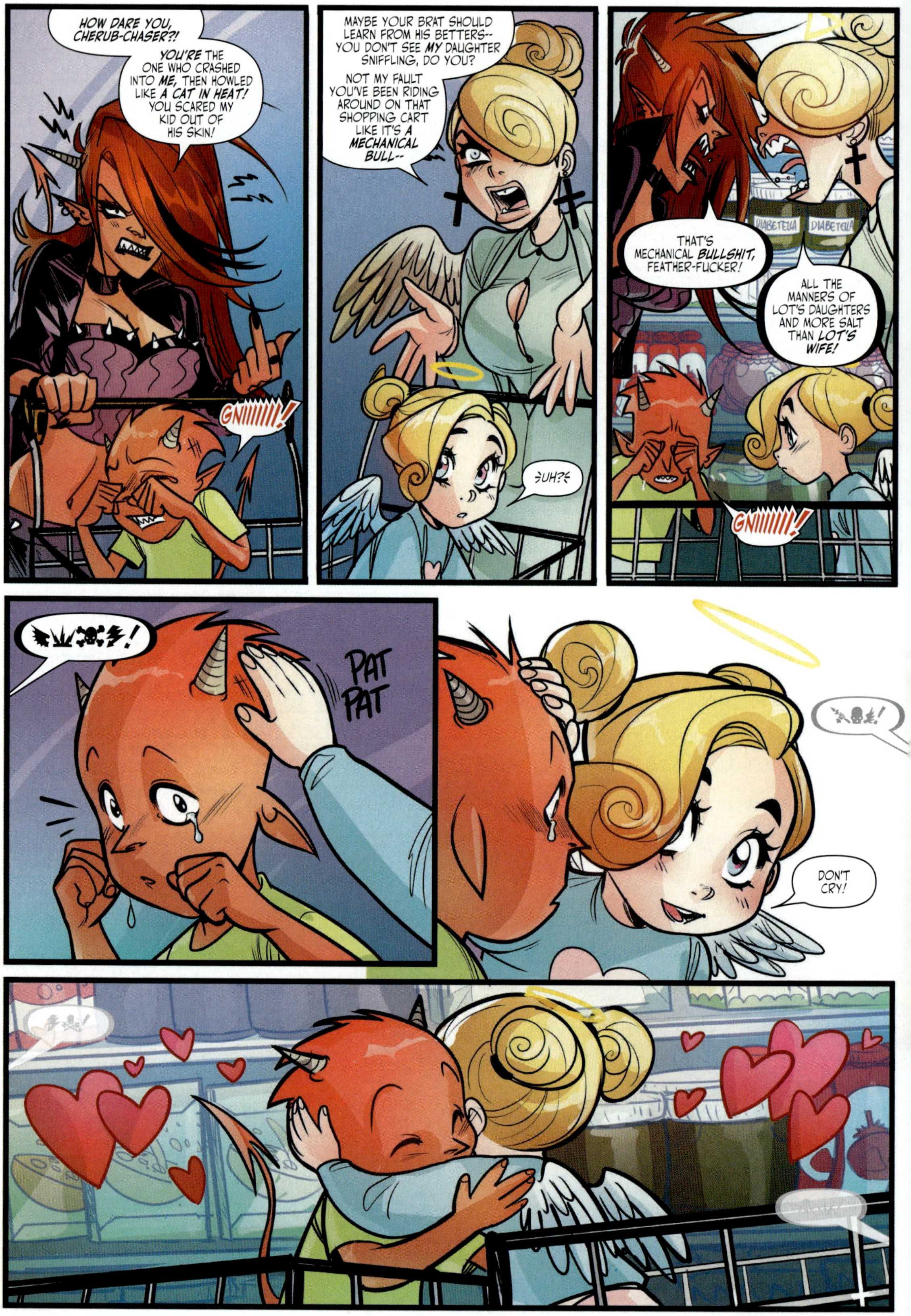
HOW DARE YOU, CHERUB-CHASER?!
YOU'RE THE ONE WHO CRASHED INTO ME, THEN HOWLED LIKE A CAT IN HEAT! YOU SCARED MY KID OUT OF HIS SKIN!
GNIIIIIII!
MAYBE YOUR BRAT SHOULD LEARN FROM HIS BETTERS-- YOU DON'T SEE MY DAUGHTER SNIFFLING, DO YOU?
NOT MY FAULT YOU'VE BEEN RIDING AROUND ON THAT SHOPPING CART LIKE IT'S A MECHANICAL BULL--
UH?
THAT'S MECHANICAL BULLSHIT, FEATHER-FUCKER!
ALL THE MANNERS OF LOT'S DAUGHTERS AND MORE SALT THAN LOT'S WIFE!
DIABETELLA
GNIIIIIII!
PAT PAT
DON'T CRY!

NO!
I'LL FIND YOU, I PROMISE!
I WON'T EVER FORGET YOUUU!
PAPRIKA
DAMIANO! HERE YOU GO, MOMMY'S LITTLE HELLION!
CAN'T CRY WITH A MOUTH FULL OF SUGAR AND SPICE--
ANGELINA! IF YOU CEASE THAT INFERNAL HOLLERING (AND SIT DOWN LIKE A GOOD LITTLE LADY), YOU CAN HAVE THIS NICE TEDDY-WEDDY-KINS.
AS LONG AS YOU SHUT UP UNTIL WE GET HOME, WHERE YOU'LL BE THE AU PAIR'S PROBLEM.
AND SO THE TWO DID NOT MEET (AND NOR DID THEY CARE) FOR THE NEXT TWENTY YEARS.
GNAM GNAM GNAM!
WIIIIII!
the end
or rather, this was... the beginning!

• INFERNO •

THROUGH ME ONE GOES INTO THE TOWN OF WOE...
THROUGH ME ONE GOES INTO ETERNAL PAIN...

WELCOME TO THE INFERNO!

BLUARGH!

PLOP!
!
WHAT'S THIS CRAP?
YOU'RE A CLOWN!
GO TO WORK, EMO SHIT!
EMO?! WHO DARED CALL US EMO? PUNKASS LITTLE--
LET IT GO, DAMIANO...IT'S NOT WORTH IT!
I UNDERSTAND, GIUDA! THIS SCUM NEEDS A LITTLE...RAZZLE DAZZLE!
YOU WON'T...
THE STAR JUMP?! NOOOOOO!
HERE I AM, PEOPLE! LOVE ME!
FUCKING ATTENTION WHORE!
BOING
SOMETHING SOFT MUST HAVE SOFTENED THE BLOW...
!
WHAT A...
OHIOHI...BE CAREFUL WHERE YOU DIVE, NEXT TIME!
I'M SORRY, SUNSHINE! NOTHING BROKEN, RIGHT? IF YOU WANT, I CAN GIVE YOU A THERAPEUTIC FULL BODY MASSAGE FOR ANY ACHES AND PAINS AND UNFULFILLED INCIDENTALS--
OH, HOW KIND!
HAHA!

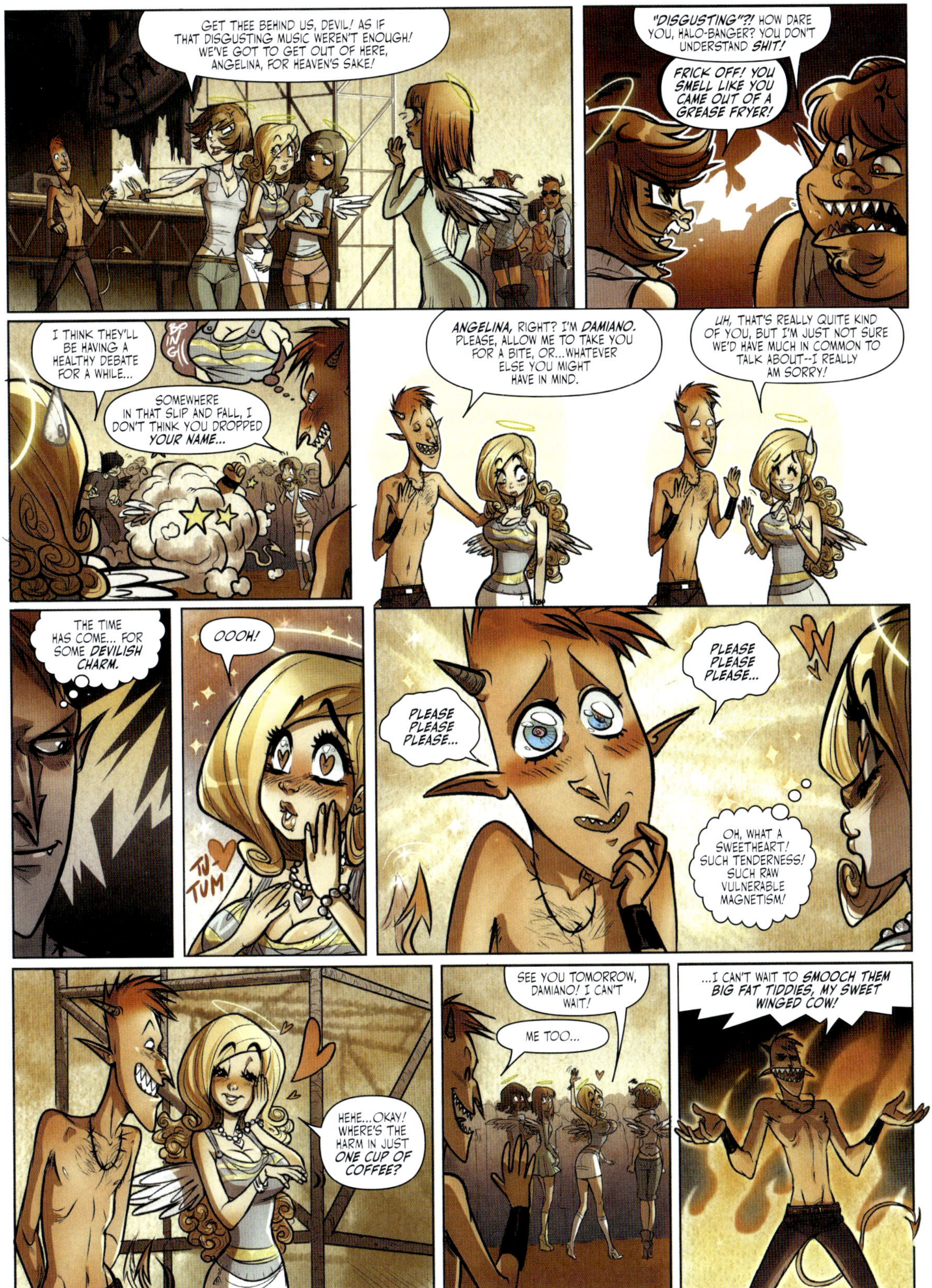
GET THEE BEHIND US, DEVIL! AS IF THAT DISGUSTING MUSIC WEREN'T ENOUGH! WE'VE GOT TO GET OUT OF HERE, ANGELINA, FOR HEAVEN'S SAKE!
"DISGUSTING"?! HOW DARE YOU, HALO-BANGER? YOU DON'T UNDERSTAND SHIT!
FRICK OFF! YOU SMELL LIKE YOU CAME OUT OF A GREASE FRYER!
I THINK THEY'LL BE HAVING A HEALTHY DEBATE FOR A WHILE...
SOMEWHERE IN THAT SLIP AND FALL, I DON'T THINK YOU DROPPED YOUR NAME...
ANGELINA, RIGHT? I'M DAMIANO. PLEASE, ALLOW ME TO TAKE YOU FOR A BITE, OR...WHATEVER ELSE YOU MIGHT HAVE IN MIND.
UH, THAT'S REALLY QUITE KIND OF YOU, BUT I'M JUST NOT SURE WE'D HAVE MUCH IN COMMON TO TALK ABOUT--I REALLY AM SORRY!
THE TIME HAS COME... FOR SOME DEVILISH CHARM.
OOOH!
TU-TUM
PLEASE PLEASE PLEASE...
PLEASE PLEASE PLEASE...
OH, WHAT A SWEETHEART! SUCH TENDERNESS! SUCH RAW VULNERABLE MAGNETISM!
HEHE...OKAY! WHERE'S THE HARM IN JUST ONE CUP OF COFFEE?
SEE YOU TOMORROW, DAMIANO! I CAN'T WAIT!
ME TOO...
...I CAN'T WAIT TO SMOOCH THEM BIG FAT TIDDIES, MY SWEET WINGED COW!

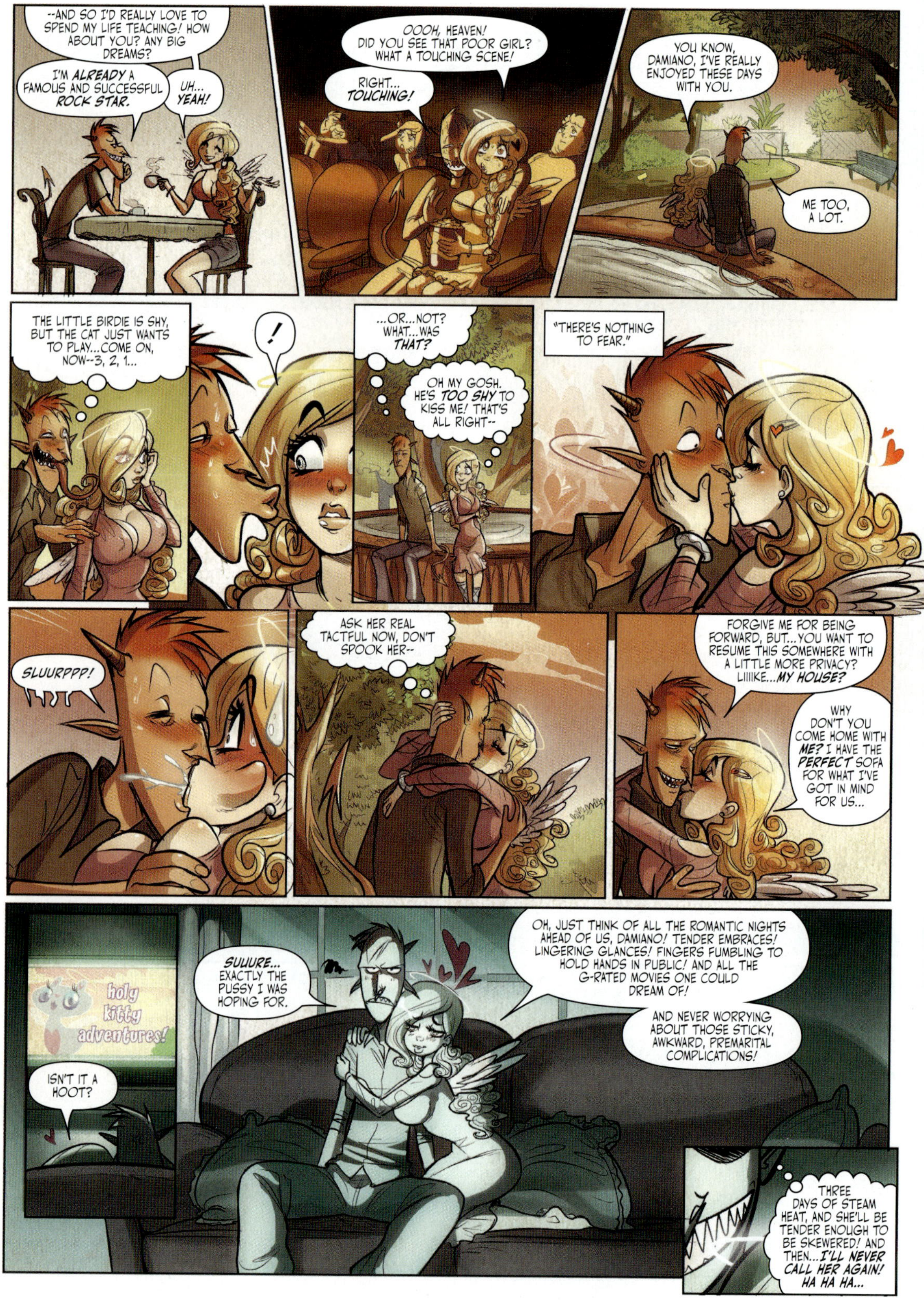
--AND SO I'D REALLY LOVE TO SPEND MY LIFE TEACHING! HOW ABOUT YOU? ANY BIG DREAMS?
I'M ALREADY A FAMOUS AND SUCCESSFUL ROCK STAR.
UH... YEAH!
OOOH, HEAVEN! DID YOU SEE THAT POOR GIRL? WHAT A TOUCHING SCENE!
RIGHT... TOUCHING!
YOU KNOW, DAMIANO, I'VE REALLY ENJOYED THESE DAYS WITH YOU.
ME TOO, A LOT.
THE LITTLE BIRDIE IS SHY, BUT THE CAT JUST WANTS TO PLAY...COME ON, NOW--3, 2, 1...
!
...OR...NOT? WHAT...WAS THAT?
OH MY GOSH. HE'S TOO SHY TO KISS ME! THAT'S ALL RIGHT--
"THERE'S NOTHING TO FEAR."
SLUURPPP!
ASK HER REAL TACTFUL NOW, DON'T SPOOK HER--
FORGIVE ME FOR BEING FORWARD, BUT...YOU WANT TO RESUME THIS SOMEWHERE WITH A LITTLE MORE PRIVACY? LIIIIKE...MY HOUSE?
WHY DON'T YOU COME HOME WITH ME? I HAVE THE PERFECT SOFA FOR WHAT I'VE GOT IN MIND FOR US...
holy kitty adventures!
ISN'T IT A HOOT?
SUUURE... EXACTLY THE PUSSY I WAS HOPING FOR.
OH, JUST THINK OF ALL THE ROMANTIC NIGHTS AHEAD OF US, DAMIANO! TENDER EMBRACES! LINGERING GLANCES! FINGERS FUMBLING TO HOLD HANDS IN PUBLIC! AND ALL THE G-RATED MOVIES ONE COULD DREAM OF!
AND NEVER WORRYING ABOUT THOSE STICKY, AWKWARD, PREMARITAL COMPLICATIONS!
THREE DAYS OF STEAM HEAT, AND SHE'LL BE TENDER ENOUGH TO BE SKEWERED! AND THEN...I'LL NEVER CALL HER AGAIN! HA HA HA...

Seven years later…

"HAPPY BIRTHDAY, ANGELINA!"

"OOOH, POOKY! HOW SWEET YOU ARE!"

"COME ON, OPEN THE PRESENT!"

"UM...IT'S CYLINDRICAL AND LONG, WHAT IS IT?"

"SOME SURPRISES ARE WHAT YOU *TAKE* OUT OF THE BOX, AND SOME SURPRISES ARE WHAT YOU *PUT* INTO THE BOX, JUST SAYIN'."

"EEEH?! BUT...BUT THIS IS..."

"HEAVEN, DAMIANO! ARE YOU CRAZY?!"

"I DON'T EVEN KNOW IF I'M ABLE TO USE IT..."

"NO PROBLEM..."

"I'LL SHOW YOU!"

"WOW, DAMIANO... *HOW IT VIBRATES!*"

VRRRRrrr VRrrrrr

"YOU LIKE IT, DON'T YOU? I KNEW YOU WOULD!"

"WAIT, DON'T GET DISTRACTED... *KEEP GOING*..."

"YES, GOOD, *LIKE THAT!* DON'T STOP... IT'S CLOSE..."

"I WON'T STOP 'TIL YOU'RE OVER THE FINISH LINE, BABY--"

VRRRr

"YAY! ALL WE NEED IS THE LAST LEVEL!"

"OH, POOKY... YOU'RE MY HERO!"

VRRRR

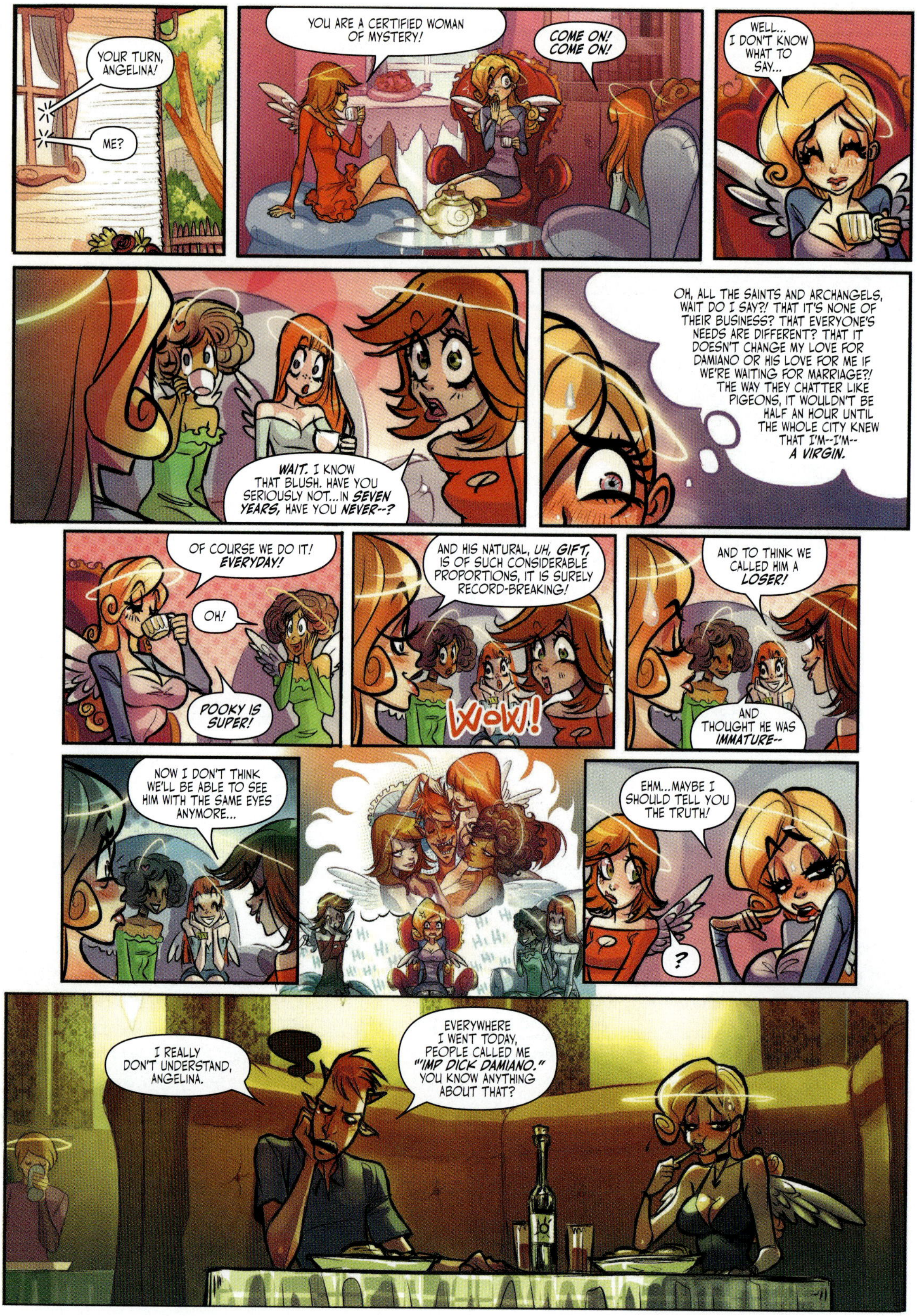
YOUR TURN, ANGELINA!
ME?
YOU ARE A CERTIFIED WOMAN OF MYSTERY!
COME ON! COME ON!
WELL... I DON'T KNOW WHAT TO SAY...
WAIT. I KNOW THAT BLUSH. HAVE YOU SERIOUSLY NOT...IN SEVEN YEARS, HAVE YOU NEVER--?
OH, ALL THE SAINTS AND ARCHANGELS, WAIT DO I SAY?! THAT IT'S NONE OF THEIR BUSINESS? THAT EVERYONE'S NEEDS ARE DIFFERENT? THAT IT DOESN'T CHANGE MY LOVE FOR DAMIANO OR HIS LOVE FOR ME IF WE'RE WAITING FOR MARRIAGE?! THE WAY THEY CHATTER LIKE PIGEONS, IT WOULDN'T BE HALF AN HOUR UNTIL THE WHOLE CITY KNEW THAT I'M--I'M-- A VIRGIN.
OF COURSE WE DO IT! EVERYDAY!
OH!
POOKY IS SUPER!
AND HIS NATURAL, UH, GIFT, IS OF SUCH CONSIDERABLE PROPORTIONS, IT IS SURELY RECORD-BREAKING!
WOW!
AND TO THINK WE CALLED HIM A LOSER!
AND THOUGHT HE WAS IMMATURE--
NOW I DON'T THINK WE'LL BE ABLE TO SEE HIM WITH THE SAME EYES ANYMORE...
EHM...MAYBE I SHOULD TELL YOU THE TRUTH!
?
I REALLY DON'T UNDERSTAND, ANGELINA.
EVERYWHERE I WENT TODAY, PEOPLE CALLED ME "IMP DICK DAMIANO." YOU KNOW ANYTHING ABOUT THAT?

MMH...
AHNNN... AH!
BIP BIP
OH HEAVEN... I'VE TO CALL HIM!
DRIIIIIN!
WHAT THE HELL...
DAMIANO, IT'S ME! I... I HAD A DREAM... I FEEL SO STRANGE!
I CAN'T RESIST... I NEED YOU, POOKY! NOW!
HELLO? DAMIANO? ARE YOU THERE?!
DLIN DLON
HERE I AM, SUGARPLUM! I KNEW THIS DAY WOULD COME! AND I AM GOING TO GIVE YOU...
...EVERYTHING YOU NEED.
COME! IN THE BEDROOM!
OOOH YES!
NO, ANGELINA... THERE'S NO MONSTERS UNDER THE BED!
OH, POOKY... IT'S THE LAST TIME I WATCH A HORROR MOVIE BEFORE I GO TO SLEEP!
WHAT NIGHTMARES!

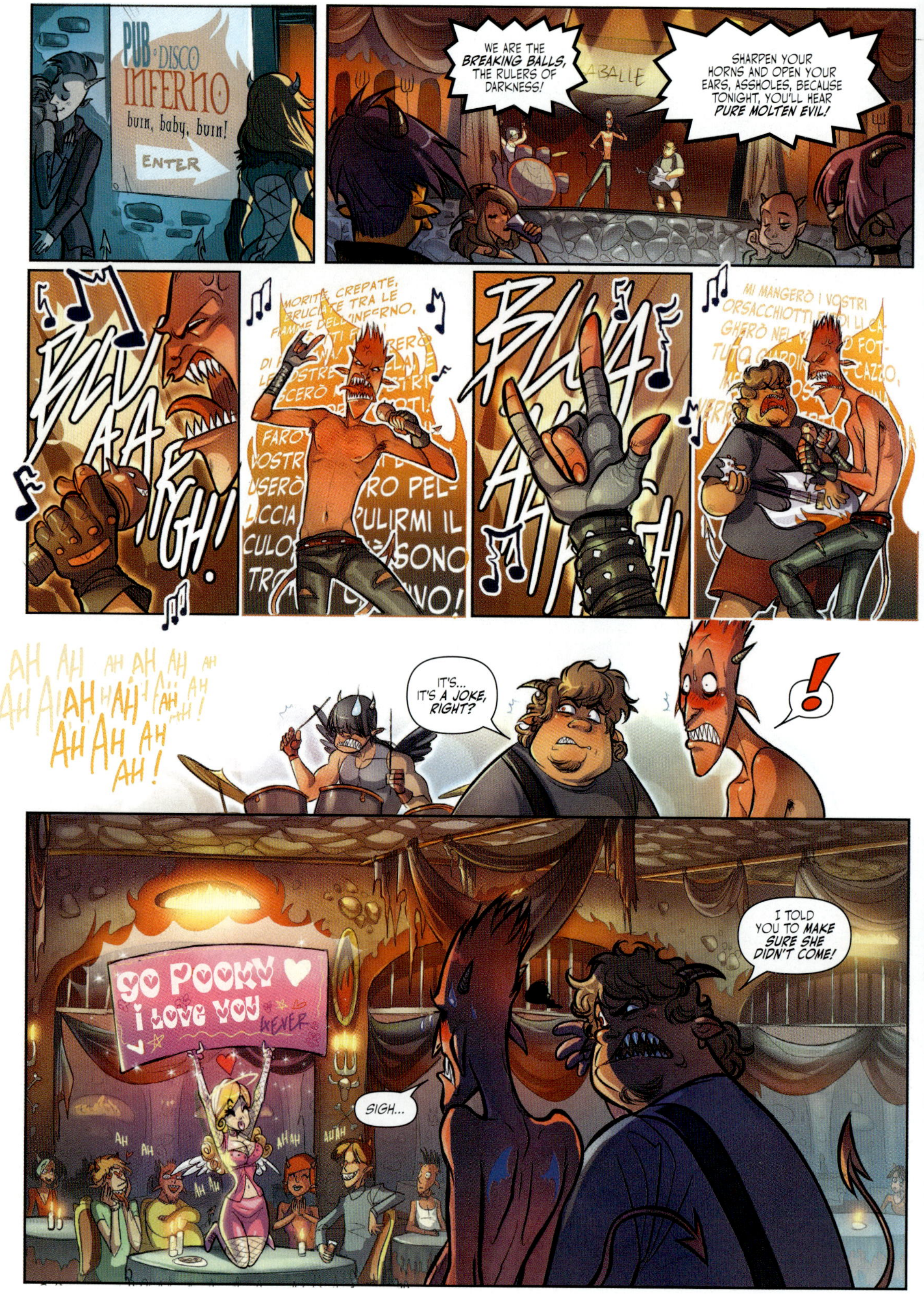
PUB DISCO INFERNO
burn, baby, burn!
ENTER
WE ARE THE BREAKING BALLS, THE RULERS OF DARKNESS!
SHARPEN YOUR HORNS AND OPEN YOUR EARS, ASSHOLES, BECAUSE TONIGHT, YOU'LL HEAR PURE MOLTEN EVIL!
BLUAAARGH!
MORITE, CREPATE, BRUCIATE TRA LE
MI MANGERÒ I VOSTRI
AH AH AH AH AH AH AH AH AH AH AH AH AH AH AH AH AH!
IT'S... IT'S A JOKE, RIGHT?
!
GO POOKY ♥ I LOVE YOU
I TOLD YOU TO MAKE SURE SHE DIDN'T COME!
SIGH...

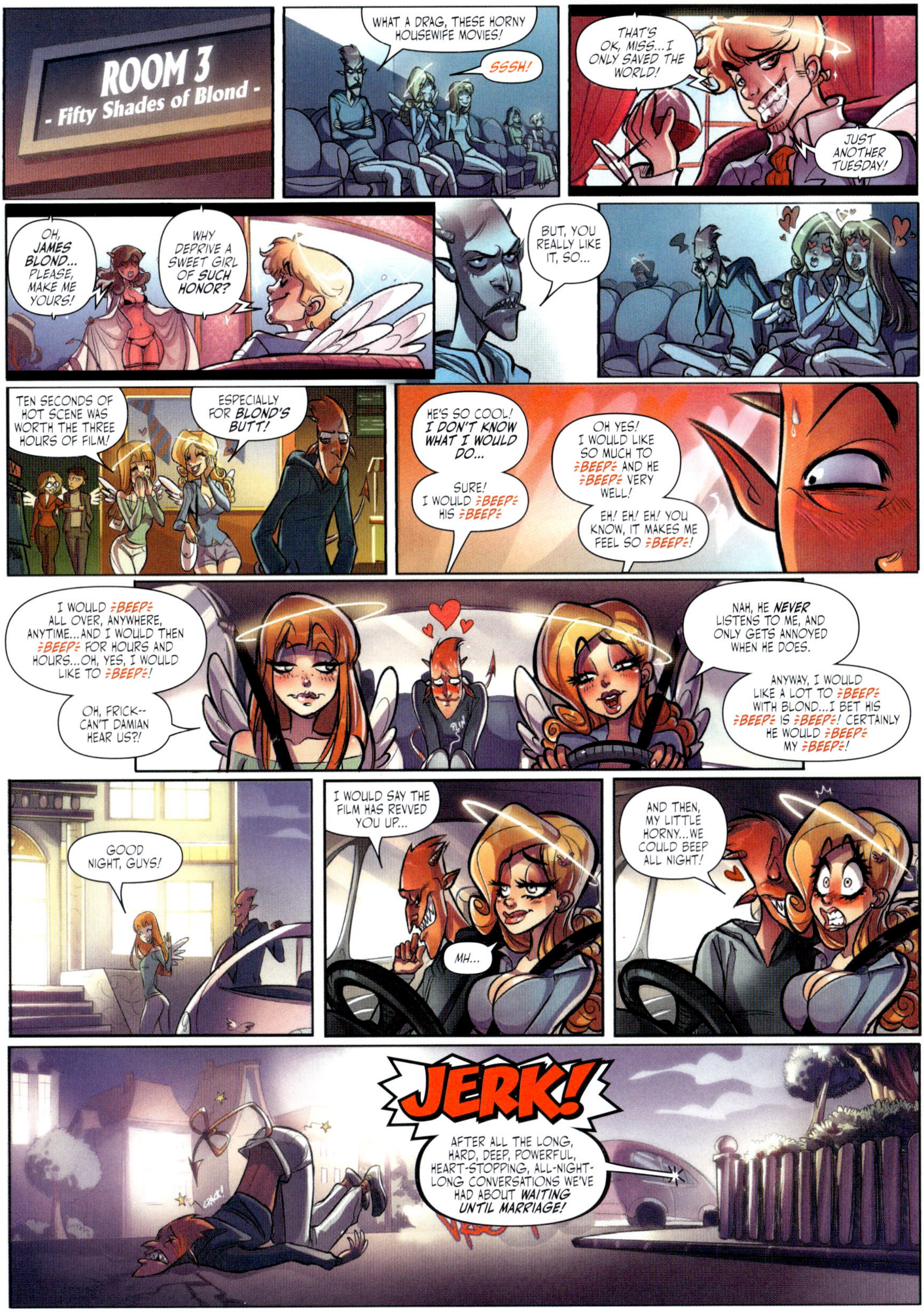
ROOM 3
- Fifty Shades of Blond -
WHAT A DRAG, THESE HORNY HOUSEWIFE MOVIES!
SSSH!
THAT'S OK, MISS... I ONLY SAVED THE WORLD!
JUST ANOTHER TUESDAY!
OH, JAMES BLOND... PLEASE, MAKE ME YOURS!
WHY DEPRIVE A SWEET GIRL OF SUCH HONOR?
BUT, YOU REALLY LIKE IT, SO...
TEN SECONDS OF HOT SCENE WAS WORTH THE THREE HOURS OF FILM!
ESPECIALLY FOR BLOND'S BUTT!
HE'S SO COOL! I DON'T KNOW WHAT I WOULD DO...
SURE! I WOULD BEEP HIS BEEP
OH YES! I WOULD LIKE SO MUCH TO BEEP AND HE BEEP VERY WELL!
EH! EH! EH! YOU KNOW, IT MAKES ME FEEL SO BEEP!
I WOULD BEEP ALL OVER, ANYWHERE, ANYTIME...AND I WOULD THEN BEEP FOR HOURS AND HOURS...OH, YES, I WOULD LIKE TO BEEP!
OH, FRICK-- CAN'T DAMIAN HEAR US?!
NAH, HE NEVER LISTENS TO ME, AND ONLY GETS ANNOYED WHEN HE DOES.
ANYWAY, I WOULD LIKE A LOT TO BEEP WITH BLOND...I BET HIS BEEP IS BEEP! CERTAINLY HE WOULD BEEP MY BEEP!
GOOD NIGHT, GUYS!
I WOULD SAY THE FILM HAS REVVED YOU UP...
MH...
AND THEN, MY LITTLE HORNY...WE COULD BEEP ALL NIGHT!
JERK!
AFTER ALL THE LONG, HARD, DEEP, POWERFUL, HEART-STOPPING, ALL-NIGHT-LONG CONVERSATIONS WE'VE HAD ABOUT WAITING UNTIL MARRIAGE!
CRACK!

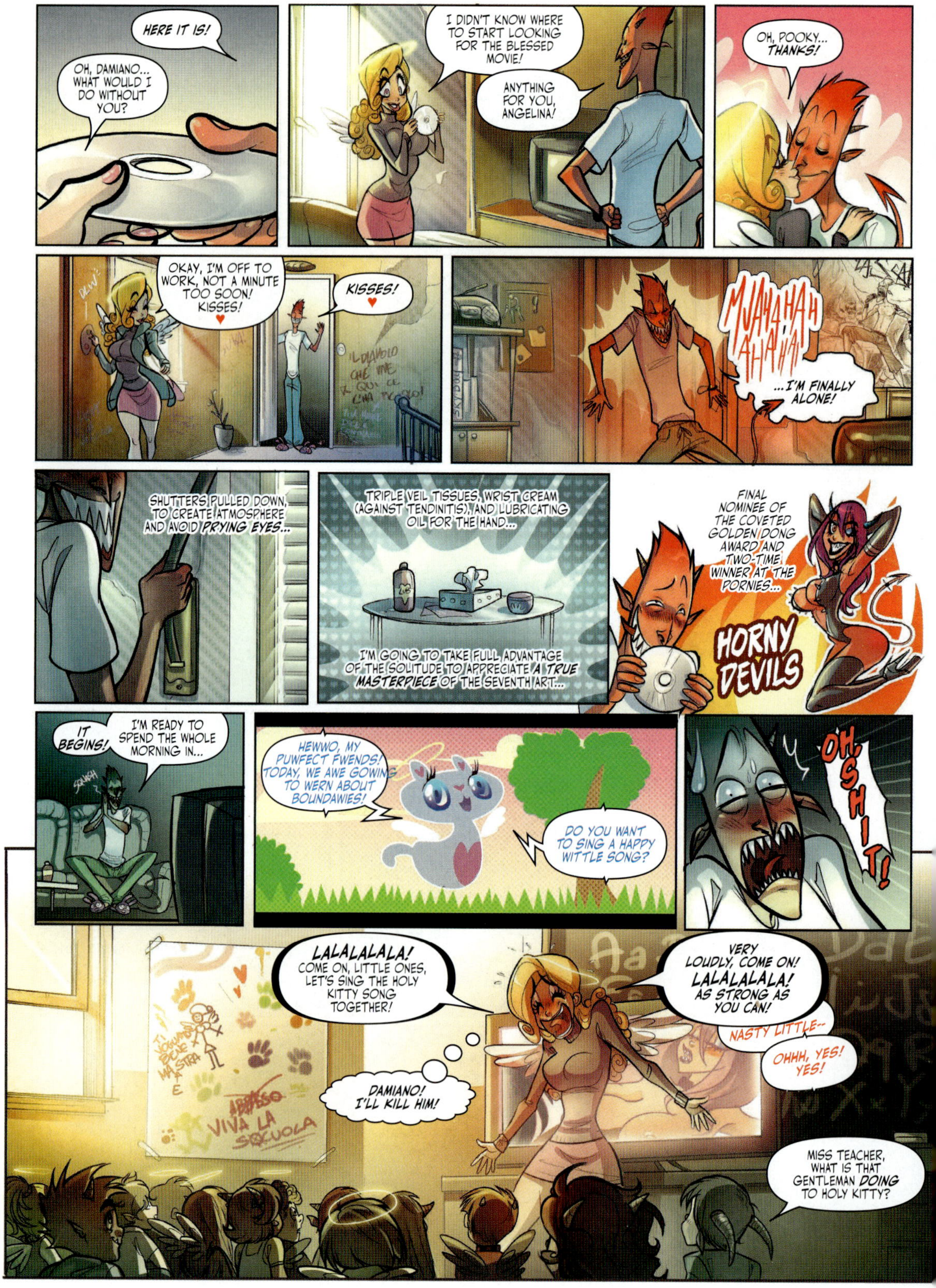
HERE IT IS!
OH, DAMIANO... WHAT WOULD I DO WITHOUT YOU?
I DIDN'T KNOW WHERE TO START LOOKING FOR THE BLESSED MOVIE!
ANYTHING FOR YOU, ANGELINA!
OH, POOKY... THANKS!
OKAY, I'M OFF TO WORK, NOT A MINUTE TOO SOON! KISSES!
KISSES!
MUAHAHAH AHAHAH
...I'M FINALLY ALONE!
SHUTTERS PULLED DOWN, TO CREATE ATMOSPHERE AND AVOID PRYING EYES...
TRIPLE VEIL TISSUES, WRIST CREAM (AGAINST TENDINITIS), AND LUBRICATING OIL FOR THE HAND...
I'M GOING TO TAKE FULL ADVANTAGE OF THE SOLITUDE TO APPRECIATE A TRUE MASTERPIECE OF THE SEVENTH ART...
FINAL NOMINEE OF THE COVETED GOLDEN DONG AWARD AND TWO-TIME WINNER AT THE PORNIES...
HORNY DEVILS
IT BEGINS!
I'M READY TO SPEND THE WHOLE MORNING IN...
HEWWO, MY PUWFECT FWENDS! TODAY, WE AWE GOWING TO WERN ABOUT BOUNDAWIES!
DO YOU WANT TO SING A HAPPY WITTLE SONG?
OH SHIT!
LALALALALA! COME ON, LITTLE ONES, LET'S SING THE HOLY KITTY SONG TOGETHER!
VERY LOUDLY, COME ON! LALALALALA! AS STRONG AS YOU CAN!
NASTY LITTLE--
OHHH, YES! YES!
DAMIANO! I'LL KILL HIM!
VIVA LA SQUOLA
MISS TEACHER, WHAT IS THAT GENTLEMAN DOING TO HOLY KITTY?

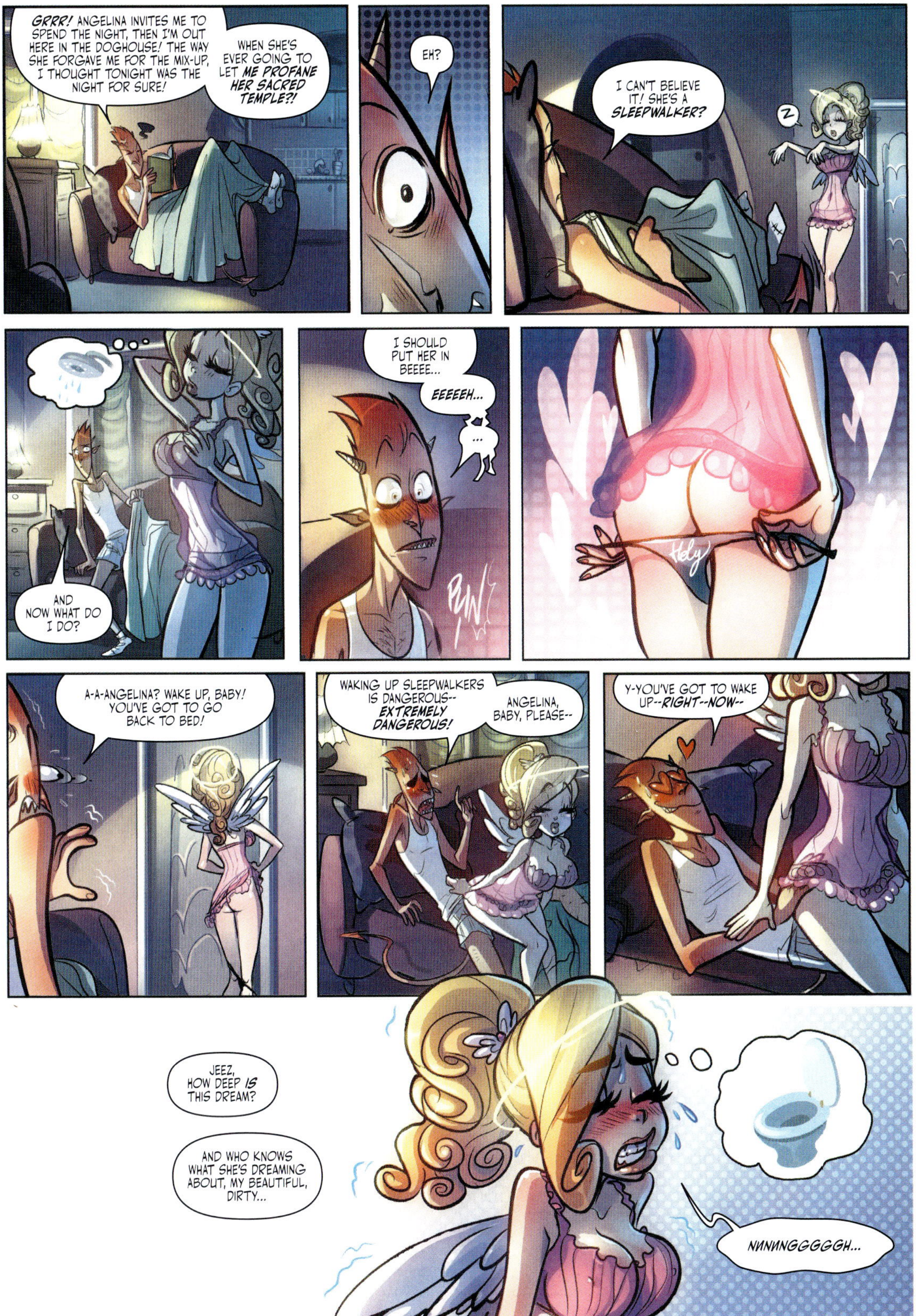
GRRR! ANGELINA INVITES ME TO SPEND THE NIGHT, THEN I'M OUT HERE IN THE DOGHOUSE! THE WAY SHE FORGAVE ME FOR THE MIX-UP, I THOUGHT TONIGHT WAS THE NIGHT FOR SURE!
WHEN SHE'S EVER GOING TO LET ME PROFANE HER SACRED TEMPLE?!
EH?
I CAN'T BELIEVE IT! SHE'S A SLEEPWALKER?
Z
AND NOW WHAT DO I DO?
I SHOULD PUT HER IN BEEEE...
EEEEEH...
...
A-A-ANGELINA? WAKE UP, BABY! YOU'VE GOT TO GO BACK TO BED!
WAKING UP SLEEPWALKERS IS DANGEROUS-- EXTREMELY DANGEROUS!
ANGELINA, BABY, PLEASE--
Y-YOU'VE GOT TO WAKE UP--RIGHT--NOW--
JEEZ, HOW DEEP IS THIS DREAM?
AND WHO KNOWS WHAT SHE'S DREAMING ABOUT, MY BEAUTIFUL, DIRTY...
NNNNNGGGGGH...

GIUDA, GRUGNO! I'VE JUST FINISHED WRITING AN AUTHENTIC *MASTERPIECE!*
I'VE HEARD THAT ONE BEFORE.
THIS TIME IT'S DIFFERENT, MY CHUMBUCKET CHUM! I HAVEN'T EATEN OR SLEPT IN INSPIRATION FOR DAYS!
OKAY, IDIOT. LET'S HEAR IT.
OKAY, A ONE, AND A TWO, AND A TH-TH-TH...
...REEEEEEEE.
OKAY, YOU'RE FREE TO BE DISCHARGED WHENEVER YOU'RE READY. BUT YOU NEED TO EAT AND SLEEP MORE AND STOP TORTURING YOURSELF IN PURSUIT OF THINGS THAT ARE CLEARLY BAD FOR YOU--
POOKY!
OH, DARLING! AS SOON AS THEY TOLD ME YOU WERE IN THE HOSPITAL, *I THREW ON THE FIRST THING I HAD* AND RODE HECK FOR LEATHER TO GET HERE!
ANGIE?
ARE YOU OKAY? I CAN'T LIVE WITHOUT MY *HORNY LITTLE TOMATO!*
IF YOU WANT SOMETHING, *I'M AT YOUR COMPLETE DISPOSAL!*
OH, REALLY...?
I DON'T KNOW HOW TO TELL YOU THIS, ANGELINA, BUT YOU SEE... *I'VE ONLY GOT A FEW HOURS TO LIVE!*
NOOO
DON'T CRY MY BELOVED! BECAUSE NOW MORE THAN EVER I NEED YOU...
I KNOW YOU ABSOLUTELY WANT TO WAIT TO GET MARRIED, BUT YOU SEE...I WOULD LIKE TO *MAKE LOVE* BEFORE I LEAVE THIS SAD WORLD! I NEED IT...
OH...
I UNDERSTAND... I KNOW JUST THE THING TO BRING YOU COMFORT!
I... I LEAVE YOU TWO ALONE!
GRRR!
SEXY DOLLY devil

IMAGINE, DAMIANO... A SPICY SALAMI APPETIZER DIPPED IN GORGONZOLA AND MASCARPONE... A DELIGHT FOR THE PALATE!
AND THEN, A NICE PLATTER OF SPAGHETTI WITH TRUFFLE OIL. WITH A LOOOT OF CREAM AND BACON, ALL GREASY AND WARM...MY MOUTH WATERS JUST THINKING ABOUT IT...
FOR THE SECOND COURSE, A NICE ROASTED PIG, COVERED WITH SALTED CARAMEL SAUCE, WITH CHOCOLATE FLAKES AND SWEET DONUTS! ON A BED OF PISTACHIO PESTO...
AS A PRE-DESSERT, TO DIGEST, SOME FRIED AND BREADED CHOCOLATE SNACKS!
YUUUMMI!
AND FINALLY...A NICE GREEN APPLE PUDDING FILLED WITH CHERRY JAM, BECAUSE A LITTLE FRUIT IS ALWAYS NEEDED, WHICH IS HEALTHY!
OOOH... I'M SO HUNGRY, MY LITTLE TOMATO! AAAHNNNNN!
TEMPTATION AND DAMNATION!
I HATE BE THE ONE TO BURST YOUR BEELZEBUBBLE, BUT THIS IS NOT WHAT I MEANT BY "DIRTY CALLS"!
Love Hotel
LOVE

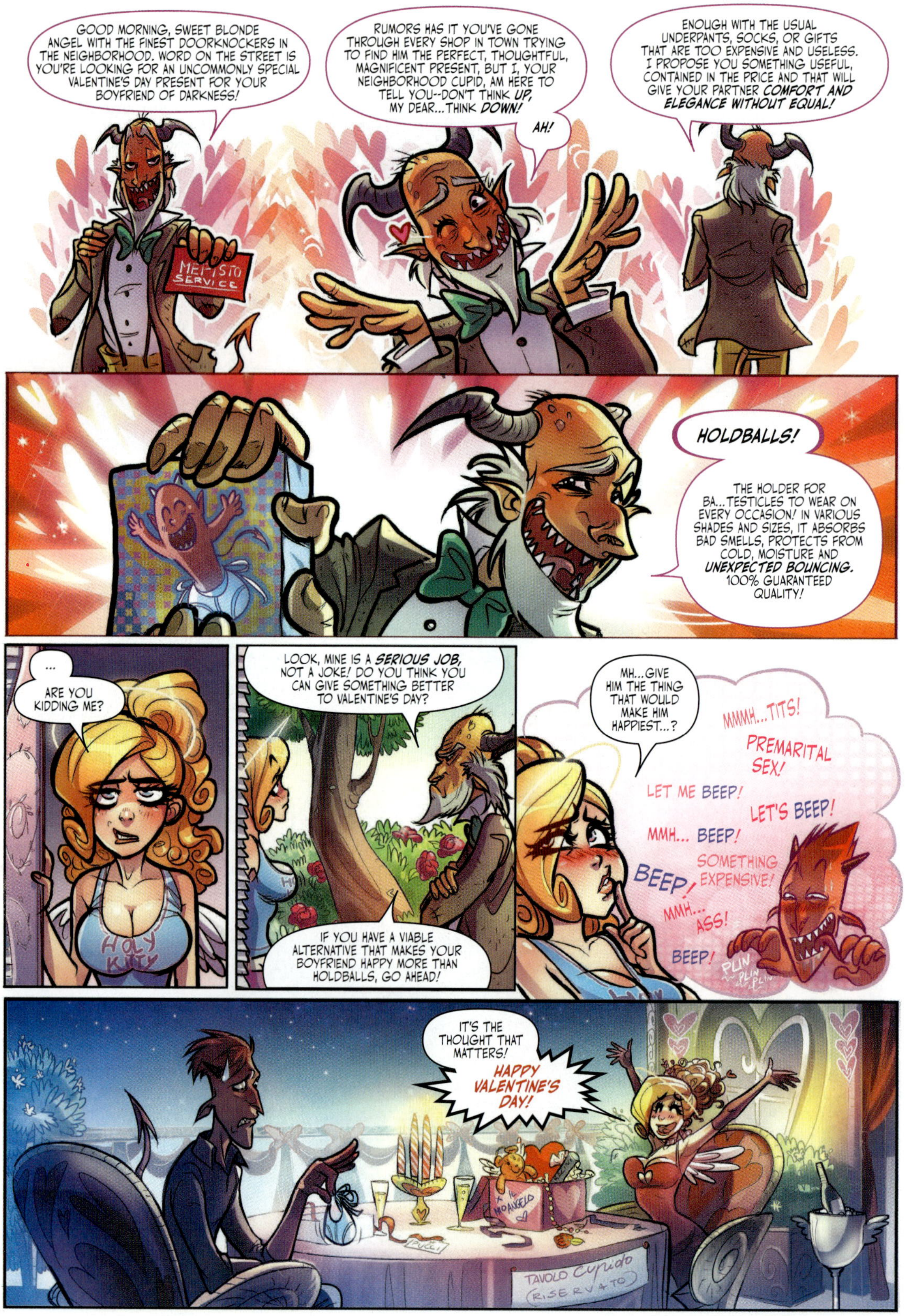
GOOD MORNING, SWEET BLONDE ANGEL WITH THE FINEST DOORKNOCKERS IN THE NEIGHBORHOOD. WORD ON THE STREET IS YOU'RE LOOKING FOR AN UNCOMMONLY SPECIAL VALENTINE'S DAY PRESENT FOR YOUR BOYFRIEND OF DARKNESS!
MEFISTO SERVICE
RUMORS HAS IT YOU'VE GONE THROUGH EVERY SHOP IN TOWN TRYING TO FIND HIM THE PERFECT, THOUGHTFUL, MAGNIFICENT PRESENT, BUT I, YOUR NEIGHBORHOOD CUPID, AM HERE TO TELL YOU--DON'T THINK UP, MY DEAR...THINK DOWN!
AH!
ENOUGH WITH THE USUAL UNDERPANTS, SOCKS, OR GIFTS THAT ARE TOO EXPENSIVE AND USELESS. I PROPOSE YOU SOMETHING USEFUL, CONTAINED IN THE PRICE AND THAT WILL GIVE YOUR PARTNER COMFORT AND ELEGANCE WITHOUT EQUAL!
HOLDBALLS!
THE HOLDER FOR BA...TESTICLES TO WEAR ON EVERY OCCASION! IN VARIOUS SHADES AND SIZES, IT ABSORBS BAD SMELLS, PROTECTS FROM COLD, MOISTURE AND UNEXPECTED BOUNCING. 100% GUARANTEED QUALITY!
... ARE YOU KIDDING ME?
HOLY KITTY
LOOK, MINE IS A SERIOUS JOB, NOT A JOKE! DO YOU THINK YOU CAN GIVE SOMETHING BETTER TO VALENTINE'S DAY?
IF YOU HAVE A VIABLE ALTERNATIVE THAT MAKES YOUR BOYFRIEND HAPPY MORE THAN HOLDBALLS, GO AHEAD!
MH...GIVE HIM THE THING THAT WOULD MAKE HIM HAPPIEST...?
MMMH...TITS!
PREMARITAL SEX!
LET ME BEEP!
LET'S BEEP!
MMH... BEEP!
BEEP!
SOMETHING EXPENSIVE!
MMH... ASS!
BEEP!
PLIN PLIN PLIN
IT'S THE THOUGHT THAT MATTERS!
HAPPY VALENTINE'S DAY!
PUCCI
TAVOLO Cupido (RISERVATO)

IN ALL MY LIFE, I HAD SEX TWICE, DAMIANO...
THE FIRST TIME WITH MY COUSIN, AND THE SECOND WITH MY MOTHER'S VACUUM CLEANER, "THE ETERNAL MAW THAT HUNGERS."
WELL, I...THE LAST TIME I DID IT, IT WAS WITH A STUFFED ANIMAL. ANGIE DOESN'T WANT TO DO IT! SHE SAYS WE HAVE TO GET MARRIED FIRST! BUT WHEN WAS THE LAST TIME YOU SAW SOMEBODY LIKE ME IN A CHURCH?!
MAYBE I DON'T TURN HER ON. IF I HAD THAT DUDE BLOND'S CHEEKBONES...
YOU THINK ANYONE WANTS TO CUDDLE WITH A PUDDLE OF JELLY LIKE ME?
BUT YOU KNOW WHAT, DAM? ENOUGH CRYING! TONIGHT WE'VE TO HAVE FUN, WITH THE HELP OF A COUPLE OF BEERS! AND THEN ANOTHER PAIR...
AND ANOTHER...
AND ANOTHER...
UGH...MY HEAD...WHERE AM I? WHAT...WHAT HAPPENED?
BLUARGH
BIP
GIUDA!
I WOKE UP IN A NO-TELL MOTEL, IN A BED COVERED IN BOOZE AND SEX TOYS! HOW DID I GET HERE? WHAT DID I DO?! I DON'T REMEMBER SHIT!
WHERE THE HELL DID YOU GO?!
IN THE BATHROOM! NO IDEA HOW I GOT HERE!
I REMEMBER SNUGGLING WITH A SWEETIE IN RED, WHO WAS INTO SOME REAL CUTE KINKY SHIT--
I DON'T CARE IF YOU THINK YOU FOUND YOUR SOUL MATE, YOU IDIOT! WHAT AM I GOING TO SAY TO ANGIE?!
THIS IS THE WORST DAY OF MY LIFE! SEVEN YEARS AND I BLOW IT IN ONE HORNY NIGHT!
HEY, I'M GONNA COME FIND YOU, BUT CALM DOWN...
"...NOBODY NEEDS TO KNOW."
...

B-BUT... BUT THAT'S URIEL!
WHO?!
YES, DAMI! HE'S THE ACTOR WHO DOES JAMES BLOND! OH, HEAVENS! I'M DREAMING! AAAH...
MONEY, OSCAR... BLAH BLAH...I'M BEAUTIFUL...BLAH... PORSCHE...
OH, BLOOOND! I'M A HUGE FAN OF YOURS, PLEASE GIVE ME AN AUTOGRAPH!
TSK!
PLEASE!
AT ONCE, YOU RADIANT ANGEL, ON ANY PART OF THE BODY YOU DESIRE! BUT ONLY IF YOU GRANT ME THE HONOR OF COMING TO VISIT MY HUGE MANSION, TONIGHT...
...I WILL SHOW YOU MY COLLECTION OF ANCIENT SWORDS, I WILL LET YOU TOUCH MY POWERFUL GOLDEN SABER, MY DEAR...
GO EASY, ASSHOLE, SHE'S WITH ME!
SHE?! WITH AN UGLY LITTLE GREMLIN LIKE YOU? SHE DESERVES THE BEST OF THE BEST...
...LIKE ME!
OH YES? LET'S SEE WHO IS THE BEST OF THE BEST...I CHALLENGE YOU TO ARM WRESTLING!
YOU GOT THE BALLS, YOU GLOW-IN-THE-DARK, COCK-OF-THE-WALK CHICKEN?!
BIG TALK WITH A BEAK LIKE THAT. I'LL SERVE YOUR SCRAWNY LITTLE ARMS WITH BUFFALO SAUCE.
POOKY, PLEASE, I SHOULDN'T HAVE SAID ANYTHING-- PLEASE DON'T GET HURT! NOTHING IS WORTH THIS!
TRUST ME...
BUT...
YOU DELUSIONAL MORON. IF YOU'D CHALLENGED ME TO CROCHET, MAYBE THEN THOSE LITTLE NEEDLES WOULD'VE STOOD A CHANCE.
NNNNNNNNNNGGGH!
?!
STRAP!
MUAH! AH! AH! AH! AH! AH! AH!
TAKE THIS, YOU UGLY SPINELESS SHOWOFF SHITSTAIN!
GO HIDE IN YOUR BIG EMPTY PLAYHOUSE AND FONDLE YOUR SABER ALL BY YOURSELF!
AAARGGGH! MERCY!
IT DOESN'T END HERE!
OH...BUT...LOVE! I DIDN'T THINK YOUR RIGHT ARM WAS SO TRAINED...
HOW DID YOU DO IT?
MY SABER ISN'T MADE OF GOLD, WHICH IS WHY IT NEEDS A LOT OF POLISHING...
?

MICHELA SAYS SHE HAS A SURPRISE FOR US!
I'M VERY CURIOUS!
RAFFY, ANGIE, GABRI, DO YOU REMEMBER THAT I STARTED WORKING AS A PRODUCT REPRESENTATIVE HERE AT RAPACIA.
DO YOU WANT TO SELL US MAKE-UP?
NOT REALLY...I ASK YOU NOT TO FEEL EMBARRASSED, OKAY?
COME ON, FOR SOME LIPSTICK? I WANT THE RED STIGMATA!
FLAP
TA-DAAAAAAAAAN! TOYS FOR LADIES! THERE'S SOMETHING FOR EVERYONE!
MICHELA! A NICE LADY LIKE YOU...
YOU SHOULD BE ASHAMED!
COME ON! IT'S SO CHIC AND... LOOK HOW IT VIBRATES!
JRRR
I SHOW YOU THE HIGHLIGHT...ONLY FOR GOURMETS!
THE DREAM OF ALL WOMEN! BOW DOWN BEFORE HIM...
LIMITED EDITION
THE MIRACULOUS EXCALIBUR! TRUST ME, ONCE HE'S IN YOUR STONE, YOU WON'T WANT TO PULL HIM OUT.
!
WOW... IT'S SO MAGICAL! I'VE GOT TO HAVE IT!
SEE ANYTHING YOU LIKE, ANGIE?
AH...SHE'S A VIRGIN...SHE DOESN'T EVEN KNOW WHAT IT'S FOR! AND WITH ONLY THAT LOSER OF A DEVIL AT HOME--
I'M A VIRGIN, BUT I'M NOT STUPID!
YOU KNOW WHAT? I WILL TAKE IT! AND I'LL USE IT, TOO, THE MINUTE MY POOKY COMES OVER!
ABOUT TIME!
A FEW HOURS LATER...
HMM...THIS MILKSHAKE IS REALLY A DELIGHT!
THANK YOU, BUT IT'S ALL DUE TO MICHELA!
SHE HAS SO MANY TOYS FOR US TO PLAY WITH--
MILK
VVVZZZ

VRRR
AH!
VRRR
NO MORE GAMES, DAMIANO! TONIGHT WE HAVE TO MEET MICHELA'S NEW BOYFRIEND AND WE'VE JUST GOT TO LOOK OUR BEST!
SO? I ALWAYS WEAR MY RATTY OLD HOODIE!
EXACTLY! TIME FOR A RESURRECTION OF THE WARDROBE!
OH, YES! YOU'RE MY POOKY'S SALVATION!
EDEN glamour
OUI VRAIMENT, MADEMOISELLE! SOON, WE'LL TURN YOUR BEAU INTO A BIJOUX!
HERE, HOW'S THIS FOR A HEAVENLY RAIMENT--
B-BUT I...
FASHION DOESN'T TOLERATE ANY "BUT"!
OOOOH, SO SEXY!
ANOTHER SOUL SAVED!
"SEXY"? ANGELINA, I FEEL AS GAUDY AS A PEACOCK--
EXACTLY! EMPHASIS ON THE CO--
"...INCIDENTAL POPULARITY OF THIS PARTICULAR PATTERN."
HEH, UH... TWINSIES, AM I RIGHT?
MUAH AH AH AH
AH AH AH AH MUAH AH AH AH AH...!

ANGELINA, I SWEAR, YOU'VE THE PRETTIEST BUST OF ANY ANGEL IN THIS CITY!
SO BIG, SO BOUNTEOUS, SO-- EXUBERANT!
I TRY NOT TO COUNT MY BLESSINGS, BUT I'M VERY LUCKY, HIHIHI!
"BLESSINGS"?! MEN OF TASTE DON'T LIKE EXAGGERATED FORMS ANY MORE--AND YOU WOULDN'T WANT TO BE PROUD OF BEING A VULGAR LITTLE SERVING WENCH, WOULD YOU?
THAT'LL TEACH HER! PUTTING ON SO MANY AIRS, SHE COULD INFLATE THOSE BEACH BALLS!
MY CHERRY TOMATO, MAY I ASK YOU A VERY PERSONAL QUESTION? MY BOSOM...YOU LIKE IT, DON'T YOU?
WHAT KIND OF QUESTION IS THAT--?!
NO, STOP! IF YOU COMPLIMENT HER, SHE'LL JUST FLOUNCE OFF AS ALOOF AS EVER ON THOSE FLUFFY LITTLE WINGS!
MY LEGENDARY PATIENCE TO THE RESCUE! I'LL SHOW HER! I'LL BE ABSOLUTELY GLACIAL!
EH, I MEAN, THEY'RE JUST MAMMARIES. EVEN COWS HAVE MAMMARIES.
B-BUT I THOUGHT YOU LIKED MY "TIDDIES"! DON'T YOU FEEL SOMETHING WHEN I DO THIS?
WHEN THEY MILK A COW I DON'T GET EXCITED, YOU KNOW?
WHAT ABOUT IF I GET THEM WET? NO REACTION?!
PLEASE, ANGIE, YOU'RE SPLASHING MY MAGAZINE--
MAYBE--MAYBE YOU JUST NEED TO SEE THEM BETTER? HOW ABOUT NOW?
LOOK, I'M GOING TO GO GET AN ICE CREAM, WHICH I'M ACTUALLY IN THE MOOD FOR.
OK?
MUAHAH! COLD AS A WITCH'S TIT! UNPRECE-DENTED SELF-CONTROL! I AM THE LITERAL COOLEST!
SNIFF!
!
LONG LIVE MY POOKY!

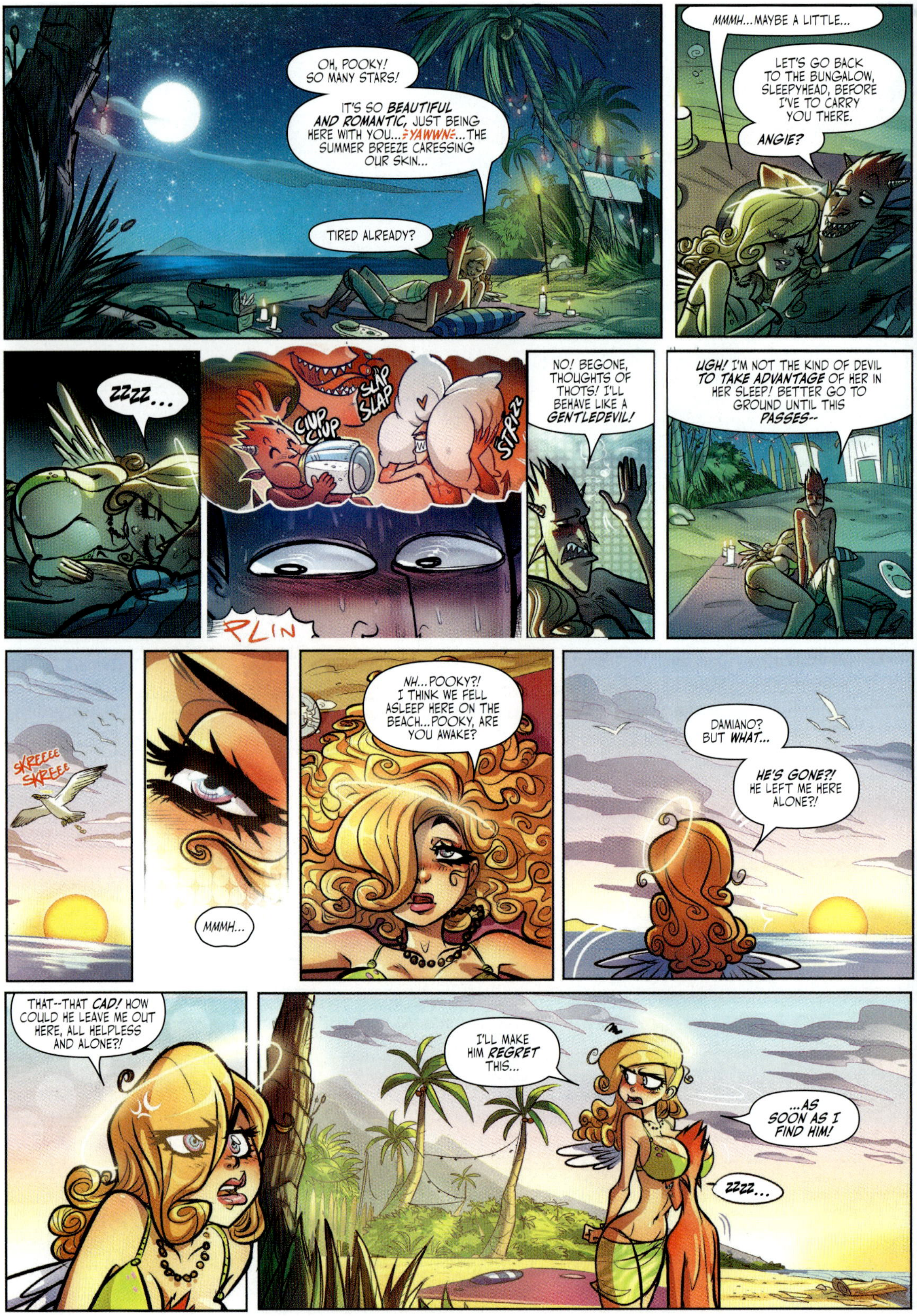
OH, POOKY! SO MANY STARS!
IT'S SO BEAUTIFUL AND ROMANTIC, JUST BEING HERE WITH YOU... ≡YAWN≡ ...THE SUMMER BREEZE CARESSING OUR SKIN...
TIRED ALREADY?
MMMH... MAYBE A LITTLE...
LET'S GO BACK TO THE BUNGALOW, SLEEPYHEAD, BEFORE I'VE TO CARRY YOU THERE.
ANGIE?
ZZZZ...
CIUP CIUP
SLAP SLAP
STRIZZ
PLIN
NO! BEGONE, THOUGHTS OF THOTS! I'LL BEHAVE LIKE A GENTLEDEVIL!
UGH! I'M NOT THE KIND OF DEVIL TO TAKE ADVANTAGE OF HER IN HER SLEEP! BETTER GO TO GROUND UNTIL THIS PASSES--
SKREEEE SKREEE
MMMH...
NH... POOKY?! I THINK WE FELL ASLEEP HERE ON THE BEACH... POOKY, ARE YOU AWAKE?
DAMIANO? BUT WHAT...
HE'S GONE?! HE LEFT ME HERE ALONE?!
THAT--THAT CAD! HOW COULD HE LEAVE ME OUT HERE, ALL HELPLESS AND ALONE?!
I'LL MAKE HIM REGRET THIS...
...AS SOON AS I FIND HIM!
ZZZZ...

HAHAHAHA!
OH, POOKY, YOU ARE ALWAYS SUCH A HOOT! BUT TONIGHT, YOU'RE EVEN FUNNIER!
I'D LOVE TO TAKE CREDIT, BUT I THINK YOU MAYBE HAD A TEE MUCH MARTOONI...
NOT AT ALL! IT'S ONLY MY THIRD COCKTAIL--BUT I FEEL A BIT STRANGE!
MAYBE IT'S BETTER IF WE GET THE CHECK--
!
WOW!
SO SORRY, DAMI, I DON'T KNOW MY OWN STRENGTH, HEHE...
I FEEL SO DIFFERENT TONIGHT...EVERYTHING WARM AND HUNGRY FOR YOU...
OH, I JUST WANT TO FEEL YOU!
BURP
IF YOU'VE GOT NEEDS, I CAN SATISFY THEM, AND THEY WON'T EVEN GET IN THE WAY OF WAITING 'TIL MARRIAGE...
OOPS! LOOKS LIKE I JUST DROPPED MY NAPKIN...
SPREAD YOUR LEGS AND MAKE YOURSELF COMFORTABLE... OKAY?
HUH?! AND WHY? IT'S OK, ANYWAY...
OH, POOKY, I DO LOVE YOU AND ALL YOUR FUNNY LITTLE... OH, BUT LOOK OVER THERE!
FOR SATAN'S SAKE, IT'S SO DARK DOWN HERE! BUT FINALLY, SHE'S AWAKENING! NOW I CAN SHOW HER WHAT SHE'S DENIED HERSELF SO LONG!
OH! SHE EVEN SPREAD HER LEGS! NO SKIRT, BUT NO PROBLEM--
SBAVVVVV TIME FOR BOTH OF US TO TASTE THAT FORBIDDEN FRUIT...
UUUUUUH... MY, THAT'S AN EVE'L TOUCH YOU'VE GOT THERE!
GOING RIGHT FOR MY SNAKE, TOO?
ZZZ
ARGH!

WELCOME TO THE AAMON'S BEAUTY FARM! I'M CRISTINA-- HOW CAN I HELP YOU?
Aamon's Beauty Farm
per il tuo benessere!
ME AND MY POOKY HAVE WON COUPONS FOR REGENERATING AND SUPER RELAXING MASSAGES!
VERY WELL, FOLLOW ME!
MH... NICE TAIL!
WHAT ARE YOU LOOKING AT?
UH...I-I? ABSOLUTELY NOTHING! YOU'VE GOT NO REASON TO BE JEALOUS!
JEALOUS, ME? PSSH!
SHE IS JEALOUS! AND IF SHE ISN'T, IT JUST SHOWS HOW THOROUGHLY SHE'S UNDER THE SPELL OF MY DARK MANLY CHARMS!
I COULD TEASE HER A LITTLE, GET HER GOOD AND STOKED--
"You get your eyes off my big sexy Pooky, you jizz-a-belle!"
HEHE HEHE!
UNFORTUNATELY ONLY ONE COT IS FREE RIGHT NOW, SO I'M AFRAID YOU'LL HAVE TO TAKE TURNS, IF THAT'S ALL RIGHT?
ABSOLUTELY NOT! I'LL START!
YOU DON'T WANT TO LET THE YOUNG LADY GO FIRST...?
NOPE!
"I'VE GOT SOME TENSION I REALLY NEED YOUR HELP TO RELEASE!"
LET'S SEE IF MY DIABOLICAL PLAN WORKS!
AH...WHAT A DELICATE YET DECISIVE TOUCH...
OH, HER HANDS ARE SCINTILLATING-- I'VE GOT CHILLS EVERYWHERE! MMMH...
OH, YES! FASTER! NOW, STRONGER! OOOH, YES, UP AND DOWN THE WHOLE LENGTH! OH, THIS IS HEAVEN!
STRAP!
THAT'S ENOUGH! GET OFF THE TABLE THIS MINUTE!
BINGO! SHE'S CRAZY ABOUT ME!
OOOOH, YOU WERE ABSOLUTELY RIGHT, MY DARLING! THIS IS UTTERLY DELICIOUS!
I COULDN'T WAIT A SECOND LONGER!

OH YES...I CAN FEEL IT, I'M GOING TO...
YOU WISH... BUT I'M FASTER!
MH!
MUAHAH! BOW BEFORE THE ONLY REAL KING OF THE TRACK, NERDS!
PLAYER: 1st SexMasterD
PLAYER: 2nd ChocoKing
PLAYER: 3rd DarkAngel
PLAY AGAIN?
REMATCH! NOW!
COME ON, GUIDA, THAT'S THE THIRD TIME I BEAT YOU! AREN'T YOU SICK OF LOSING? AND I'VE GOT ANGIE WAITING!
BUT IT'S OUR GAME NIGHT! WE'VE HAD THIS SCHEDULE FOR YEARS!
I KNOW, YOU JELLYBELLY (GET IT? 'CAUSE YOU'RE JEALOUS), BUT ANGIE WANTS TO PLAY TOO!
SERIOUSLY?! SHE CAN'T EVEN BEAT HOLY KITTY, BUT SHE GETS A WHOLE GAME NIGHT?
MPFH!
IN THE WORDS OF MOZART: LICK MY ASS! LATER, HATERS--!
I DON'T FRIGGIN' GET IT, GRUGNO! THE ONLY THING SHE'LL LET HIM PLUG IN IS THE CONTROLLER! WHAT'S SO SPECIAL ABOUT GAME NIGHT WITH HER?
VRRRR
VRRR
I WIN AGAIN! I WIN AGAIN! HEEHEEHEE!
BOING
PLIN

MICHELA, WHAT ARE WE DOING OUT HERE? THERE'S NOTHING BUT STONES ON THIS PATH!
TRUST ME, THESE STONES ARE GONNA ROCK YOUR WORLD! STAND UP STRAIGHT WITH YOUR BACK AND TIGHTEN YOUR LEGS!
WHY?!
HERE'S WHY!
VRRRRR
MMMMMH...FANTASTIC!
SEE? JUST LIKE RIDING A BIKE! WHAT AN ORGASM!
I--I--I JUST HAD AN... ORGASM?!
HERE'S WHAT YOU MISS BY BEING A VIRGIN!
I--I'VE TO GO TO DAMIANO!
ANGIE, WAIT! YOU CAN'T WALK FROM HERE!
LET HER GO TO HER "POOKY"...I THINK THAT DEVIL OWES US A FAVOR!
OOOH... YES, MY LOVE... GO...FASTER!
AND WHY WASN'T THE PARK GOOD ENOUGH? IT'S ALL ROCKY HERE!
VRRRR!
OH, POOKY! KEEP PEDALING!

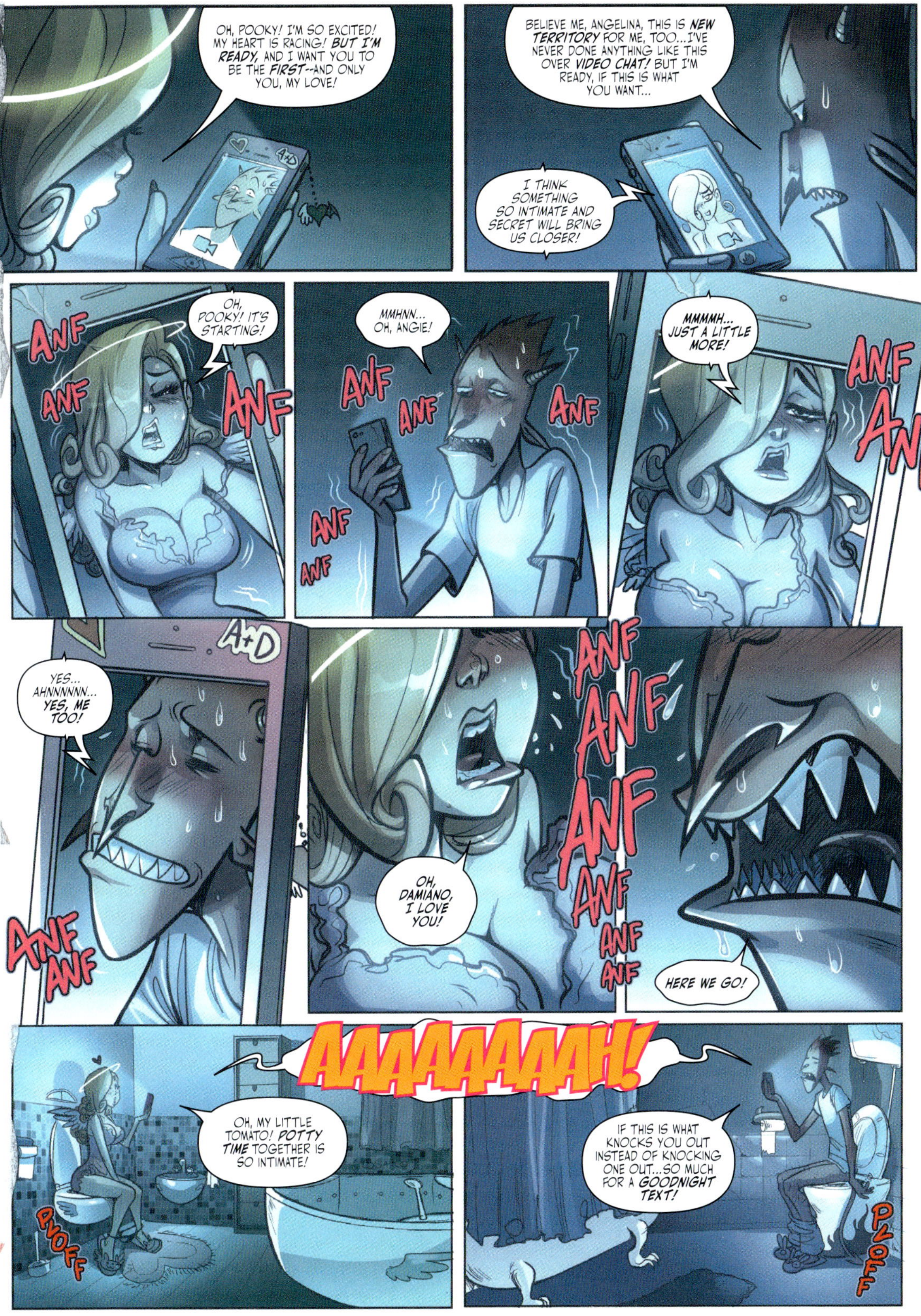
OH, POOKY! I'M SO EXCITED! MY HEART IS RACING! BUT I'M READY, AND I WANT YOU TO BE THE FIRST--AND ONLY YOU, MY LOVE!
A+D
BELIEVE ME, ANGELINA, THIS IS NEW TERRITORY FOR ME, TOO...I'VE NEVER DONE ANYTHING LIKE THIS OVER VIDEO CHAT! BUT I'M READY, IF THIS IS WHAT YOU WANT...
I THINK SOMETHING SO INTIMATE AND SECRET WILL BRING US CLOSER!
ANF
ANF
OH, POOKY! IT'S STARTING!
ANF
MMHNN... OH, ANGIE!
ANF
ANF
ANF
ANF
ANF
MMMMH... JUST A LITTLE MORE!
ANF
ANF
A+D
YES... AHNNNNNN... YES, ME TOO!
ANF
ANF
OH, DAMIANO, I LOVE YOU!
ANF
ANF
ANF
ANF
ANF
ANF
HERE WE GO!
AAAAAAAAH!
OH, MY LITTLE TOMATO! POTTY TIME TOGETHER IS SO INTIMATE!
PLOFF
IF THIS IS WHAT KNOCKS YOU OUT INSTEAD OF KNOCKING ONE OUT...SO MUCH FOR A GOODNIGHT TEXT!
PLOFF

NO, SEVERINO! YOU CAN'T EAT CHALK!
TEACHERAAAAAAH, PLEASEPLEASE PLEASEPLEASE PLEASEPLEASE...
OH, DAMIANO... I ADORE CHILDREN, BUT SOMETIMES THEY JUST DRIVE ME UP THE WEEPING WALL! THEY CAN JUST BE SO-- SO--CHILDISH!
HAHA, I CAN ONLY IMAGINE! NOW THAT YOU'RE AROUND GROWNUPS, YOU CAN FINALLY RELAX!
YOU'RE SO BEAUTIFUL! I'VE SEEN ALL YOUR MOVIES!
OH, HEAVENS! IS THAT THE PORN ACTRESS WHO WAS ON THE COVER OF WHORE OF BABE-YLON LAST YEAR? GRACIOUS!
HERE YOU GO, DEAR!
LOOK HOW QUICKLY THOSE MEN ABANDON THEIR WIVES AND GIRLFRIENDS TO GO SNIFF AFTER HER! SO SHAMELESS AND DISLOYAL!
I DON'T KNOW...
PLIN
I'M SO GLAD YOU'RE DIFFERENT, POOKY! I BET YOU DON'T EVEN KNOW HER NAME!
LILITH, CLASS '85, TEN YEARS OF CAREER IN FETISH LESBIAN PORN. MISS BIG BOOBS OF THE YEAR. UNDISPUTED STAR OF THE "HORNY DEVILS" TRILOGY! I MUST...I MUST RESISTS! Y-YES! I'M NOT SOME SLOBBERING DOG IN RUT! SHE'S JUST A WORKING DEVIL LIKE ANY OF THEM!
WHO WANTS AN AUTOGRAPH DOWN BELOW, BOYS? I'VE BEEN PRACTICING MY JOHN HAN-COCK!
OH, ANGIE, I WANT THE AUTOGRAPH TOO, PLEASEPLEASE PLEASEPLEASE PLEASEPLEASE...

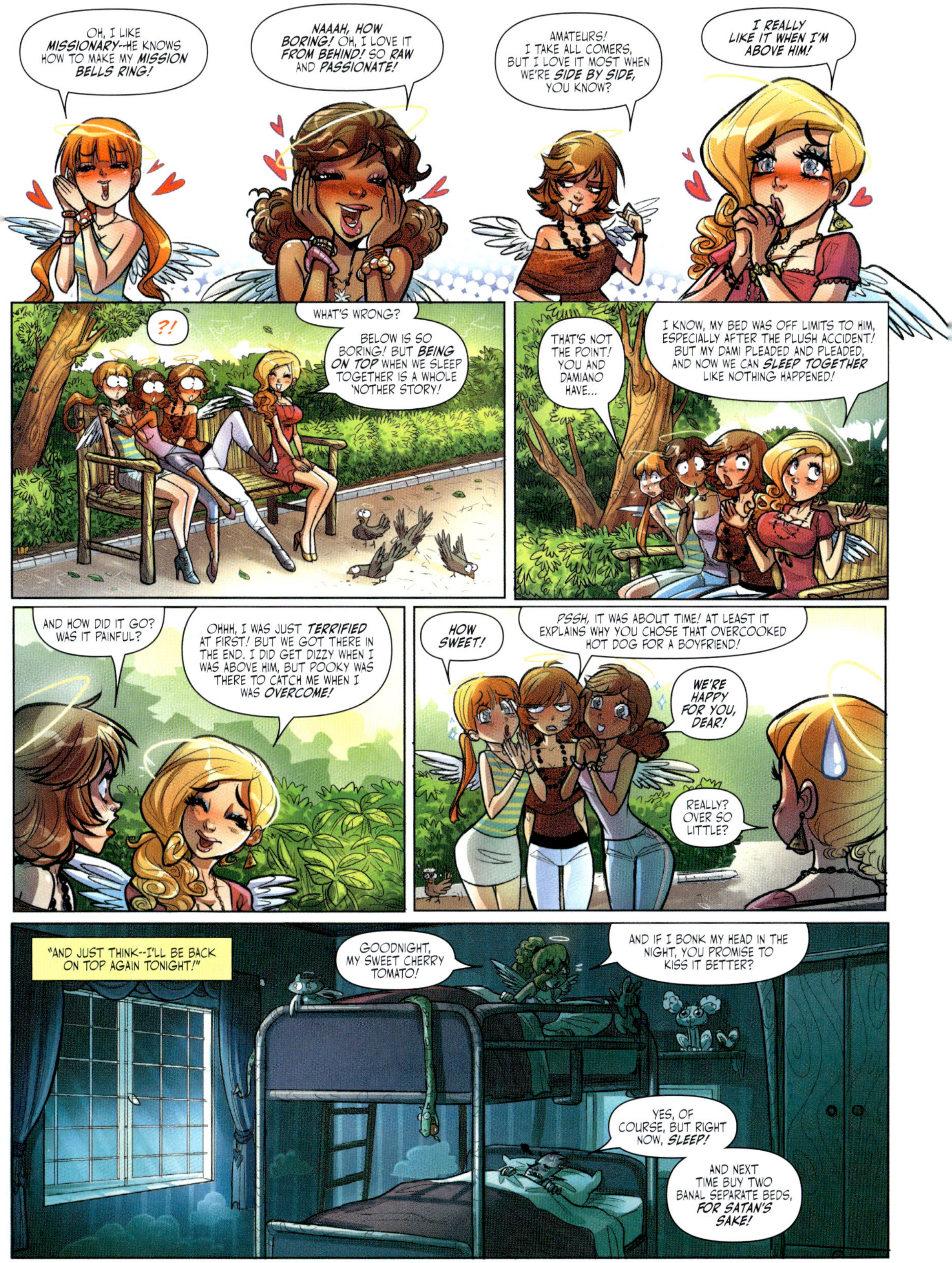
OH, I LIKE MISSIONARY--HE KNOWS HOW TO MAKE MY MISSION BELLS RING!
NAAAH, HOW BORING! OH, I LOVE IT FROM BEHIND! SO RAW AND PASSIONATE!
AMATEURS! I TAKE ALL COMERS, BUT I LOVE IT MOST WHEN WE'RE SIDE BY SIDE, YOU KNOW?
I REALLY LIKE IT WHEN I'M ABOVE HIM!
?!
WHAT'S WRONG?
BELOW IS SO BORING! BUT BEING ON TOP WHEN WE SLEEP TOGETHER IS A WHOLE 'NOTHER STORY!
THAT'S NOT THE POINT! YOU AND DAMIANO HAVE...
I KNOW, MY BED WAS OFF LIMITS TO HIM, ESPECIALLY AFTER THE PLUSH ACCIDENT! BUT MY DAMI PLEADED AND PLEADED, AND NOW WE CAN SLEEP TOGETHER LIKE NOTHING HAPPENED!
AND HOW DID IT GO? WAS IT PAINFUL?
OHHH, I WAS JUST TERRIFIED AT FIRST! BUT WE GOT THERE IN THE END. I DID GET DIZZY WHEN I WAS ABOVE HIM, BUT POOKY WAS THERE TO CATCH ME WHEN I WAS OVERCOME!
HOW SWEET!
PSSH, IT WAS ABOUT TIME! AT LEAST IT EXPLAINS WHY YOU CHOSE THAT OVERCOOKED HOT DOG FOR A BOYFRIEND!
WE'RE HAPPY FOR YOU, DEAR!
REALLY? OVER SO LITTLE?
"AND JUST THINK--I'LL BE BACK ON TOP AGAIN TONIGHT!"
GOODNIGHT, MY SWEET CHERRY TOMATO!
AND IF I BONK MY HEAD IN THE NIGHT, YOU PROMISE TO KISS IT BETTER?
YES, OF COURSE, BUT RIGHT NOW, SLEEP!
AND NEXT TIME BUY TWO BANAL SEPARATE BEDS, FOR SATAN'S SAKE!

SEE YOU TOMORROW, LITTLE ONES!
SEE YOU, TEACHER!
SEVERINO, WHAT ARE YOU STILL DOING HERE? DIDN'T YOU HAVE ANOTHER CHALKING FIT?
THIS IS FOR YOU!
IF IT'S ONE OF YOUR USUAL JOKES, I SWEAR...
YOU DO YOU WOANT TO BE MY GIRLXFRIEND?
YES OR NO
MARK WITH "X"
SWEET SEVERINO! I'VE MISJUDGED YOU, PLEASE FORGIVE ME, YOU DEAR LITTLE DEVIL DUMPLING!
TELL ME YES, TEACHER! I LIKE YOU SO MUCH!
POOR PUPPY! I CERTAINLY CAN'T BREAK HIS LITTLE HEART BY REFUSING HIM! MAYBE I SHOULD GO ALONG WITH IT FOR A WHILE, UNTIL HE FORGETS AND HAS OTHER HOBBIES...
OK, BUT THIS STAYS BETWEEN ME AND YOU! IF DAMIANO DISCOVERS HE'LL BE JEALOUS, AND HE'LL CRY! WE DON'T WANT THAT, DO WE?
HOORAY!
SMACK
HEHEHE! I LOVE CHILDREN! THEY'RE SO SWEET, INNOCENT...SO PURE!
BIP BIP
UGH, I'M SO BORED...LET'S SEE WHAT'S ON FACEBIBLE...OOOH, A NEW PRIVATE MESSAGE?
diavoli, luoghi e oggetti
Damiano
+ Nuovo messaggio
Azioni
Severino
From now on, I'm gonna be the one plowing your girlfriend.

OHHH, POOKY! DID YOU COME GALLOPING IN ON YOUR WHITE STEED FOR OUR WEDDING DAY!
I CAN'T WAIT TO START A FAMILY!
WELL...
?!
AFTER YOU REFUSED TO TAKE MY NEEDS SERIOUSLY, I WOUND UP LOOKING ELSEWHERE, AND DISCOVERED A SIDE OF MYSELF I NEVER KNEW EXISTED... ISN'T THAT TRUE, MY SWEET GUIDA?
NNOOOoOoOoOoOoOOOoOoOoOoOo!
DAMIANO, CHOOSE ME!
FEEL, POOKY, WHAT A SOFT SKIN YOUR ANGIE'S GOT! GUIDA DOESN'T FEEL LIKE THAT!
YOU LIKE ME, RIGHT? I'M THE ONE YOU CHOSE, DIDN'T YOU?!
PLIN!
OH, MY...I, UH, "FEEL" YOU VERY CONFIDENT ABOUT ME...ABSOLUTELY ADAMANT, IN FACT.
YOU CAN BET!
OH, WHAT A RELIEF! IF WE HAVEN'T ANY DOUBTS, THEN WE HAVEN'T ANYTHING TO PROVE BY EXPERIMENTAL INTERCOURSE! WELP, GOOD NIGHT!
00:20
AHHH, FINALLY, SOME SOLID BEAUTY SLEEP!
04:25

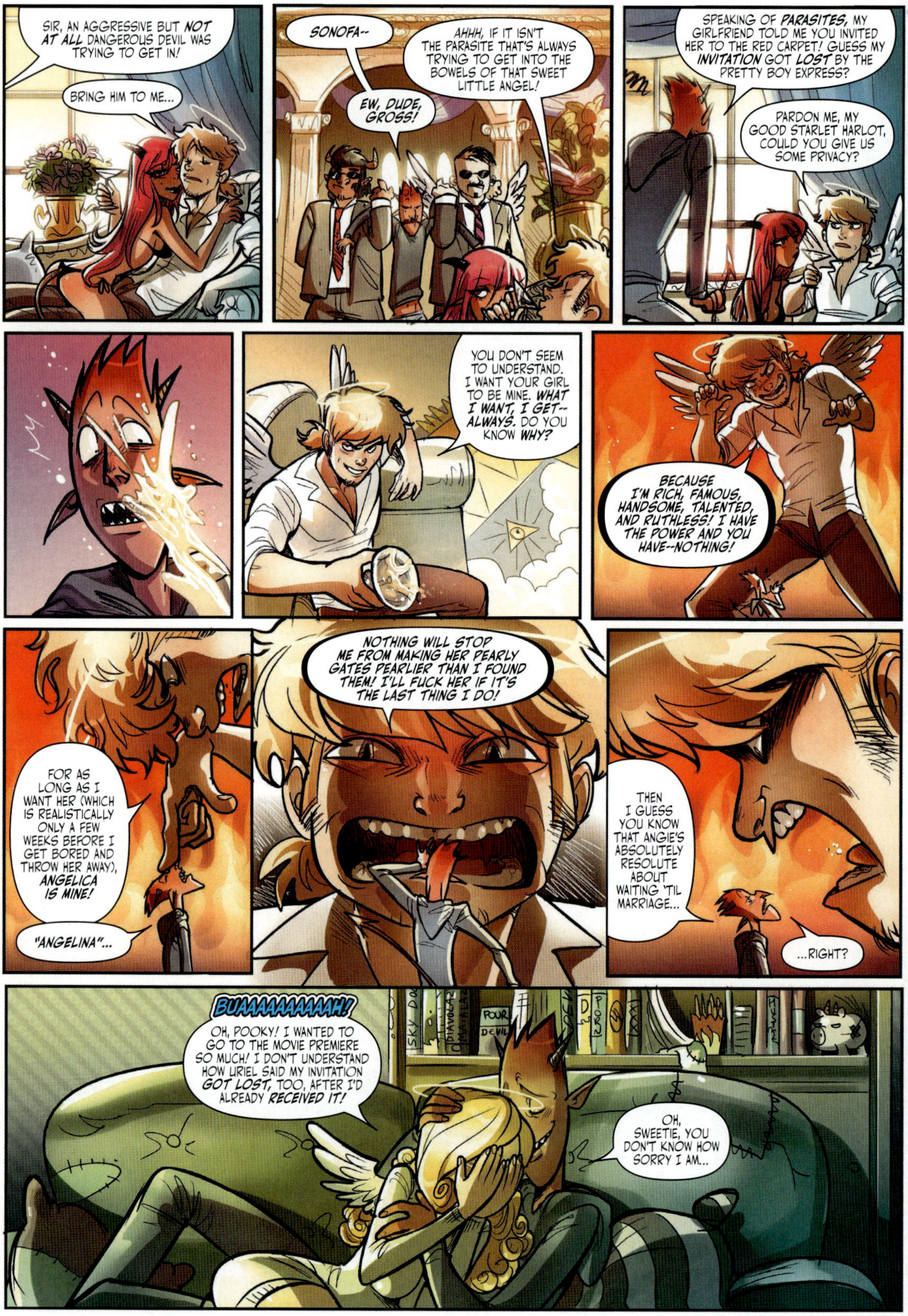
SIR, AN AGGRESSIVE BUT NOT AT ALL DANGEROUS DEVIL WAS TRYING TO GET IN!
BRING HIM TO ME...
SONOFA--
AHHH, IF IT ISN'T THE PARASITE THAT'S ALWAYS TRYING TO GET INTO THE BOWELS OF THAT SWEET LITTLE ANGEL!
EW, DUDE, GROSS!
SPEAKING OF PARASITES, MY GIRLFRIEND TOLD ME YOU INVITED HER TO THE RED CARPET! GUESS MY INVITATION GOT LOST BY THE PRETTY BOY EXPRESS?
PARDON ME, MY GOOD STARLET HARLOT, COULD YOU GIVE US SOME PRIVACY?
YOU DON'T SEEM TO UNDERSTAND. I WANT YOUR GIRL TO BE MINE. WHAT I WANT, I GET--ALWAYS. DO YOU KNOW WHY?
BECAUSE I'M RICH, FAMOUS, HANDSOME, TALENTED, AND RUTHLESS! I HAVE THE POWER AND YOU HAVE--NOTHING!
FOR AS LONG AS I WANT HER (WHICH IS REALISTICALLY ONLY A FEW WEEKS BEFORE I GET BORED AND THROW HER AWAY), ANGELICA IS MINE!
"ANGELINA"...
NOTHING WILL STOP ME FROM MAKING HER PEARLY GATES PEARLIER THAN I FOUND THEM! I'LL FUCK HER IF IT'S THE LAST THING I DO!
THEN I GUESS YOU KNOW THAT ANGIE'S ABSOLUTELY RESOLUTE ABOUT WAITING 'TIL MARRIAGE...
...RIGHT?
BUAAAAAAAAAAH!
OH, POOKY! I WANTED TO GO TO THE MOVIE PREMIERE SO MUCH! I DON'T UNDERSTAND HOW URIEL SAID MY INVITATION GOT LOST, TOO, AFTER I'D ALREADY RECEIVED IT!
OH, SWEETIE, YOU DON'T KNOW HOW SORRY I AM...

GET OFF MY TITS AND QUIT CALLING ME, YOU NEEDY SLIMEBALL!
IS SOMETHING WRONG, MICHELA?
UGH, HE'S JUST A STICKY FRIEND WITH BENEFITS...HE THINKS I'M HIS GIRLFRIEND!
TOO PATHETIC!
"FRIEND WITH BENEFITS"?
SOMEONE YOU CAN HAVE SEX WITH, WITH NO FEELINGS. HE'S ACTUALLY SOMEONE YOU KNOW--
GUIDA!
WHAT?! BUT DON'T YOU PREFER THE RICH, HANDSOME COUNTRY CLUB BOYS?
ABSOLUTELY!
I NEVER THOUGHT I'D EVER WANT SOMEONE LIKE HIM, BUT WE HOOKED UP WHEN I WAS BUZZED AND...
WELL, SINCE I'M THE COOLEST GIRL HE'S EVER SCORED WITH, HE FUCKS ME LIKE THERE'S NO TOMORROW! I'VE NEVER HAD IT THIS GOOD!
AHH, SPARE ME THE DETAILS...
HE LASTS LONGER THAN ANY LOVER I'VE EVER HAD! AND HOW ENDOWED! LIKE THIS! IT'S NOT A PENIS, IT'S A DIVINE INSTRUMENT OF FEMALE PLEASURE!
AND THE ORAL SEX IS SPECTACULAR!
BUT YOU DON'T WANT TO HAVE ANYTHING TO DO WITH HIM. RIGHT?
...
HELLO, YOU HUSKY HERCULES... IT'S TEN MINUTES SINCE YOU CALLED ME... WHY DON'T YOU COME TO SEE ME?
I MISS YOU SO MUCH...

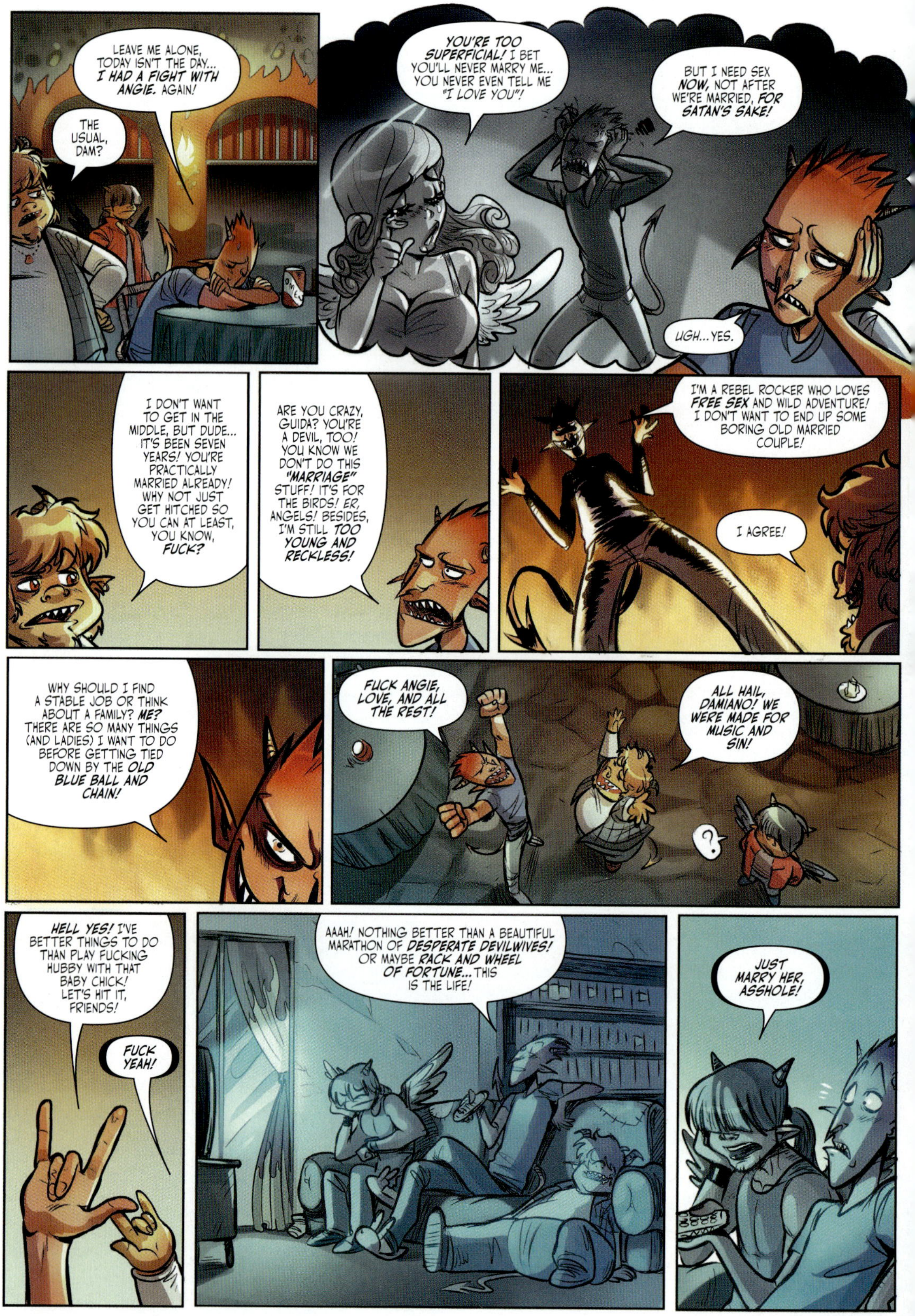
LEAVE ME ALONE, TODAY ISN'T THE DAY... I HAD A FIGHT WITH ANGIE. AGAIN!
THE USUAL, DAM?
YOU'RE TOO SUPERFICIAL! I BET YOU'LL NEVER MARRY ME... YOU NEVER EVEN TELL ME "I LOVE YOU"!
BUT I NEED SEX NOW, NOT AFTER WE'RE MARRIED, FOR SATAN'S SAKE!
UGH... YES.
I DON'T WANT TO GET IN THE MIDDLE, BUT DUDE... IT'S BEEN SEVEN YEARS! YOU'RE PRACTICALLY MARRIED ALREADY! WHY NOT JUST GET HITCHED SO YOU CAN AT LEAST, YOU KNOW, FUCK?
ARE YOU CRAZY, GUIDA? YOU'RE A DEVIL, TOO! YOU KNOW WE DON'T DO THIS "MARRIAGE" STUFF! IT'S FOR THE BIRDS! ER, ANGELS! BESIDES, I'M STILL TOO YOUNG AND RECKLESS!
I'M A REBEL ROCKER WHO LOVES FREE SEX AND WILD ADVENTURE! I DON'T WANT TO END UP SOME BORING OLD MARRIED COUPLE!
I AGREE!
WHY SHOULD I FIND A STABLE JOB OR THINK ABOUT A FAMILY? ME? THERE ARE SO MANY THINGS (AND LADIES) I WANT TO DO BEFORE GETTING TIED DOWN BY THE OLD BLUE BALL AND CHAIN!
FUCK ANGIE, LOVE, AND ALL THE REST!
ALL HAIL, DAMIANO! WE WERE MADE FOR MUSIC AND SIN!
?
HELL YES! I'VE BETTER THINGS TO DO THAN PLAY FUCKING HUBBY WITH THAT BABY CHICK! LET'S HIT IT, FRIENDS!
FUCK YEAH!
AAAH! NOTHING BETTER THAN A BEAUTIFUL MARATHON OF DESPERATE DEVILWIVES! OR MAYBE RACK AND WHEEL OF FORTUNE... THIS IS THE LIFE!
JUST MARRY HER, ASSHOLE!

WHAT ABOUT THE DRESSING ROOM, ANGIE?
WOW! TONIGHT YOU'LL BE A REAL ROCK STAR!
RIGHT...I BET YOU WANT TO HAVE SEX, DRUGS AND ROCK & ROLL IN HERE...THAT FIRST ONE ABOVE ALL!
COME ON, DAMI...YOU'VE TO CONCENTRATE FOR THE CONCERT!
SEE YOU LATER, MY LITTLE POOKY PUCCINI!
UGH...
BUT WHO IS THAT?
OH, MY LITTLE DEVIL HAS A LOT OF GROUPIES, LIKE ALL THE STARS!
UAAAARGH!
NO CAR, NO CASH, NO JOB, NO LUCK! I'D SELL MY SOUL, JUST LET ME FU--!
DAMIANO, I LOVE YOU! PLEASE, DEFLOWER ME!
DAMIANOOO? YOU SANG DELICIOUSLY AS USUAL...
OH?
URGH! ER...WELL... I CAN EXPLAIN EVERYTHING...
OH, BUT I'M NOT JEALOUS...GO AHEAD AND I SEE YOU TOMORROW!
?!
HEEHEE! SHE EVEN GAVE ME HER PERMISSION! THIS IS THE BEST DAY OF MY LIFE!
STRAAAPPP
ANGELINA IS REALLY UNIQUE, IT'S ALSO FOR THIS REASON THAT I LOV...
UH...
?
AFTER TONIGHT, I THOUGHT I'D BE THE ONE, SHALL I SAY, "WEARING THE HORNS"...?
SGRUNT! ON THE OTHER HAND, SOONER OR LATER I'LL GET A FUCKING HALO!
DE SCARTAVETRAMENTUM MARONES
CONCERT OF SACRED MUSIC FOR WHITE VOICES AND PERCUSSION BUT WITHOUT TRIANGLE
BLINK

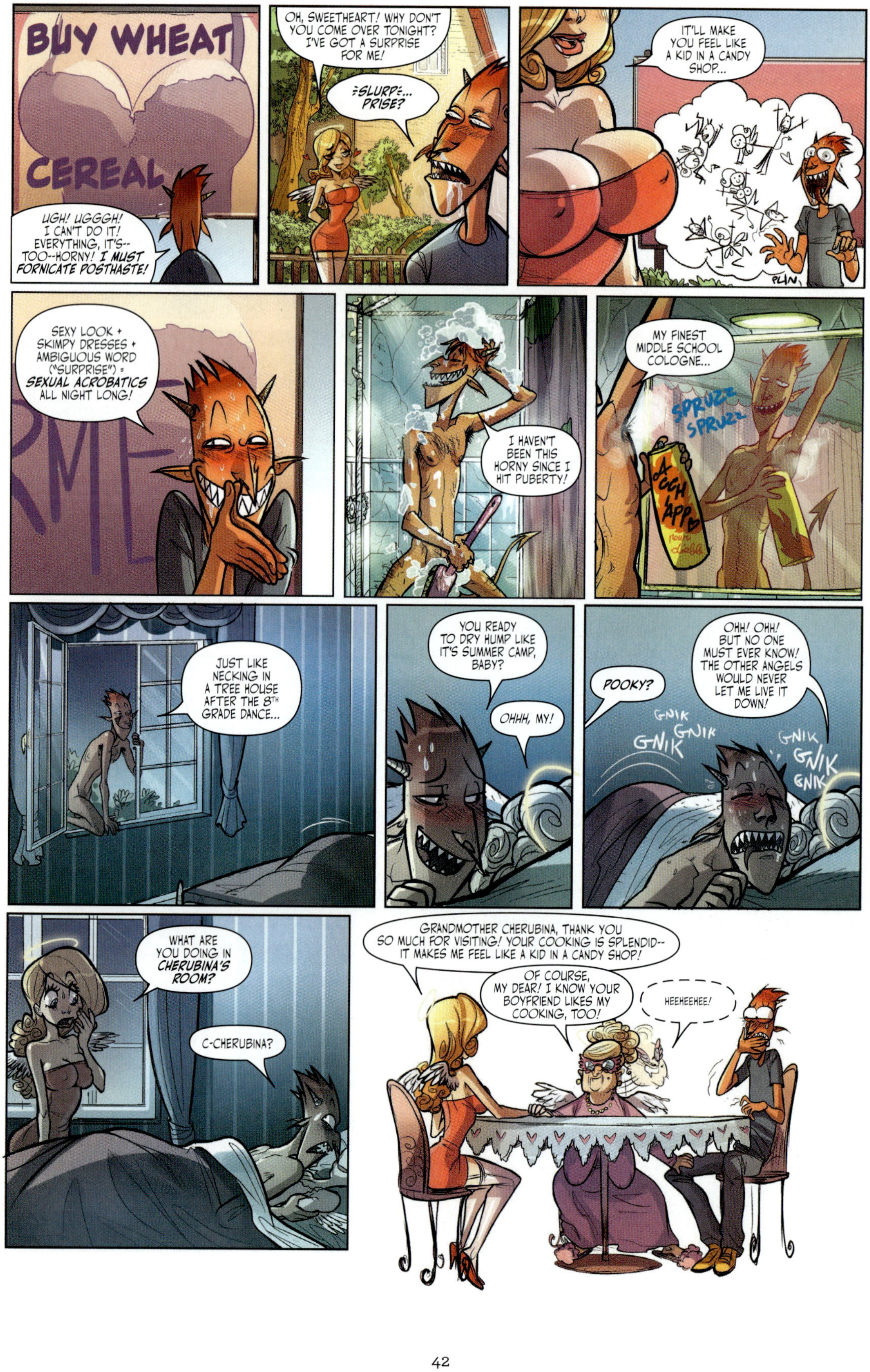
BUY WHEAT
CEREAL
UGH! UGGGH! I CAN'T DO IT! EVERYTHING, IT'S-- TOO--HORNY! I MUST FORNICATE POSTHASTE!
OH, SWEETHEART! WHY DON'T YOU COME OVER TONIGHT? I'VE GOT A SURPRISE FOR ME!
SLURP... PRISE?
IT'LL MAKE YOU FEEL LIKE A KID IN A CANDY SHOP...
PLIN
SEXY LOOK + SKIMPY DRESSES + AMBIGUOUS WORD ("SURPRISE") = SEXUAL ACROBATICS ALL NIGHT LONG!
I HAVEN'T BEEN THIS HORNY SINCE I HIT PUBERTY!
MY FINEST MIDDLE SCHOOL COLOGNE...
SPRUZZ SPRUZZ
JUST LIKE NECKING IN A TREE HOUSE AFTER THE 8TH GRADE DANCE...
YOU READY TO DRY HUMP LIKE IT'S SUMMER CAMP, BABY?
OHHH, MY!
POOKY?
OHH! OHH! BUT NO ONE MUST EVER KNOW! THE OTHER ANGELS WOULD NEVER LET ME LIVE IT DOWN!
GNIK GNIK GNIK
GNIK GNIK GNIK
WHAT ARE YOU DOING IN CHERUBINA'S ROOM?
C-CHERUBINA?
GRANDMOTHER CHERUBINA, THANK YOU SO MUCH FOR VISITING! YOUR COOKING IS SPLENDID-- IT MAKES ME FEEL LIKE A KID IN A CANDY SHOP!
OF COURSE, MY DEAR! I KNOW YOUR BOYFRIEND LIKES MY COOKING, TOO!
HEEHEEHEE!

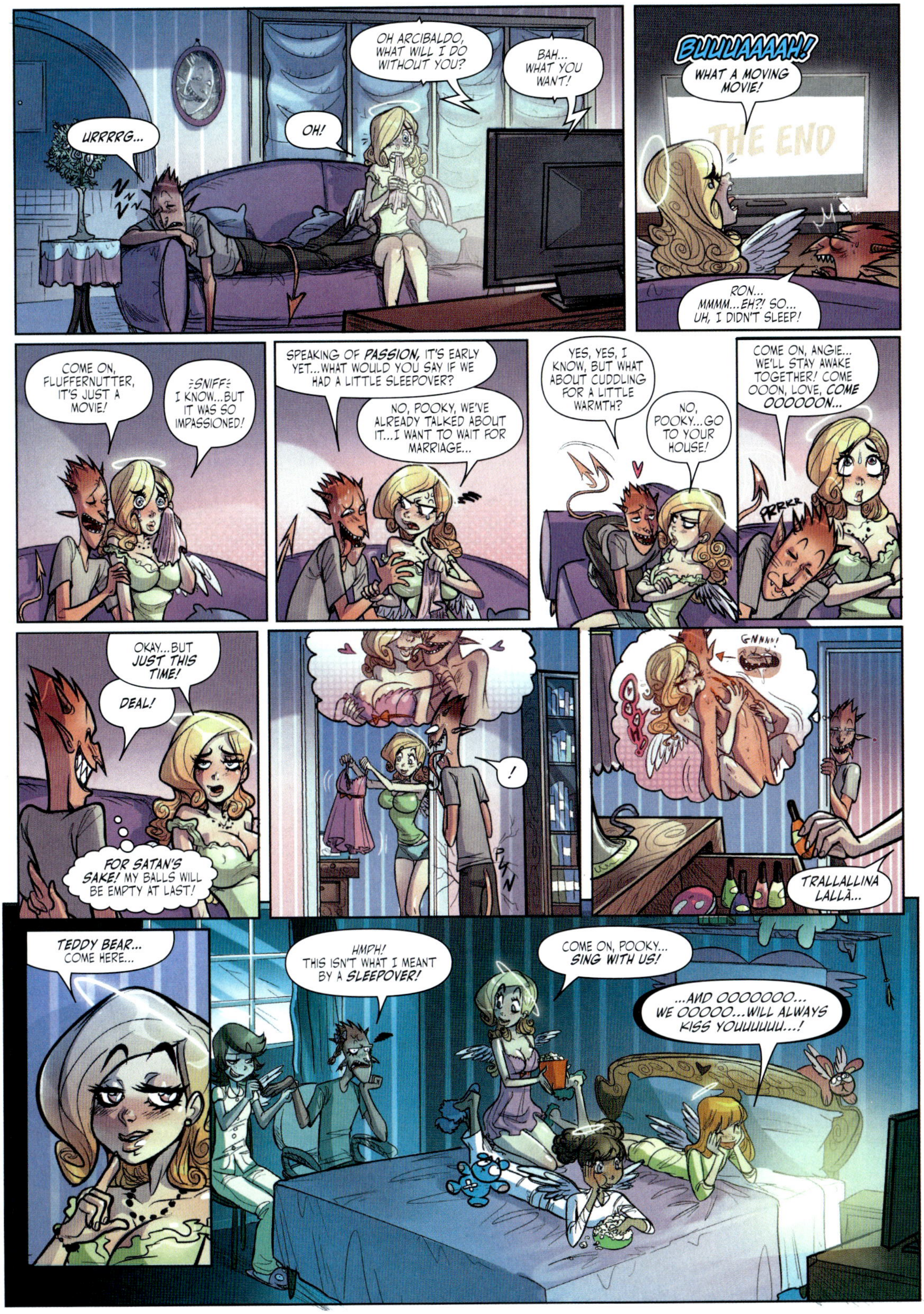
URRRRG...
OH!
OH ARCIBALDO, WHAT WILL I DO WITHOUT YOU?
BAH... WHAT YOU WANT!
BUUUAAAAH!
WHAT A MOVING MOVIE!
THE END
RON...
MMMM...EH?! SO... UH, I DIDN'T SLEEP!
COME ON, FLUFFERNUTTER, IT'S JUST A MOVIE!
SNIFF I KNOW...BUT IT WAS SO IMPASSIONED!
SPEAKING OF PASSION, IT'S EARLY YET...WHAT WOULD YOU SAY IF WE HAD A LITTLE SLEEPOVER?
NO, POOKY, WE'VE ALREADY TALKED ABOUT IT...I WANT TO WAIT FOR MARRIAGE...
YES, YES, I KNOW, BUT WHAT ABOUT CUDDLING FOR A LITTLE WARMTH?
NO, POOKY...GO TO YOUR HOUSE!
COME ON, ANGIE... WE'LL STAY AWAKE TOGETHER! COME OOON, LOVE, COME OOOOOON...
OKAY...BUT JUST THIS TIME!
DEAL!
FOR SATAN'S SAKE! MY BALLS WILL BE EMPTY AT LAST!
!
TRALLALLINA LALLÀ...
TEDDY BEAR... COME HERE...
HMPH! THIS ISN'T WHAT I MEANT BY A SLEEPOVER!
COME ON, POOKY... SING WITH US!
...AND OOOOOOO... WE OOOOO...WILL ALWAYS KISS YOUUUUUU...!

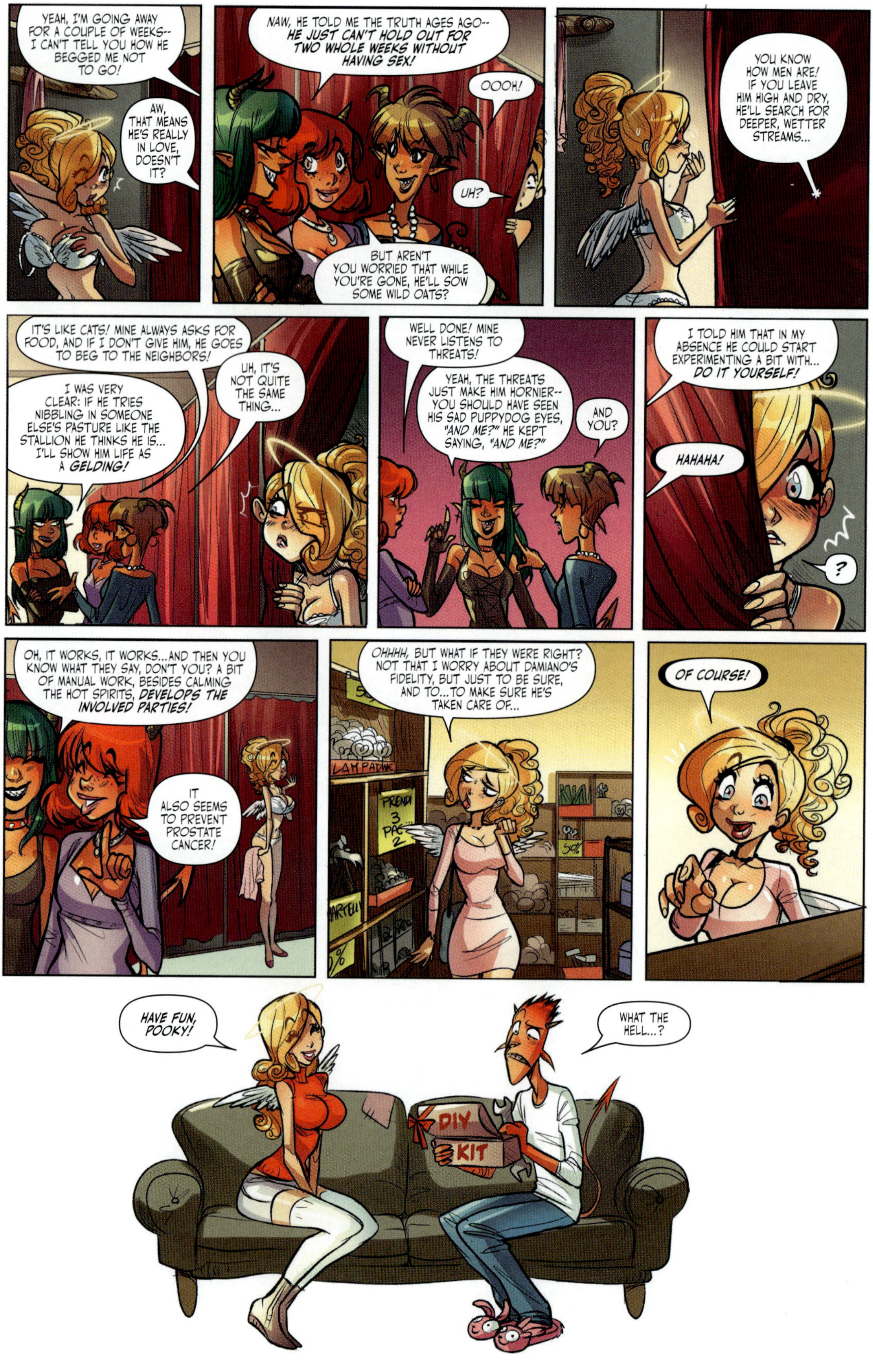
YEAH, I'M GOING AWAY FOR A COUPLE OF WEEKS--I CAN'T TELL YOU HOW HE BEGGED ME NOT TO GO!
AW, THAT MEANS HE'S REALLY IN LOVE, DOESN'T IT?
NAW, HE TOLD ME THE TRUTH AGES AGO--**HE JUST CAN'T HOLD OUT FOR TWO WHOLE WEEKS WITHOUT HAVING SEX!**
OOOH!
UH?
BUT AREN'T YOU WORRIED THAT WHILE YOU'RE GONE, HE'LL SOW SOME WILD OATS?
YOU KNOW HOW MEN ARE! IF YOU LEAVE HIM HIGH AND DRY, HE'LL SEARCH FOR DEEPER, WETTER STREAMS...
IT'S LIKE CATS! MINE ALWAYS ASKS FOR FOOD, AND IF I DON'T GIVE HIM, HE GOES TO BEG TO THE NEIGHBORS!
I WAS VERY CLEAR: IF HE TRIES NIBBLING IN SOMEONE ELSE'S PASTURE LIKE THE STALLION HE THINKS HE IS... I'LL SHOW HIM LIFE AS A *GELDING!*
UH, IT'S NOT QUITE THE SAME THING...
WELL DONE! MINE NEVER LISTENS TO THREATS!
YEAH, THE THREATS JUST MAKE HIM HORNIER--YOU SHOULD HAVE SEEN HIS SAD PUPPYDOG EYES, *"AND ME?"* HE KEPT SAYING, *"AND ME?"*
AND YOU?
I TOLD HIM THAT IN MY ABSENCE HE COULD START EXPERIMENTING A BIT WITH... ***DO IT YOURSELF!***
HAHAHA!
?
OH, IT WORKS, IT WORKS...AND THEN YOU KNOW WHAT THEY SAY, DON'T YOU? A BIT OF MANUAL WORK, BESIDES CALMING THE HOT SPIRITS, ***DEVELOPS THE INVOLVED PARTIES!***
IT ALSO SEEMS TO PREVENT PROSTATE CANCER!
OHHHH, BUT WHAT IF THEY WERE RIGHT? NOT THAT I WORRY ABOUT DAMIANO'S FIDELITY, BUT JUST TO BE SURE, AND TO...TO MAKE SURE HE'S TAKEN CARE OF...
LAMPADINE
PRENDI 3 PAG 2
30%
OF COURSE!
HAVE FUN, POOKY!
WHAT THE HELL...?
DIY KIT

Holy Kitty Land
SO, IS THE SURPRISE READY?
OH, POOKY! WHAT A SWEET THOUGHT TO TAKE ME TO HOLYKITTYLAND!
FOR MY SWEET LITTLE ANGEL, THIS AND MORE...
SCREW BUYING DINNERS AND DRINKS AND TRIPS TO THE OPERA! AFTER THIS, SHE'LL PUT OUT FOR SURE!
LET'S GO!
"--TAKE THE PLUNGE!"
I'M A BIT SCARED, POOKY...
NEVER FEAR, I'M WITH YOU!
WII!
SLURP!
PLIN!
PURRRATES OF THE CARIBBEAN
HOW BEAUTIFUL!
UUUH... IT'S COLD!
PLIN!
I HAD A LOT OF FUN!
LET'S GET SOUVENIR T-SHIRTS!
Holy Kitty Land SHOP
OF COURSE, IT'LL LOOK EVEN BETTER FLUNG AT THE END OF MY BED...
OH, BUT IT'S NOT MY SIZE!
OH, NO! IT DOESN'T LOOK AT ALL LIKE IT DID ON THE RACK!
TRUST ME, BABE...
THIS RACK... IS THE ONLY ONE YOU'LL EVER NEED.
PLIN!

DRIIIN
HAPPY HOLIDAYS AND MERRY CHRISTMAS! SEE YOU IN JANUARY!
UHM...
SOMETHING SHADY IS HAPPENING DOWN THERE!
?!
...AND IF YOU DO ME THIS FAVOR, I'LL GIVE YOU A NICE BAG FULL OF CANDY! BUT YOU'LL HAVE TO BE GOOD, DISCREET, AND DO EXACTLY WHAT I TOLD YOU!
OK!
OH HEAVEN! WE'VE TO DO SOMETHING, AND NOW!
I'LL HANDLE THAT!
UAHÀÀ
SBAM
I'LL MAKE CHRISTMAS PUDDING OUTTA YOU!
STAND BY ME AND DON'T LOOK! IT'S NOT A GOOD SHOW, BUT THAT DESPICABLE BEING DESERVES IT ALL!
GO SO, ERMENEGILDA, BREAK THAT UGLY PERVERT'S FACE!
BUT TEACHER, ISN'T THAT THE DEVIL I SAW YOU KISSING UNDER THE MISTLETOE?
?!
CRUNCH CRUNCH
OH NO! ERMY, STOP! THAT'S MY BOYFRIEND, DAMIANO!
WHAT, THIS LUMP OF COAL?
HANGIHEH, THEHREH WAHS AH MIHSUHNDEHR-STAHNDIHNG!

TEACHER, THE UGLY DEVIL-MAN TOLD US TO GIVE YOU THIS!
WHY DIDN'T THOSE LITTLE BASTARDS MOVE FASTER?
EH?
HE SAYS THAT SANTA CLAUS CHOSE US FOR A SPECIAL MISSION!
"DA...DARLING ANGEL...INA! SINCE YOU HAVE BIG...BOO..." UHM, NO IT'S CROSSED OUT.
"...YOU ARE SO G... GOOD AND NICE WITH DA..."
"...WITH DAMIANO, I DECIDED TO SEND YOU A NICE CHRISTMAS PRESENT IN ADVANCE!"
"ME, I MEAN SANTA CLAUS, I SEND YOU THIS... THIS GIFT FOR HIM! HE DOESN'T...HAVE THE COUGAR..." I MEAN "THE COURAGE...BECAUSE HE IS A LITTLE STUPID!" HEHEHE! THERE IS WRITTEN STUPID!
"HE TOOK SO MANY YEARS... TO DECIDE, SO I D...I DID IT FOR HIM!"
!
"...HE LOVES YOU VERY MUCH, EVEN IF...HE DOES NOT SAY IT...BECAUSE HE IS SHY! BUT HE LOVES YOU SO MUCH...
"...HE HAS DE... DECIDED THAT HE WANTS TO SPEND ALL HIS LIFE...WITH YOU! AND I WOULD BE...WOULD BE...HAPPY IF AS A CHRISTMAS GIFT, YOU WOULD SAY 'YES' AND MA..." UM, HOW DO YOU READ THIS?
"MARRY HIM," STUPID IDIOT!
MISSION ACCOMPLISHED!
HOORAY!
DO YOU SEE HOW ROMANTIC IS SANTA CLAUS? HEHEHE! SORRY IF IT TOOK ME A WHILE TO UNDERSTAND THAT I'M NOT A KID ANYMORE, AND THAT IT'S TIME FOR US TO GET SERIOUS... YOU'RE TOO IMPORTANT TO ME! SO WHAT DO YOU THINK, UH... "POOKY"?

YUP! YES, MY CHERRY TOMATO! I LOVE YOU!
I CAN'T WAIT TO TELL MICHELA AND--
OH, I SENT HER A MESSAGE BEFORE. SHE KNOWS!
UH? WHY?
"WELL...I WANTED TO HAVE SOME SATISFACTION!"
THAT LITTLE VIRGIN IS GETTING MARRIED BEFORE ME?! THE ONLY RING I'VE GOT IS A HALO!
AAAH! SO CUTE! LIKE ME AND MY GIANGIOVANNI!
"LIKE"?!
BE READY FOR THE WEDDING NIGHT, EH! A YEAR PASSES QUICKLY! PAH HA HA HA!
I DON'T SEE WHY WE SHOULD WAIT THAT LONG.
EH?
I WAS A FOOL, DAMIANO!
I BELIEVED THAT TO STRENGTHEN A RELATIONSHIP, YOU HAD TO WAIT...
BUT IT'S NOT SO! YOU'VE BEEN WITH ME FOR SEVEN YEARS, RESPECTING MY WISHES. AND TODAY, ALL THIS... AT THIS POINT, WHY WAIT ANY LONGER? ANY TIME IS THE RIGHT ONE, NOW!
CAN YOU EVER FORGIVE ME FOR HAVING UNDERSTOOD IT SO LATE?
SO YOU'RE TELLING ME, AFTER YEARS OF STUFFING MY OWN STOCKING, YOU'VE SUDDENLY UNDERSTOOD THIS. NOW THAT I'VE PROPOSED TO YOU.
YUP!
MH.
SO IF I COME TO YOUR HOUSE TONIGHT, I HAVE PERMISSION TO DEFLOWER YOU. RIGHT?
I WOULD LIKE THAT VERY MUCH!
FORGIVEEEN...
PLIIIIN!

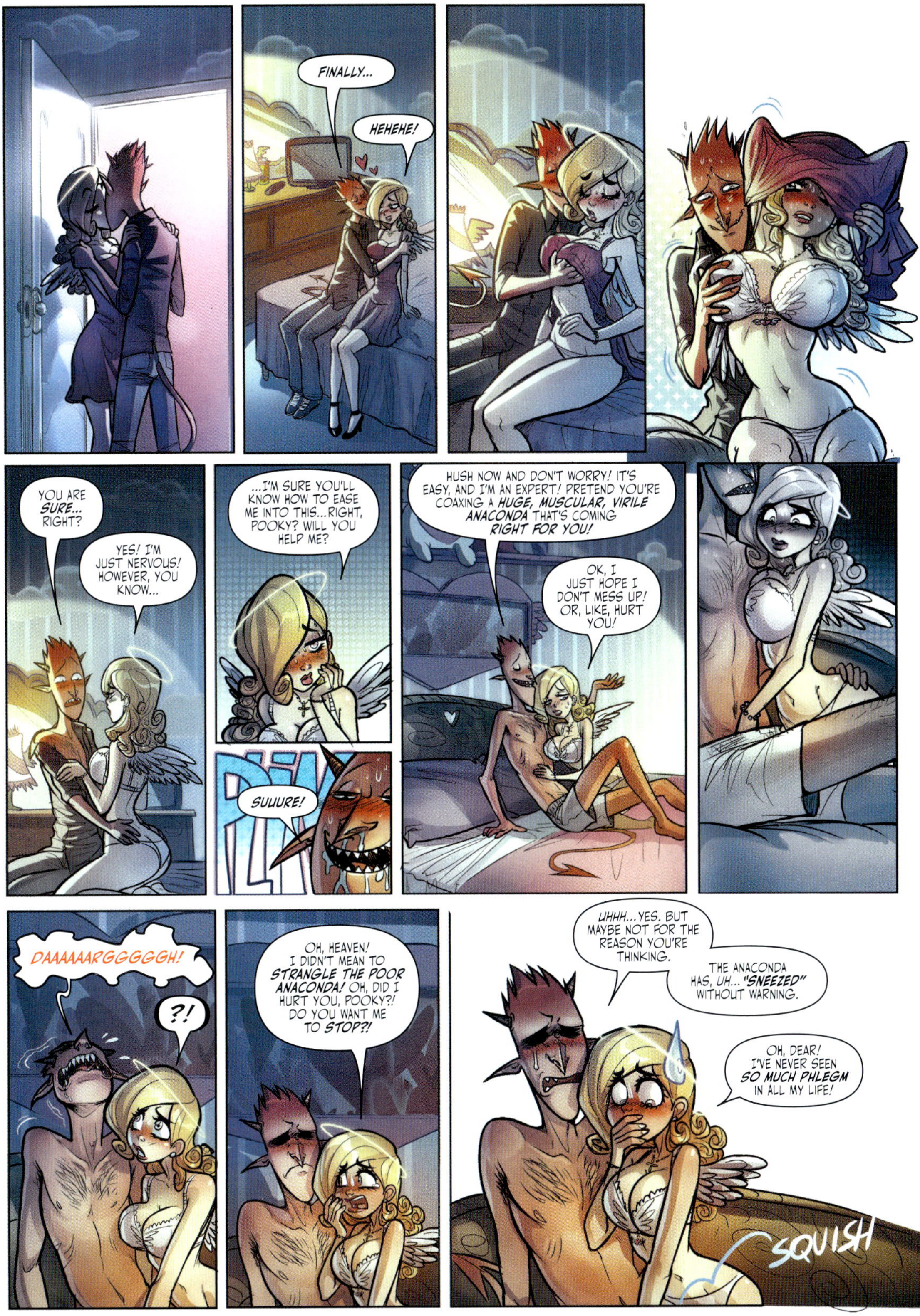
FINALLY...
HEHEHE!
YOU ARE SURE... RIGHT?
YES! I'M JUST NERVOUS! HOWEVER, YOU KNOW...
...I'M SURE YOU'LL KNOW HOW TO EASE ME INTO THIS...RIGHT, POOKY? WILL YOU HELP ME?
SUUURE!
HUSH NOW AND DON'T WORRY! IT'S EASY, AND I'M AN EXPERT! PRETEND YOU'RE COAXING A HUGE, MUSCULAR, VIRILE ANACONDA THAT'S COMING RIGHT FOR YOU!
OK, I JUST HOPE I DON'T MESS UP! OR, LIKE, HURT YOU!
DAAAAAARGGGGGH!
?!
OH, HEAVEN! I DIDN'T MEAN TO STRANGLE THE POOR ANACONDA! OH, DID I HURT YOU, POOKY?! DO YOU WANT ME TO STOP?!
UHHH...YES. BUT MAYBE NOT FOR THE REASON YOU'RE THINKING.
THE ANACONDA HAS, UH... "SNEEZED" WITHOUT WARNING.
OH, DEAR! I'VE NEVER SEEN SO MUCH PHLEGM IN ALL MY LIFE!
SQUISH

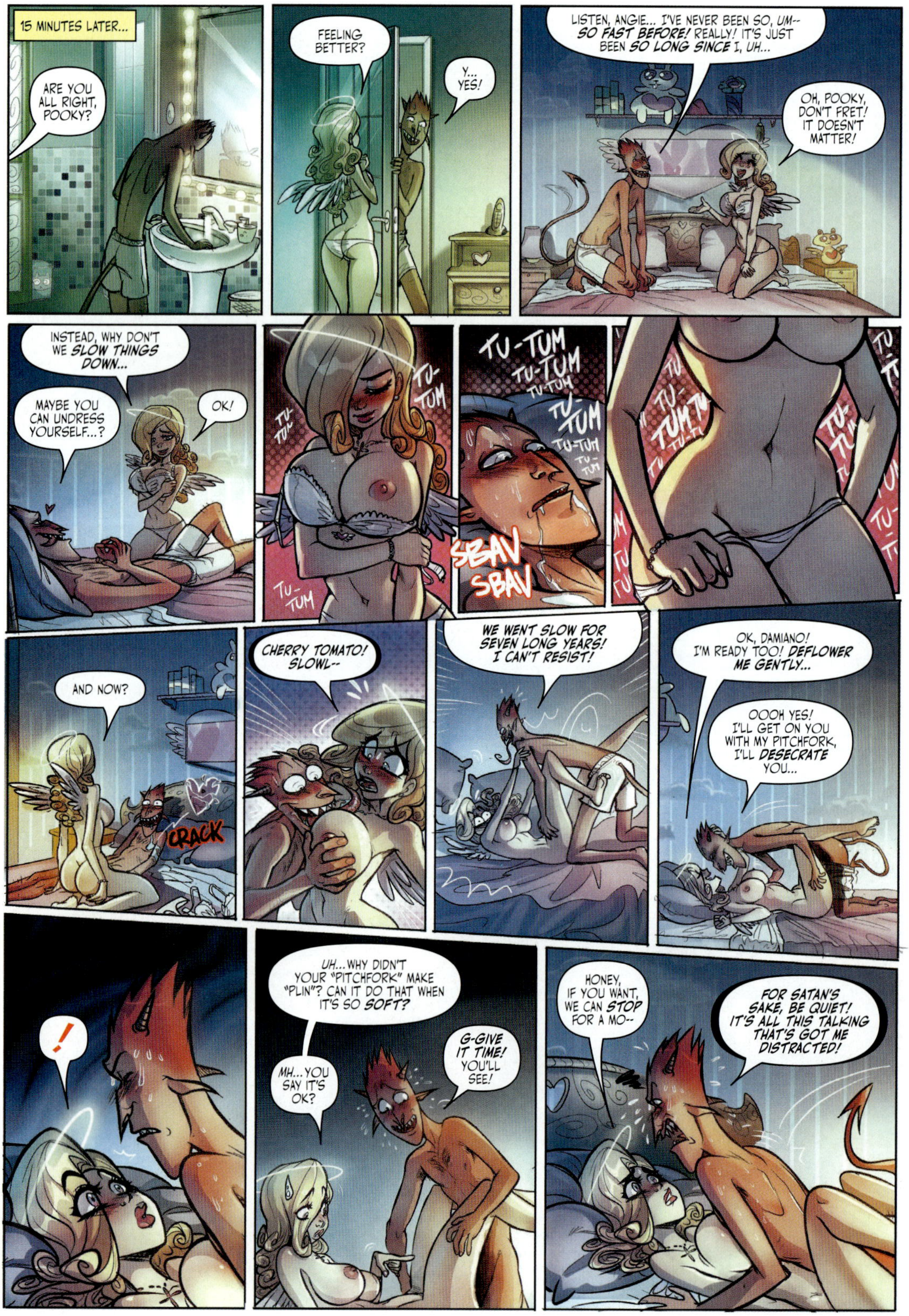
15 MINUTES LATER...
ARE YOU ALL RIGHT, POOKY?
FEELING BETTER?
Y... YES!
LISTEN, ANGIE... I'VE NEVER BEEN SO, UM-- SO FAST BEFORE! REALLY! IT'S JUST BEEN SO LONG SINCE I, UH...
OH, POOKY, DON'T FRET! IT DOESN'T MATTER!
INSTEAD, WHY DON'T WE SLOW THINGS DOWN...
MAYBE YOU CAN UNDRESS YOURSELF...?
OK!
TU-TUM
TU-TUM
TU-TUM TU-TUM
SBAV SBAV
AND NOW?
CRACK
CHERRY TOMATO! SLOWL--
WE WENT SLOW FOR SEVEN LONG YEARS! I CAN'T RESIST!
OK, DAMIANO! I'M READY TOO! DEFLOWER ME GENTLY...
OOOH YES! I'LL GET ON YOU WITH MY PITCHFORK, I'LL DESECRATE YOU...
!
UH... WHY DIDN'T YOUR "PITCHFORK" MAKE "PLIN"? CAN IT DO THAT WHEN IT'S SO SOFT?
MH... YOU SAY IT'S OK?
G-GIVE IT TIME! YOU'LL SEE!
HONEY, IF YOU WANT, WE CAN STOP FOR A MO--
FOR SATAN'S SAKE, BE QUIET! IT'S ALL THIS TALKING THAT'S GOT ME DISTRACTED!

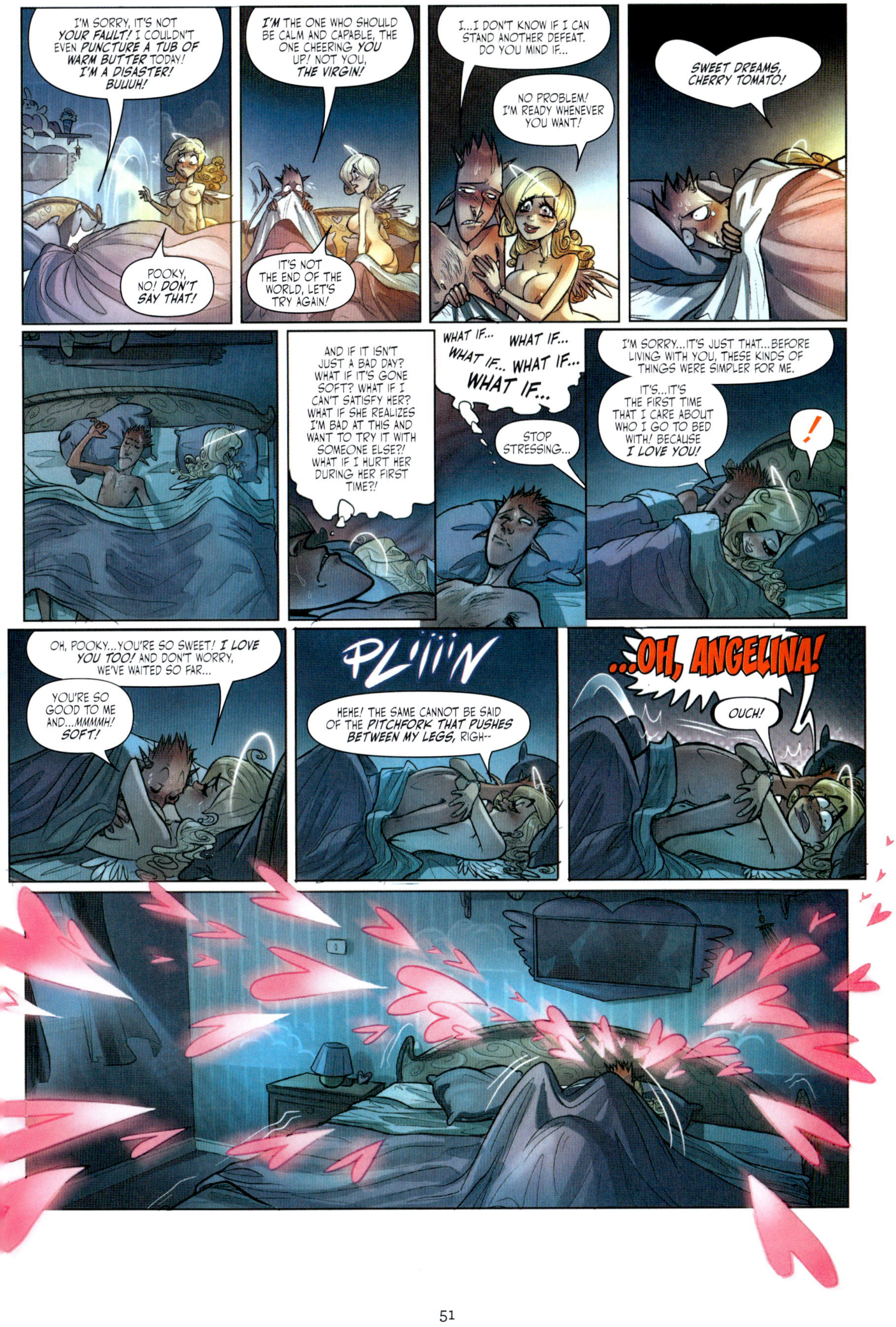
I'M SORRY, IT'S NOT YOUR FAULT! I COULDN'T EVEN PUNCTURE A TUB OF WARM BUTTER TODAY! I'M A DISASTER! BUUUH!
POOKY, NO! DON'T SAY THAT!
I'M THE ONE WHO SHOULD BE CALM AND CAPABLE, THE ONE CHEERING YOU UP! NOT YOU, THE VIRGIN!
IT'S NOT THE END OF THE WORLD, LET'S TRY AGAIN!
I...I DON'T KNOW IF I CAN STAND ANOTHER DEFEAT. DO YOU MIND IF...
NO PROBLEM! I'M READY WHENEVER YOU WANT!
SWEET DREAMS, CHERRY TOMATO!
AND IF IT ISN'T JUST A BAD DAY? WHAT IF IT'S GONE SOFT? WHAT IF I CAN'T SATISFY HER? WHAT IF SHE REALIZES I'M BAD AT THIS AND WANT TO TRY IT WITH SOMEONE ELSE?! WHAT IF I HURT HER DURING HER FIRST TIME?!
WHAT IF... WHAT IF... WHAT IF... WHAT IF... WHAT IF...
STOP STRESSING...
I'M SORRY...IT'S JUST THAT...BEFORE LIVING WITH YOU, THESE KINDS OF THINGS WERE SIMPLER FOR ME.
IT'S...IT'S THE FIRST TIME THAT I CARE ABOUT WHO I GO TO BED WITH! BECAUSE I LOVE YOU!
!
OH, POOKY...YOU'RE SO SWEET! I LOVE YOU TOO! AND DON'T WORRY, WE'VE WAITED SO FAR...
YOU'RE SO GOOD TO ME AND...MMMMH! SOFT!
PLIIIN
HEHE! THE SAME CANNOT BE SAID OF THE PITCHFORK THAT PUSHES BETWEEN MY LEGS, RIGH--
...OH, ANGELINA!
OUCH!

ANF ANF ANF ANF ANF
AND SO YOU SUCCEEDED IN FUCKING THE ANGEL AFTER SEVEN YEARS OF HELL!
YOU'VE GOT TO TELL US EVERYTHING! FROM WHEN YOU ENTERED HER ROOM, WHEN YOU SLIPPED OUT (OF HER!), THE COLOR OF HER PANTIES, THE SCENT OF HER PU--
ANF ANF ANF ANF ANF ANF
NO!
"FUCKING" IS NOT THE EXACT TERM, AND IT'S NONE OF YOUR DAMN BUSINESS! I'M NOT TELLING YOU ANYTHING, YOU PIGS!
YOU'RE KIDDING, RIGHT?
THE RARE TIMES WE'VE MATED WITH LIVING BEINGS, WE'VE ALWAYS SHARED EVERYTHING, DAMIANO/D!
ONCE, MAYBE! NOW I'M A GENTLEDEVIL, AND THEN WE'RE TALKING ABOUT MY FUTURE WIFE, GIUDA!
STOP ASKING! I'M NOT TELLING YOU FUCK-ALL ABOUT LAST NIGHT, ESPECIALLY SINCE YOU'D JUST CRAM IT IN YOUR SPANK BANK, THE SAME AS I WOULD'VE DONE! HAVE A LITTLE RESPECT, FOR SATAN'S SAKE!
YOU'RE RIGHT, POOKY! BETTER NOT TELL THE GORY DETAILS OF OUR FIRST AND SWEET PENETRATION! OF YOUR LITTLE STINGER IN MY TINKLEFLOWER! OOOH!
OR MAAAYBE... YOU DON'T WANT TO TELL US ANYTHING BECAUSE THE ONLY THING YOU FUCKED UP WAS YOUR CHANCE! AND MAYBE YOUR STINGER COULDN'T EVEN GO IN FOR THE KILL...
I MEAN, YOU'VE GOT NO PROOF, NOT EVEN AFTER SEVEN YEARS! ANYTHING COULD'VE HAPPENED--OR NOTHING!
...
...OK, OK! WE'LL MIND OUR BUSINESS!

•PURGATORY•

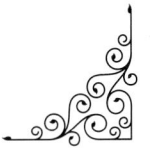

MOMMY, WHO IS MY DADDY? WHAT DOES HE DO? WHERE IS HE?

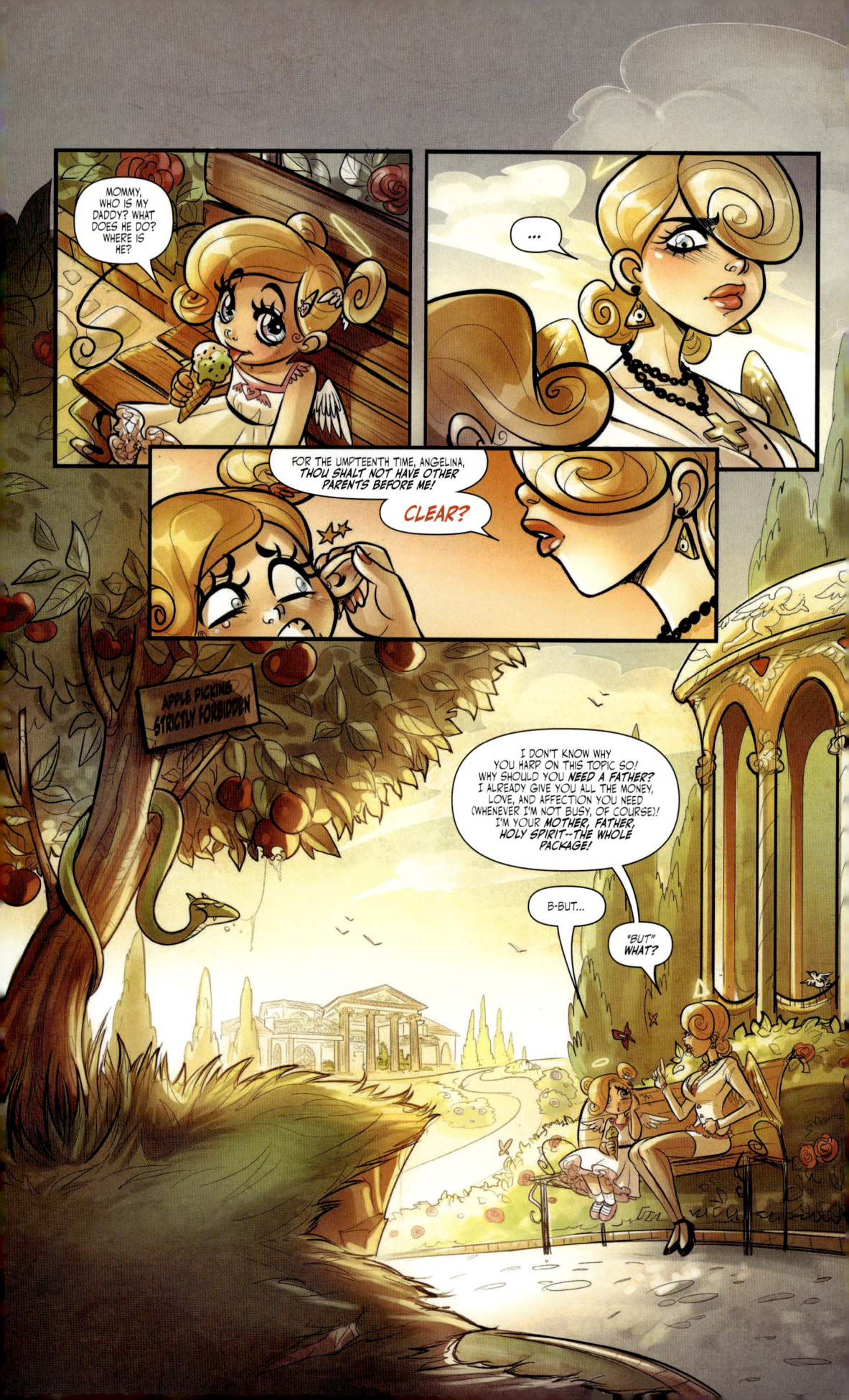

...

FOR THE UMPTEENTH TIME, ANGELINA, THOU SHALT NOT HAVE OTHER PARENTS BEFORE ME! CLEAR?

APPLE PICKING STRICTLY FORBIDDEN

I DON'T KNOW WHY YOU HARP ON THIS TOPIC SO! WHY SHOULD YOU NEED A FATHER? I ALREADY GIVE YOU ALL THE MONEY, LOVE, AND AFFECTION YOU NEED (WHENEVER I'M NOT BUSY, OF COURSE)! I'M YOUR MOTHER, FATHER, HOLY SPIRIT—THE WHOLE PACKAGE!

B-BUT...

"BUT" WHAT?

BUT ALL MY FRIENDS HAVE DADDIES, LITTLE BROTHERS, AND SMALL HOUSES...AND STILL THEY HAVE BIG FAMILIES! I BET I DON'T HAVE A DADDY BECAUSE I'VE DONE SOMETHING WRONG, MOMMY! IT'S MY FAULT, ISN'T IT?
DON'T SAY SUCH NONSENSE! BABBLING LIKE THE TOWER OF BABEL!
YOUR FATHER...HE WAS FROM THE LOWER ORDERS OF ANGELS. AND I WAS TOO MUCH IN LOVE TO UNDERSTAND THAT ONCE HE GOT WHAT HE WANTED, HE WASN'T THE KIND TO FEATHER A NEST. THE ONLY GOOD THING HE LEFT ME WAS YOU!
AND WHAT DID HE WANT?
WHEN YOU GROW UP AND FALL IN LOVE, THEN YOU'LL UNDERSTAND!
I'LL FALL IN LOVE WITH A HANDSOME AND SOPHISTICATED ANGEL CHARMING!
OBVIOUSLY! BUT NO MAN CAN BE TRUSTED! PROMISE ME THAT YOU WON'T MAKE THE MISTAKES I DID, THAT YOU'LL NEVER BE SO OVERWHELMED BY YOUR EMOTIONS! IF HE LOVES YOU, HE WILL MARRY YOU!
THAT'S THE ONLY WAY IT CAN WORK, DO YOU UNDERSTAND ME?!
PROMISE ME, ANGELINA!
BUT... MY TEACHER SAYS THAT THE MOST IMPORTANT THING OF ALL IS LOVE, AND IF THERE IS LOVE THEN IT MEANS THAT YOU'RE FOLLOWING YOUR HEART, AND...
DON'T LISTEN TO SUCH A BLASPHEMOUS CRETIN! I'M THE ONE IN THE RIGHT HERE! PROMISE!
I-I DON'T WANT YOU TO GET MAD AT ME! I...UHM...
"...I PROMISE!"
MOMMY! UH...WHY ARE YOU CALLING ME SO EARLY IN THE MORNING?

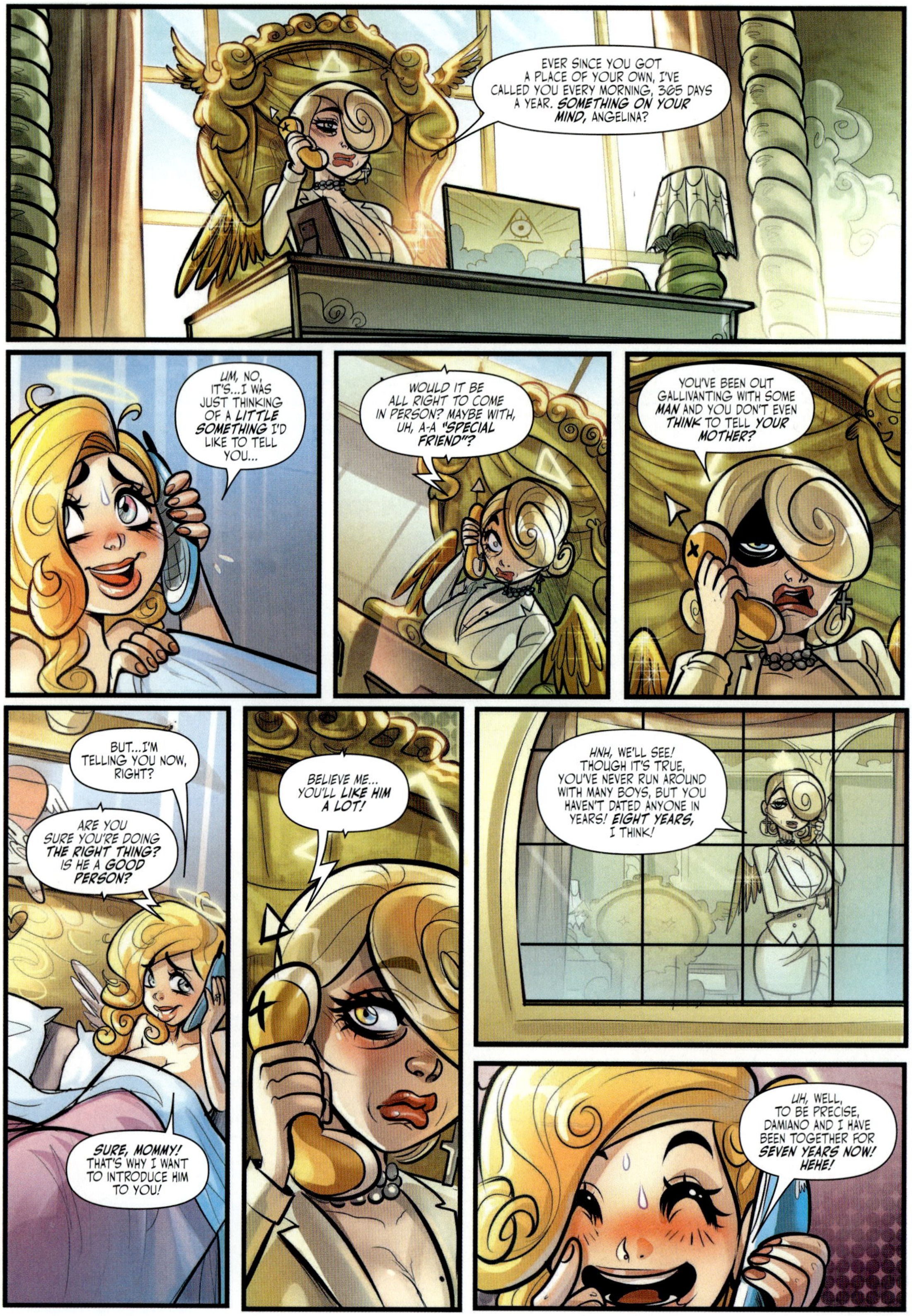
EVER SINCE YOU GOT A PLACE OF YOUR OWN, I'VE CALLED YOU EVERY MORNING, 365 DAYS A YEAR. SOMETHING ON YOUR MIND, ANGELINA?
UM, NO, IT'S...I WAS JUST THINKING OF A LITTLE SOMETHING I'D LIKE TO TELL YOU...
WOULD IT BE ALL RIGHT TO COME IN PERSON? MAYBE WITH, UH, A-A "SPECIAL FRIEND"?
YOU'VE BEEN OUT GALLIVANTING WITH SOME MAN AND YOU DON'T EVEN THINK TO TELL YOUR MOTHER?
BUT...I'M TELLING YOU NOW, RIGHT?
ARE YOU SURE YOU'RE DOING THE RIGHT THING? IS HE A GOOD PERSON?
SURE, MOMMY! THAT'S WHY I WANT TO INTRODUCE HIM TO YOU!
BELIEVE ME... YOU'LL LIKE HIM A LOT!
HNH, WE'LL SEE! THOUGH IT'S TRUE, YOU'VE NEVER RUN AROUND WITH MANY BOYS, BUT YOU HAVEN'T DATED ANYONE IN YEARS! EIGHT YEARS, I THINK!
UH, WELL, TO BE PRECISE, DAMIANO AND I HAVE BEEN TOGETHER FOR SEVEN YEARS NOW! HEHE!

WHAAAT?!
AND YOU TELL ME THAT THERE'S NOTHING WRONG?
N-NO, MOM! I JUST WANTED TO WAIT FOR THE RIGHT MOMENT!
IS HE POOR? UGLY? BORING? DOES HE PRESSURE YOU FOR UNTOWARD CONSUMMATIONS BEFORE HOLY MATRIMONY? OR WORSE...
...IS HE A DEVIL? A FILTHY, RANDY, DISGUSTING OLD GOAT?
I-I'VE TO GO! KISSES!
WELL, DAMI, YOU'VE GOT TO MEET MY MOTHER SOON ENOUGH!
IS SHE AS FAR AWAY AS JERUSALEM FROM JERICHO?
ER...SHE'S BACK!
NOW, OF ALL TIMES? RIGHT WHEN WE'RE SO HAPPY?
ABSOLUTELY! JUST IN TIME FOR THE WEDDING!

MERRY CHRISTMAS, POOKY!
MERRY CHRISTMAS, ANGELINA!
BEING IN THIS COTTAGE WITH YOU IS A DREAM! AND THEN I GOT YOU A VERY SPECIAL AND ROMANTIC GIFT...
IT'LL DRIVE YOU CRAZY! HEEHEE!
MMMH... I'M CURIOUS!
PANTIES, PLEASE SAY HER PANTIES--BACK-BOW BANDED BRAZILIAN TANGAS, PREFERABLY USED!
UH...HEART-SHAPED EARRINGS?
AND, UM... WHAT DO THESE MEAN?
WHAT... DO THEY MEAN?
ER...
STRIZZ
HOW INSENSITIVE! THOSE ARE THE EARRINGS I WAS WEARING WHEN WE FIRST MET! BOOHOOH!
ER... YEAH, UH...I REMEMBER!
I THINK...
LIAR! YOU DON'T KNOW WHAT LOVE IS! I REMEMBER EVERY DETAIL, WHILE YOU...WELL, FOR YOU IT WAS JUST ANOTHER DAY LIKE ANY OTHER, AM I RIGHT?! NOTHING SPECIAL!
DON'T SAY THAT!
MAYBE THE EARRINGS ESCAPED ME, BUT IT'S ONLY BECAUSE THEY WERE COVERED BY YOUR MAGNIFICENT GOLDEN HAIR, BUT I REMEMBER OTHER THINGS! LIKE YOUR BLUE AND PINK EYES, YOUR LOVELY DRESS AND YOUR BEAUTIFUL PEARL NECKLACE!
SNIFF... REALLY?
AND NOT JUST THAT! I CAN LIST EVERY NECKLACE THAT HAS WRAPPED YOUR DELICIOUS NECK, UP UNTIL TODAY! THE ONE WITH THE HEART PENDANT, A STAR, A KITTEN...I LOOK AT ALL THOSE DETAILS! BECAUSE I LOVE YOU!
SO ROMANTIC!
BUT WHY ALL THE NECKLACES, POOKY?
HEHE! THAT'S A SECRET!
SPLUUW

THAT'S RIGHT, YOU PLAYED LIKE CRAP! YOU GOT A PROBLEM?!
bip
YOU SHOULD TURN OFF YOUR CELL PHONE WHEN WE'RE PRACTICING. THAT'S THE TENTH TEXT YOU'VE GOTTEN!
IT'S ANGIE...
I BET SHE'S NOT HAPPY UNLESS SHE'S SLOPPING YOU IN SYRUPY MESSAGES, RIGHT?
AH, WOMEN!
OTHER THAN "POOCHIE-POOKY-POO"... THERE'S ONLY ONE THING THAT COUNTS—OR, WELL, TWO! BIG, THICK, AND FIRM, HAHA!
SAY GOODBYE AS WE DANCE WITH THE DEVIL TONIGHT...
READY? YES... OK, I UNDERSTAND. MESSAGE RECEIVED!
HEY, IS EVERYTHING OK? THE LOOK ON YOUR FACE...
YEAH, BUT I NEED TO GO!
STAFF ONLY
I'M ALONE. SPEAK!
OOOH, POOKY! WHO IS MY SWEET HORNY CHERRY TOMATO?
ME, ME, MEEE!
PURR!

SO, HE ASKED YOU TO MARRY HIM? WOW!
AND, AFTER HE ASKED YOU, YOU TWO...
OH, HEAVEN, I'M BLUSHING!
FINALLY! WE WANT ALL THE DETAILS, EX-VIRGIN!
ALRIGHT THEN! AT FIRST IT WAS EMBARRASSING AND PAINFUL, BUT THEN IT WAS ALL SO SWEET!
POOKY WAS SO...OH HEAVEN, SO TENDER! HE SAID HE WAS SO, SO EXCITED, AND THAT HIS LITTLE HEART WAS GOING "BOOM-BOOM-BOOM". HIS WORDS!
PFFF... "BUM-BUM-BUM," MORE LIKE.
YES! AND THEN, HIS PENIS IS SOOO CUUUTE! LOOKS LIKE A LITTLE VIENNA SAUSAGE!
HEEHEE!
HA HA! PLEASE TELL ME MORE DETAILS ABOUT THIS...SO-CALLED "NIGHT OF PASSION"!
OH, AT THE END HE HUGGED ME, AND THEN...
...HE CRIED! WEPT WITH JOY! HEAVEN, HE'S SO SENSITIVE!
HEEEHEEE!
HOW DEAR OF MICHELA! SHE'S CRYING WITH JOY FOR ME, TOO!
AHAHAH AHAWAH!
FINALLY DAMIANO HAS BECOME THE SWEET AND SENSITIVE GENTLEDEVIL YOU ALWAYS DREAMED OF!
OH YES! HE'S NO LONGER A NAUGHTY PIG...HE'S A REAL PRINCE, AND HE TREATS ME LIKE A PRINCESS!
HIC! AND THEN SHE TOLD ME "HARPOON ME WITH YOUR BEAUTIFUL, MAJESTIC...HIC! PITCHFORK!".
AND I: "SURE...HIC! MY BEAUTIFUL FEATHERY FUCKDOLL!" AND I WILDLY RAVISHED HER!

PANT! POOF! MY BACK!
CHOP THE CARROTS, CUT THE PEPPERS... THE POTATOES ARE READY...
THE MEATLOAF MUST REMAIN IN THE OVEN FOR HALF AN HOUR AND THEN THERE WE ARE!
CRYSTAL GLASSES FROM GREAT-AUNT LIUTPRANDA...SILK NAPKINS, AND VOILA!
PHEW... EVERYTHING IS READY!
GOOD SILVER IS ON THE TABLE, DISHES ARE READY, HANDMADE DECORATIONS...
I SPENT A BIBLICAL KING'S RANSOM, BUT IT'S A PITTANCE COMPARED TO MY LOVE FOR MY POOKY-- NOTHING WILL RUIN THIS VALENTINE'S DAY!
ONE LAST TOUCH, AND...
DLIN DLON
POOKY!
HELLOOO!
PLIN
YOU'RE BEAUTIFUL! WHAT A DELECTABLE AROMA...
MUST BE THE MEATLOAF! COME ON, LET'S EAT!
I WAS ACTUALLY REFERRING TO YOUR PERFUME!
GOOD, POOKY! FIRST DINNER, THEN THE BED!
BED? DINNER? TO HELL WITH THIS CRAP! LET'S DO IT ON THE TABLE!
!
CRASH!

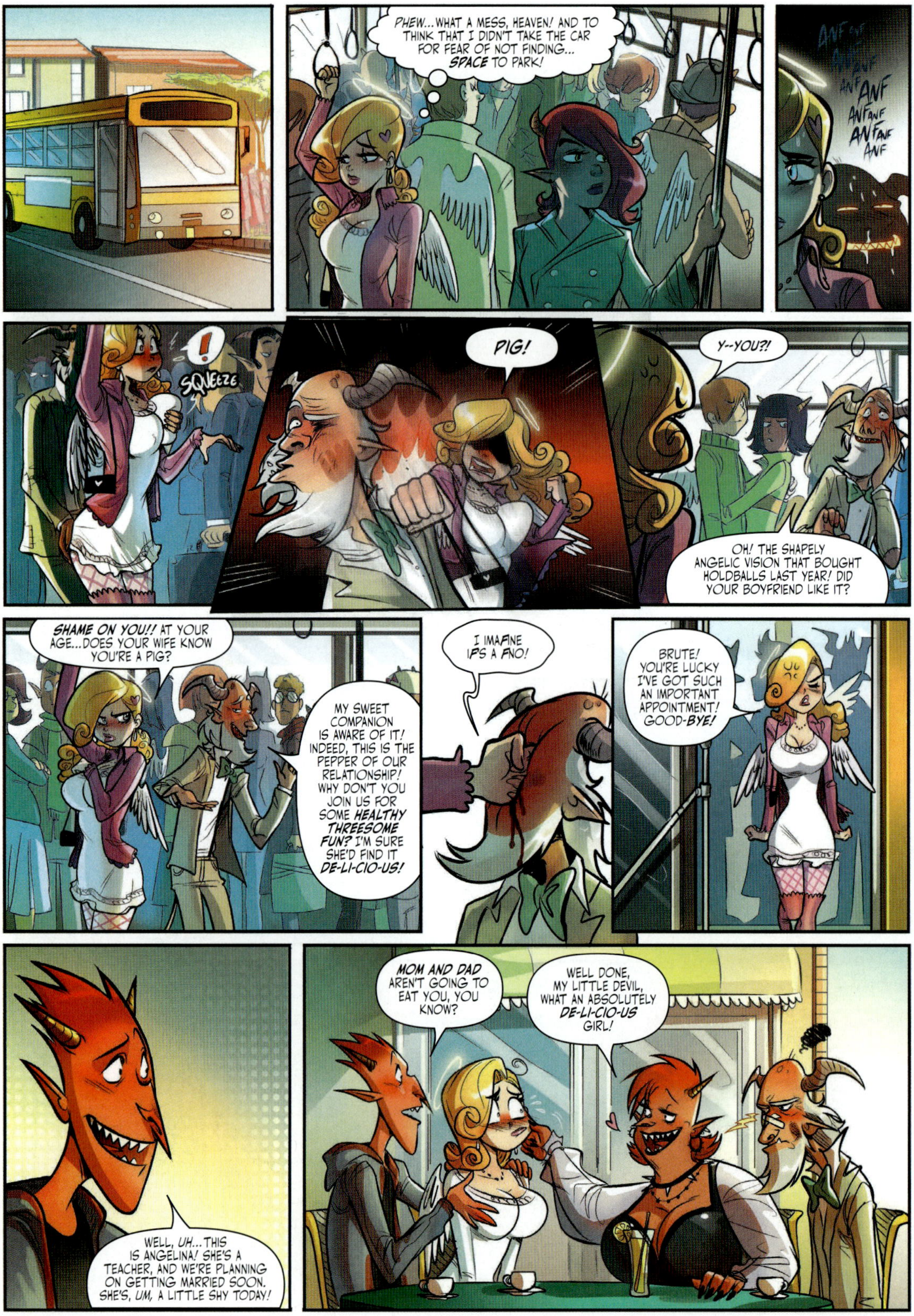
PHEW... WHAT A MESS, HEAVEN! AND TO THINK THAT I DIDN'T TAKE THE CAR FOR FEAR OF NOT FINDING... SPACE TO PARK!
ANF ANF ANF ANF ANF ANF ANF ANF ANF ANF
SQUEEZE
!
PIG!
Y--YOU?!
OH! THE SHAPELY ANGELIC VISION THAT BOUGHT HOLDBALLS LAST YEAR! DID YOUR BOYFRIEND LIKE IT?
SHAME ON YOU!! AT YOUR AGE... DOES YOUR WIFE KNOW YOU'RE A PIG?
MY SWEET COMPANION IS AWARE OF IT! INDEED, THIS IS THE PEPPER OF OUR RELATIONSHIP! WHY DON'T YOU JOIN US FOR SOME HEALTHY THREESOME FUN? I'M SURE SHE'D FIND IT DE-LI-CIO-US!
I IMAFINE IF'S A FNO!
BRUTE! YOU'RE LUCKY I'VE GOT SUCH AN IMPORTANT APPOINTMENT! GOOD-BYE!
WELL, UH... THIS IS ANGELINA! SHE'S A TEACHER, AND WE'RE PLANNING ON GETTING MARRIED SOON. SHE'S, UM, A LITTLE SHY TODAY!
MOM AND DAD AREN'T GOING TO EAT YOU, YOU KNOW?
WELL DONE, MY LITTLE DEVIL, WHAT AN ABSOLUTELY DE-LI-CIO-US GIRL!

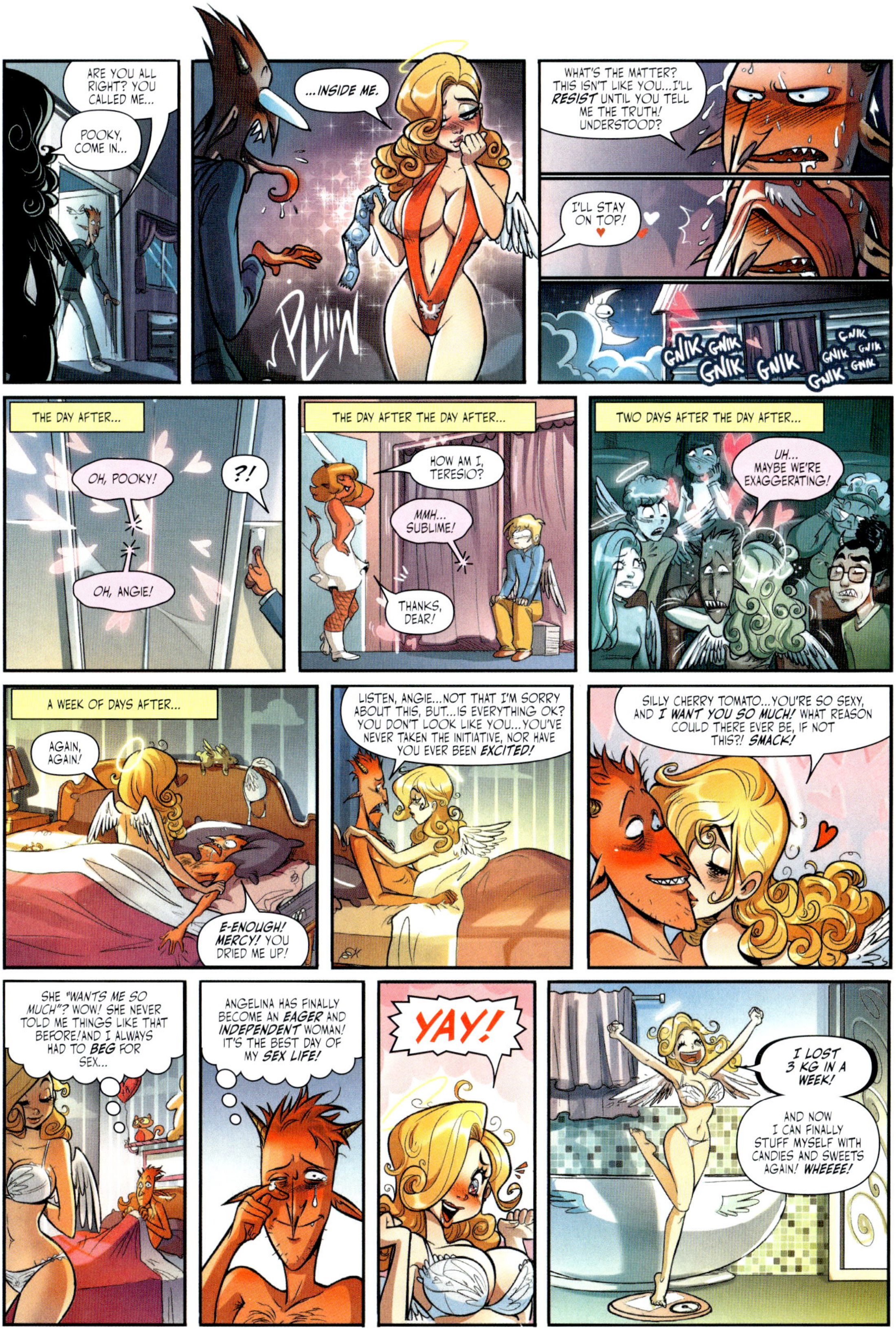
ARE YOU ALL RIGHT? YOU CALLED ME...
POOKY, COME IN...
...INSIDE ME.
PLIIIN
WHAT'S THE MATTER? THIS ISN'T LIKE YOU...I'LL RESIST UNTIL YOU TELL ME THE TRUTH! UNDERSTOOD?
I'LL STAY ON TOP!
GNIK GNIK GNIK GNIK GNIK GNIK GNIK GNIK GNIK
THE DAY AFTER...
OH, POOKY!
?!
OH, ANGIE!
THE DAY AFTER THE DAY AFTER...
HOW AM I, TERESIO?
MMH... SUBLIME!
THANKS, DEAR!
TWO DAYS AFTER THE DAY AFTER...
UH... MAYBE WE'RE EXAGGERATING!
A WEEK OF DAYS AFTER...
AGAIN, AGAIN!
E-ENOUGH! MERCY! YOU DRIED ME UP!
LISTEN, ANGIE...NOT THAT I'M SORRY ABOUT THIS, BUT...IS EVERYTHING OK? YOU DON'T LOOK LIKE YOU...YOU'VE NEVER TAKEN THE INITIATIVE, NOR HAVE YOU EVER BEEN EXCITED!
SILLY CHERRY TOMATO...YOU'RE SO SEXY, AND I WANT YOU SO MUCH! WHAT REASON COULD THERE EVER BE, IF NOT THIS?! SMACK!
SHE "WANTS ME SO MUCH"? WOW! SHE NEVER TOLD ME THINGS LIKE THAT BEFORE! AND I ALWAYS HAD TO BEG FOR SEX...
ANGELINA HAS FINALLY BECOME AN EAGER AND INDEPENDENT WOMAN! IT'S THE BEST DAY OF MY SEX LIFE!
YAY!
I LOST 3 KG IN A WEEK!
AND NOW I CAN FINALLY STUFF MYSELF WITH CANDIES AND SWEETS AGAIN! WHEEEE!

UFF!
LOOK, POOKY, IT DOESN'T FIT!
CHOKE!
MPFH!
GNN!
OPS!
STRAAAP!
BUUUUUH! BUT I TRIED SO HAAAARD!
NO, MY LOVE! I'M GOING TO GET YOU A BIGGER SIZE!
THIS TIME BRING ME A SUPER-MEGA-ULTRA-EXTRA-SMALL!
EVEN TIGHTER? YOU SURE?
VERY SHORT, AND TIGHT ON THE CHEST, THANK YOU!
STAFF

YOU LIKE IT?
OH, POOKY!
YOU ARE FANTASTIC, SUPER... FABULOUS... NO...
SUPER-FANTASTI-BULOUS... OOH!
YOU'VE BEEN WEARING THAT EXPRESSION FOR AT LEAST A WEEK. DID YOU HAVE A STROKE?
NOPE! "SELF-CONFIDENCE!"
I KNOW I'M THE GOD OF SEX!
ANGIE IS THE ONLY ONE, THE ONLY VERY FORTUNATE GIRL TO WHOM I GRANT THE HONOR OF ENJOYING MY GIFT!
BEHOLD, UNLUCKY ONES, BE SATISFIED!
PCIU'
SHE SAID THAT I'M "SUPER-FANTASTI-BULOUS"! MR. SUPER-FANTASTI-BULOUS!
DISTRIBUTOR OF MULTIPLE ORGASMS AND CHAMPION OF COITUS!
DON'T BE SO COCKY, O PRINCE OF PUSSY.
JEALOUS?
SHE CALLS A SINGLE SCOOP OF VANILLA THE SAME THING!
OOOH...SUPER-FANTASTIBULOUS!

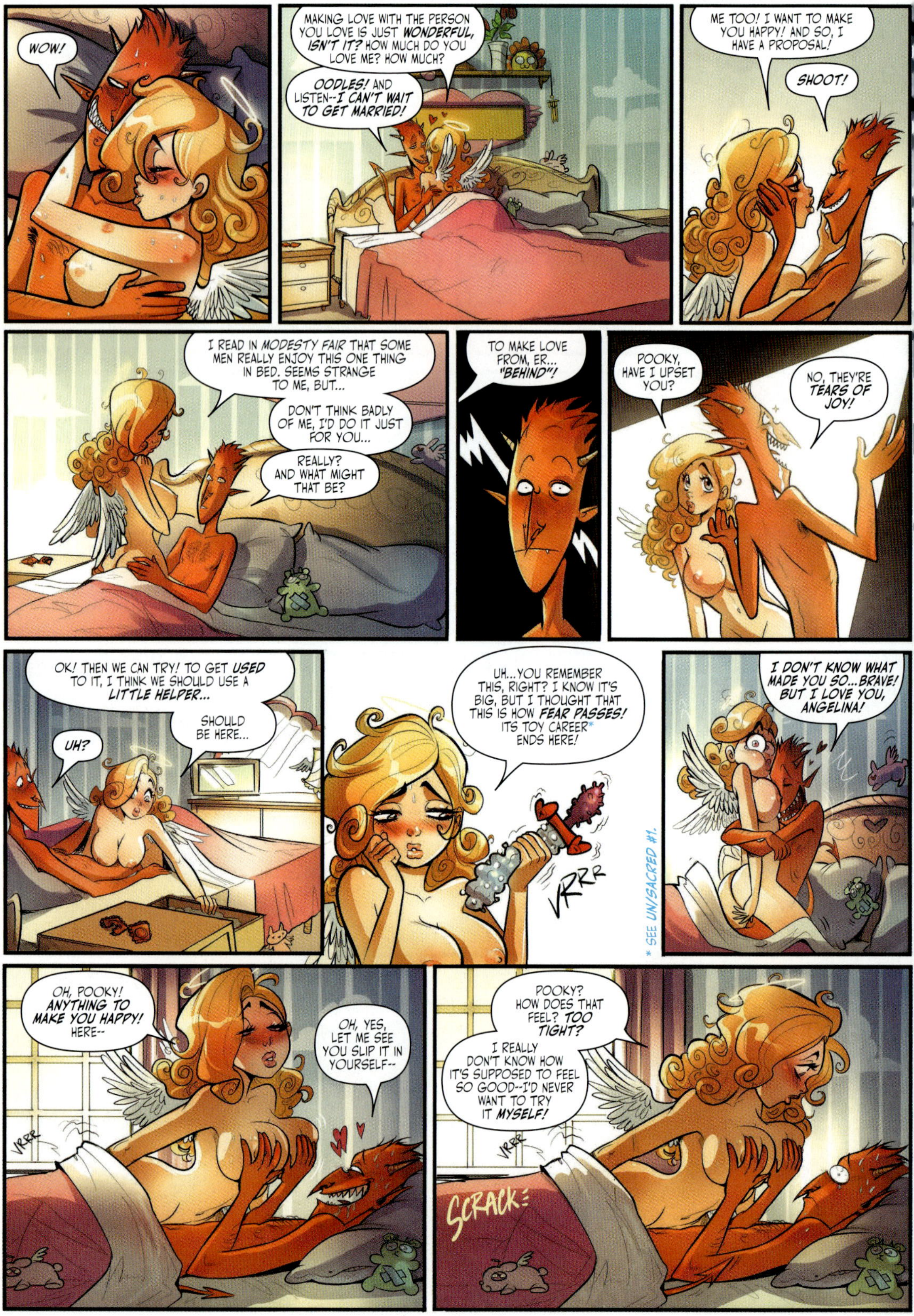
WOW!
MAKING LOVE WITH THE PERSON YOU LOVE IS JUST WONDERFUL, ISN'T IT? HOW MUCH DO YOU LOVE ME? HOW MUCH?
OODLES! AND LISTEN--I CAN'T WAIT TO GET MARRIED!
ME TOO! I WANT TO MAKE YOU HAPPY! AND SO, I HAVE A PROPOSAL!
SHOOT!
I READ IN MODESTY FAIR THAT SOME MEN REALLY ENJOY THIS ONE THING IN BED. SEEMS STRANGE TO ME, BUT...
DON'T THINK BADLY OF ME, I'D DO IT JUST FOR YOU...
REALLY? AND WHAT MIGHT THAT BE?
TO MAKE LOVE FROM, ER... "BEHIND"!
POOKY, HAVE I UPSET YOU?
NO, THEY'RE TEARS OF JOY!
OK! THEN WE CAN TRY! TO GET USED TO IT, I THINK WE SHOULD USE A LITTLE HELPER...
UH?
SHOULD BE HERE...
UH...YOU REMEMBER THIS, RIGHT? I KNOW IT'S BIG, BUT I THOUGHT THAT THIS IS HOW FEAR PASSES! ITS TOY CAREER* ENDS HERE!
VRRR
* SEE UN/SACRED #1.
I DON'T KNOW WHAT MADE YOU SO...BRAVE! BUT I LOVE YOU, ANGELINA!
OH, POOKY! ANYTHING TO MAKE YOU HAPPY! HERE--
OH, YES, LET ME SEE YOU SLIP IT IN YOURSELF--
VRRR
POOKY? HOW DOES THAT FEEL? TOO TIGHT?
I REALLY DON'T KNOW HOW IT'S SUPPOSED TO FEEL SO GOOD--I'D NEVER WANT TO TRY IT MYSELF!
VRRR
SCRACK

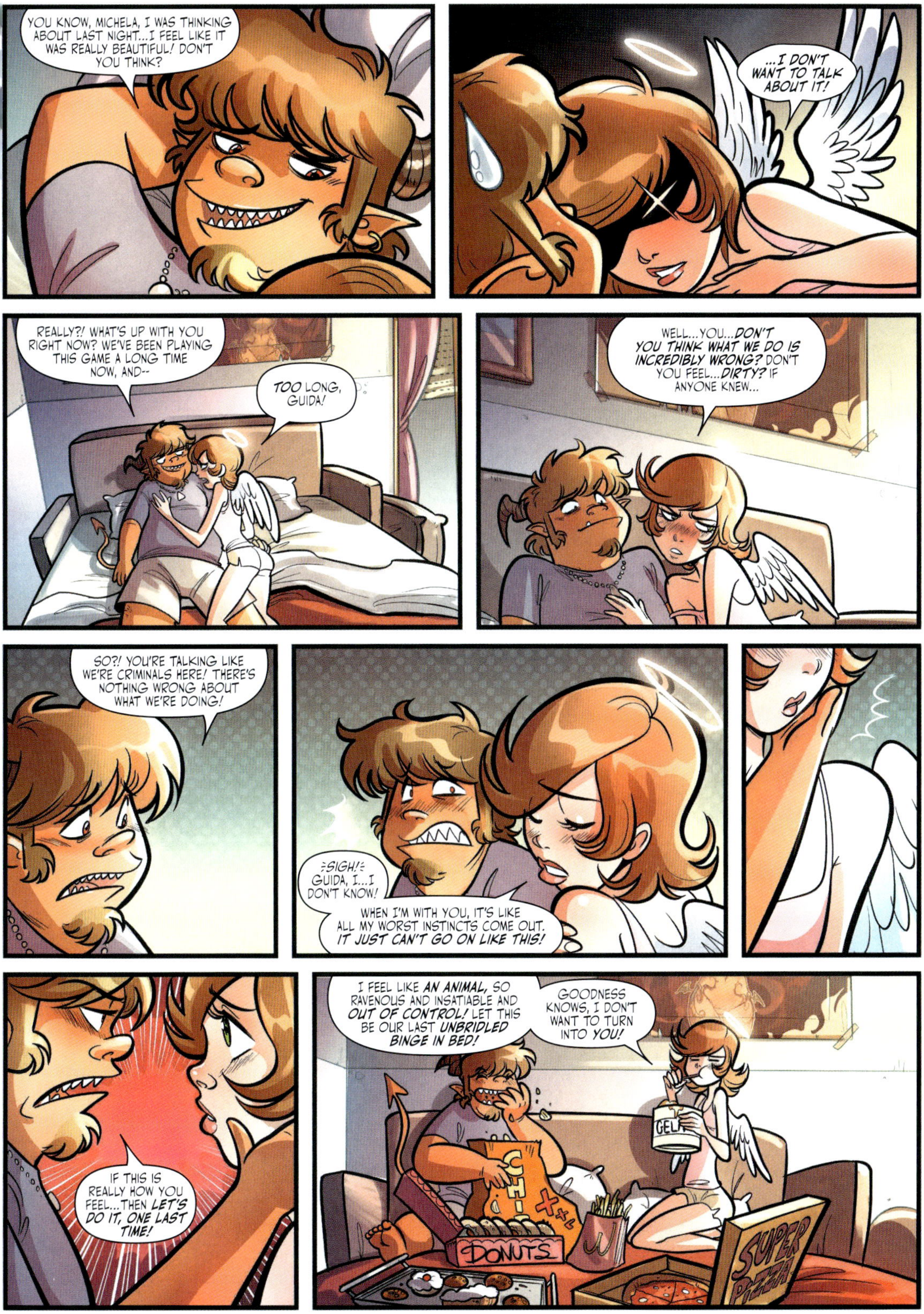

YOU KNOW, MICHELA, I WAS THINKING ABOUT LAST NIGHT...I FEEL LIKE IT WAS REALLY BEAUTIFUL! DON'T YOU THINK?
...I DON'T WANT TO TALK ABOUT IT!
REALLY?! WHAT'S UP WITH YOU RIGHT NOW? WE'VE BEEN PLAYING THIS GAME A LONG TIME NOW, AND--
TOO LONG, GUIDA!
WELL...YOU...DON'T YOU THINK WHAT WE DO IS INCREDIBLY WRONG? DON'T YOU FEEL...DIRTY? IF ANYONE KNEW...
SO?! YOU'RE TALKING LIKE WE'RE CRIMINALS HERE! THERE'S NOTHING WRONG ABOUT WHAT WE'RE DOING!
=SIGH!= GUIDA, I...I DON'T KNOW!
WHEN I'M WITH YOU, IT'S LIKE ALL MY WORST INSTINCTS COME OUT. IT JUST CAN'T GO ON LIKE THIS!
IF THIS IS REALLY HOW YOU FEEL...THEN LET'S DO IT, ONE LAST TIME!
I FEEL LIKE AN ANIMAL, SO RAVENOUS AND INSATIABLE AND OUT OF CONTROL! LET THIS BE OUR LAST UNBRIDLED BINGE IN BED!
GOODNESS KNOWS, I DON'T WANT TO TURN INTO YOU!
DONUTS
SUPER PIZZA

HELLO, MY LITTLE BIRD OF PARADISE! YOU READY TO GO?
HELLO, DAMIANO! JUST A MINUTE MORE, I'M SETTING UP THE ARTS AND CRAFTS FOR THE CHILDREN'S EASTER PROJECT!
DO YOU LIKE IT?
ER, ANGIE...
OH NO... DON'T YOU LIKE IT?!
IT MUST NEED A BIGGER *TUFT!*
NO, THE...ER... TUFTS OF GRASS ARE GOOD... BUT *LOOK CAREFULLY* AND YOU'LL *UNDERSTAND!*
...
OH HEAVEN!
YOU'RE RIGHT, POOKY! HOW COULD I BE SO *BLIND?* LET ME GIVE IT SOME QUICK HANDS-ON ATTENTION--
I'D SAY IT'S BETTER!
READY!
NOW IT'S NICE AND STRAIGHT!
CIAFF

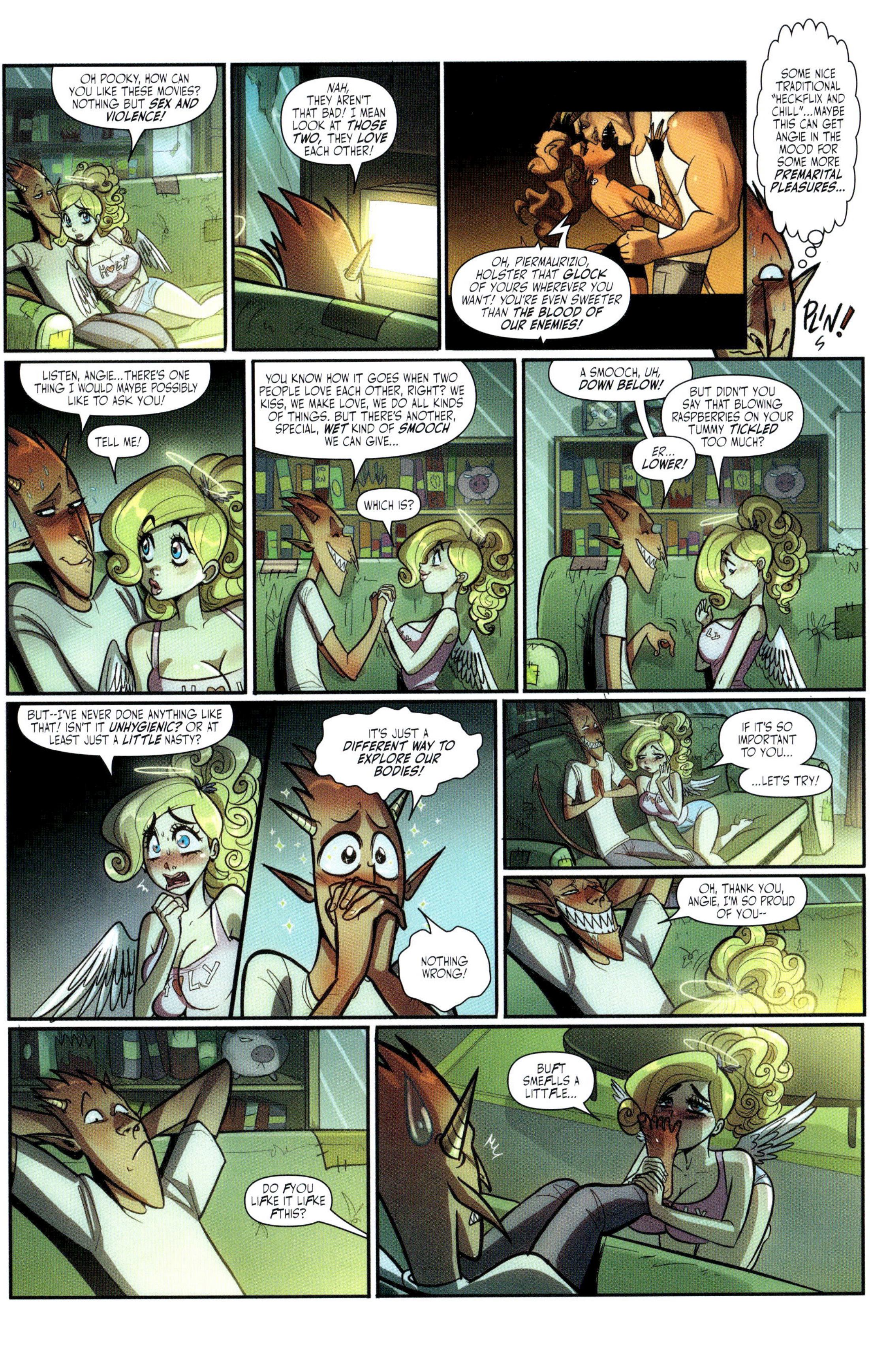
OH POOKY, HOW CAN YOU LIKE THESE MOVIES? NOTHING BUT SEX AND VIOLENCE!
NAH, THEY AREN'T THAT BAD! I MEAN LOOK AT THOSE TWO, THEY LOVE EACH OTHER!
OH, PIERMAURIZIO, HOLSTER THAT GLOCK OF YOURS WHEREVER YOU WANT! YOU'RE EVEN SWEETER THAN THE BLOOD OF OUR ENEMIES!
SOME NICE TRADITIONAL "HECKFLIX AND CHILL"...MAYBE THIS CAN GET ANGIE IN THE MOOD FOR SOME MORE PREMARITAL PLEASURES...
PLIN!
LISTEN, ANGIE...THERE'S ONE THING I WOULD MAYBE POSSIBLY LIKE TO ASK YOU!
TELL ME!
YOU KNOW HOW IT GOES WHEN TWO PEOPLE LOVE EACH OTHER, RIGHT? WE KISS, WE MAKE LOVE, WE DO ALL KINDS OF THINGS. BUT THERE'S ANOTHER, SPECIAL, WET KIND OF SMOOCH WE CAN GIVE...
WHICH IS?
A SMOOCH, UH, DOWN BELOW!
BUT DIDN'T YOU SAY THAT BLOWING RASPBERRIES ON YOUR TUMMY TICKLED TOO MUCH?
ER... LOWER!
BUT--I'VE NEVER DONE ANYTHING LIKE THAT! ISN'T IT UNHYGIENIC? OR AT LEAST JUST A LITTLE NASTY?
IT'S JUST A DIFFERENT WAY TO EXPLORE OUR BODIES!
NOTHING WRONG!
IF IT'S SO IMPORTANT TO YOU...
...LET'S TRY!
OH, THANK YOU, ANGIE, I'M SO PROUD OF YOU--
BUFT SMEFLLS A LITTFLE...
DO FYOU LIFKE IT LIFKE FTHIS?

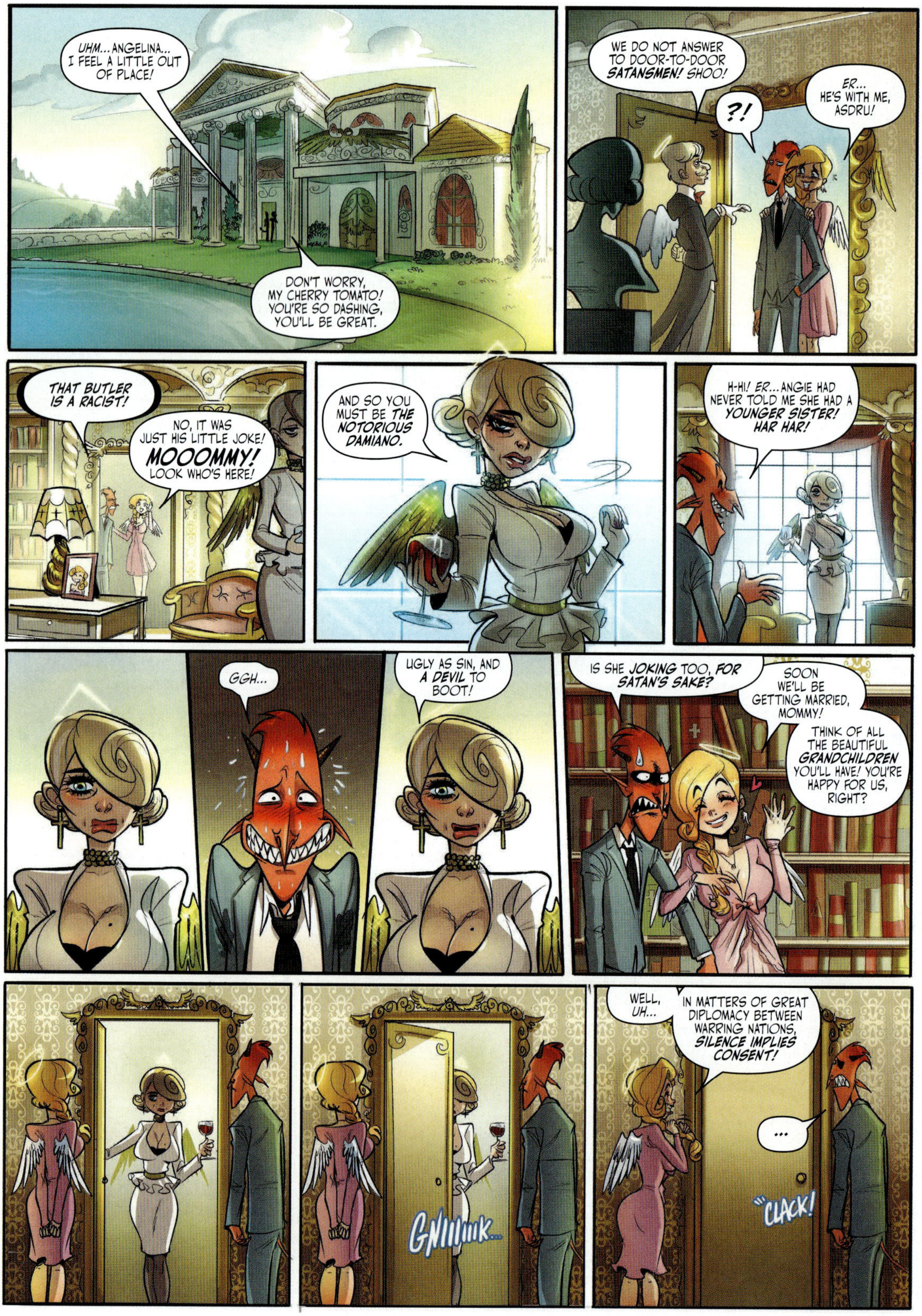
UHM... ANGELINA... I FEEL A LITTLE OUT OF PLACE!
DON'T WORRY, MY CHERRY TOMATO! YOU'RE SO DASHING, YOU'LL BE GREAT.
WE DO NOT ANSWER TO DOOR-TO-DOOR SATANSMEN! SHOO!
?!
ER... HE'S WITH ME, ASDRU!
THAT BUTLER IS A RACIST!
NO, IT WAS JUST HIS LITTLE JOKE! MOOOMMY! LOOK WHO'S HERE!
AND SO YOU MUST BE THE NOTORIOUS DAMIANO.
H-HI! ER... ANGIE HAD NEVER TOLD ME SHE HAD A YOUNGER SISTER! HAR HAR!
GGH...
UGLY AS SIN, AND A DEVIL TO BOOT!
IS SHE JOKING TOO, FOR SATAN'S SAKE?
SOON WE'LL BE GETTING MARRIED, MOMMY!
THINK OF ALL THE BEAUTIFUL GRANDCHILDREN YOU'LL HAVE! YOU'RE HAPPY FOR US, RIGHT?
GNIIIIIK...
WELL, UH...
IN MATTERS OF GREAT DIPLOMACY BETWEEN WARRING NATIONS, SILENCE IMPLIES CONSENT!
...
CLACK!

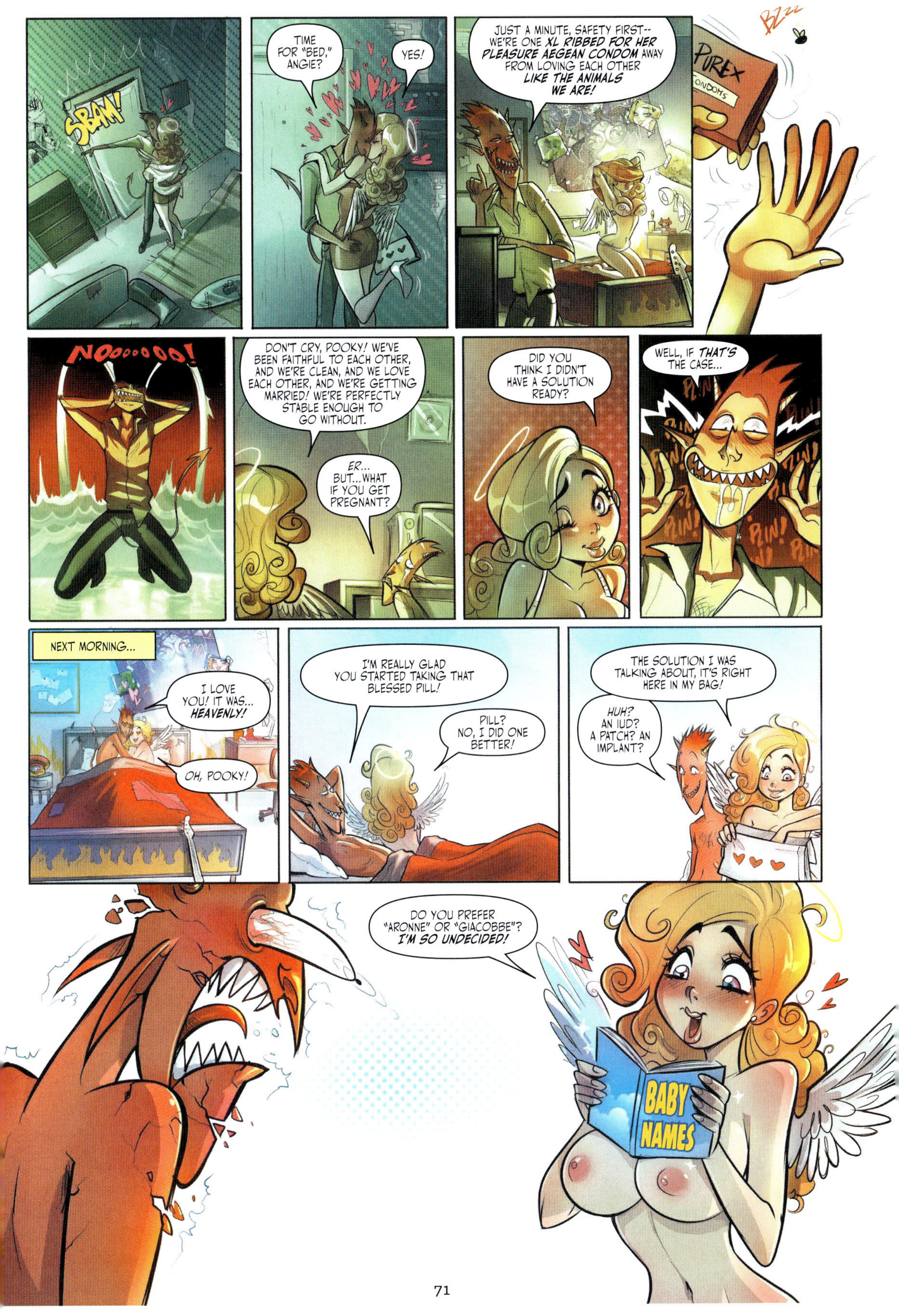
SBAM!
TIME FOR "BED," ANGIE?
YES!
JUST A MINUTE, SAFETY FIRST-- WE'RE ONE XL RIBBED FOR HER PLEASURE AEGEAN CONDOM AWAY FROM LOVING EACH OTHER LIKE THE ANIMALS WE ARE!
PUREX CONDOMS
BZzz
NOooooOO!
DON'T CRY, POOKY! WE'VE BEEN FAITHFUL TO EACH OTHER, AND WE'RE CLEAN, AND WE LOVE EACH OTHER, AND WE'RE GETTING MARRIED! WE'RE PERFECTLY STABLE ENOUGH TO GO WITHOUT.
ER... BUT...WHAT IF YOU GET PREGNANT?
DID YOU THINK I DIDN'T HAVE A SOLUTION READY?
WELL, IF THAT'S THE CASE...
NEXT MORNING...
I LOVE YOU! IT WAS... HEAVENLY!
OH, POOKY!
I'M REALLY GLAD YOU STARTED TAKING THAT BLESSED PILL!
PILL? NO, I DID ONE BETTER!
THE SOLUTION I WAS TALKING ABOUT, IT'S RIGHT HERE IN MY BAG!
HUH? AN IUD? A PATCH? AN IMPLANT?
DO YOU PREFER "ARONNE" OR "GIACOBBE"? I'M SO UNDECIDED!
BABY NAMES

ANGIE DID WHAT?!
I'M SERIOUS, GIUDA! I'M PRETTY SURE SHE WANTS TO GET PREGNANT ASAP!
REALLY! ISN'T SHE AFRAID OF NOT FITTING INTO HER WEDDING DRESS? WHY HURRY NOW OF ALL TIMES?
I THINK HER MOM'S REJECTION TRIGGERED SOMETHING IN HER!
THIS TIME SHE FAILED, BUT THIS JUST MEANS SHE WILL TRY AGAIN...AND AGAIN... AND AGAIN!
LOOK, I'M SURE THERE WAS A LITTLE MISUNDERSTANDING. I MEAN, WE'RE OVERTHINKING THIS!
TALK TO HER! CLARIFY!
UM...IT'S ALSO THAT...THERE'S SOMETHING I NEVER TOLD YOU!
WHILE SHE'S ALWAYS DREAMED OF HAVING A FAMILY WITH LOTS OF KIDS, I...UH...WELL, WHEN I MET HER, I DIDN'T THINK WE'D GET TO THIS POINT!
SO?!
I ALWAYS THOUGHT THAT I WOULD CARRY ON A SINFUL LIFE LIKE A SEXY GIGOLO! I DON'T KNOW IF I EVER EVEN THOUGHT ABOUT HAVING KIDS! AND NOW I DON'T KNOW IF I WANT THEM! AND MAYBE I WON'T EVER... AND IF I TOLD HER THE TRUTH--I DON'T KNOW WHAT COULD HAPPEN!
MAMMA MIA, YOU DON'T NEED KIDS IF YOU'RE GONNA BE HER BIG MELODRAMATIC BABY!
TRUST ME, YOU'RE OVERTHINKING!
YOU SO SURE ABOUT THAT?
TOTALLY, DUDE!
MOMMYYYY'S SWEET LITTLE POOOKYS! DOES ONE OF MY BEAUTIFUL BABIES WANT A NICE BOTTLE OF CHOCOLATE MILK?
GNAGNA! ME!

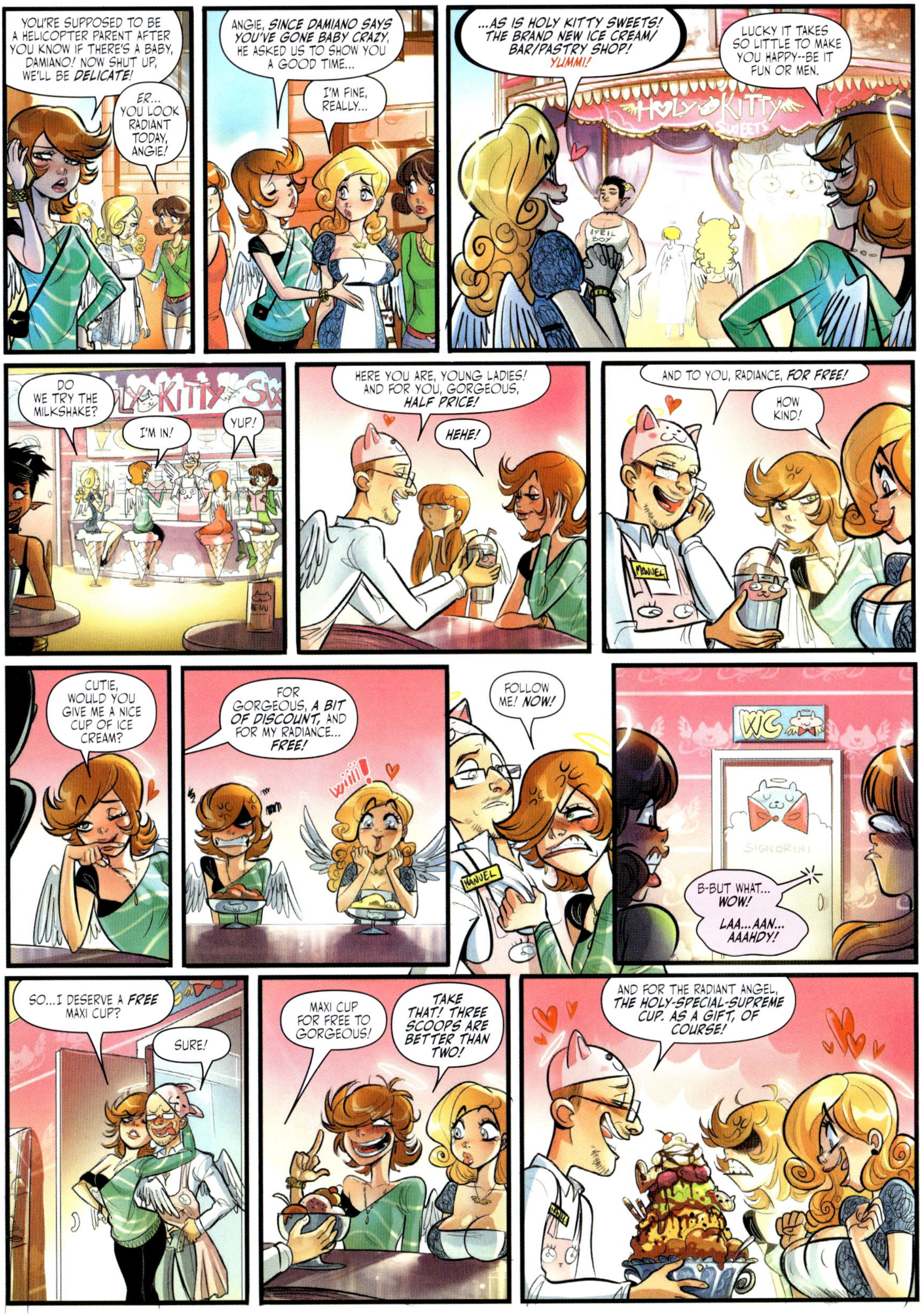
YOU'RE SUPPOSED TO BE A HELICOPTER PARENT AFTER YOU KNOW IF THERE'S A BABY, DAMIANO! NOW SHUT UP, WE'LL BE DELICATE!
ER... YOU LOOK RADIANT TODAY, ANGIE!
ANGIE, SINCE DAMIANO SAYS YOU'VE GONE BABY CRAZY, HE ASKED US TO SHOW YOU A GOOD TIME...
I'M FINE, REALLY...
...AS IS HOLY KITTY SWEETS! THE BRAND NEW ICE CREAM/ BAR/PASTRY SHOP! YUMMI!
LUCKY IT TAKES SO LITTLE TO MAKE YOU HAPPY--BE IT FUN OR MEN.
HOLY KITTY
DO WE TRY THE MILKSHAKE?
I'M IN!
YUP!
HERE YOU ARE, YOUNG LADIES! AND FOR YOU, GORGEOUS, HALF PRICE!
HEHE!
AND TO YOU, RADIANCE, FOR FREE!
HOW KIND!
MANUEL
CUTIE, WOULD YOU GIVE ME A NICE CUP OF ICE CREAM?
FOR GORGEOUS, A BIT OF DISCOUNT, AND FOR MY RADIANCE... FREE!
FOLLOW ME! NOW!
MANUEL
WC
SIGNORINI
B-BUT WHAT... WOW!
LAA...AAN... AAAHDY!
SO...I DESERVE A FREE MAXI CUP?
SURE!
MAXI CUP FOR FREE TO GORGEOUS!
TAKE THAT! THREE SCOOPS ARE BETTER THAN TWO!
AND FOR THE RADIANT ANGEL, THE HOLY-SPECIAL-SUPREME CUP. AS A GIFT, OF COURSE!

I'VE GOT TO GO TO THE POWDER ROOM! WHILE I'M GONE, WHY DON'T YOU AND MOMMY GET TO KNOW EACH OTHER?
YOU REALLY DO HAVE A WONDERFUL HOME, MY SOON-TO-BE MOM-IN-LAW...
SHUT UP, HELLSPAWN.
YES, MA'AM...
I DON'T LIKE YOU, DAMIANO. YOU DON'T HAVE A JOB...
I'M... A SINGER...
THE. ARTS. ARE. NOT. A. JOB.
YOU'RE NOT CULTURED, YOU DON'T HAVE A DRIVER'S LICENSE, YOU DON'T KNOW HOW TO DRESS, YOU DON'T KNOW HOW TO DO HOUSEWORK, AND YOU WOULDN'T KNOW HOW TO FIND YOUR TAIL EVEN WITH A DETAILED MAP.
YOU'RE NOT BEAUTIFUL, YOU'RE NOT RELIABLE, YOU'VE AN INDOLENT, MALNOURISHED BODY, WITHOUT A SHRED OF MUSCLE OR CHARM! AND WORSE, BUT REALLY, REALLY WORSE...
...YOU'RE A DEVIL! YOUR ONLY REDEEMING QUALITY, DAMIANO, IS THAT YOU'LL DIE ONE DAY.
YET THERE'S ONLY ONE THING THAT MAKES ME TOLERATE YOUR PRESENCE...
YOU RESPECT THE PURITY, THE BLESSED VIRGINITY OF MY LITTLE ONE!
ER... I...
YES... SURE!
I'M SURE IF YOU'D PUT YOUR DIRTY HANDS ON HER, ANGELINA WOULD'VE TOLD ME. IN SHORT, WITH DUE TACT... SHE KNOWS HOW IMPORTANT THIS THING IS TO ME!
OF COURSE SHE KNOWS!
THE OTHERS JUST WANT THE TEMPTING, WOMANLY BODY OF MY BABY! BUT YOU'RE...DIFFERENT! YOU HAVEN'T TRIED TO INVOLVE HER ABERRANT, ABHORRENT, PREMARITAL SEX!
THANK YOU.
YOU'VE NO IDEA HOW HAPPY I AM! AND THAT'S WHY I DECIDED TO GIVE YOU A CHANCE... WELCOME TO THE FAMILY.
NO BABIES THIS TIME, POOKY, I JUST GOT MY PERIOD! I'M SURE YOU'RE RELIEVED *SIGH*...
CRACK

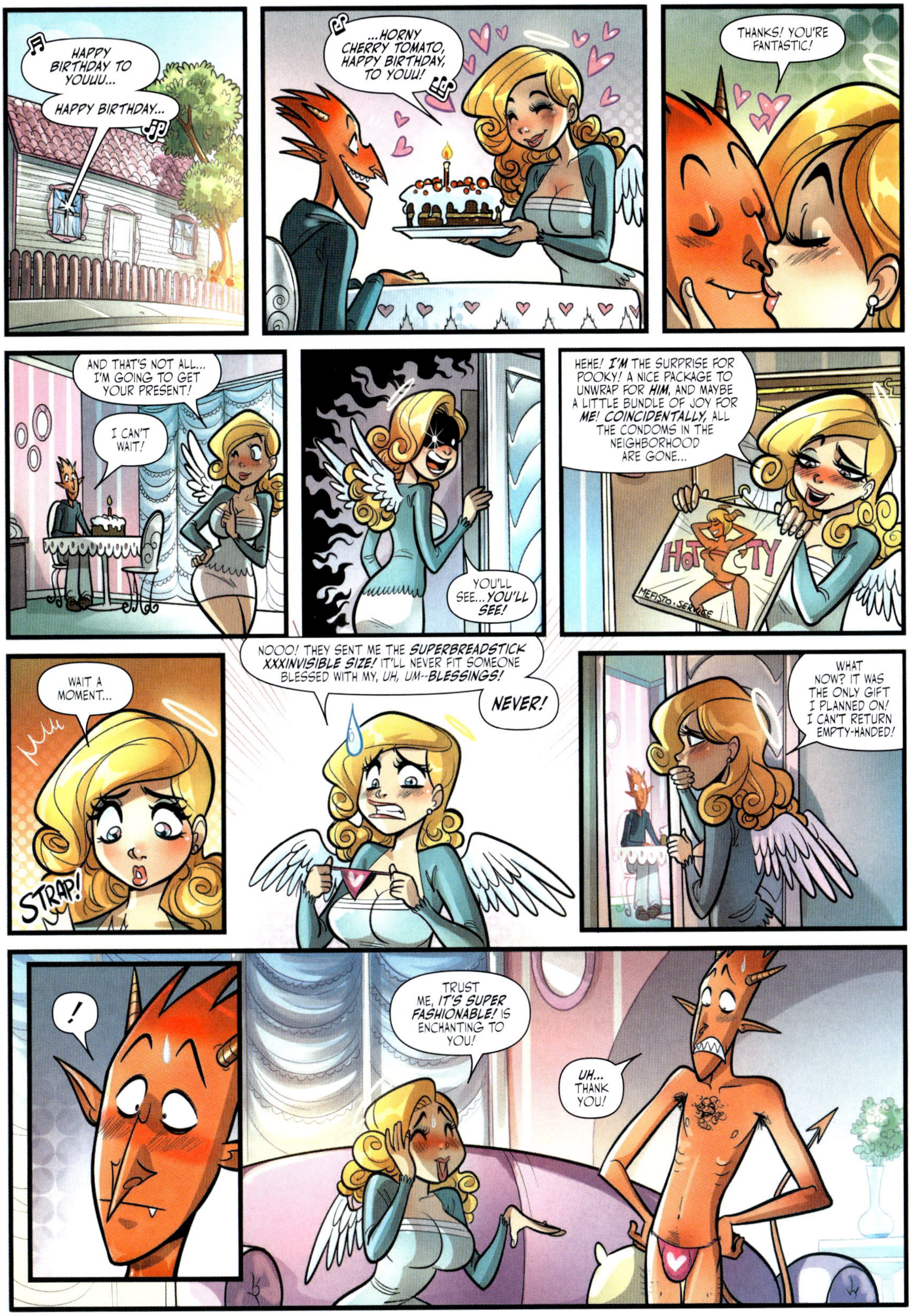
HAPPY BIRTHDAY TO YOUUU...
HAPPY BIRTHDAY...
...HORNY CHERRY TOMATO, HAPPY BIRTHDAY, TO YOUU!
THANKS! YOU'RE FANTASTIC!
AND THAT'S NOT ALL... I'M GOING TO GET YOUR PRESENT!
I CAN'T WAIT!
YOU'LL SEE... YOU'LL SEE!
HEHE! I'M THE SURPRISE FOR POOKY! A NICE PACKAGE TO UNWRAP FOR HIM, AND MAYBE A LITTLE BUNDLE OF JOY FOR ME! COINCIDENTALLY, ALL THE CONDOMS IN THE NEIGHBORHOOD ARE GONE...
MEFISTO . SERVICE
WAIT A MOMENT...
STRAP!
NOOO! THEY SENT ME THE SUPERBREADSTICK XXXINVISIBLE SIZE! IT'LL NEVER FIT SOMEONE BLESSED WITH MY, UH, UM--BLESSINGS!
NEVER!
WHAT NOW? IT WAS THE ONLY GIFT I PLANNED ON! I CAN'T RETURN EMPTY-HANDED!
!
TRUST ME, IT'S SUPER FASHIONABLE! IS ENCHANTING TO YOU!
UH... THANK YOU!

WHAT A JOY TO FINALLY BE ABLE TO MEET, MISSUS! I HOPE YOU LIKE OUR HUMBLE ABODE!
MPFH!
PRRR
MOMMY! PLEASE!
PLEAD ALL YOU WANT! BUT THIS HOLE LOOKS LIKE A FUNERAL HOME WHERE THEY CAME TO BURY BAD TASTE ITSELF!
NOT TO MENTION THE QUALITY OF THE POTABLES AND--AND POTTAGE.
POPA POLA
ARE YOU READY TO TASTE MY TEN GORGONZOLAS POTATOES WITH ONION AND BACON?!
VADE RETRO! THEY WILL HAVE AT LEAST A MILLION CALORIES!
PURRR
I WONDER HOW HER HUSBAND AND HER SON CAN BE SO SKINNY, AND NOT LIKE...HER!
IS THIS WHY YOU'VE BECOME SO GELATINOUS? THESE DEMONS OF THE PIT ARE MISLEADING YOU! YOU'RE BECOMING A SAVAGE, TO EAT SUCH SLOP!
GNAM!
SON, CAN I PLEASE TELL HER TO GO FUCK HERSELF?
NO, DAD, BE QUIET!
WELL, I DON'T KNOW ABOUT THAT, BUT MY SON SURE "MISLED" HER SEVERAL TIMES LAST WEEK...SINCE WHEN YOU'RE NOT BEING SATISFIED, TO BE SO SOUR?
NOW, HONEY, WE SHOULDN'T ANSWER RUDENESS WITH RUDENESS!
WHEW! AT LEAST YOU UNDERSTAND!
CRASH!
IT'S BEST TO LEAD BY EXAMPLE--AND USE GOOD TABLE MANNERS.

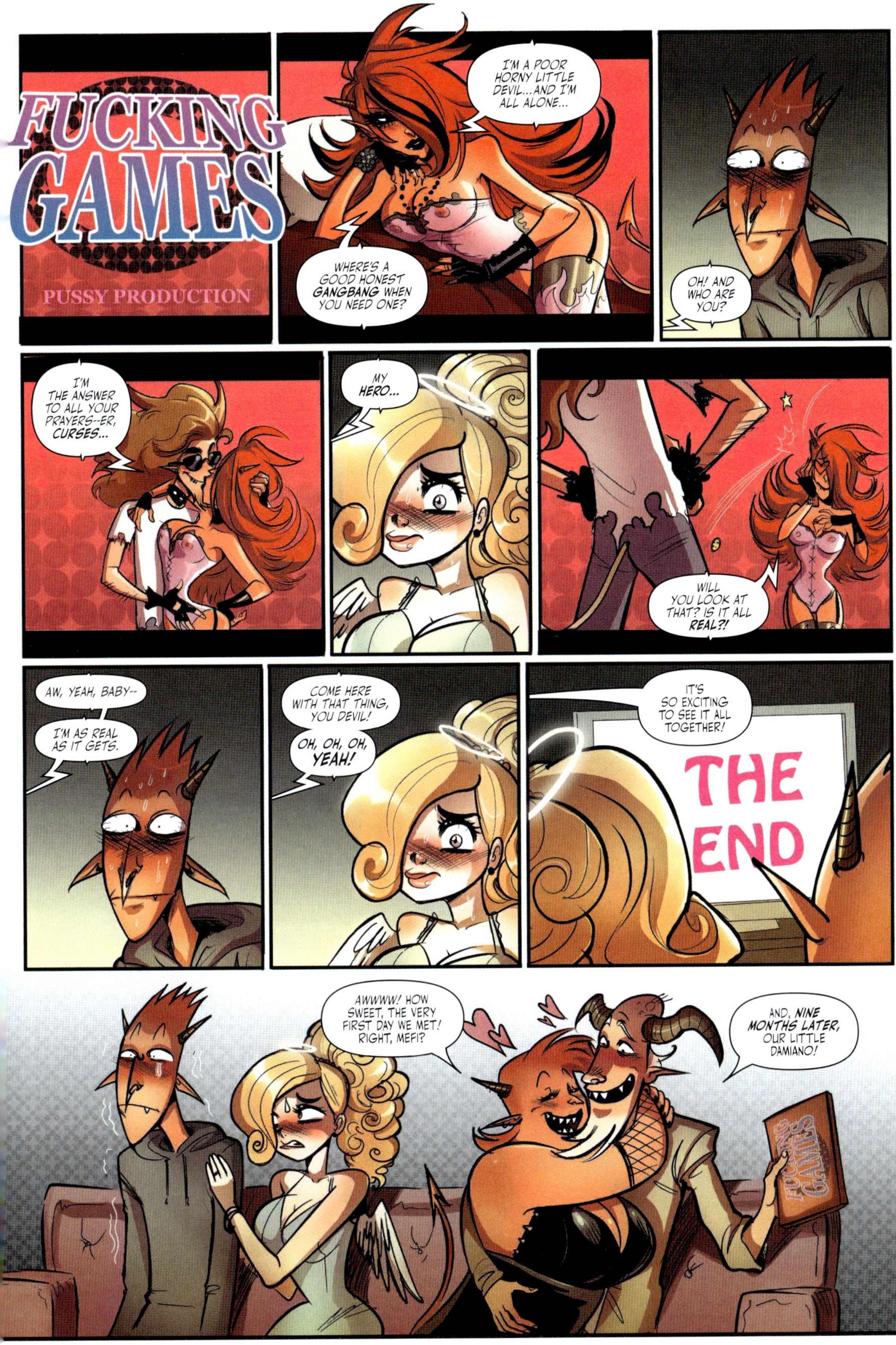

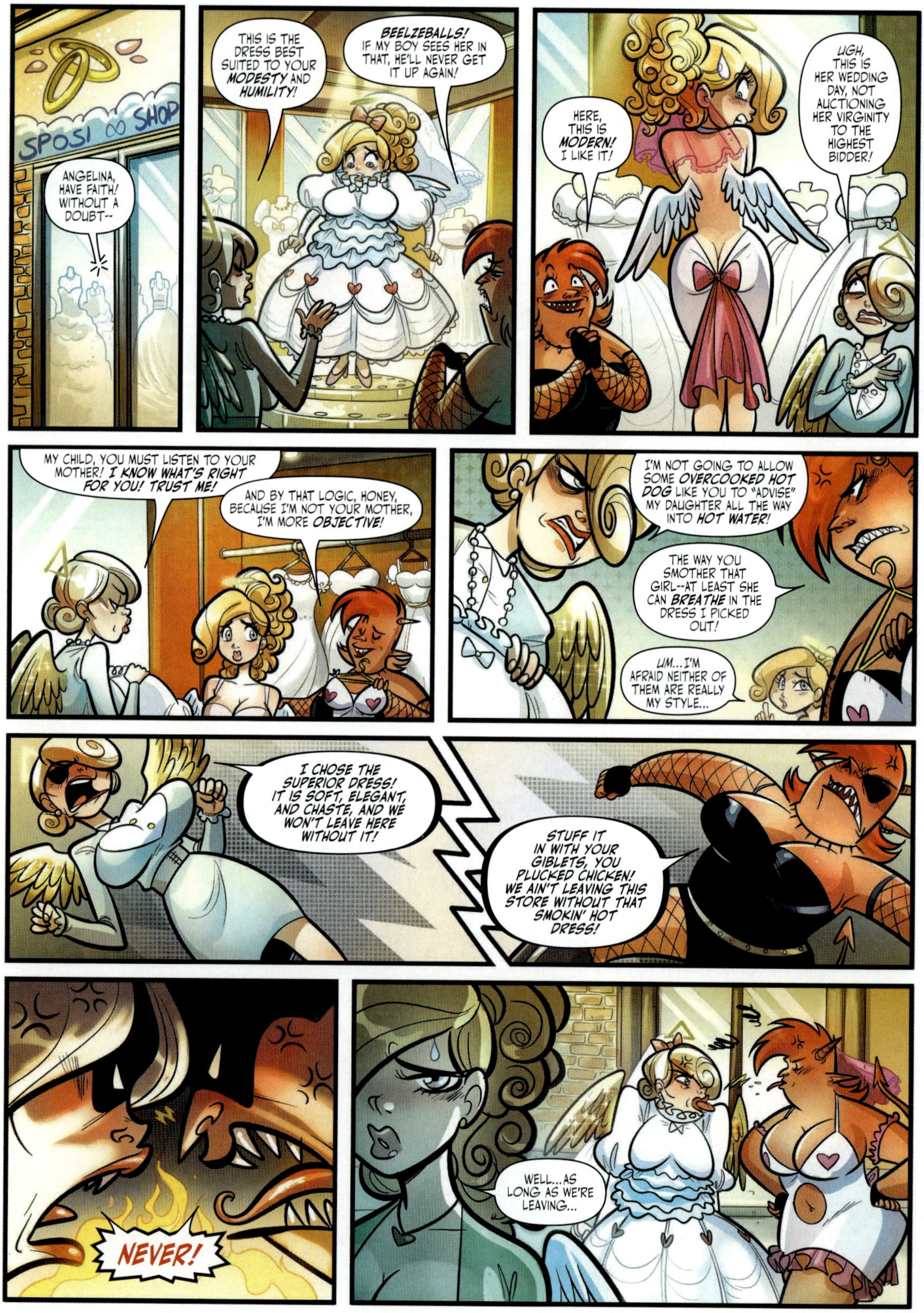
SPOSI ∞ SHOP
ANGELINA, HAVE FAITH! WITHOUT A DOUBT--
THIS IS THE DRESS BEST SUITED TO YOUR MODESTY AND HUMILITY!
BEELZEBALLS! IF MY BOY SEES HER IN THAT, HE'LL NEVER GET IT UP AGAIN!
HERE, THIS IS MODERN! I LIKE IT!
UGH, THIS IS HER WEDDING DAY, NOT AUCTIONING HER VIRGINITY TO THE HIGHEST BIDDER!
MY CHILD, YOU MUST LISTEN TO YOUR MOTHER! I KNOW WHAT'S RIGHT FOR YOU! TRUST ME!
AND BY THAT LOGIC, HONEY, BECAUSE I'M NOT YOUR MOTHER, I'M MORE OBJECTIVE!
I'M NOT GOING TO ALLOW SOME OVERCOOKED HOT DOG LIKE YOU TO "ADVISE" MY DAUGHTER ALL THE WAY INTO HOT WATER!
THE WAY YOU SMOTHER THAT GIRL--AT LEAST SHE CAN BREATHE IN THE DRESS I PICKED OUT!
UM...I'M AFRAID NEITHER OF THEM ARE REALLY MY STYLE...
I CHOSE THE SUPERIOR DRESS! IT IS SOFT, ELEGANT, AND CHASTE, AND WE WON'T LEAVE HERE WITHOUT IT!
STUFF IT IN WITH YOUR GIBLETS, YOU PLUCKED CHICKEN! WE AIN'T LEAVING THIS STORE WITHOUT THAT SMOKIN' HOT DRESS!
NEVER!
WELL...AS LONG AS WE'RE LEAVING...

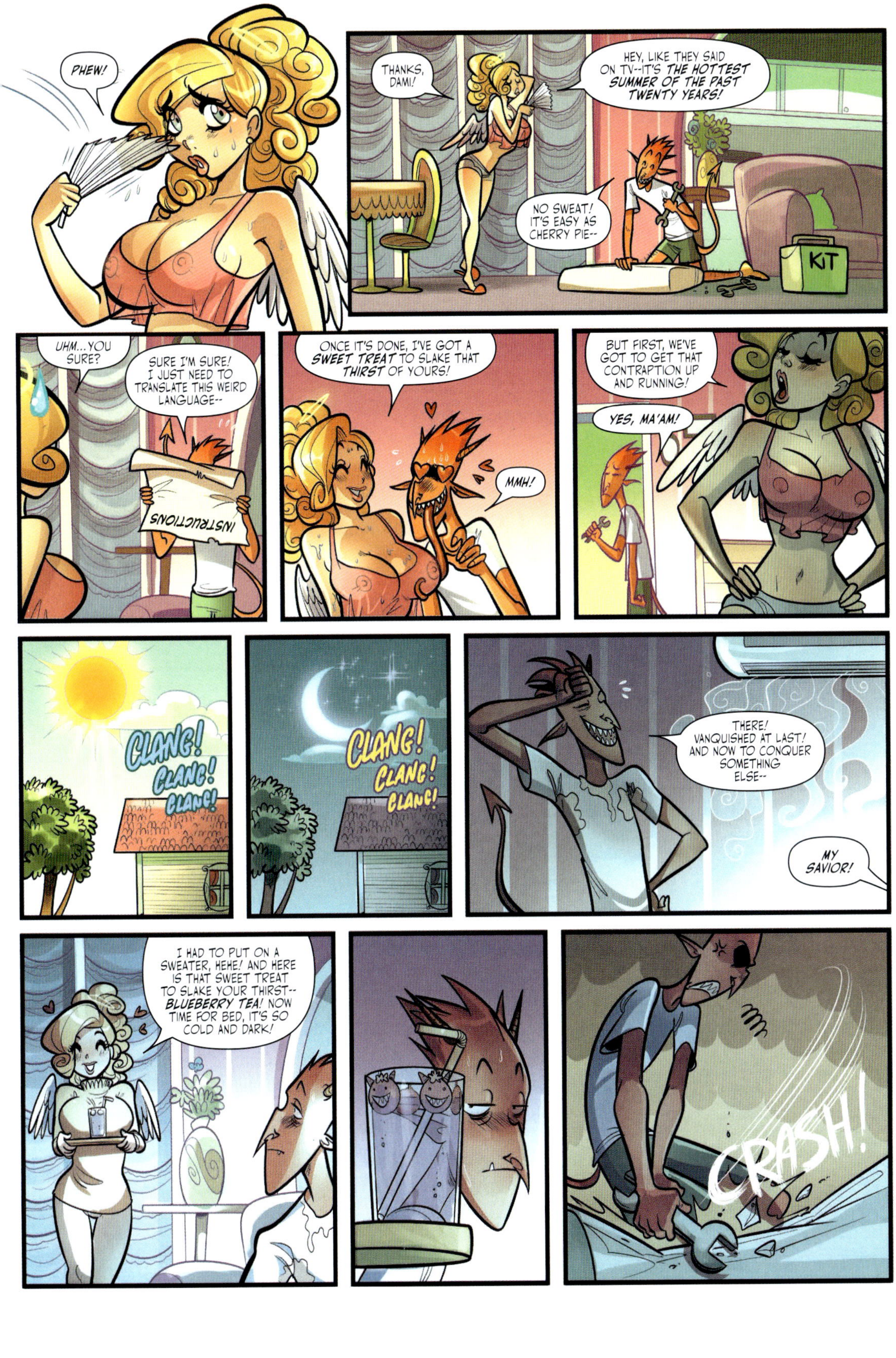
PHEW!
THANKS, DAMI!
HEY, LIKE THEY SAID ON TV--IT'S THE HOTTEST SUMMER OF THE PAST TWENTY YEARS!
NO SWEAT! IT'S EASY AS CHERRY PIE--
KIT
UHM...YOU SURE?
SURE I'M SURE! I JUST NEED TO TRANSLATE THIS WEIRD LANGUAGE--
INSTRUCTIONS
ONCE IT'S DONE, I'VE GOT A SWEET TREAT TO SLAKE THAT THIRST OF YOURS!
MMH!
BUT FIRST, WE'VE GOT TO GET THAT CONTRAPTION UP AND RUNNING!
YES, MA'AM!
CLANG! CLANG! CLANG!
CLANG! CLANG! CLANG!
THERE! VANQUISHED AT LAST! AND NOW TO CONQUER SOMETHING ELSE--
MY SAVIOR!
I HAD TO PUT ON A SWEATER, HEHE! AND HERE IS THAT SWEET TREAT TO SLAKE YOUR THIRST-- BLUEBERRY TEA! NOW TIME FOR BED, IT'S SO COLD AND DARK!
CRASH!

COME HERE, LITTLE DARLINGS! RECESS IS OVER!
?
WHAT BEAUTIFUL COLORS!
WOW!
WHAT ARE YOU DOING...?
LOOK, TEACHER! YOU LIKE IT? THIS BIG I BET IT'S BIGGER THAN EVEN YOUR BOYFRIEND'S! HAHAHA!
WHERE DID YOU GET THAT?!
HEY! IT WAS IN MUM'S DRAWER! YOU CAN'T USE IT!
GASP SEVERINO! YOU'LL BE LUCKY IF YOUR MOTHER DOESN'T PADDLE YOU WITH A FLAMING SWORD!
YES, MA'AM! AS SOON AS POSSIBLE! I'LL WAIT FOR YOU!
WHAT DID HE DO THIS TIME? I HOPE NOTHING SERIOUS!
I'M AFRAID IT IS. YOU KNOW HOW LIVELY YOU SON IS!
UNFORTUNATELY...
HERE...I'M AFRAID HE STOLE SOMETHING VERY PERSONAL!
DAMN! IT HAD TO BE A SURPRISE FOR HIS BIRTHDAY! FOR MONTHS HE HAD ASKED ME TO BUY HIM THE PISTOL LASERGALAXY 4000! ALL HIS FRIENDS HAVE ONE!
ZAP! ZAP!
THE IDEAL GIFT FOR THE EXCELLENT GRADES HE WILL RECEIVE FOR SHUT U...ER...FOR GOOD BEHAVIOR! I REALLY WANTED TO TELL HIM!
PAT PAT

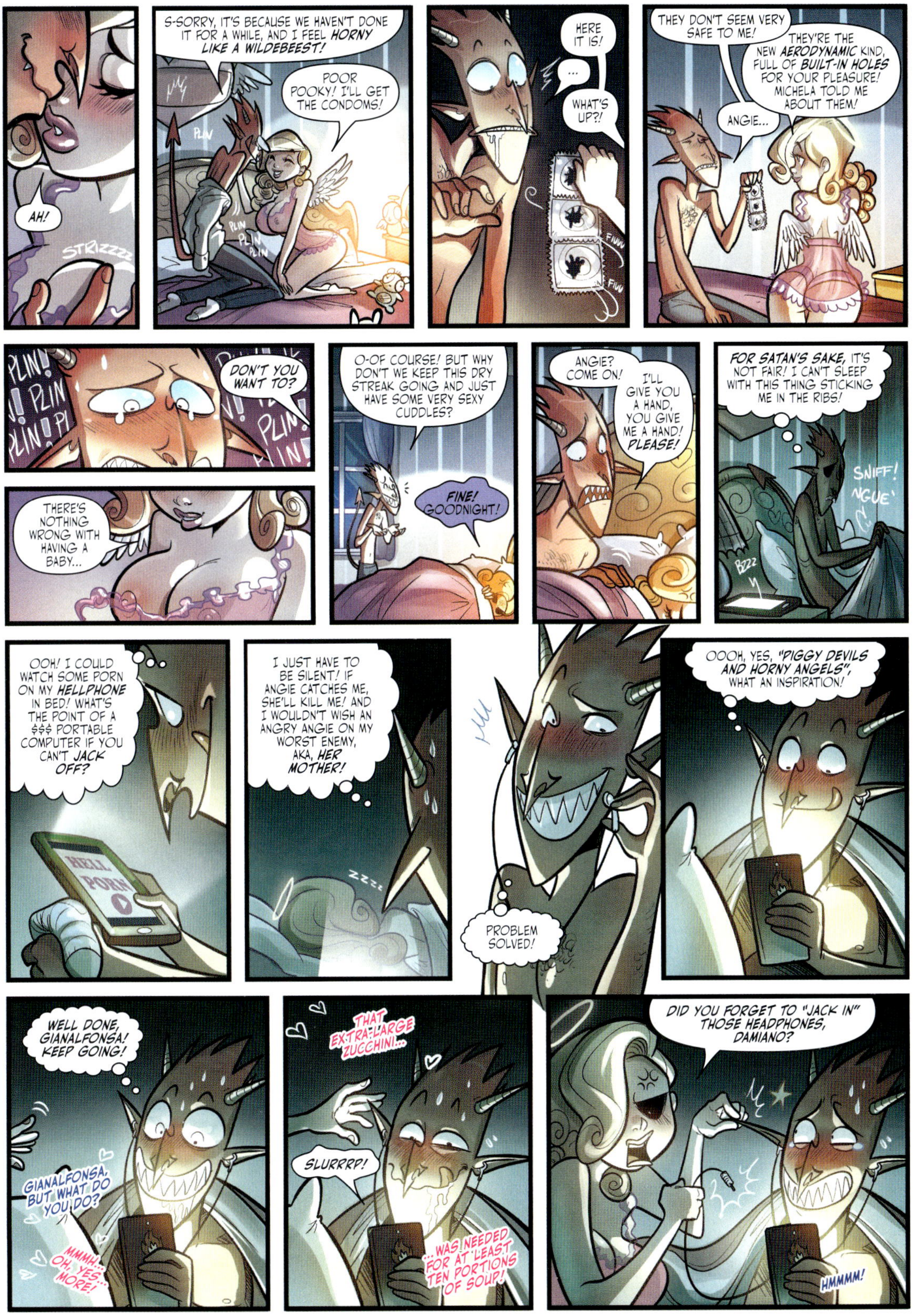
AH!
STRIZZZZ
S-SORRY, IT'S BECAUSE WE HAVEN'T DONE IT FOR A WHILE, AND I FEEL HORNY LIKE A WILDEBEEST!
POOR POOKY! I'LL GET THE CONDOMS!
PLIN
PLIN
PLIN
PLIN
HERE IT IS!
...
WHAT'S UP?!
FIUUU
FIUU
THEY DON'T SEEM VERY SAFE TO ME!
ANGIE...
THEY'RE THE NEW AERODYNAMIC KIND, FULL OF BUILT-IN HOLES FOR YOUR PLEASURE! MICHELA TOLD ME ABOUT THEM!
DON'T YOU WANT TO?
THERE'S NOTHING WRONG WITH HAVING A BABY...
O-OF COURSE! BUT WHY DON'T WE KEEP THIS DRY STREAK GOING AND JUST HAVE SOME VERY SEXY CUDDLES?
FINE! GOODNIGHT!
ANGIE? COME ON!
I'LL GIVE YOU A HAND, YOU GIVE ME A HAND! PLEASE!
FOR SATAN'S SAKE, IT'S NOT FAIR! I CAN'T SLEEP WITH THIS THING STICKING ME IN THE RIBS!
SNIFF!
NGUE'
BZZZ
OOH! I COULD WATCH SOME PORN ON MY HELLPHONE IN BED! WHAT'S THE POINT OF A $$$ PORTABLE COMPUTER IF YOU CAN'T JACK OFF?
HELL PORN
I JUST HAVE TO BE SILENT! IF ANGIE CATCHES ME, SHE'LL KILL ME! AND I WOULDN'T WISH AN ANGRY ANGIE ON MY WORST ENEMY, AKA, HER MOTHER!
ZZZZ
PROBLEM SOLVED!
OOOH, YES, "PIGGY DEVILS AND HORNY ANGELS", WHAT AN INSPIRATION!
WELL DONE, GIANALFONSA! KEEP GOING!
GIANALFONSA, BUT WHAT DO YOU DO?
MMMH... OH, YES... MORE!
THAT EXTRA-LARGE ZUCCHINI...
SLURRRP!
...WAS NEEDED FOR AT LEAST TEN PORTIONS OF SOUP!
DID YOU FORGET TO "JACK IN" THOSE HEADPHONES, DAMIANO?
HMMMM!

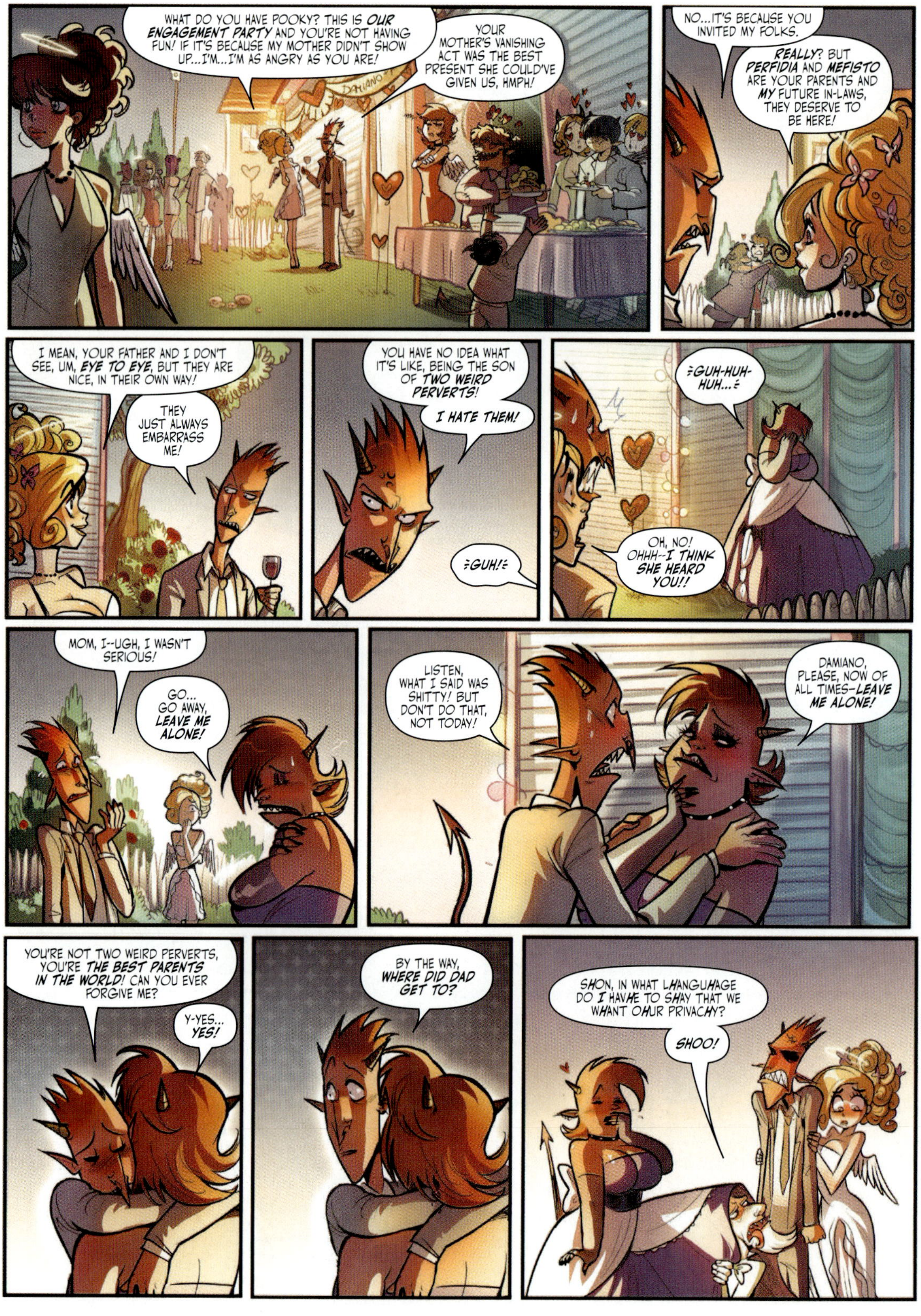

WHAT DO YOU HAVE POOKY? THIS IS OUR ENGAGEMENT PARTY AND YOU'RE NOT HAVING FUN! IF IT'S BECAUSE MY MOTHER DIDN'T SHOW UP...I'M...I'M AS ANGRY AS YOU ARE!
YOUR MOTHER'S VANISHING ACT WAS THE BEST PRESENT SHE COULD'VE GIVEN US, HMPH!
DAMIANO
NO...IT'S BECAUSE YOU INVITED MY FOLKS.
REALLY? BUT PERFIDIA AND MEFISTO ARE YOUR PARENTS AND MY FUTURE IN-LAWS, THEY DESERVE TO BE HERE!
I MEAN, YOUR FATHER AND I DON'T SEE, UM, EYE TO EYE, BUT THEY ARE NICE, IN THEIR OWN WAY!
THEY JUST ALWAYS EMBARRASS ME!
YOU HAVE NO IDEA WHAT IT'S LIKE, BEING THE SON OF TWO WEIRD PERVERTS!
I HATE THEM!
GUH!
GUH-HUH-HUH...
OH, NO! OHHH--I THINK SHE HEARD YOU!!
MOM, I--UGH, I WASN'T SERIOUS!
GO... GO AWAY, LEAVE ME ALONE!
LISTEN, WHAT I SAID WAS SHITTY! BUT DON'T DO THAT, NOT TODAY!
DAMIANO, PLEASE, NOW OF ALL TIMES--LEAVE ME ALONE!
YOU'RE NOT TWO WEIRD PERVERTS, YOU'RE THE BEST PARENTS IN THE WORLD! CAN YOU EVER FORGIVE ME?
Y-YES... YES!
BY THE WAY, WHERE DID DAD GET TO?
SHON, IN WHAT LHANGUHAGE DO I HAVHE TO SHAY THAT WE WHANT OHUR PRIVACHY?
SHOO!

WHAT A GREAT IDEA, A BACHELORETTE PARTY WITH JUST THE GIRLS IN THE FAMILY! ALL WHILE THE BOYS SIT AT HOME SMASHED WITH FUPA 15 ON SEXBOX ONE!
LET'S ROCK THIS TOWN!
"ROCK THIS TOWN"? GET STONED FOR SUCH INDECENCY, MORE LIKE! ANGELINA IS ABOUT TO BECOME A MARRIED MATRON, FOR GOODNESS SAKE!
COME ON, I'M NOT TALKING ABOUT GOING TO A STRIP CLUB! YOU SAID NO THE FIRST SIX TIMES I ASKED!
WHAT ABOUT THAT?
I SAW IT ON TV, IT SEEMS TO BE A VERY HOT AND HAPPENING PLACE!
PURGATORY
HMM, EXCLUSIVITY IS GOOD. A LITTLE "TIP" FOR THE DOORMAN...
WHO NEEDS A TIP WHEN YOU CAN HAVE A TIT! TONIGHT'S ON ME, GIRLS!
...WITH MY FEMININITY! I OFFER! DO YOU LIKE THE SHOW, CUTE?
SWISSSH
PATHETIC! CAN SHE SEE HOW SHE DEGRADES HERSELF! SHE'S GIVING IT AWAY AND THEY AVERT THEIR EYES!
WELL...
...DIFFERENT CURRENCY FOR DIFFERENT CUSTOMERS!
FORGIVE MY DEPARTURE, RED GODDESS, I HAD TO CAPTURE YOUR VOLUPTUOUS BEAUTY! YOU AND YOUR LITTLE FRIENDS ARE MOST WELCOME!

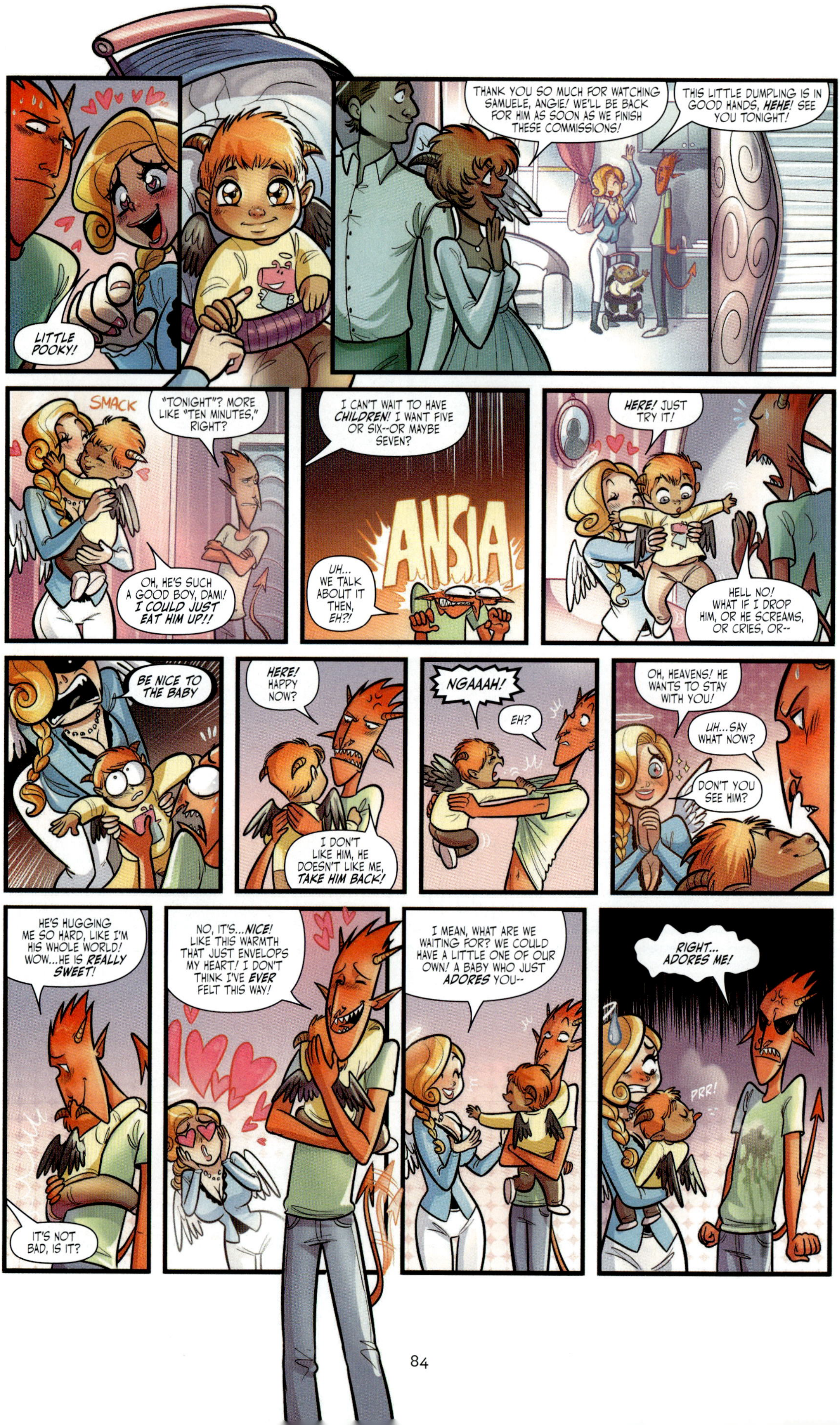
LITTLE POOKY!
THANK YOU SO MUCH FOR WATCHING SAMUELE, ANGIE! WE'LL BE BACK FOR HIM AS SOON AS WE FINISH THESE COMMISSIONS!
THIS LITTLE DUMPLING IS IN GOOD HANDS, HEHE! SEE YOU TONIGHT!
SMACK
"TONIGHT"? MORE LIKE "TEN MINUTES," RIGHT?
OH, HE'S SUCH A GOOD BOY, DAMI! I COULD JUST EAT HIM UP!!
I CAN'T WAIT TO HAVE CHILDREN! I WANT FIVE OR SIX--OR MAYBE SEVEN?
ANSIA
UH... WE TALK ABOUT IT THEN, EH?!
HERE! JUST TRY IT!
HELL NO! WHAT IF I DROP HIM, OR HE SCREAMS, OR CRIES, OR--
BE NICE TO THE BABY
HERE! HAPPY NOW?
I DON'T LIKE HIM, HE DOESN'T LIKE ME, TAKE HIM BACK!
NGAAAH!
EH?
OH, HEAVENS! HE WANTS TO STAY WITH YOU!
UH...SAY WHAT NOW?
DON'T YOU SEE HIM?
HE'S HUGGING ME SO HARD, LIKE I'M HIS WHOLE WORLD! WOW...HE IS REALLY SWEET!
IT'S NOT BAD, IS IT?
NO, IT'S...NICE! LIKE THIS WARMTH THAT JUST ENVELOPS MY HEART! I DON'T THINK I'VE EVER FELT THIS WAY!
I MEAN, WHAT ARE WE WAITING FOR? WE COULD HAVE A LITTLE ONE OF OUR OWN! A BABY WHO JUST ADORES YOU--
RIGHT... ADORES ME!
PRR!

PASTICCERIA
IL BOMBOLONE D'OR
OPEN
IT WAS HARD, BUT I DID IT, AND HER WEDDING CAKE WILL HAVE THE SPECIAL DECORATIONS SHE WANTED! WHAT DO YOU THINK?
...AREN'T THEY BEAUTIFUL?
OH YES! MY ANGIE IS DELICIOUS! PERFECT IN EVERY DETAIL...
PLOP
JUST A LITTLE... TOP-HEAVY.
URGH!
LET'S FIX IT NOW! JUST REDUCE THE MEASUREMENTS AND...
AAAAAAGH! ARE YOU CRAZY?! NEVER! PUT A COUNTERWEIGHT SOMEWHERE!
YOU'RE THE BOSS! I'LL PUT SOME SUGAR PASTE BACK HERE, AND...
"REDUCE HER MEASUREMENTS," FOR SATAN'S SAKE, MY POOR POINTED EARS...
...IT'S DONE! WHAT DO YOU THINK?
!
MY FIANCÉE DOESN'T HAVE SUCH A BIG BUTT!
PLOP
UHM...I CAN ADD WEIGHT HERE AND THERE TO BALANCE EVERYTHING WITHOUT LOSING SIGHT OF THE PROPORTIONS, BUT IT WON'T BE EASY, I WARN YOU...
WHAT ARE YOU WAITING FOR? DO SOMETHING!
ER...CLEARLY THERE ARE STILL A COUPLE OF DETAILS TO FIX!
CLEARLY.
IN THE MEANTIME, YOU CAN USE HER AS A PILLOW TONIGHT-- WHEN YOU SLEEP ON THE COUCH.

THERE'S SOMETHING IN THE AIR TONIGHT, GUIDA... HIC!
EVERY NOW AND THEN, IT'S NICE TO HAVE A BOYS' NIGHT OUT, NO GIRLS ALLOWED!
YUP, AND WITH SUCH A BEAUTIFUL MOON IN THE SKY!
I'LL DRINK TO THAT!
I'M SO GLAD I'VE GOT A FRIEND LIKE YOU, DAMIANO... HIC! WE'VE BEEN FRIENDS SO LONG, AND YOU "KNOW" ME LIKE NO ONE ELSE--
NO! YOU DISGUSTING, DRUNKEN OAF! YOU'VE GOT THIS PUSSY ON SPEED DIAL AND--AHEM--I V-VERY MAGNANIMOUSLY ALLOW TO YOU BE FRIENDS WITH BENEFITS, AND YOU WANT TO RUT WITH THIS OVERCOOKED CHILI PEPPER HELLSPAWN?!
COME ON, CALM DOWN, MICHELA! HIC!
HEY, BABY, WHAT'S WRONG? HIC!
YOU ALWAYS GET SO MAD THAT LOVE MAKES OTHER PEOPLE HAPPY IN WAYS IT DOESN'T MAKE YOU HAPPY!
DID YOU THINK YOU PUT A RING ON MY COCK AND A CHASTITY BELT ON MY FINGER? "IF LOST--"
GRRR!
"--RETURN TO MICHELA'?"
SQUASH
REMEMBER, GUIDA, THAT REVENGE IS A DISH BEST SERVED COLD... AND WET!
CRACK

SNAP! SNAP! SNAP!

WHY AM I HERE? BUT ABOVE ALL: WHERE IS IT HERE?

ANGELINA, HOW DID WE GET TO THIS PLACE?

ANGELINA? I'M NOT ANGELINA... I'M ANNA, AND I'M HER COUSIN.

OTTO DEIFIED ANNA!

YOU PERFIDIOUS PSYCHOPOMP OF A DWARF! WHAT IS THIS LYNCHIAN NIGHTMARE? WHERE ARE HAVE TAKEN US? WHY ISN'T ANGELINA ANGELINA?

OTTO DEIFIED ANNA... OTTO DEIFIED ANNA...

I DON'T UNDERSTAND IF YOU TALK BACKWARDS...

OTTO DEIFIED ANNA...OTTO DEIFIED ANNA...

RUSTLE RUSTLE

AAARGH!

OH, ANGELINA! PLEASE, I BEG OF YOU--

ANYTHING, MY CHERRY TOMATO!

FOR THE SAKE OF MY SANITY, PLEASE DON'T WEAR THOSE CELLOPHANE SLIMMING SUITS TO BED ANYMORE!

?

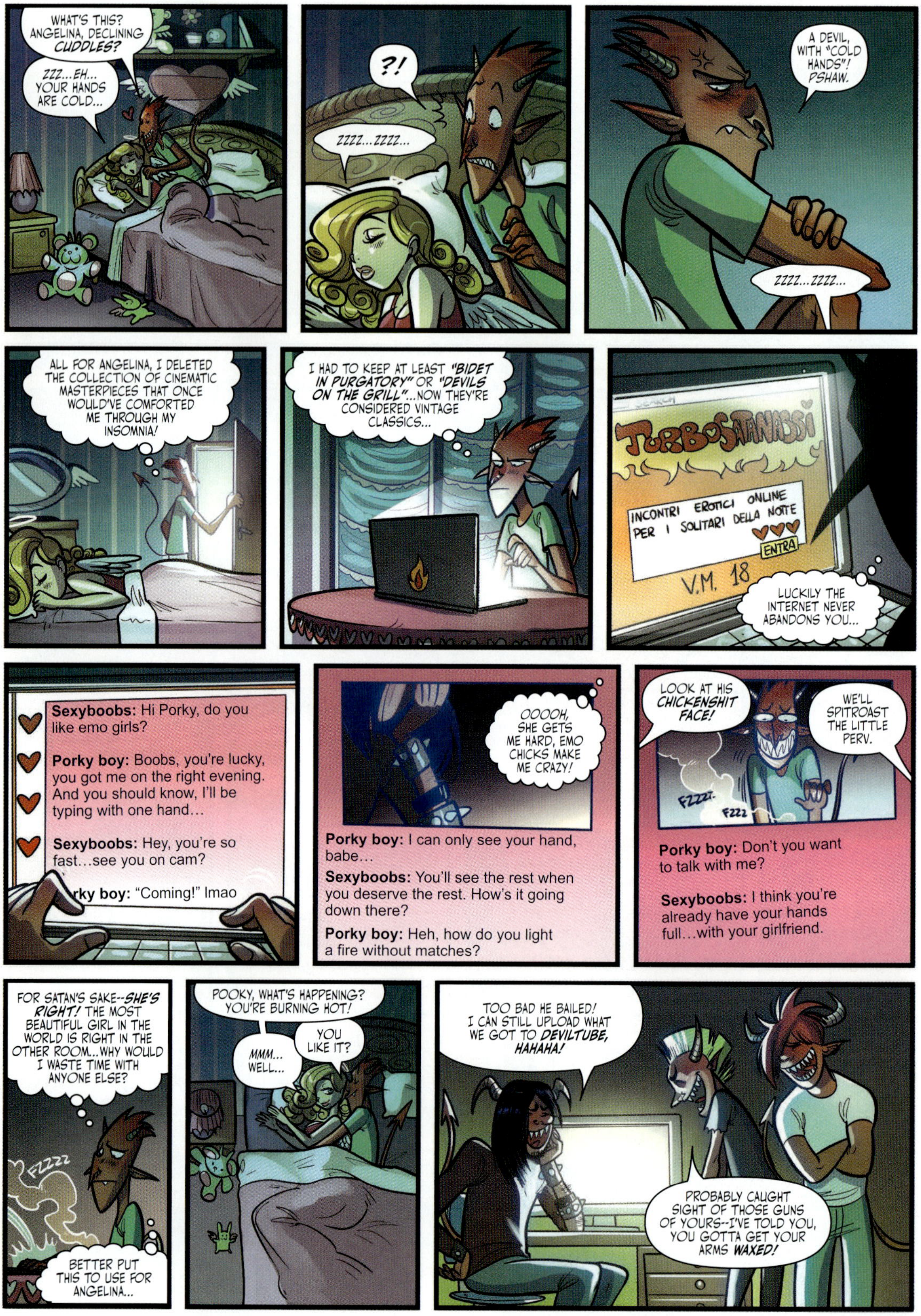
WHAT'S THIS? ANGELINA, DECLINING CUDDLES?
ZZZ...EH... YOUR HANDS ARE COLD...
?!
ZZZZ...ZZZZ...
A DEVIL, WITH "COLD HANDS"! PSHAW.
ZZZZ...ZZZZ...
ALL FOR ANGELINA, I DELETED THE COLLECTION OF CINEMATIC MASTERPIECES THAT ONCE WOULD'VE COMFORTED ME THROUGH MY INSOMNIA!
I HAD TO KEEP AT LEAST "BIDET IN PURGATORY" OR "DEVILS ON THE GRILL"...NOW THEY'RE CONSIDERED VINTAGE CLASSICS...
TURBOSATANASSI
INCONTRI EROTICI ONLINE PER I SOLITARI DELLA NOTTE
ENTRA
V.M. 18
LUCKILY THE INTERNET NEVER ABANDONS YOU...
Sexyboobs: Hi Porky, do you like emo girls?
Porky boy: Boobs, you're lucky, you got me on the right evening. And you should know, I'll be typing with one hand…
Sexyboobs: Hey, you're so fast…see you on cam?
rky boy: "Coming!" lmao
OOOOH, SHE GETS ME HARD, EMO CHICKS MAKE ME CRAZY!
Porky boy: I can only see your hand, babe…
Sexyboobs: You'll see the rest when you deserve the rest. How's it going down there?
Porky boy: Heh, how do you light a fire without matches?
LOOK AT HIS CHICKENSHIT FACE!
WE'LL SPITROAST THE LITTLE PERV.
FZZZT.
FZZZ
Porky boy: Don't you want to talk with me?
Sexyboobs: I think you're already have your hands full…with your girlfriend.
FOR SATAN'S SAKE--SHE'S RIGHT! THE MOST BEAUTIFUL GIRL IN THE WORLD IS RIGHT IN THE OTHER ROOM...WHY WOULD I WASTE TIME WITH ANYONE ELSE?
FZZZZ
BETTER PUT THIS TO USE FOR ANGELINA...
POOKY, WHAT'S HAPPENING? YOU'RE BURNING HOT!
MMM... WELL...
YOU LIKE IT?
TOO BAD HE BAILED! I CAN STILL UPLOAD WHAT WE GOT TO DEVILTUBE, HAHAHA!
PROBABLY CAUGHT SIGHT OF THOSE GUNS OF YOURS--I'VE TOLD YOU, YOU GOTTA GET YOUR ARMS WAXED!

CHERRY TOMATO! HERE I AM! HOW DO I LOOK?
OH, ANGIE, YOU'RE FANTASTIC! BUT...
"BUT" WHAT? DON'T YOU LIKE ME? DON'T MAKE ME PARANOID, POOKY!
OH, IT'S NOTHING BIG! LOOK DOWN, AND YOU'LL SEE FOR YOURSELF...
UM...IT SEEMS ALL RIGHT TO ME. COME ON, TELL ME!
DO YOU REALLY NEED ME TO TELL YOU? ANYONE WHO LOOKS AT YOU CAN SEE...
YOU REALLY DON'T SEE THAT THEY'RE DIFFERENT FROM EACH OTHER?
POOKY, DON'T WORRY ME! THEY LOOK PERFECTLY IDENTICAL TO ME!
IDENTICAL?!
FOR SATAN'S SAKE! THEY'RE DIFFERENT! THEY'RE AS DIFFERENT AS SHEEP AND GOATS! BUT WHERE ARE YOU LOOKING?
"WHERE AM I LOOKING?" WHERE YOU TOLD ME TO LOOK, DOWN! AND THEY LOOK PERFECTLY IDENTICAL!
IDENTICAL?! OH, FORGET IT, COME ON!
MEMO TO DAMIANO: WHEN YOU TALK TO WOMEN ABOUT SHOES, REMEMBER: YOU ARE ALWAYS IN THE WRONG!

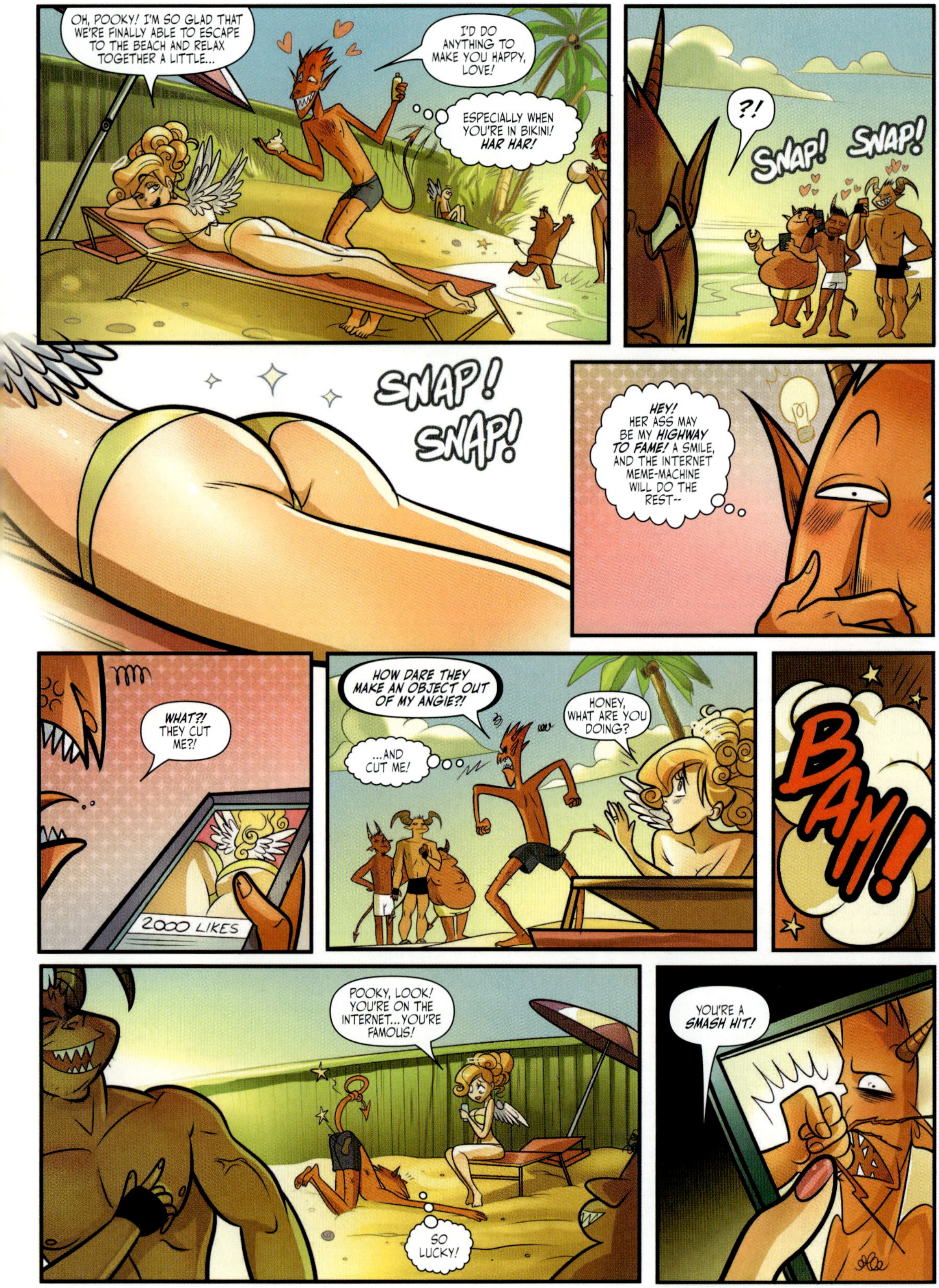
OH, POOKY! I'M SO GLAD THAT WE'RE FINALLY ABLE TO ESCAPE TO THE BEACH AND RELAX TOGETHER A LITTLE...
I'D DO ANYTHING TO MAKE YOU HAPPY, LOVE!
ESPECIALLY WHEN YOU'RE IN BIKINI! HAR HAR!
?!
SNAP! SNAP!
SNAP! SNAP!
HEY! HER ASS MAY BE MY HIGHWAY TO FAME! A SMILE, AND THE INTERNET MEME-MACHINE WILL DO THE REST--
WHAT?! THEY CUT ME?!
2000 LIKES
HOW DARE THEY MAKE AN OBJECT OUT OF MY ANGIE?!
...AND CUT ME!
HONEY, WHAT ARE YOU DOING?
BAM!
POOKY, LOOK! YOU'RE ON THE INTERNET...YOU'RE FAMOUS!
SO LUCKY!
YOU'RE A SMASH HIT!

DIIIN DOON

HAHA! LOOK AT DAMIANO! HE'S SO NERVOUS, HE'S SWEATING LIKE, UH, WELL, A DEVIL IN CHURCH!

DON'T YOU KNOW?

DEVILS ARE ALL *ALLERGIC TO CHURCHES*! HE'S IN THE *DEEP FRYER* NOW!

OH... I THOUGHT IT WAS THE SMELL OF *FAST FOOD* ON THE CORNER!

I'M *S-SO* ITCHY! I CAN'T LAST ANOTHER MINUTE!

DON'T BREAK MY BALLS, YOU'RE NOT THE ONLY ONE!

WHY THIS RIDICULOUS CUSTOM? WHY NOT GET MARRIED IN CITY HALL, AT HOME, AT THE *BAR*... WHY DO ANGELS WANT TO GET MARRIED HERE?

DO YOU WANT TO ESCAPE?

EVEN IF I WANTED, IT'S *TOO LATE!*

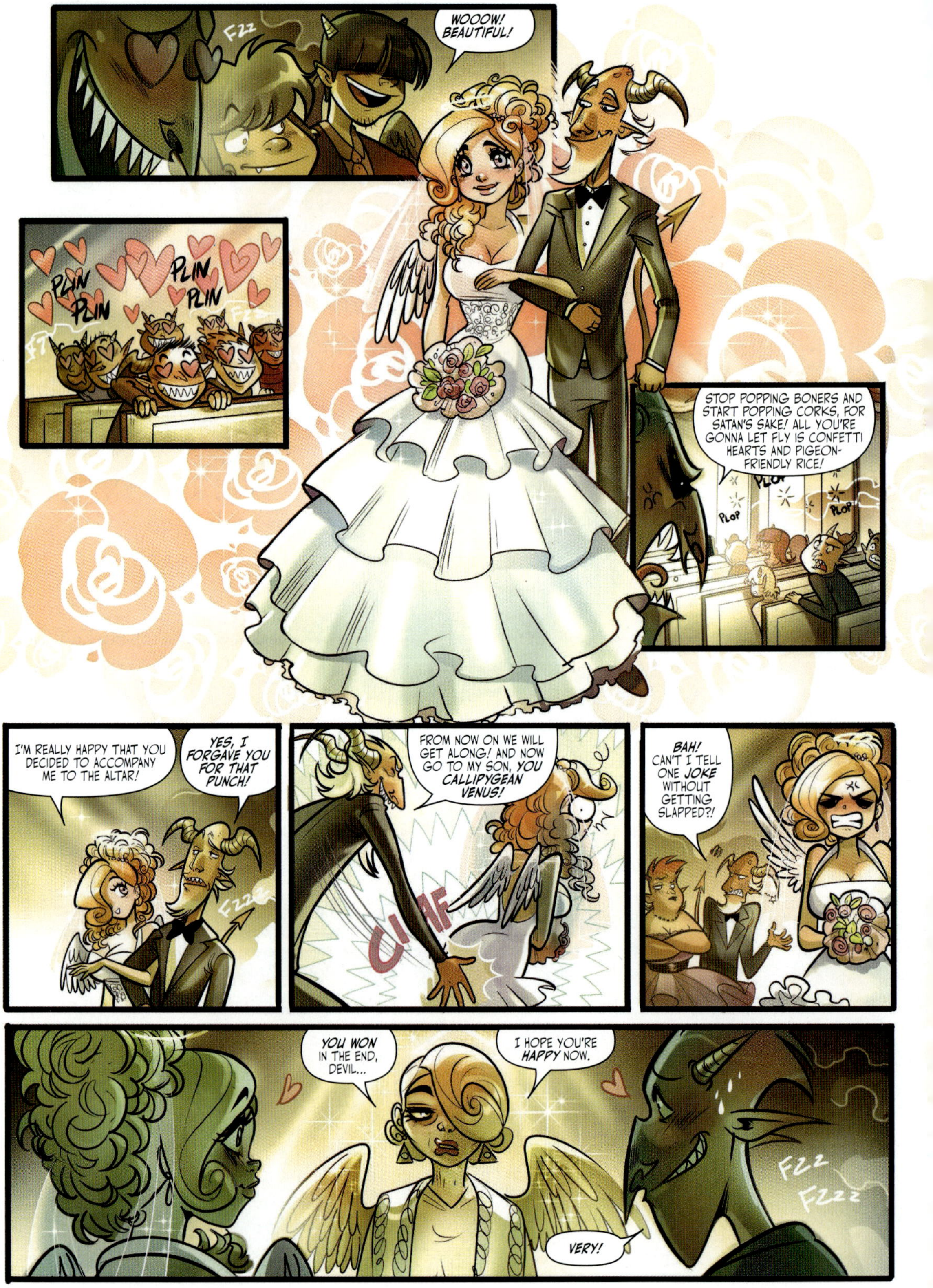
FZZ
WOOOW! BEAUTIFUL!
PLIN
PLIN
PLIN
PLIN
STOP POPPING BONERS AND START POPPING CORKS, FOR SATAN'S SAKE! ALL YOU'RE GONNA LET FLY IS CONFETTI HEARTS AND PIGEON-FRIENDLY RICE!
PLOP
PLOP
PLOP
I'M REALLY HAPPY THAT YOU DECIDED TO ACCOMPANY ME TO THE ALTAR!
YES, I FORGAVE YOU FOR THAT PUNCH!
FROM NOW ON WE WILL GET ALONG! AND NOW GO TO MY SON, YOU CALLIPYGEAN VENUS!
BAH! CAN'T I TELL ONE JOKE WITHOUT GETTING SLAPPED?!
YOU WON IN THE END, DEVIL...
I HOPE YOU'RE HAPPY NOW.
VERY!
FZZ
FZZZ

AND SO BE IT...
TODAY WE ARE GATHERED HERE TO WITNESS THE SPIRITUAL UNION OF TWO DISTINCT HALVES. A RITUAL THAT WE ANGELS BELIEVE TO BE OF FUNDAMENTAL IMPORTANCE, AND WHICH BINDS TWO HEARTS TOGETHER FOREVER, MAKING THEM A A SINGLE ENTITY FOR ETERNITY.
HIT THE LIGHTS!
SNAP!
WE DON'T KNOW WHY WE ARE HERE, OR WHERE WE COME FROM. WE ONLY KNOW THAT THIS IS PROBABLY NOT OUR ONLY FORM OF EXISTENCE.
FOR THIS WE MUST LIVE IN THE PRESENT WITH DIGNITY AND LIVE IT TO THE END WITH OUR OTHER HALF. PROMISING IT BEFORE FAMILY AND FRIENDS. A PROMISE THAT LASTS FOREVER!
IN THE NEXT LIFE, WE MAY HAVE NO WINGS OR HALOES, HORNS AND TAILS. AND WE DON'T KNOW WHAT AWAITS US.
DO YOU WANT, ANGELINA, TAKE...URGH... DAMIANO AS YOUR HUSBAND AND VICE VERSA?
I'VE LOVED YOU EVER SINCE YOU FIRST LOOKED AT ME WITH THOSE PERFECT PUPPYDOG EYES AT THE CONCERT EIGHT YEARS AGO. I KNEW I'D NEVER LOVE ANYONE ELSE!
I DO!
HOW WOULD I EVER LIVE WITHOUT THE ANGEL WHO CALLS ME "POOKY" IN FRONT OF ALL AND SUNDRY?
I DO!
FZZZ
FZZZ
FZZZZ
AND WITH GREAT PREJUDICE, ER...WITH GREAT JOY, I PRONOUNCE YOU HUSBAND AND WIFE!

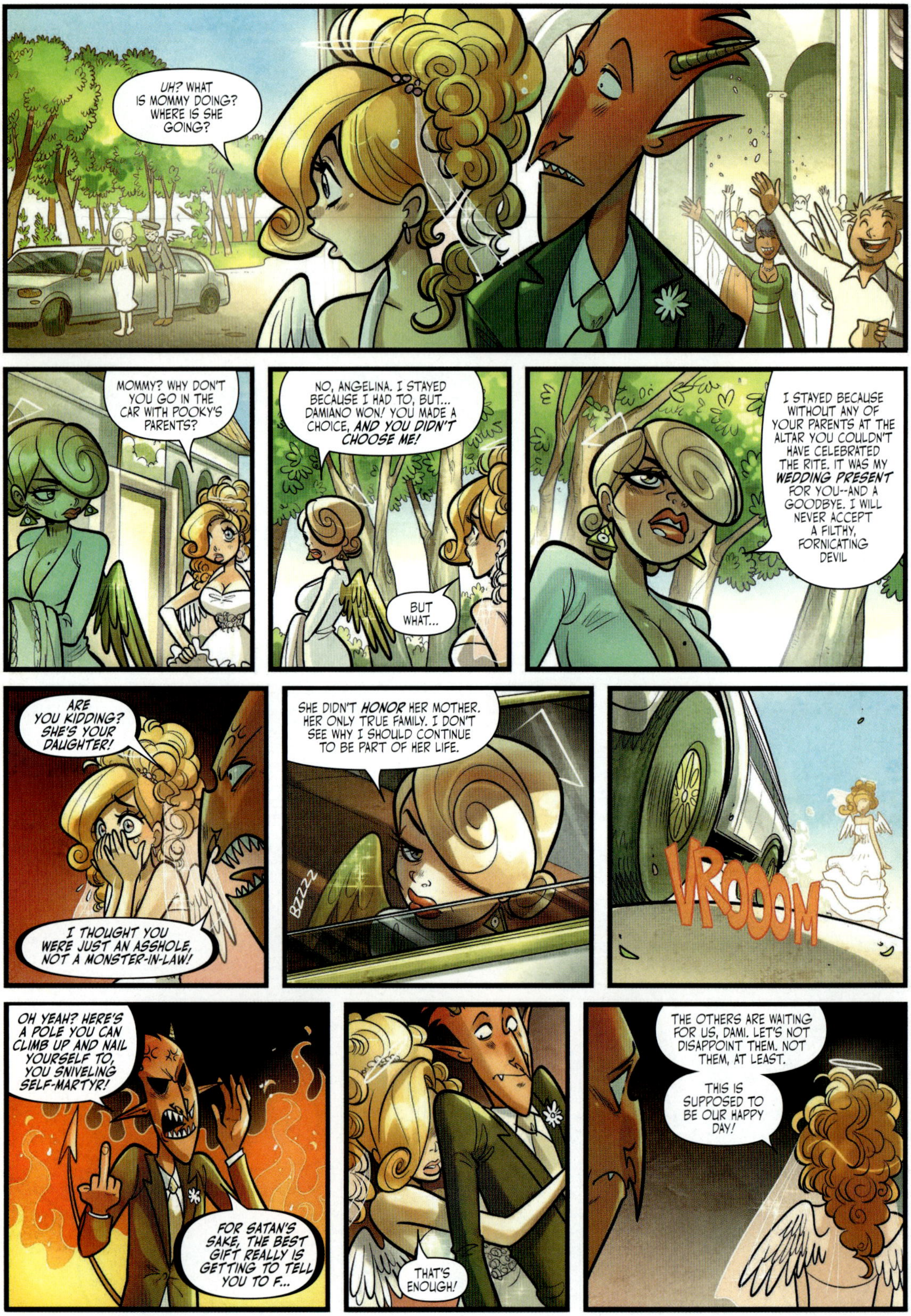
UH? WHAT IS MOMMY DOING? WHERE IS SHE GOING?
MOMMY? WHY DON'T YOU GO IN THE CAR WITH POOKY'S PARENTS?
NO, ANGELINA. I STAYED BECAUSE I HAD TO, BUT... DAMIANO WON! YOU MADE A CHOICE, AND YOU DIDN'T CHOOSE ME!
BUT WHAT...
I STAYED BECAUSE WITHOUT ANY OF YOUR PARENTS AT THE ALTAR YOU COULDN'T HAVE CELEBRATED THE RITE. IT WAS MY WEDDING PRESENT FOR YOU--AND A GOODBYE. I WILL NEVER ACCEPT A FILTHY, FORNICATING DEVIL
ARE YOU KIDDING? SHE'S YOUR DAUGHTER!
I THOUGHT YOU WERE JUST AN ASSHOLE, NOT A MONSTER-IN-LAW!
SHE DIDN'T HONOR HER MOTHER. HER ONLY TRUE FAMILY. I DON'T SEE WHY I SHOULD CONTINUE TO BE PART OF HER LIFE.
BZZZZ
VROOOM
OH YEAH? HERE'S A POLE YOU CAN CLIMB UP AND NAIL YOURSELF TO, YOU SNIVELING SELF-MARTYR!
FOR SATAN'S SAKE, THE BEST GIFT REALLY IS GETTING TO TELL YOU TO F...
THAT'S ENOUGH!
THE OTHERS ARE WAITING FOR US, DAMI. LET'S NOT DISAPPOINT THEM. NOT THEM, AT LEAST.
THIS IS SUPPOSED TO BE OUR HAPPY DAY!

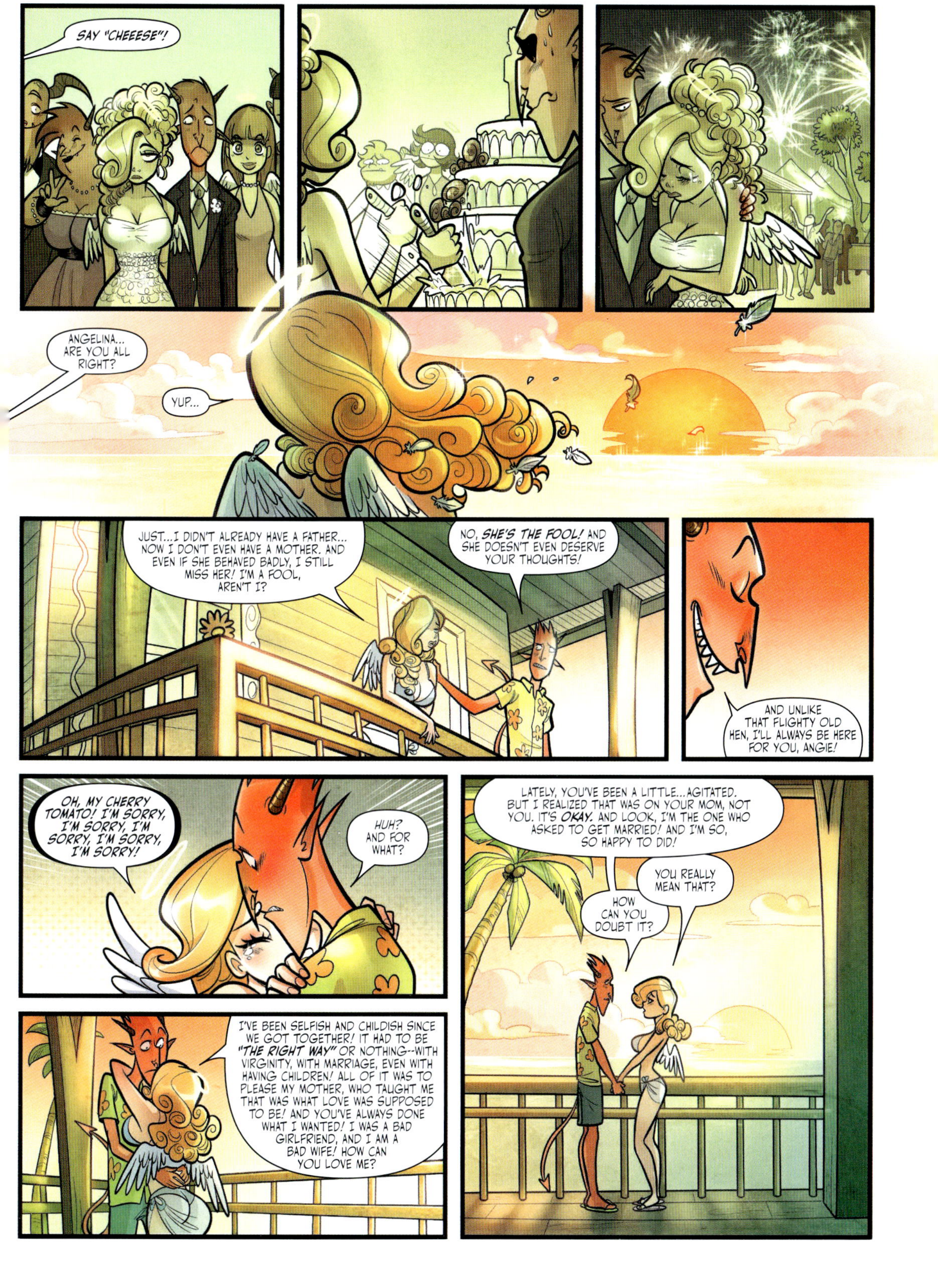
SAY "CHEEESE"!
ANGELINA... ARE YOU ALL RIGHT?
YUP...
JUST...I DIDN'T ALREADY HAVE A FATHER... NOW I DON'T EVEN HAVE A MOTHER. AND EVEN IF SHE BEHAVED BADLY, I STILL MISS HER! I'M A FOOL, AREN'T I?
NO, SHE'S THE FOOL! AND SHE DOESN'T EVEN DESERVE YOUR THOUGHTS!
AND UNLIKE THAT FLIGHTY OLD HEN, I'LL ALWAYS BE HERE FOR YOU, ANGIE!
OH, MY CHERRY TOMATO! I'M SORRY, I'M SORRY, I'M SORRY, I'M SORRY, I'M SORRY!
HUH? AND FOR WHAT?
I'VE BEEN SELFISH AND CHILDISH SINCE WE GOT TOGETHER! IT HAD TO BE "THE RIGHT WAY" OR NOTHING--WITH VIRGINITY, WITH MARRIAGE, EVEN WITH HAVING CHILDREN! ALL OF IT WAS TO PLEASE MY MOTHER, WHO TAUGHT ME THAT WAS WHAT LOVE WAS SUPPOSED TO BE! AND YOU'VE ALWAYS DONE WHAT I WANTED! I WAS A BAD GIRLFRIEND, AND I AM A BAD WIFE! HOW CAN YOU LOVE ME?
LATELY, YOU'VE BEEN A LITTLE...AGITATED. BUT I REALIZED THAT WAS ON YOUR MOM, NOT YOU. IT'S OKAY. AND LOOK, I'M THE ONE WHO ASKED TO GET MARRIED! AND I'M SO, SO HAPPY TO DID!
YOU REALLY MEAN THAT?
HOW CAN YOU DOUBT IT?

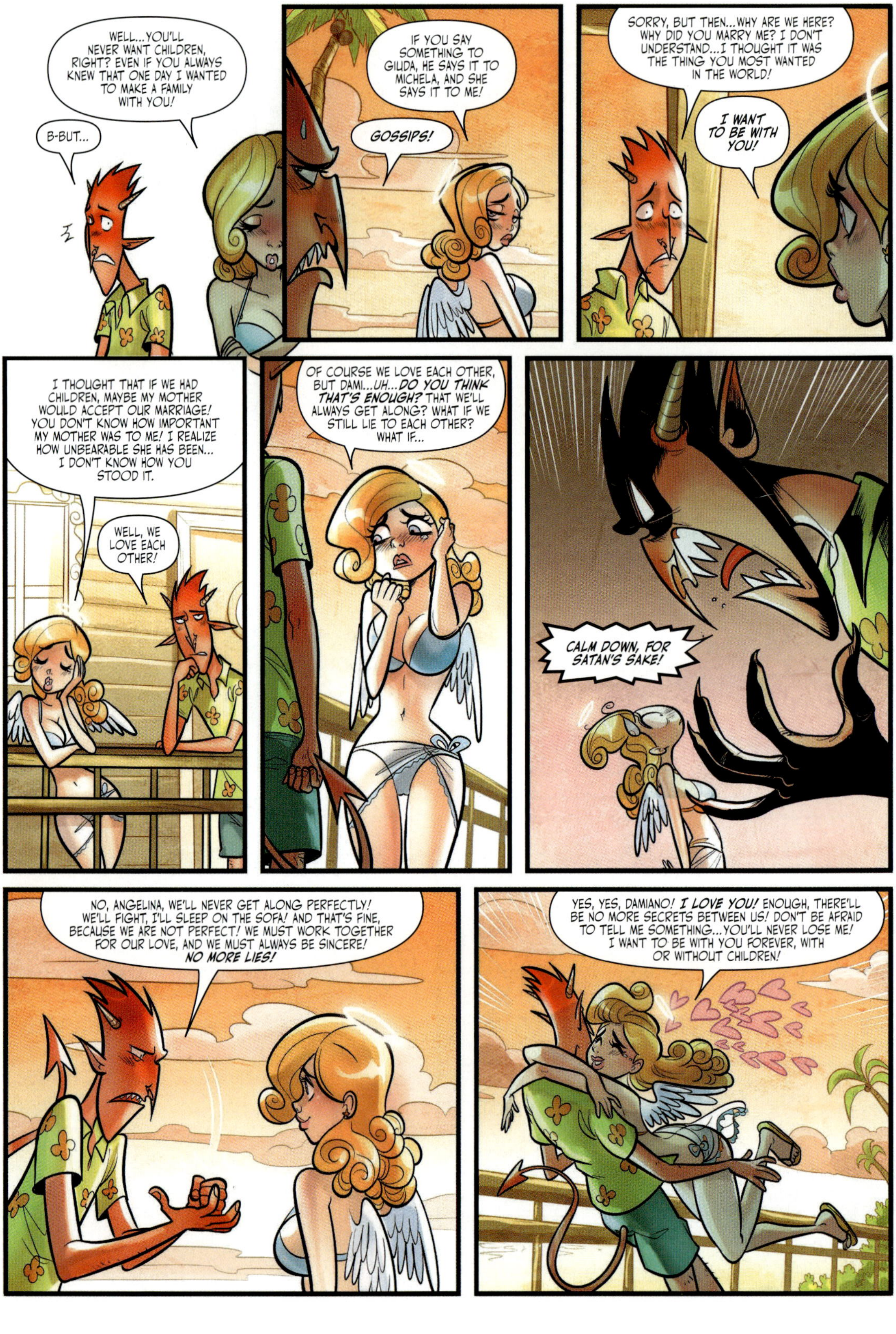
WELL...YOU'LL NEVER WANT CHILDREN, RIGHT? EVEN IF YOU ALWAYS KNEW THAT ONE DAY I WANTED TO MAKE A FAMILY WITH YOU!
B-BUT...
IF YOU SAY SOMETHING TO GIUDA, HE SAYS IT TO MICHELA, AND SHE SAYS IT TO ME!
GOSSIPS!
SORRY, BUT THEN...WHY ARE WE HERE? WHY DID YOU MARRY ME? I DON'T UNDERSTAND...I THOUGHT IT WAS THE THING YOU MOST WANTED IN THE WORLD!
I WANT TO BE WITH YOU!
I THOUGHT THAT IF WE HAD CHILDREN, MAYBE MY MOTHER WOULD ACCEPT OUR MARRIAGE! YOU DON'T KNOW HOW IMPORTANT MY MOTHER WAS TO ME! I REALIZE HOW UNBEARABLE SHE HAS BEEN... I DON'T KNOW HOW YOU STOOD IT.
WELL, WE LOVE EACH OTHER!
OF COURSE WE LOVE EACH OTHER, BUT DAMI...UH...DO YOU THINK THAT'S ENOUGH? THAT WE'LL ALWAYS GET ALONG? WHAT IF WE STILL LIE TO EACH OTHER? WHAT IF...
CALM DOWN, FOR SATAN'S SAKE!
NO, ANGELINA, WE'LL NEVER GET ALONG PERFECTLY! WE'LL FIGHT, I'LL SLEEP ON THE SOFA! AND THAT'S FINE, BECAUSE WE ARE NOT PERFECT! WE MUST WORK TOGETHER FOR OUR LOVE, AND WE MUST ALWAYS BE SINCERE! NO MORE LIES!
YES, YES, DAMIANO! I LOVE YOU! ENOUGH, THERE'LL BE NO MORE SECRETS BETWEEN US! DON'T BE AFRAID TO TELL ME SOMETHING...YOU'LL NEVER LOSE ME! I WANT TO BE WITH YOU FOREVER, WITH OR WITHOUT CHILDREN!

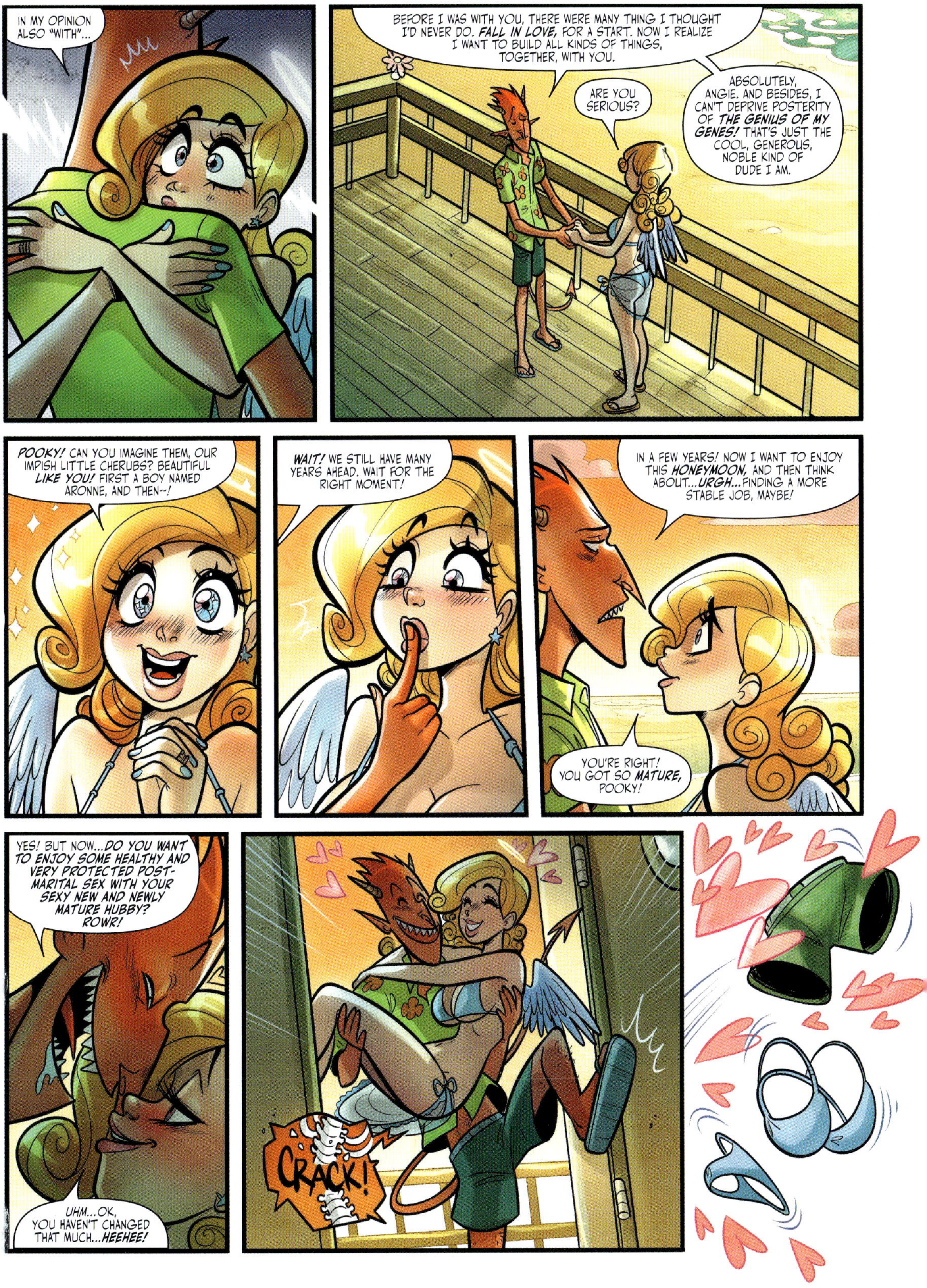
IN MY OPINION ALSO "WITH"...
BEFORE I WAS WITH YOU, THERE WERE MANY THING I THOUGHT I'D NEVER DO. FALL IN LOVE, FOR A START. NOW I REALIZE I WANT TO BUILD ALL KINDS OF THINGS, TOGETHER, WITH YOU.
ARE YOU SERIOUS?
ABSOLUTELY, ANGIE. AND BESIDES, I CAN'T DEPRIVE POSTERITY OF THE GENIUS OF MY GENES! THAT'S JUST THE COOL, GENEROUS, NOBLE KIND OF DUDE I AM.
POOKY! CAN YOU IMAGINE THEM, OUR IMPISH LITTLE CHERUBS? BEAUTIFUL LIKE YOU! FIRST A BOY NAMED ARONNE, AND THEN--!
WAIT! WE STILL HAVE MANY YEARS AHEAD. WAIT FOR THE RIGHT MOMENT!
IN A FEW YEARS! NOW I WANT TO ENJOY THIS HONEYMOON, AND THEN THINK ABOUT...URGH...FINDING A MORE STABLE JOB, MAYBE!
YOU'RE RIGHT! YOU GOT SO MATURE, POOKY!
YES! BUT NOW...DO YOU WANT TO ENJOY SOME HEALTHY AND VERY PROTECTED POST-MARITAL SEX WITH YOUR SEXY NEW AND NEWLY MATURE HUBBY? ROWR!
UHM...OK, YOU HAVEN'T CHANGED THAT MUCH...HEEHEE!
CRACK!

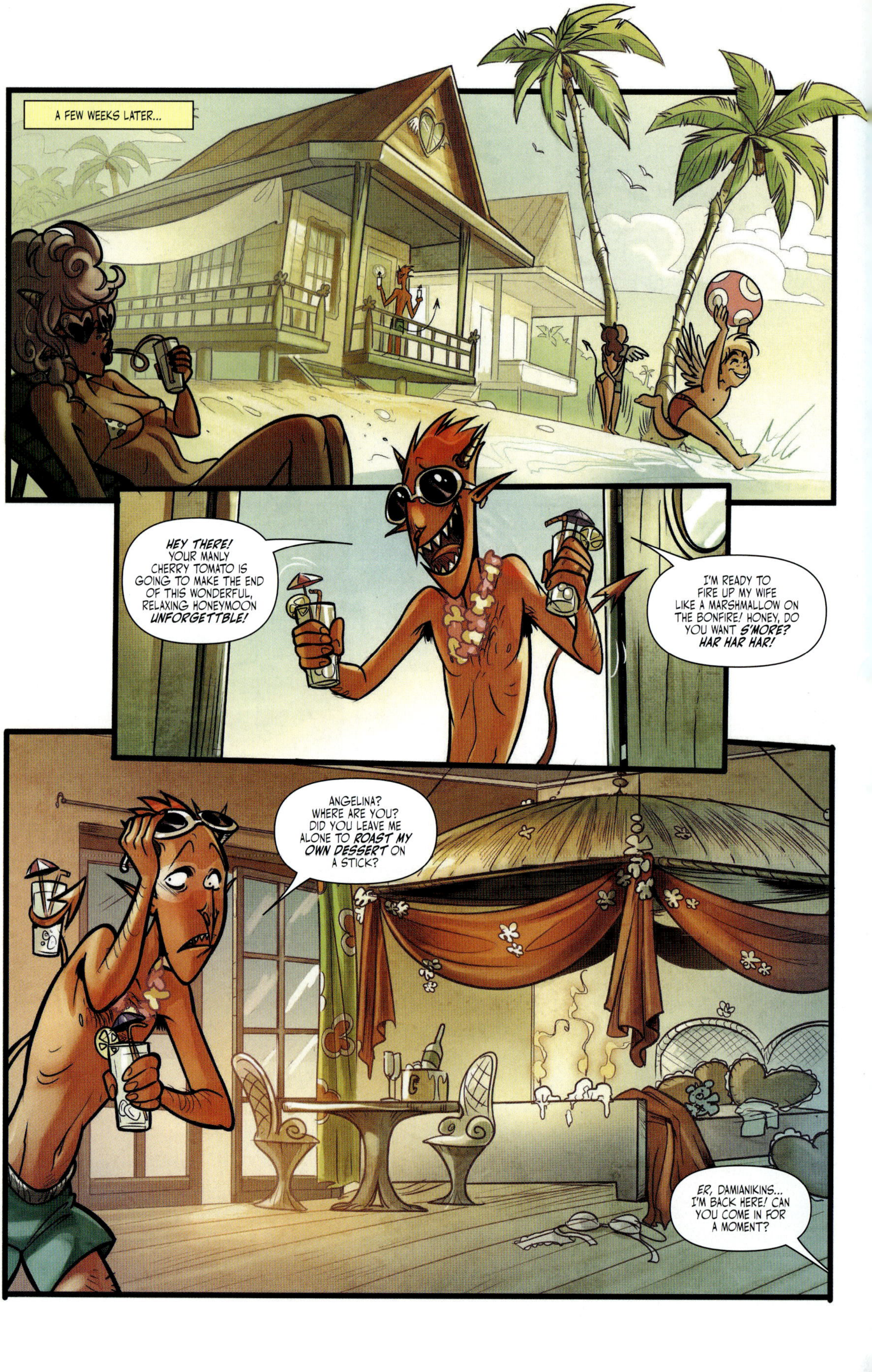
A FEW WEEKS LATER...
HEY THERE! YOUR MANLY CHERRY TOMATO IS GOING TO MAKE THE END OF THIS WONDERFUL, RELAXING HONEYMOON UNFORGETTBLE!
I'M READY TO FIRE UP MY WIFE LIKE A MARSHMALLOW ON THE BONFIRE! HONEY, DO YOU WANT S'MORE? HAR HAR HAR!
ANGELINA? WHERE ARE YOU? DID YOU LEAVE ME ALONE TO ROAST MY OWN DESSERT ON A STICK?
ER, DAMIANIKINS... I'M BACK HERE! CAN YOU COME IN FOR A MOMENT?

STILL IN THE BATHROOM?! FOR SATAN'S SAKE, I TOLD YOU NOT TO FILL UP WITH CLAM AND PESTO SOUP FOR BREAKFAST!
DAMIANO... UH...
I THINK WE WILL RETURN FROM THIS TRIP WITH AN UNEXPECTED LITTLE SOUVENIR!
PURR
SCRIII
SCRIII
CRASH!
CRASH!
CRASH!

•PARADISE•

THREE...

...TWO...

...ONE...

BLUAAAARGH!!

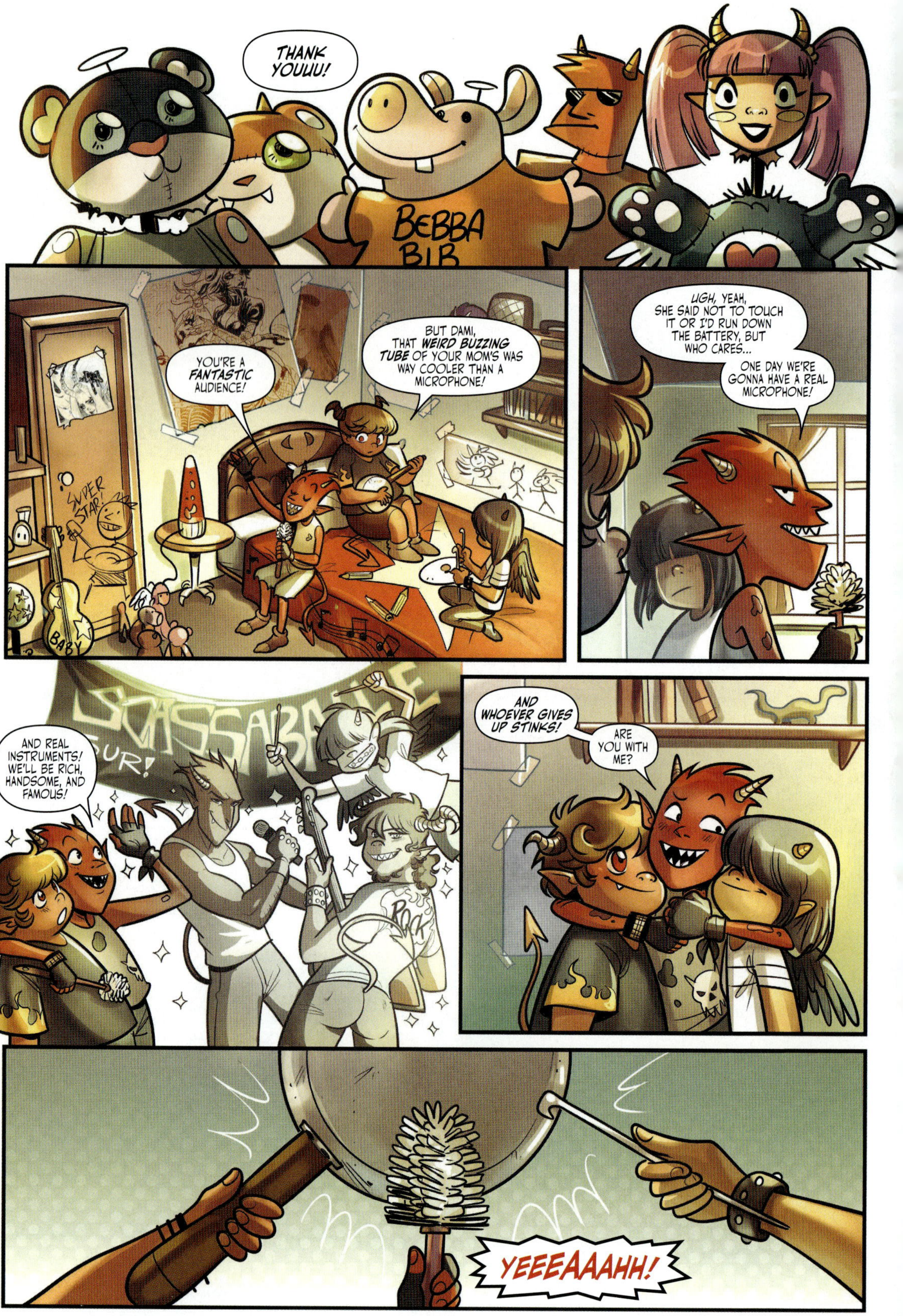
THANK YOUUU!
BEBBA BIB
YOU'RE A FANTASTIC AUDIENCE!
BUT DAMI, THAT WEIRD BUZZING TUBE OF YOUR MOM'S WAS WAY COOLER THAN A MICROPHONE!
SUPER STAR!
BABY
UGH, YEAH, SHE SAID NOT TO TOUCH IT OR I'D RUN DOWN THE BATTERY, BUT WHO CARES...
ONE DAY WE'RE GONNA HAVE A REAL MICROPHONE!
AND REAL INSTRUMENTS! WE'LL BE RICH, HANDSOME, AND FAMOUS!
ROCK
AND WHOEVER GIVES UP STINKS!
ARE YOU WITH ME?
YEEEAAAHH!

CHEERS!
TO MY LAST DAYS OF PEACEFUL SLEEP! BEFORE DEALING WITH DIAPERS AND BURPS...
...A BIT LIKE WITH MY GRANDFATHER ERMENUALDO!
HEHE!
DONUTS
HEY THERE! YOU HAVING FUN?
OF COURSE YES!
TO TOP IT OFF WE SHOULD PLAY! WHAT DO YOU SAY, DAM?
I DON'T KNOW... IT'S SUCH A PEACEFUL EVENING...
A LITTLE TOO PEACEFUL, DON'T YOU THINK?
COME ON, WE'VE ALREADY TAKEN A LONG BREAK AFTER YOUR WEDDING...

HAHA! COME ON, GIUDA! YOU KNOW IT CAN'T BE JUST A "BREAK". I HAVE MORE IMPORTANT THINGS TO THINK ABOUT NOW...
I HAVE TO FIND A REAL JOB!
BUT, POOKY... I'M SURE YOU CAN STILL PLAY!
DON'T JOKE, ANGIE! I'M AN ADULT, I CAN'T THINK ABOUT THIS BULLSHIT ANYMORE...
AS YOU WISH! I'LL SUPPORT YOU, WHATEVER YOU PICK!
WHO'D HAVE THOUGHT I'D GIVE UP ON THESE GARAGE BAND DREAMS? WE CARED SO MUCH... RIGHT, GUYS?
UH?

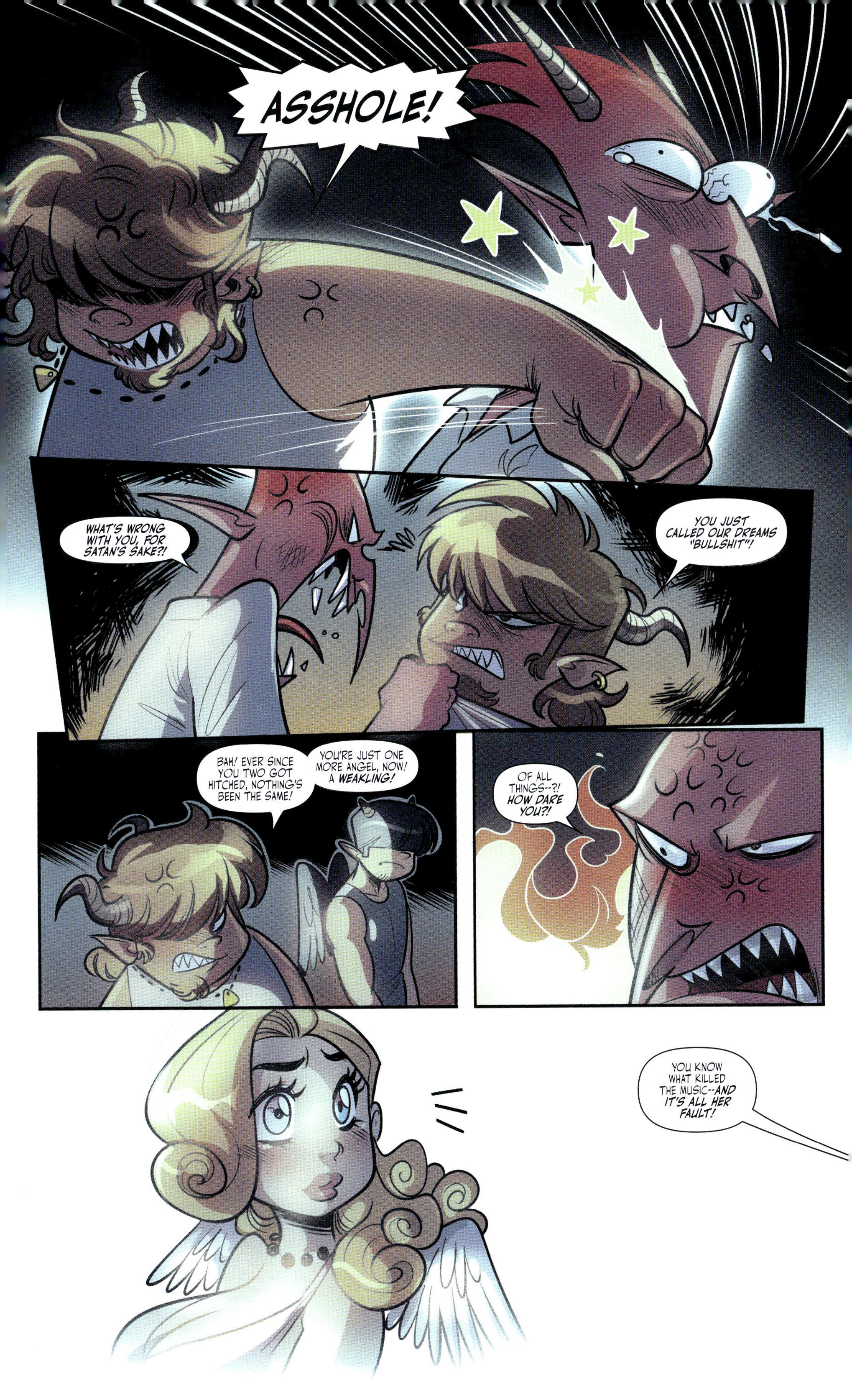
ASSHOLE!
WHAT'S WRONG WITH YOU, FOR SATAN'S SAKE?!
YOU JUST CALLED OUR DREAMS "BULLSHIT"!
BAH! EVER SINCE YOU TWO GOT HITCHED, NOTHING'S BEEN THE SAME!
YOU'RE JUST ONE MORE ANGEL, NOW! A *WEAKLING!*
OF ALL THINGS--?! *HOW DARE YOU?!*
YOU KNOW WHAT KILLED THE MUSIC--*AND IT'S ALL HER FAULT!*

SAINT BEACH
HEY!
PIECE OF #%@¢...
POOKY! TAKE IT EASY!
I WILL CALM DOWN WHEN THEY LEAVE!
HAVE IT YOUR WAY! WE'LL MAKE LIKE YOUR MOM'S BOOBS AND BOUNCE!
SAINT BEACH
OH NO! WE CAN'T TELL HIM, MEFY!
MH... MAYBE IT'S NOT THE TIME TO SPEAK TO DAMIANO, IS IT?!
DEFINITELY NOT TONIGHT.
BUT WE SHOULD TELL HIM, SOONER OR LATER... SOMEHOW!
RIGHT... BUT FOR NOW LET'S GO HOME!

MERRY CHRISTMAS, ANGELINA!
OOOOOH, POOKY...HOW SWEET YOU ARE!
YOU KNOW IT'S OUR FIRST CHRISTMAS AS A MARRIED COUPLE? EEEEEE!
I'M GOING TO GET YOUR GIFT!
ALREADY?! DON'T YOU WANT TO SEE YOURS FIRST?
NAW, I DON'T WANT IT TO BE A WASH! JUST YOU WAIT UNTIL YOU SEE WHAT I'VE GOT FOR YOU!
REALLY? NOW I'M VERY CURIOUS...
HEHEHE! YOU'LL SEE! I GOT IT JUST FOR YOU--IT'LL CHANGE YOUR LIFE!
BUT POOKY, IT'S HUGE! WHAT IS THAT?
THAT'S THE SAME THING YOU SAID WHEN YOU SAW ME NAKED! OPEN IT...
I...I DON'T KNOW WHAT TO IMAGINE!
WE GOTTA CELEBRATE THE BEGINNING OF OUR WONDERFUL LIFE TOGETHER, RIGHT?
TA-DAAAAAAH! THE EZEKIEL 36:25! THE BEST WASHING MACHINE MONEY CAN BUY (AT LEAST ON CLEARANCE SALE)!
BETWEEN YOUR JOB, CHORES, ERRANDS, AND ALL THE HOUSEWORK, NOT TO MENTION TAKING CARE FOR YOUR DARLING HUSBAND--YOU'LL NEED A LITTLE EXTRA HELP! HAPPY, ANGIE?
WHEN YOU'VE DRIED OUT, YOU CAN HELP TIDY UP AROUND THE COUCH--SINCE THAT'S WHERE YOU'LL BE SLEEPING FOR THE NEXT FEW WEEKS, "HUBBY"!

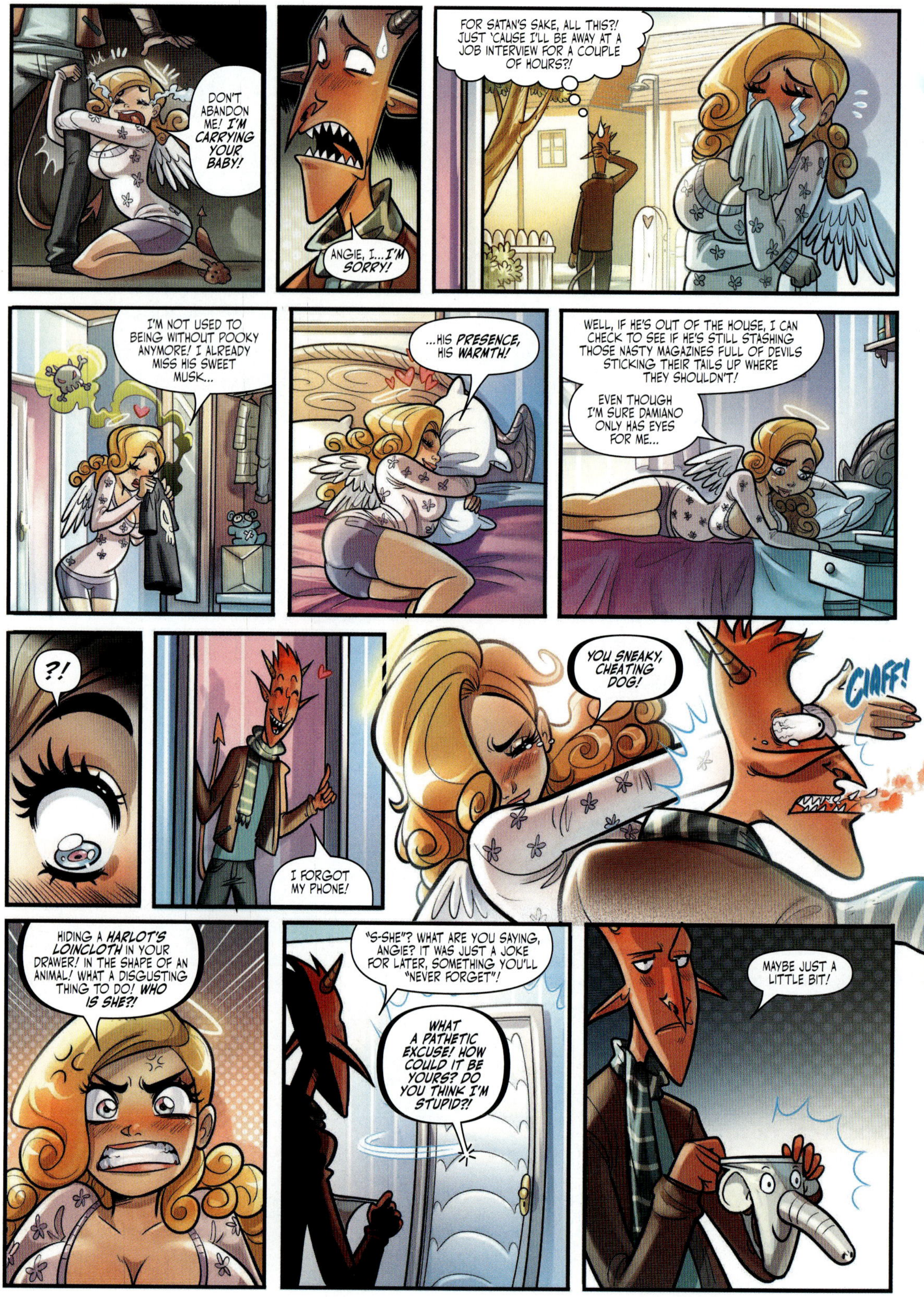
DON'T ABANDON ME! I'M CARRYING YOUR BABY!
ANGIE, I... I'M SORRY!
FOR SATAN'S SAKE, ALL THIS?! JUST 'CAUSE I'LL BE AWAY AT A JOB INTERVIEW FOR A COUPLE OF HOURS?!
I'M NOT USED TO BEING WITHOUT POOKY ANYMORE! I ALREADY MISS HIS SWEET MUSK...
...HIS PRESENCE, HIS WARMTH!
WELL, IF HE'S OUT OF THE HOUSE, I CAN CHECK TO SEE IF HE'S STILL STASHING THOSE NASTY MAGAZINES FULL OF DEVILS STICKING THEIR TAILS UP WHERE THEY SHOULDN'T!
EVEN THOUGH I'M SURE DAMIANO ONLY HAS EYES FOR ME...
?!
I FORGOT MY PHONE!
YOU SNEAKY, CHEATING DOG!
CIAFF!
HIDING A HARLOT'S LOINCLOTH IN YOUR DRAWER! IN THE SHAPE OF AN ANIMAL! WHAT A DISGUSTING THING TO DO! WHO IS SHE?!
"S-SHE"? WHAT ARE YOU SAYING, ANGIE? IT WAS JUST A JOKE FOR LATER, SOMETHING YOU'LL "NEVER FORGET"!
WHAT A PATHETIC EXCUSE! HOW COULD IT BE YOURS? DO YOU THINK I'M STUPID?!
MAYBE JUST A LITTLE BIT!

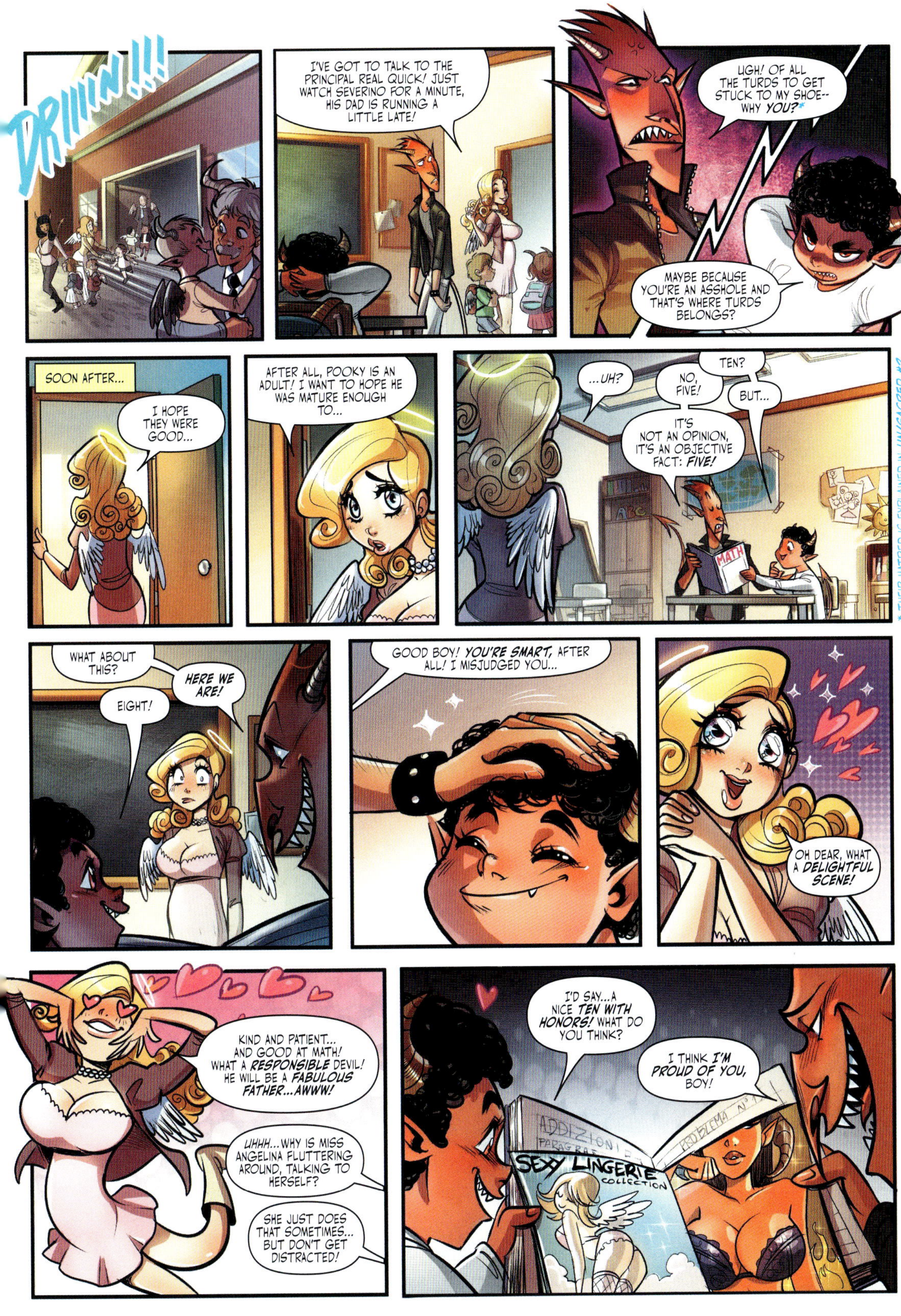

* THEIR HATRED IS EXPLAINED IN *UN/SACRED #2.*

I THINK THE BABY WILL HAVE BLONDE CURLS LIKE YOU AND A COMPLEXION LIKE DAMIANO!
OR IMAGINE IT HAS YOUR BLUE AND PINK EYES, AND YOUR HUSBAND'S LONG HORNS!
I BET THE BRAT IS GONNA HAVE A HONKER OF NOSE, JUST LIKE ITS *PUSSYHOUND FATHER!*
ONE GIANT NOSE! LIKE FATHER, LIKE... GIANT NOSE! *HAHA!*
ER... JOKING ASIDE, THERE'S A GOOD CHANCE THAT IT WILL HAVE *THE FAMILY MOLE!*
BAR HALO
THE FAMILY MOLE?!
YUP! IT'S A BEAUTY MARK WE'VE HAD FOR GENERATIONS! MY MOTHER HAD IT ON HER *DÉCOLLETAGE.*
BUT...WE'VE SEEN YOU NAKED A TON OF TIMES! I DON'T EVER REMEMBER YOU HAVING A MOLE!
HEHEHE, WELL, FOR ME, IT'S SOMEWHERE ONLY MY POOKY CAN SEE, AND THEN FROM A VERY *RARE* POSITION...
HI HI HI HI HI HI HI HI HI
"...WHEN, AT THE STROKE OF MIDNIGHT, HE MAKES ME FEEL JUST LIKE *CINDERELLA!"*
OOOOH, YES, THAT'S THE SPOT!
BUT I'VE BEEN GOING ON FOR *TWO HOURS...* THEN WE HAVE SEX, DON'T WE?

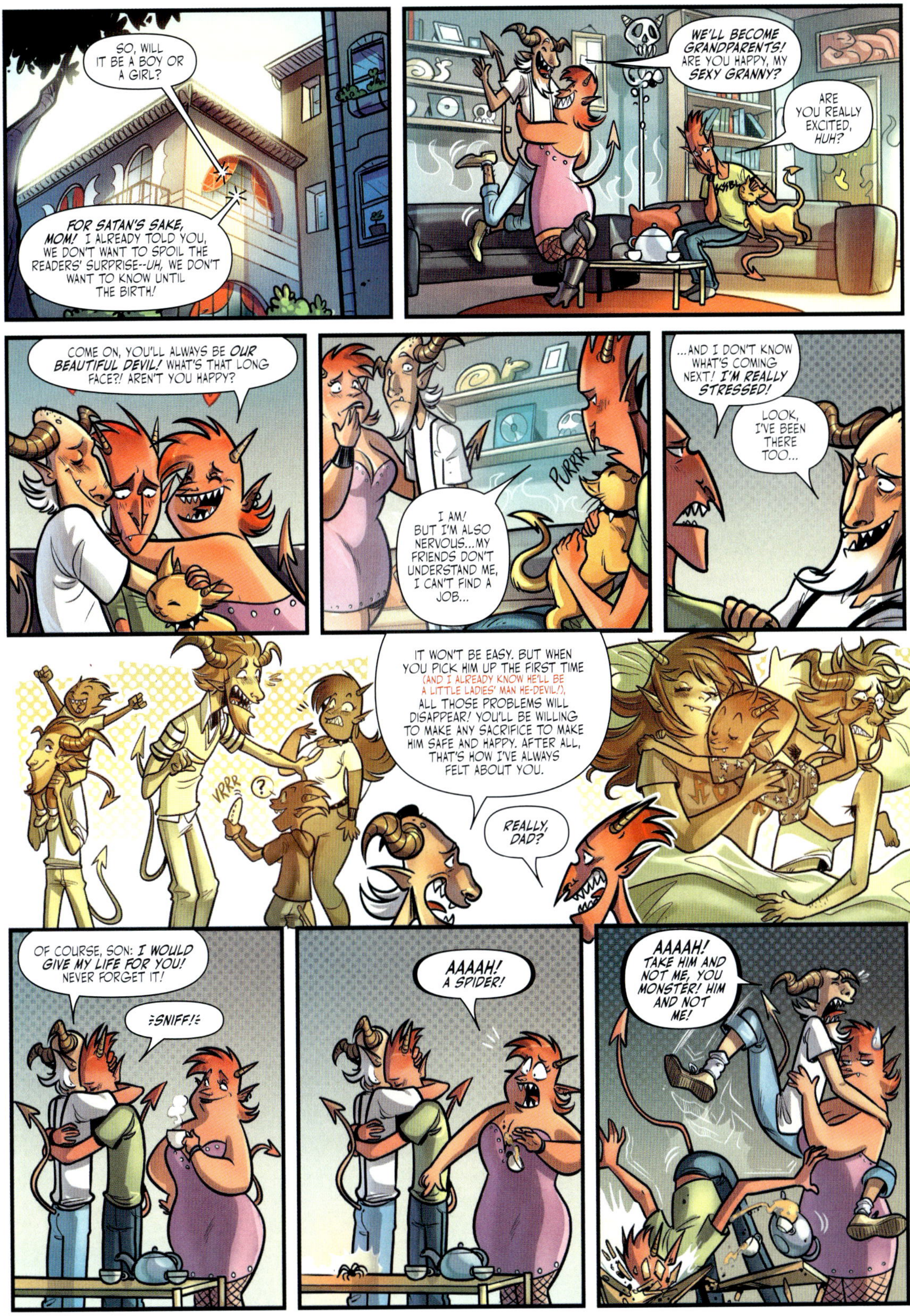
SO, WILL IT BE A BOY OR A GIRL?
FOR SATAN'S SAKE, MOM! I ALREADY TOLD YOU, WE DON'T WANT TO SPOIL THE READERS' SURPRISE--UH, WE DON'T WANT TO KNOW UNTIL THE BIRTH!
WE'LL BECOME GRANDPARENTS! ARE YOU HAPPY, MY SEXY GRANNY?
ARE YOU REALLY EXCITED, HUH?
COME ON, YOU'LL ALWAYS BE OUR BEAUTIFUL DEVIL! WHAT'S THAT LONG FACE?! AREN'T YOU HAPPY?
PURRR
I AM! BUT I'M ALSO NERVOUS...MY FRIENDS DON'T UNDERSTAND ME, I CAN'T FIND A JOB...
...AND I DON'T KNOW WHAT'S COMING NEXT! I'M REALLY STRESSED!
LOOK, I'VE BEEN THERE TOO...
IT WON'T BE EASY. BUT WHEN YOU PICK HIM UP THE FIRST TIME (AND I ALREADY KNOW HE'LL BE A LITTLE LADIES' MAN HE-DEVIL!), ALL THOSE PROBLEMS WILL DISAPPEAR! YOU'LL BE WILLING TO MAKE ANY SACRIFICE TO MAKE HIM SAFE AND HAPPY. AFTER ALL, THAT'S HOW I'VE ALWAYS FELT ABOUT YOU.
VRRR
?
REALLY, DAD?
OF COURSE, SON: I WOULD GIVE MY LIFE FOR YOU! NEVER FORGET IT!
SNIFF!
AAAAH! A SPIDER!
AAAAH! TAKE HIM AND NOT ME, YOU MONSTER! HIM AND NOT ME!

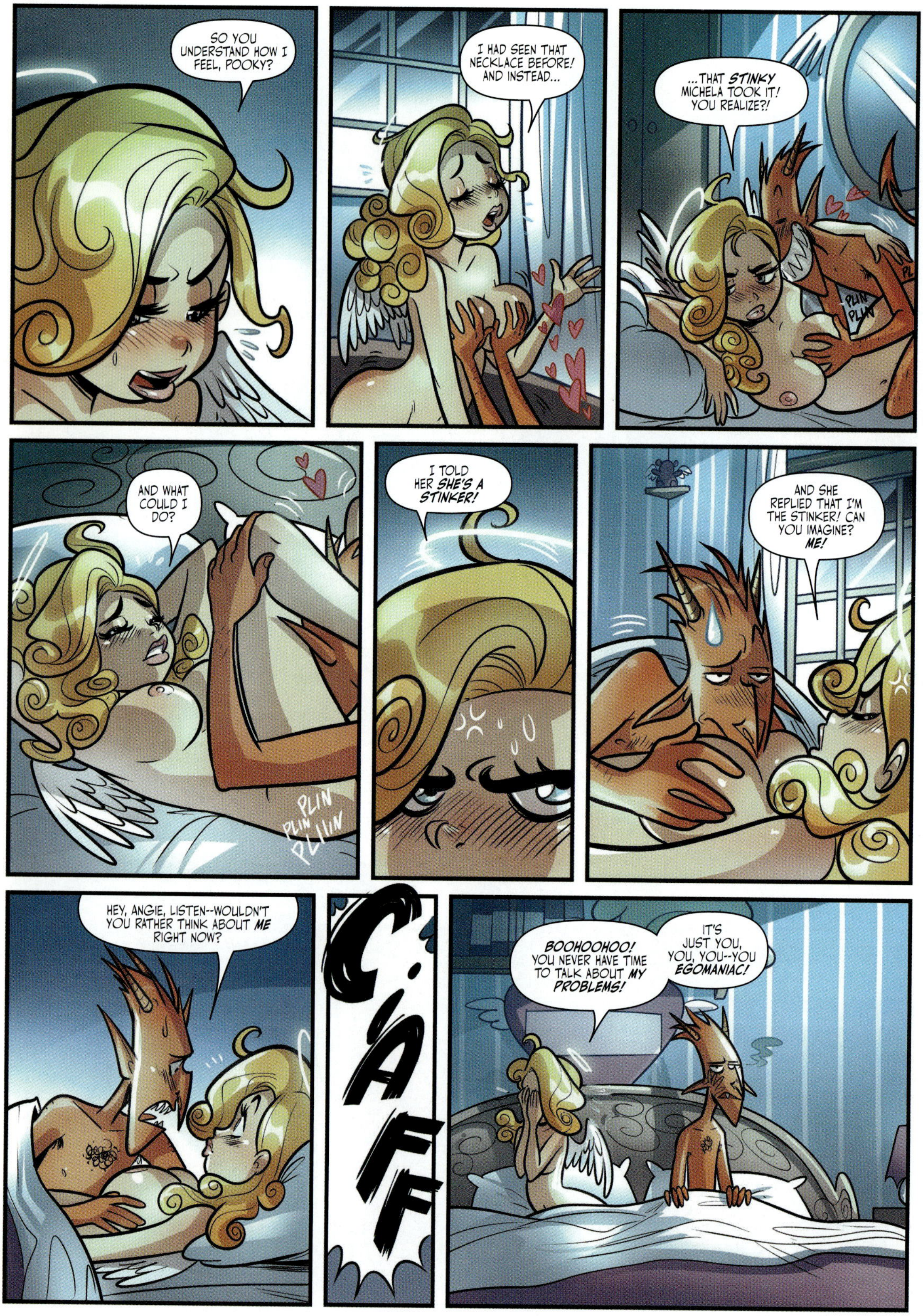
SO YOU UNDERSTAND HOW I FEEL, POOKY?
I HAD SEEN THAT NECKLACE BEFORE! AND INSTEAD...
...THAT STINKY MICHELA TOOK IT! YOU REALIZE?!
PLIN PLIN
AND WHAT COULD I DO?
PLIN PLIN PLIIIN
I TOLD HER SHE'S A STINKER!
AND SHE REPLIED THAT I'M THE STINKER! CAN YOU IMAGINE? ME!
HEY, ANGIE, LISTEN--WOULDN'T YOU RATHER THINK ABOUT ME RIGHT NOW?
CIAFF
BOOHOOHOO! YOU NEVER HAVE TIME TO TALK ABOUT MY PROBLEMS!
IT'S JUST YOU, YOU, YOU--YOU EGOMANIAC!

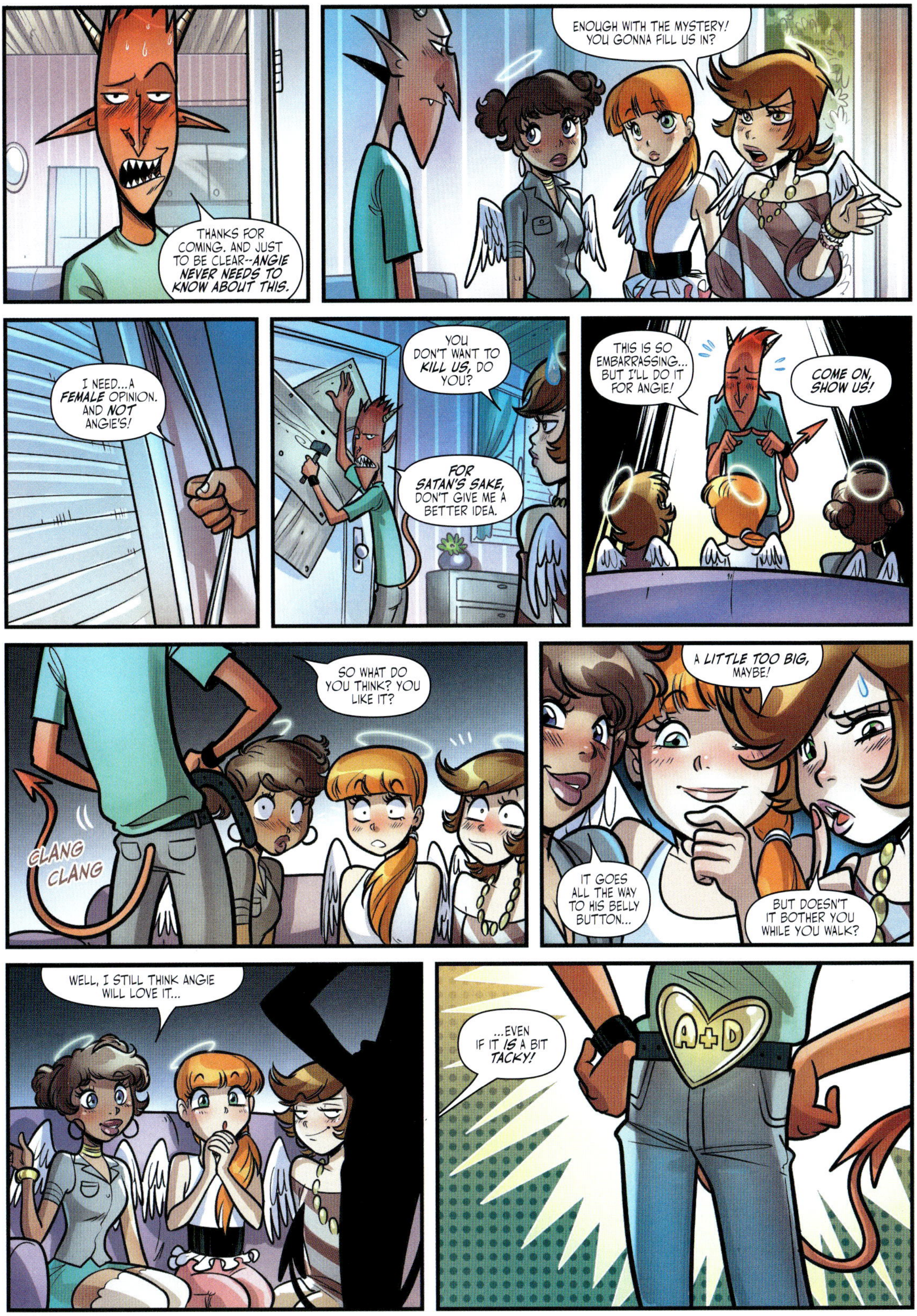

THANKS FOR COMING. AND JUST TO BE CLEAR--ANGIE NEVER NEEDS TO KNOW ABOUT THIS.
ENOUGH WITH THE MYSTERY! YOU GONNA FILL US IN?
I NEED...A FEMALE OPINION. AND NOT ANGIE'S!
YOU DON'T WANT TO KILL US, DO YOU?
FOR SATAN'S SAKE, DON'T GIVE ME A BETTER IDEA.
THIS IS SO EMBARRASSING... BUT I'LL DO IT FOR ANGIE!
COME ON, SHOW US!
SO WHAT DO YOU THINK? YOU LIKE IT?
CLANG CLANG
A LITTLE TOO BIG, MAYBE!
IT GOES ALL THE WAY TO HIS BELLY BUTTON...
BUT DOESN'T IT BOTHER YOU WHILE YOU WALK?
WELL, I STILL THINK ANGIE WILL LOVE IT...
...EVEN IF IT IS A BIT TACKY!
A+D

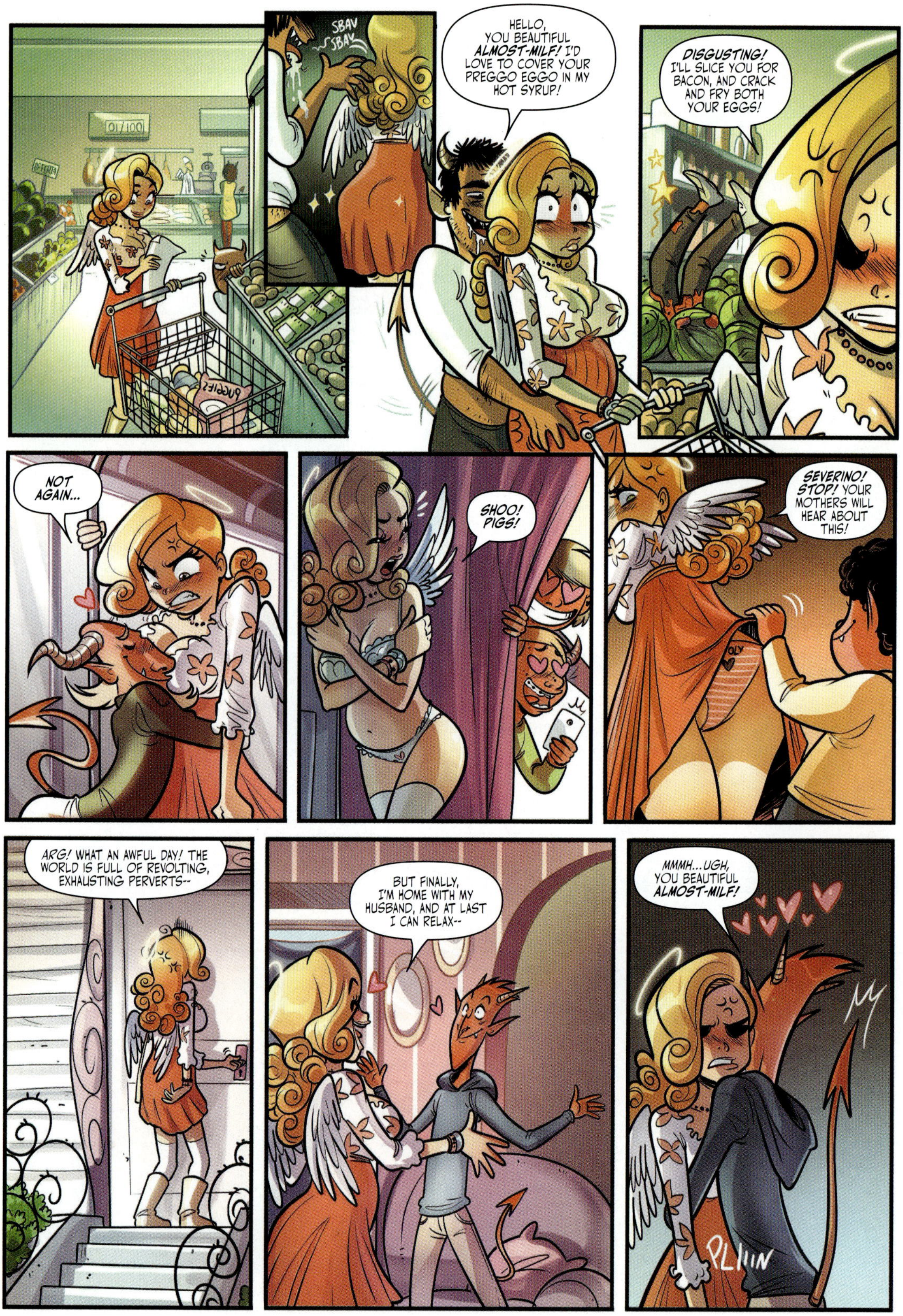
SBAV SBAV
HELLO, YOU BEAUTIFUL ALMOST-MILF! I'D LOVE TO COVER YOUR PREGGO EGGO IN MY HOT SYRUP!
DISGUSTING! I'LL SLICE YOU FOR BACON, AND CRACK AND FRY BOTH YOUR EGGS!
NOT AGAIN...
SHOO! PIGS!
SEVERINO! STOP! YOUR MOTHERS WILL HEAR ABOUT THIS!
ARG! WHAT AN AWFUL DAY! THE WORLD IS FULL OF REVOLTING, EXHAUSTING PERVERTS--
BUT FINALLY, I'M HOME WITH MY HUSBAND, AND AT LAST I CAN RELAX--
MMMH...UGH, YOU BEAUTIFUL ALMOST-MILF!
MY
PLIIIN

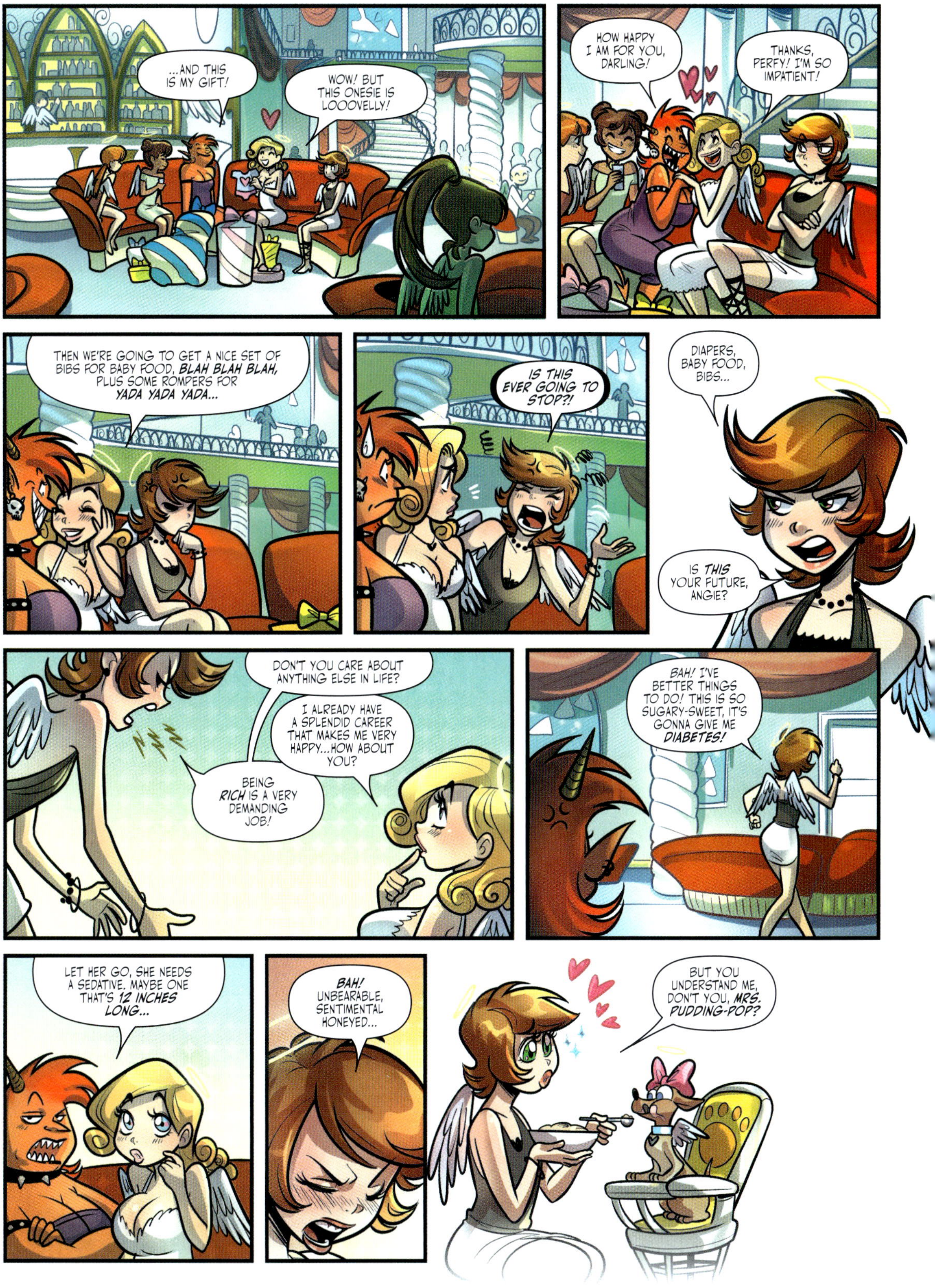
...AND THIS IS MY GIFT!
WOW! BUT THIS ONESIE IS LOOOVELLY!
HOW HAPPY I AM FOR YOU, DARLING!
THANKS, PERFY! I'M SO IMPATIENT!
THEN WE'RE GOING TO GET A NICE SET OF BIBS FOR BABY FOOD, BLAH BLAH BLAH, PLUS SOME ROMPERS FOR YADA YADA YADA...
IS THIS EVER GOING TO STOP?!
DIAPERS, BABY FOOD, BIBS...
IS THIS YOUR FUTURE, ANGIE?
DON'T YOU CARE ABOUT ANYTHING ELSE IN LIFE?
I ALREADY HAVE A SPLENDID CAREER THAT MAKES ME VERY HAPPY...HOW ABOUT YOU?
BEING RICH IS A VERY DEMANDING JOB!
BAH! I'VE BETTER THINGS TO DO! THIS IS SO SUGARY-SWEET, IT'S GONNA GIVE ME DIABETES!
LET HER GO, SHE NEEDS A SEDATIVE. MAYBE ONE THAT'S 12 INCHES LONG...
BAH! UNBEARABLE, SENTIMENTAL HONEYED...
BUT YOU UNDERSTAND ME, DON'T YOU, MRS. PUDDING-POP?

OOOH! LOOK WHO'S THERE! ***MY BEST FRIENDS!***
HOW NICE TO SEE YOU!
DID YOU KNOW YOUR CELL PHONES AREN'T WORKING? YOUR LANDLINES, TOO!
IT'S OKAY! HOW ABOUT WE GAME TONIGHT, MY PLACE?
ME AND GRUGNO ARE DONE WITH YOU!
GUYS, IF IT'S GOT ANYTHING TO DO WITH THAT BALL-BUSTING INCIDENT--
WHY DON'T YOU MAKE LIKE HORSE SHIT AND HIT THE TRAIL?
BEHOLD, AS A SIGN OF PEACE!
YOU KNOW WHAT HAPPENS WITH PREGNANT WOMEN, DON'T YOU? I'VE GOT A HOUSE ***FILL OF MILK,*** AND I DON'T KNOW WHERE TO PUT IT ANYMORE!
HUH?! ARE YOU ***KIDDING?***
NOT AT ALL! IT'S THE HIGHEST QUALITY! AND STILL
GLU GLU GLU
LUKEWARM!
SLURP SLURP
BURP
FRESH MILK!
COME ON... EVEN IF YOU NEVER ADMIT IT, YOU KNOW YOU WANT IT...
ONE SIP FROM THAT COW AND I'LL TURN YOU FROM A BULL INTO A STEER!
YOU'RE DISGUSTING! DOES ANGIE EVEN KNOW YOU DID THIS? YOU'RE BUSTING MY GUT!
NO, ANGIE, I CAN'T GO BACK TO THE MILKMAN, I WAS JUST THERE TWO HOURS AGO. ANYTHING ***ELSE*** YOU WANT?

CIP CIP
GOOD MORNING, CHERRY TOMATO! IT'S SATURDAY, DO YOU KNOW WHAT THAT MEANS? NO WORK...
HEHEHE, WHICH MEANS WE CAN MAKE LOVE AAAALL DAY! WE'VE HAD SO LITTLE TIME SINCE YOU GOT--
PLIN
NOT NOW! LOOK, WHAT A BEAUTIFUL DAY! WE HAVE LOTS OF LITTLE CHORES FIRST--
SIGH...
A DELICIOUS BREAKFAST...
SHOPPING AT THE MALL...
NATAL
50%
THAT CRADLE IS GORGEOUS!
VISIT FRIENDS...
ALL VERY NICE, BUT ANGIE AND I HAVE TO GO TO FU...TO MAKE AN IMPORTANT CONNECTION, SO BYE!
NOT NOW!
A NICE DINNER...
CHEST OR THIGH?
ER...
PLIN PLIN
A MOVIE IN THE EVENING...
MMH...THIS POPCORN IS KIND OF GOOEY!
ANF SBAV ANF
SBAV
PLIN PLIN PLIN
AND FINALLY...
DO YOU LIKE MY NEW PYJAMAS?
OHHH YESSS...
PLIN
PLIN
PLIN
I'M GLAD YOU LIKE IT, BECAUSE I'VE BEEN WAITING FOR THIS MOMENT ALL DAY...
YOU DON'T SAY?!
PLIN PLIN PLIN PLIN
SIGH! OH, AFTER A LONG, EXHAUSTING DAY, THERE'S NOTHING BETTER THAN A GOOD NIGHT'S SLEEP!

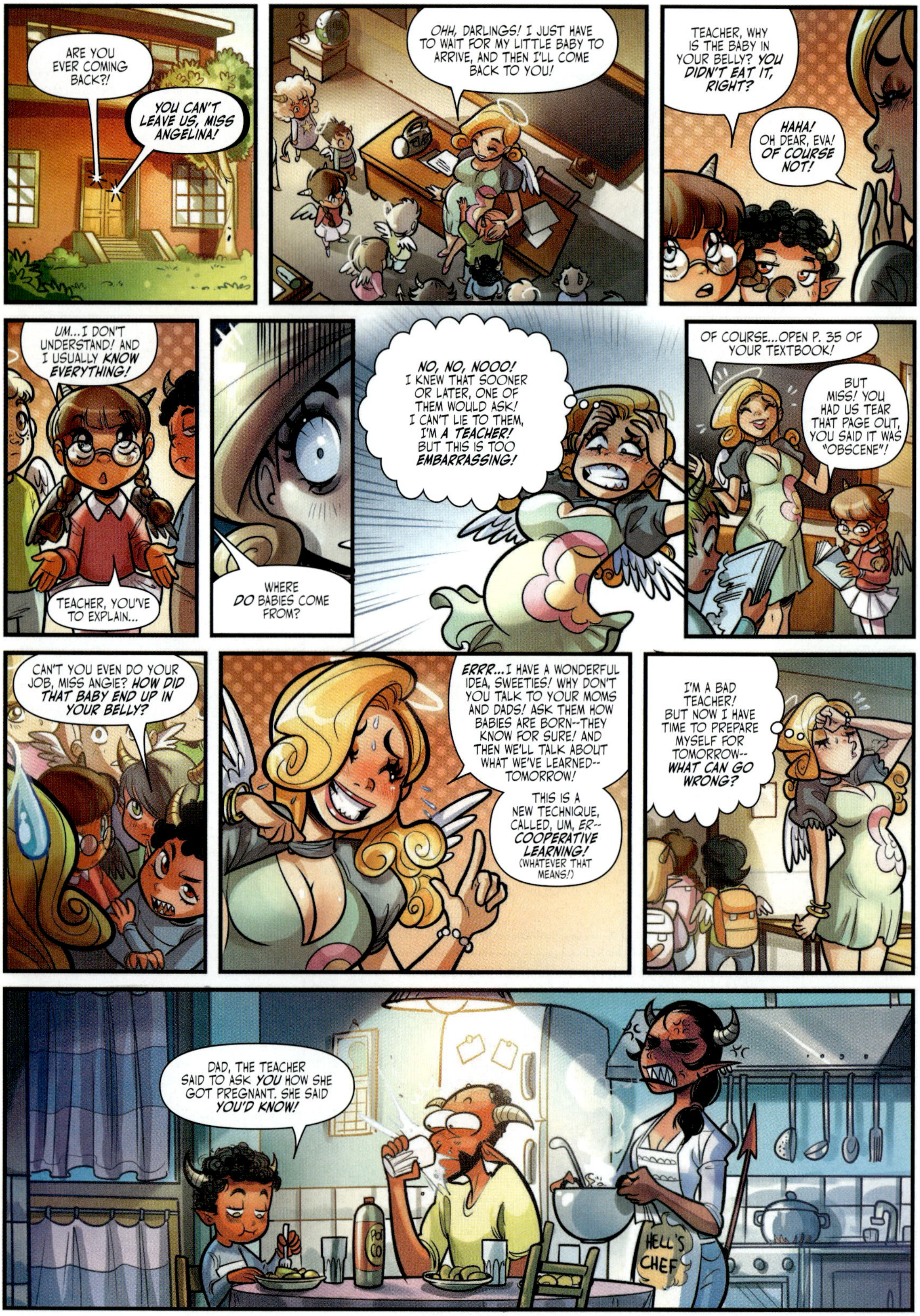
ARE YOU EVER COMING BACK?!
YOU CAN'T LEAVE US, MISS ANGELINA!
OHH, DARLINGS! I JUST HAVE TO WAIT FOR MY LITTLE BABY TO ARRIVE, AND THEN I'LL COME BACK TO YOU!
TEACHER, WHY IS THE BABY IN YOUR BELLY? YOU DIDN'T EAT IT, RIGHT?
HAHA! OH DEAR, EVA! OF COURSE NOT!
UM...I DON'T UNDERSTAND! AND I USUALLY KNOW EVERYTHING!
TEACHER, YOU'VE TO EXPLAIN...
WHERE DO BABIES COME FROM?
NO, NO, NOOO! I KNEW THAT SOONER OR LATER, ONE OF THEM WOULD ASK! I CAN'T LIE TO THEM, I'M A TEACHER! BUT THIS IS TOO EMBARRASSING!
OF COURSE...OPEN P. 35 OF YOUR TEXTBOOK!
BUT MISS! YOU HAD US TEAR THAT PAGE OUT, YOU SAID IT WAS "OBSCENE"!
CAN'T YOU EVEN DO YOUR JOB, MISS ANGIE? HOW DID THAT BABY END UP IN YOUR BELLY?
ERRR...I HAVE A WONDERFUL IDEA, SWEETIES! WHY DON'T YOU TALK TO YOUR MOMS AND DADS! ASK THEM HOW BABIES ARE BORN--THEY KNOW FOR SURE! AND THEN WE'LL TALK ABOUT WHAT WE'VE LEARNED--TOMORROW!
THIS IS A NEW TECHNIQUE, CALLED, UM, ER--COOPERATIVE LEARNING! (WHATEVER THAT MEANS!)
I'M A BAD TEACHER! BUT NOW I HAVE TIME TO PREPARE MYSELF FOR TOMORROW--WHAT CAN GO WRONG?
DAD, THE TEACHER SAID TO ASK YOU HOW SHE GOT PREGNANT. SHE SAID YOU'D KNOW!
HELL'S CHEF

GORGEOUS AND HEALTHY MANE!
TOTAL BODY HAIR REMOVAL.
ONE OF THE MOST TRAUMATIZING EXPERIENCES OF MY LIFE...
HOT!
AND I'M READY TO BREAK HEARTS!
HOT!
PER FOTOMODEL
DIVENTA UNA STA
AHAHAHA! RIDICULOUS! DIDN'T YOU WANT A "SERIOUS" JOB?
BELLEZZA INTERI
UNA
TELL ME, "DEAR" GUIDA, ARE YOU HERE TO WIN THIS "RIDICULOUS" JOB, TOO?
ER, WE... HERE...
...WE'RE ONLY HERE TO WATCH YOU GO DOWN IN FLAMES, WHERE YOU BELONG!
CONGRATULATIONS TO THE PROTAGONIST OF OUR NEXT COMMERCIAL! DO YOU HAVE ANYTHING TO SAY?
AS THE SAYING GOES, "ONLY WINNERS WIN, AND ONLY IDIOTS PARTICIPATE!"
I-IT'S IMPOSSIBLE!
A-HA! WHO LAUGHS NOW, HATERS? AND NOW, PLEASE EXCUSE ME...
...I'M GOING TO ENJOY MY SUCCESS AND BEAUTY!
BEFORE...
LEVEL
UP
...AFTER!
ENERGY DRINK

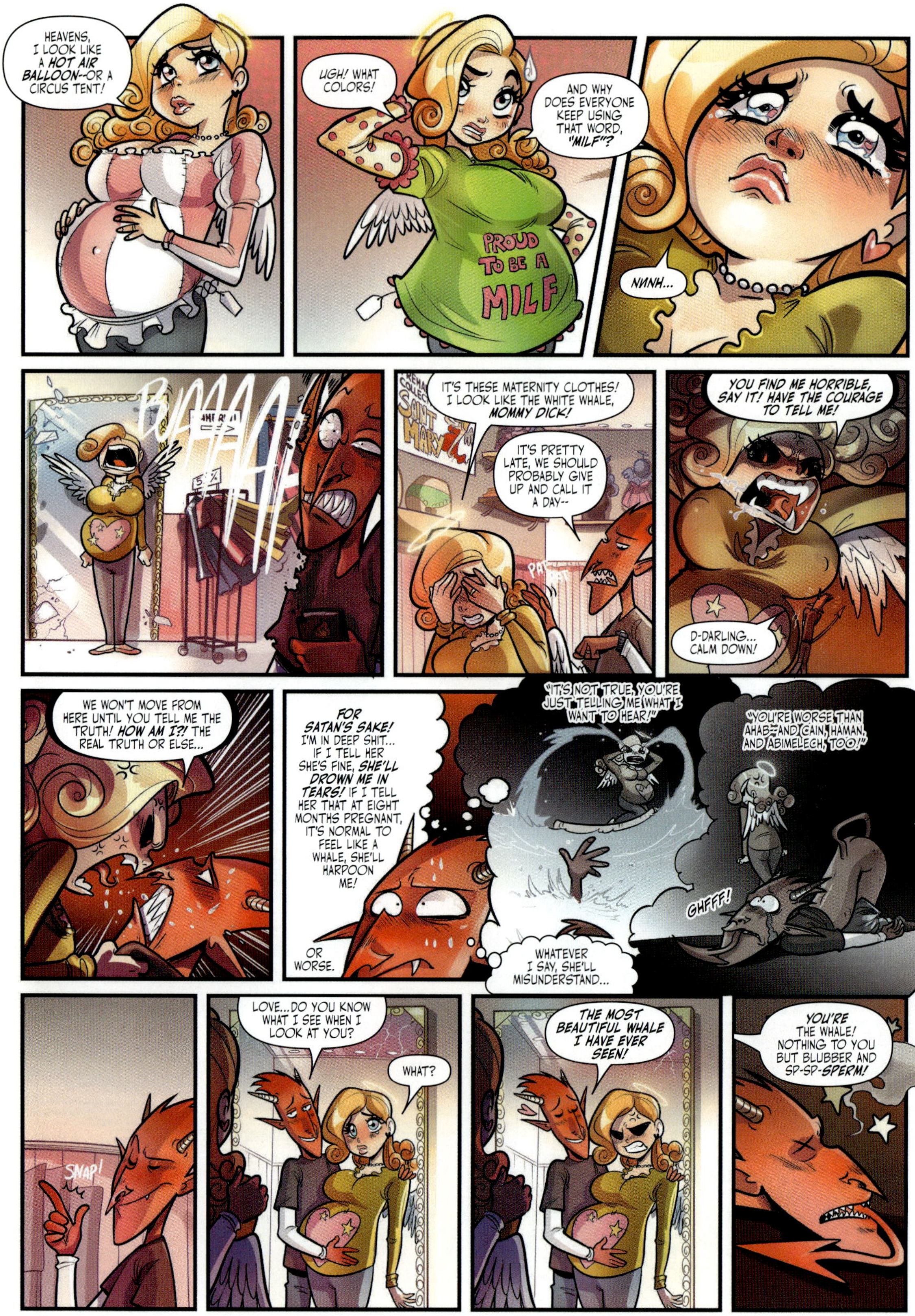
HEAVENS, I LOOK LIKE A HOT AIR BALLOON--OR A CIRCUS TENT!
UGH! WHAT COLORS!
AND WHY DOES EVERYONE KEEP USING THAT WORD, "MILF"?
PROUD TO BE A MILF
NNNH...
BWAAAH!
IT'S THESE MATERNITY CLOTHES! I LOOK LIKE THE WHITE WHALE, MOMMY DICK!
IT'S PRETTY LATE, WE SHOULD PROBABLY GIVE UP AND CALL IT A DAY--
PAT PAT
YOU FIND ME HORRIBLE, SAY IT! HAVE THE COURAGE TO TELL ME!
D-DARLING... CALM DOWN!
WE WON'T MOVE FROM HERE UNTIL YOU TELL ME THE TRUTH! HOW AM I?! THE REAL TRUTH OR ELSE...
FOR SATAN'S SAKE! I'M IN DEEP SHIT... IF I TELL HER SHE'S FINE, SHE'LL DROWN ME IN TEARS! IF I TELL HER THAT AT EIGHT MONTHS PREGNANT, IT'S NORMAL TO FEEL LIKE A WHALE, SHE'LL HARPOON ME!
OR WORSE.
"IT'S NOT TRUE, YOU'RE JUST TELLING ME WHAT I WANT TO HEAR!"
"YOU'RE WORSE THAN AHAB--AND CAIN, HAMAN, AND ABIMELECH, TOO!"
GHFFF!
WHATEVER I SAY, SHE'LL MISUNDERSTAND...
SNAP!
LOVE...DO YOU KNOW WHAT I SEE WHEN I LOOK AT YOU?
WHAT?
THE MOST BEAUTIFUL WHALE I HAVE EVER SEEN!
YOU'RE THE WHALE! NOTHING TO YOU BUT BLUBBER AND SP-SP-SPERM!

YOU'RE ASHAMED OF GOING OUT WITH ME, RIGHT?
BUT INSTEAD OF SAYING BULLSHIT, LET'S MOVE, I'M HUNGRY! AND THAT ISOLATED RESTAURANT THAT I TOLD YOU IS VERY FAR AWAY, IN THAT NEIGHBORHOOD WHERE WE DON'T KNOW ANYONE!
AND THIS IS HOW YOU DRESS FOR A DATE? LIKE AN UNDERCOVER SPY?
UM--BRRR! DOESN'T IT FEEL COLD OUT TO YOU?
ICE CREAM
FINE! YOU WANT THE TRUTH? IT'S DEGRADING FOR A CATCH LIKE ME TO BE SEEN WITH THE LOW-TIDE BLOBFISH LIKE YOU!
URGH!
WHERE ARE WE GOING?
TO YOUR OWN PERSONAL HELL: THE GYM!
IF YOU WANT TO GO OUT WITH ME IN THE SUNLIGHT, GET BUSY!
PUFF...PANT... PANT...FOR MICHELA, FOR MICHELA!
MONTHS LATER...
WOW!
SUPER!
HERE IS A BRAND NEW GIUDA, TO SHOW OFF AT PARTIES, GROUP OUTINGS AND DINNERS WITH FRIENDS!
HEHEHE! THIS AND MORE FOR YOU!
I HAD NEVER NOTICED THAT YOU WERE SO... SEXY!
YES, WITH THAT BEARD. SOME HINT OF MUSCLE... MH!
SLURP...BUT ARE YOU REALLY SURE? WHY DID YOU CHANGE YOUR MIND?
WHAT A SILLY QUESTION! BECAUSE I LIKE YOU JUST THE WAY YOU ARE!

CHOMP
GNOM
SLURP
CHICKEN
FOR SATAN'S SAKE...YOU ARE INHALING EVERYTHING AS IF YOU HAVEN'T EATEN FOR MONTHS!
OOPS! YOU KNOW... I DO IT FOR OUR LITTLE BUNDLE OF JOY!
I HAD TO WALK FOR TWO HOURS BEFORE FINDING A DEVILBUCKS OPEN AT THIS HOUR...
THANK YOU! OUR LITTLE BUNDLE WANTED IT SO MUCH!
COME ON, MY CHERRY TOMATO, ANOTHER HOUR. MY ANKLES ARE SO SWOLLEN! OTHERWISE, HOW COULD I CARRY OUR LITTLE BUNDLE AROUND?
BY THE WAY, HE REALLY WANTS TO SEE "HEAVEN'S KITCHEN"!
IT'S NOT FOR MY STUFFED ANIMAL COLLECTION, OF COURSE NOT! IT'S A PLAYMATE FOR THE LITTLE BUNDLE! (MAYBE!)
CAPPELLI
I HEARD A LITTLE VOICE IN MY BELLY SAY "BUY EVERYTHING"!
POOKY? THE LITTLE BUNDLE OF JOY WANTS...
METAL GEAR DEVIL
PRESS PLAY
PS 2000
OH, YEAH, I HEARD IT! THE LITTLE BUNDLE DEFINITELY WANTED ME TO THE SPEND THIS MONTH'S SALARY ON THE VIDEOGAME WORKSTATION OF MY DREAMS.
ONE DAY, IT WILL THANK ME!

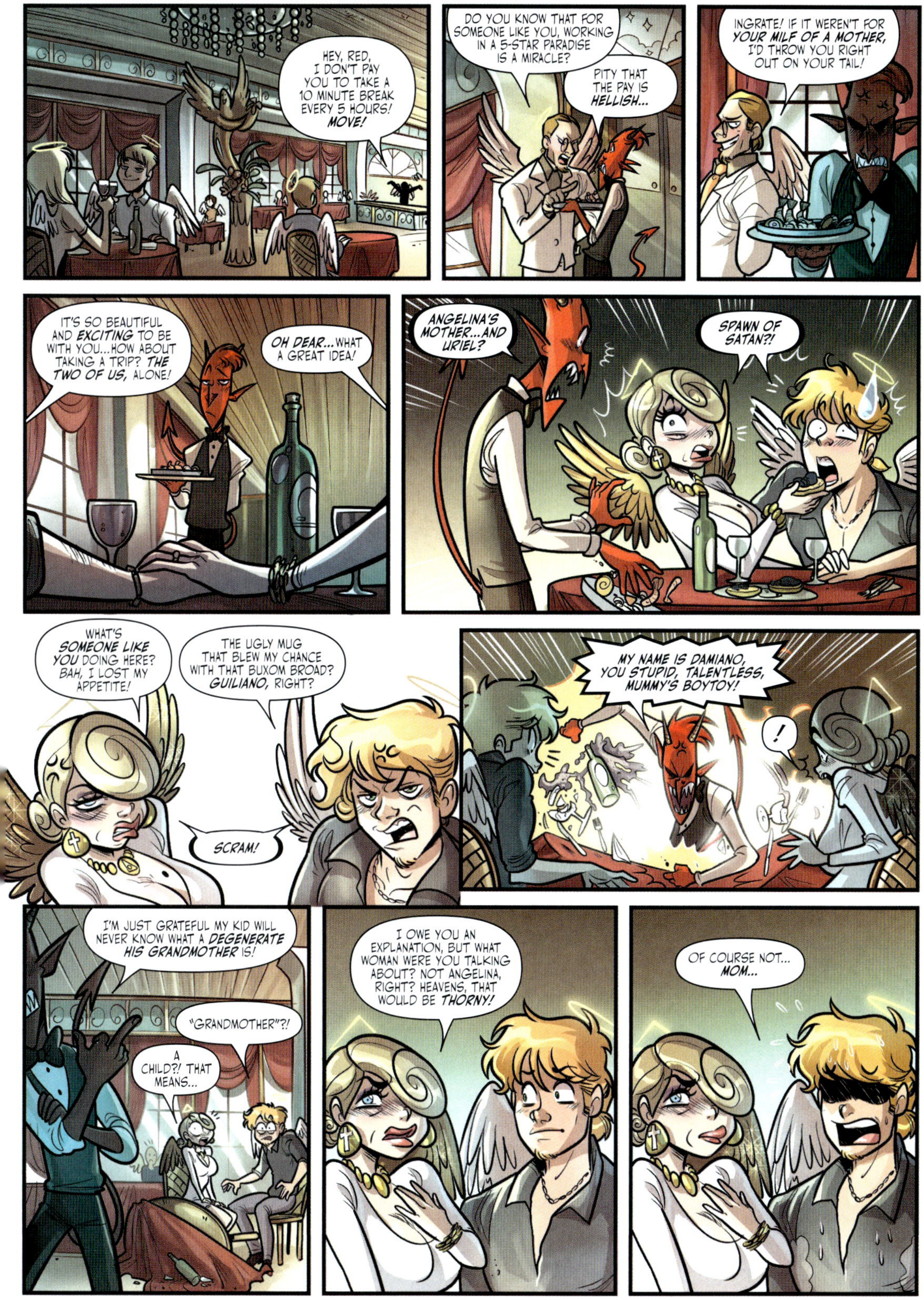
HEY, RED, I DON'T PAY YOU TO TAKE A 10 MINUTE BREAK EVERY 5 HOURS! MOVE!
DO YOU KNOW THAT FOR SOMEONE LIKE YOU, WORKING IN A 5-STAR PARADISE IS A MIRACLE?
PITY THAT THE PAY IS HELLISH...
INGRATE! IF IT WEREN'T FOR YOUR MILF OF A MOTHER, I'D THROW YOU RIGHT OUT ON YOUR TAIL!
IT'S SO BEAUTIFUL AND EXCITING TO BE WITH YOU...HOW ABOUT TAKING A TRIP? THE TWO OF US, ALONE!
OH DEAR...WHAT A GREAT IDEA!
ANGELINA'S MOTHER...AND URIEL?
SPAWN OF SATAN?!
WHAT'S SOMEONE LIKE YOU DOING HERE? BAH, I LOST MY APPETITE!
THE UGLY MUG THAT BLEW MY CHANCE WITH THAT BUXOM BROAD? GUILIANO, RIGHT?
SCRAM!
MY NAME IS DAMIANO, YOU STUPID, TALENTLESS, MUMMY'S BOYTOY!
!
I'M JUST GRATEFUL MY KID WILL NEVER KNOW WHAT A DEGENERATE HIS GRANDMOTHER IS!
"GRANDMOTHER"?!
A CHILD?! THAT MEANS...
I OWE YOU AN EXPLANATION, BUT WHAT WOMAN WERE YOU TALKING ABOUT? NOT ANGELINA, RIGHT? HEAVENS, THAT WOULD BE THORNY!
OF COURSE NOT... MOM...

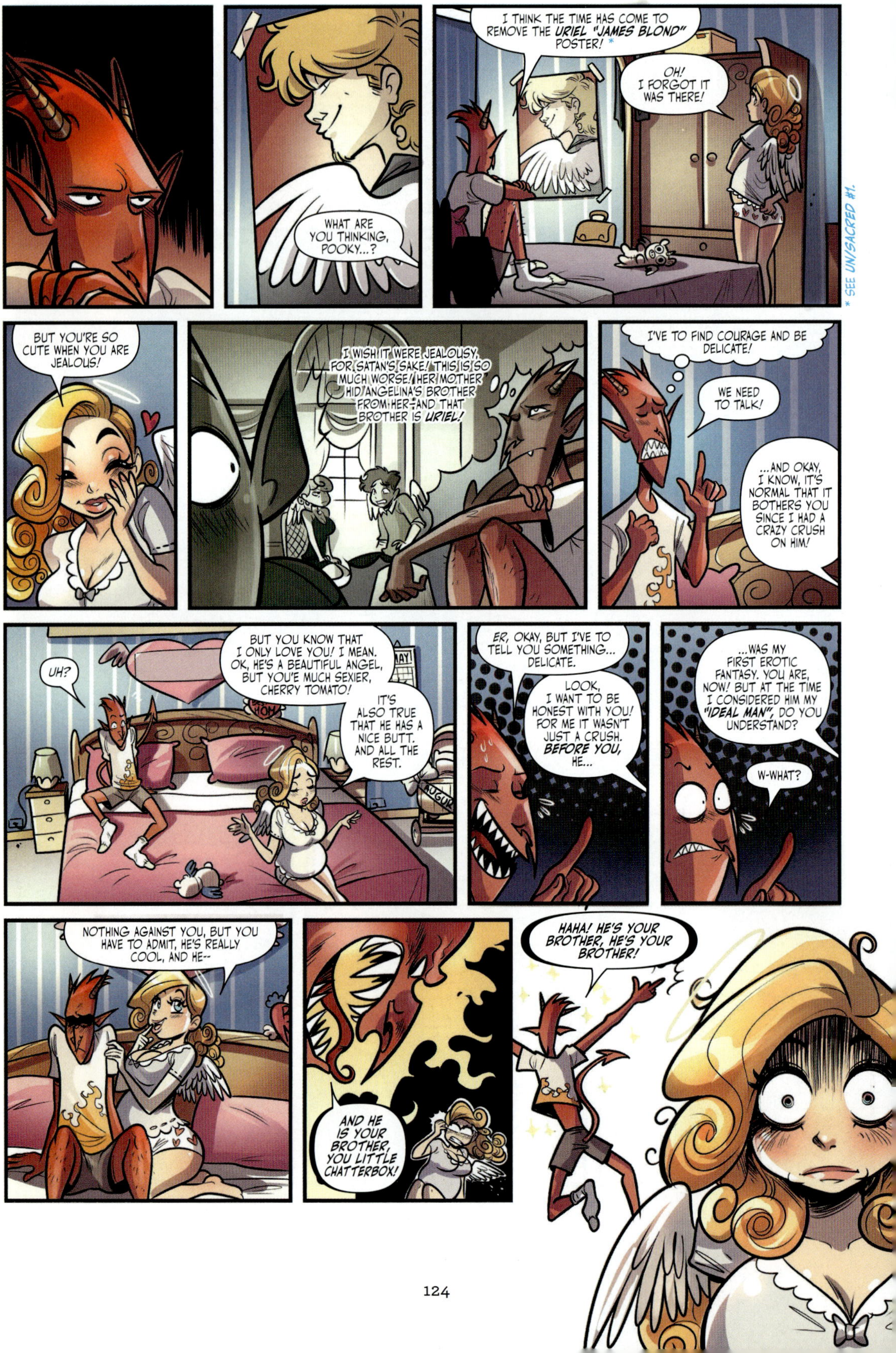

WHAT ARE YOU THINKING, POOKY...?
I THINK THE TIME HAS COME TO REMOVE THE URIEL "JAMES BLOND" POSTER! *
OH! I FORGOT IT WAS THERE!
* SEE UN/SACRED #1.
BUT YOU'RE SO CUTE WHEN YOU ARE JEALOUS!
I WISH IT WERE JEALOUSY, FOR SATAN'S SAKE! THIS IS SO MUCH WORSE! HER MOTHER HID ANGELINA'S BROTHER FROM HER- AND THAT BROTHER IS URIEL!
I'VE TO FIND COURAGE AND BE DELICATE!
WE NEED TO TALK!
...AND OKAY, I KNOW, IT'S NORMAL THAT IT BOTHERS YOU SINCE I HAD A CRAZY CRUSH ON HIM!
UH?
BUT YOU KNOW THAT I ONLY LOVE YOU! I MEAN. OK, HE'S A BEAUTIFUL ANGEL, BUT YOU'RE MUCH SEXIER, CHERRY TOMATO!
IT'S ALSO TRUE THAT HE HAS A NICE BUTT. AND ALL THE REST.
ER, OKAY, BUT I'VE TO TELL YOU SOMETHING... DELICATE.
LOOK, I WANT TO BE HONEST WITH YOU! FOR ME IT WASN'T JUST A CRUSH. BEFORE YOU, HE...
...WAS MY FIRST EROTIC FANTASY. YOU ARE, NOW! BUT AT THE TIME I CONSIDERED HIM MY "IDEAL MAN", DO YOU UNDERSTAND?
W-WHAT?
NOTHING AGAINST YOU, BUT YOU HAVE TO ADMIT, HE'S REALLY COOL, AND HE--
AND HE IS YOUR BROTHER, YOU LITTLE CHATTERBOX!
HAHA! HE'S YOUR BROTHER, HE'S YOUR BROTHER!

THE FABULOUS 80S!
LAST MONDAY WE HAD SEX FOUR TIMES...
FOUR, THEREFORE: A...B...C...D!
TUESDAY, UNFORTUNATELY, ONLY ONCE...
SOB... WHAT A SADNESS... THEN WE PUT ONE IN...
BUT ON WEDNESDAY WE MADE UP FOR IT. THIRTEEN TIMES, REMEMBER?
AND HOW COULD I FORGET IT, MY STALLION?
THE THIRTEEN CORRESPONDS TO THE LETTER M, RIGHT?
QUITE RIGHT! THURSDAY INSTEAD NINE TIMES, SO WE PUT A NICE I...
D-A-M-I...
"ONE MOMENT!"
YOU WANT TO TELL ME THAT THIS IS THE SYSTEM YOU USED TO CHOOSE MY NAME?!
WELL, YES... SO WHAT?
OOOH, IT'S SO ROMANTIC...
IT'S NOT ROMANTIC! IT'S CRAZY!
WHY? DON'T YOU LIKE DAMIANO?
THAT'S NOT THE POINT!
IF YOU HAD SEX A DIFFERENT NUMBER OF TIMES THAT WEEK I COULD BE CALLED FLHTMGG...
OR BGLAKNG!
RIGHT. BUT IT DIDN'T HAPPEN. SO WHAT'S THE PROBLEM?
LET'S SEE... MONDAY, IF I'M NOT MISTAKEN...
THE PROBLEM IS THAT YOU'RE IRRESPONSIBLE!
POOKY! POOKY!
THINK HOW FUNNY! ACCORDING TO YOUR PARENTS' SYSTEM...
THE LITTLE WOULD BE CALLED AAAABAA...
A-A-A-A-B-A-A... BLUE BA'AL.
D-A-M-I-A-N-O... MOLDY DICK.

NOW'S THE COME-TO-SATAN MOMENT, THIS IS A "KILL OR BE KILLED" MATCH! THE WINNER GETS THE RIGHT TO BE PISSED AT THE LOSER FOR ALL TIME, KAPEESH?!
GET READY TO BE HATED FOR ALL ETERNITY, GUIDA!
DRIIIN
WHO'S BREAKING MY BALLS NOW?! MY PHONE'S SUPPOSED TO BE ON SILENT!
CALENDAR ALERT: You are LATE for [ANGELINA'S ULTRASOUND]
AAARGH! I'M DONE FOR!
IF I'M LATE FOR THIS, I'LL BE IN THE DOGHOUSE 'TIL THE END OF OLD YELLER!
PLEASE, GUIDA! EVEN THOUGH WE NOW HAVE A BLOOD DEBT OF EVERLASTING HATRED BETWEEN US, IN THE NAME OF THE FRIENDSHIP WE ONCE HAD-- LEND ME YOUR CAR!
BUT YOU DON'T EVEN KNOW HOW TO DRIVE! UGH, YOU CAN TAKE MY COUSIN'S RIDE--
YOUR TEN-YEAR-OLD COUSIN, HUH?
I'M ALMOST THERE!
CLOSED FOR RENOVATION
DRIIIN
DRIIN
I tried to call you several times to tell you the ultrasound was postponed. Have fun and bury the hatchet with your friends, my sweet cherry tomato! <3
CLOSED FOR RENOVATION
WHOOOSSSH
FIUU FIUUU

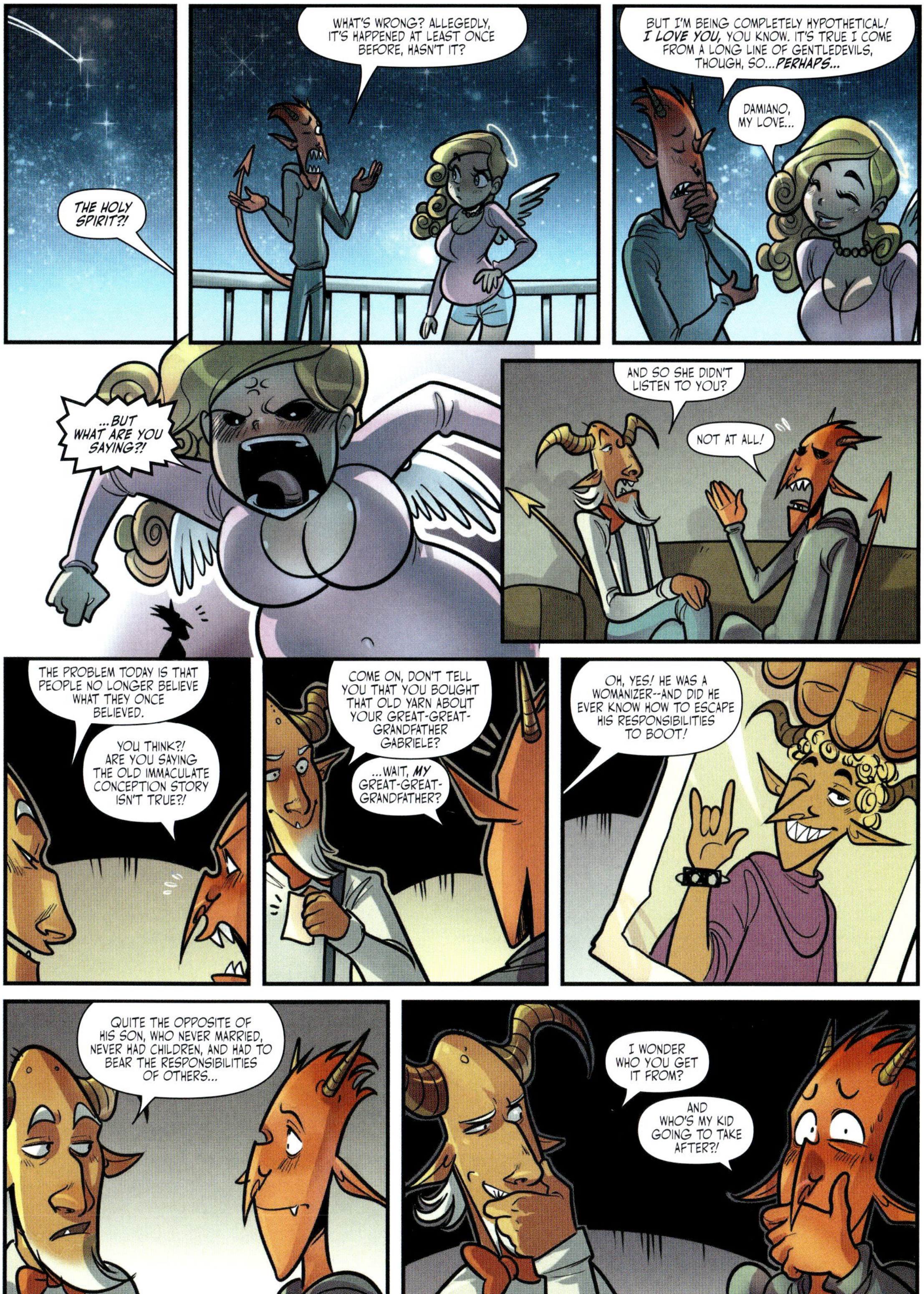
THE HOLY SPIRIT?!
WHAT'S WRONG? ALLEGEDLY, IT'S HAPPENED AT LEAST ONCE BEFORE, HASN'T IT?
BUT I'M BEING COMPLETELY HYPOTHETICAL! I LOVE YOU, YOU KNOW. IT'S TRUE I COME FROM A LONG LINE OF GENTLEDEVILS, THOUGH, SO...PERHAPS...
DAMIANO, MY LOVE...
...BUT WHAT ARE YOU SAYING?!
AND SO SHE DIDN'T LISTEN TO YOU?
NOT AT ALL!
THE PROBLEM TODAY IS THAT PEOPLE NO LONGER BELIEVE WHAT THEY ONCE BELIEVED.
YOU THINK?! ARE YOU SAYING THE OLD IMMACULATE CONCEPTION STORY ISN'T TRUE?!
COME ON, DON'T TELL YOU THAT YOU BOUGHT THAT OLD YARN ABOUT YOUR GREAT-GREAT-GRANDFATHER GABRIELE?
...WAIT, MY GREAT-GREAT-GRANDFATHER?
OH, YES! HE WAS A WOMANIZER--AND DID HE EVER KNOW HOW TO ESCAPE HIS RESPONSIBILITIES TO BOOT!
QUITE THE OPPOSITE OF HIS SON, WHO NEVER MARRIED, NEVER HAD CHILDREN, AND HAD TO BEAR THE RESPONSIBILITIES OF OTHERS...
I WONDER WHO YOU GET IT FROM?
AND WHO'S MY KID GOING TO TAKE AFTER?!

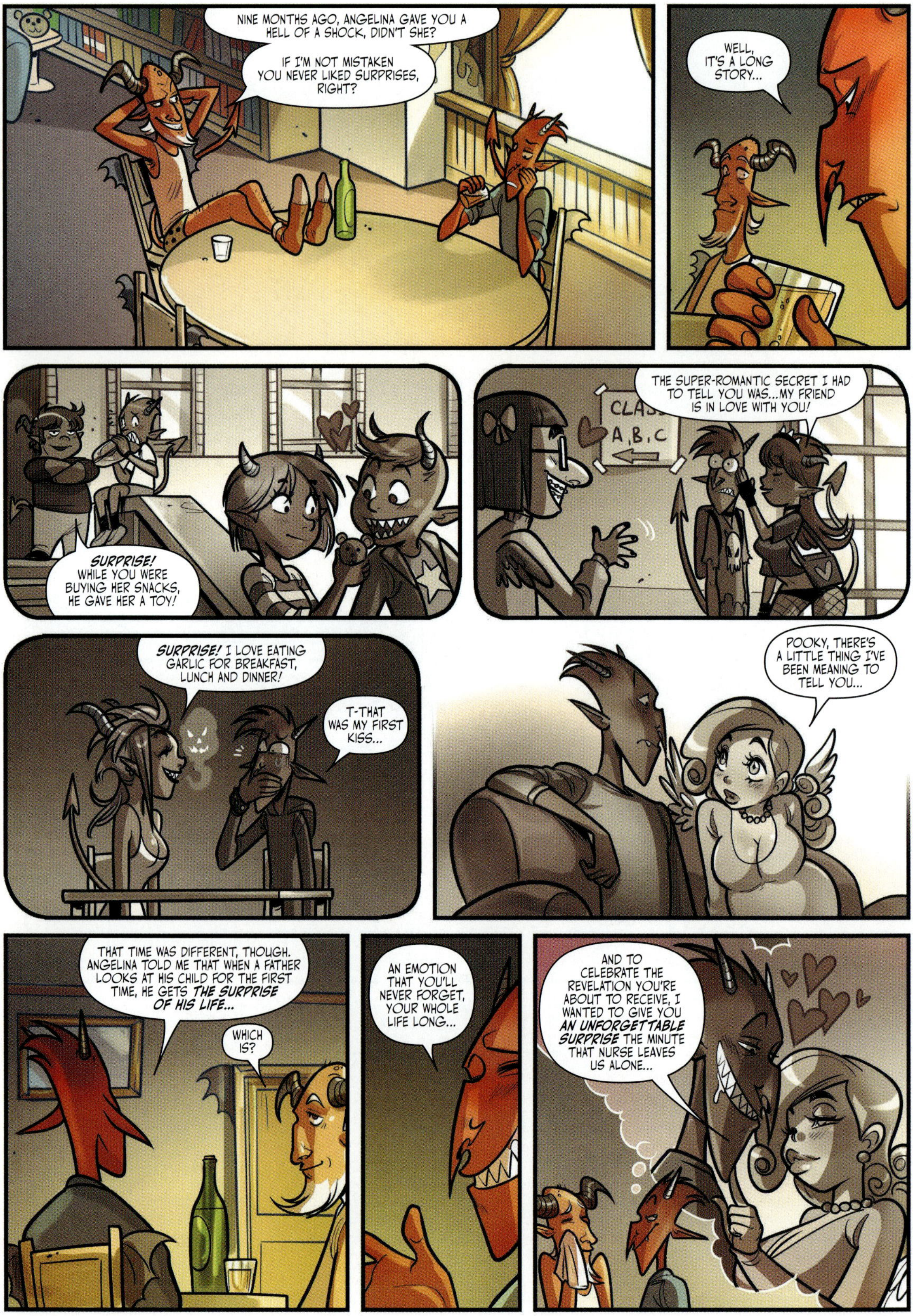
NINE MONTHS AGO, ANGELINA GAVE YOU A HELL OF A SHOCK, DIDN'T SHE?
IF I'M NOT MISTAKEN YOU NEVER LIKED SURPRISES, RIGHT?
WELL, IT'S A LONG STORY...
SURPRISE! WHILE YOU WERE BUYING HER SNACKS, HE GAVE HER A TOY!
THE SUPER-ROMANTIC SECRET I HAD TO TELL YOU WAS...MY FRIEND IS IN LOVE WITH YOU!
CLASS A, B, C
SURPRISE! I LOVE EATING GARLIC FOR BREAKFAST, LUNCH AND DINNER!
T-THAT WAS MY FIRST KISS...
POOKY, THERE'S A LITTLE THING I'VE BEEN MEANING TO TELL YOU...
THAT TIME WAS DIFFERENT, THOUGH. ANGELINA TOLD ME THAT WHEN A FATHER LOOKS AT HIS CHILD FOR THE FIRST TIME, HE GETS THE SURPRISE OF HIS LIFE...
WHICH IS?
AN EMOTION THAT YOU'LL NEVER FORGET, YOUR WHOLE LIFE LONG...
AND TO CELEBRATE THE REVELATION YOU'RE ABOUT TO RECEIVE, I WANTED TO GIVE YOU AN UNFORGETTABLE SURPRISE THE MINUTE THAT NURSE LEAVES US ALONE...

MY POOKY-LOVE, CAN YOU IMAGINE HOW LOVELY THESE WALKS WILL BE WHEN WE'RE NO LONGER TWO, BUT THREE?
...OR MAYBE FOUR OR FIVE! I WANT A WHOLE ENTOURAGE!
LOOK HOW CUTE!
WHAT A SET OF LUNGS! HE SHOULD START HIS OWN BAND! HE COULD CALL IT THE--
CIP CIP CIP
UUAAAAAAHHH
UUUEEEHHH AAARGHH!
MAYBE ONE IS ENOUGH...
THREE'S A MELODY, MORE'S A RACKET...

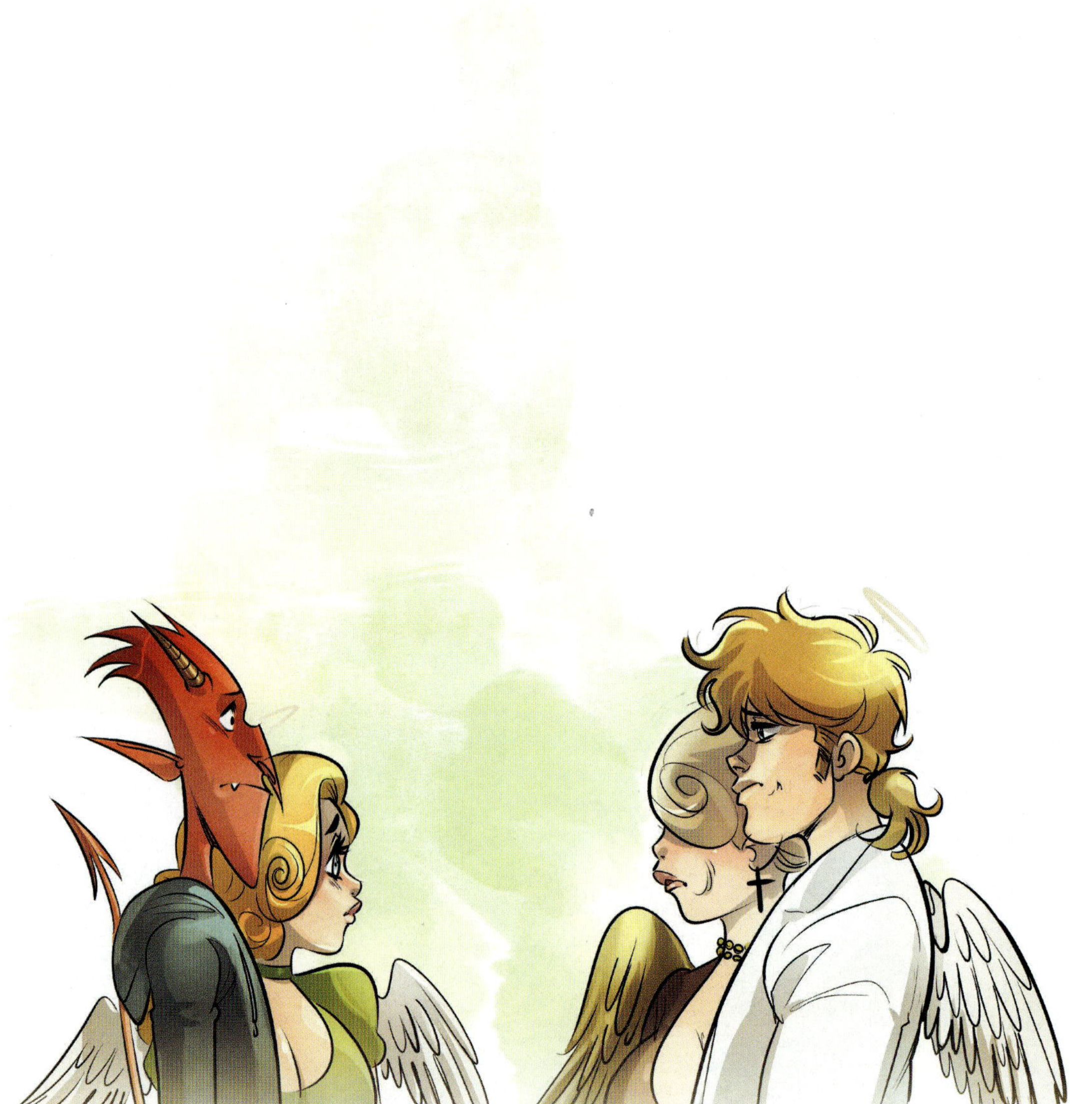

AND SO WE MEET AGAIN, MY "DEAR"...
...WITH UTMOST DISGUST AND DISPLEASURE, AS ALWAYS.
ANGELINA, LET ME INTRODUCE YOU TO YOUR FATHER.
IN HIS PRESENT FORM, PASSIVE AND SILENT. MY FAVOURITE.
POOKY, ARE YOU CRYING?! OH, YOU'RE SO SWEET AND EMPATHETIC!
I'VE BEEN WONDERING WHO ANGIE'S DAD IS FOR A DECADE! THERE'S NOT EVEN A PICTURE OF HIS UGLY FRIGGIN' MUG, FOR SATAN'S SAKE!
IT'S NOT RIGHT!
OH, MY SWEET EMOTIONAL POOKY!

MOMMY, BUT, I DON'T UNDERSTAND! WHEN DID HE DIED? WHY DIDN'T YOU EVER LET ME GET TO KNOW HIM?!
A HEART ATTACK, JUST AROUND WHEN YOU LEFT ON YOUR HONEYMOON.
I NEVER WANTED TO INTRODUCE YOU TO HIM AFTER ALL THE PAIN AND HURT HE PUT ME THROUGH. IT WAS BETTER THIS WAY!
CALM DOWN, MOMMY!
IT WASN'T "BETTER"! I HAD THE RIGHT TO MEET MY FATHER!
WELL, IT'S TOO LATE NOW, ANGIE! NO ONE COULD HAVE PREDICTED IT WOULD TURN OUT THIS WAY! AND BELIEVE ME, IT'S FOR THE BEST THAT YOU REMAINED STRANGERS...
"HE MADE ME FALL IN LOVE WITH HIM, JUST SO HE COULD GET HIS TALONS ON MY MONEY! I WAS SO STUPID AND NAÏVE–WHEN I WOKE UP, WE BROKE UP, BUT WE ALREADY HAD TWO HATCHLINGS ON THE WAY--AND HE WANTED YOU BOTH FOR HIMSELF!
"AFTER ENDLESS LAWSUITS, I MANAGED TO KEEP YOU WITH ME, BUT HE GOT CUSTODY OF URIEL, AND ALWAYS KEPT ME FROM SEEING HIM.
"AND THEN AFTER ALL THAT TIME, URIEL AND I MET AT LAST, AND THERE WAS IMMEDIATE UNDERSTANDING BETWEEN US!"
BUT WITH ANGELINA, YOU'VE ALWAYS BEEN A "MUMMY DEAREST." WHY MAKE AN EXCEPTION FOR URIEL? SCARED OF MAKING THE SAME MISTAKES?
GUILT HAS EATEN ME ALIVE FOR THE LAST SIX MONTHS! ONCE I KNEW I WAS ABOUT TO BECOME A GRANDMOTHER, I KNEW IT WAS A SIGN.
Y-YES...

MOM...
I...I FELT BETRAYED, ANGELINA! FIRST YOUR FATHER, AND THEN YOU, WITH THAT LAVA-LICKING HELLSPAWN--ER, DEVIL!
I'M SORRY! I REALIZED I'LL NEVER BE ABLE TO CUT YOU OUT OF MY LIFE, EVEN IF I WANTED TO! PLEASE, FORGIVE ME! I JUST WANT TO BE WITH YOU AND URIEL!
I'M SORRY I NEVER INTRODUCED YOU TO YOUR FATHER AND NEVER TOLD YOU ABOUT YOUR BROTHER, PLEASE, PLEASE FORGIVE ME!
FOR SATAN'S SAKE, EITHER THIS IS UNHOLY WATER OR I'M ACTUALLY CRYING...
OHH...I FEEL... STRANGE...
I KNOW THIS WAS AN EMOTIONAL SCENE, BUT DON'T YOU THINK YOU'RE A LITTLE OLD FOR AN "ACCIDENT," ANGIE--?
AH...AAAH! IT HURTS!
IMBECILE! SHE'S IN LABOR!
B-BUT THERE'S STILL A WEEK...
DON'T WORRY, URIEL TO THE RESCUE! I'VE GOT A MAGNIFICENT FEATHER-RARI 2000--
DRIVE NOW, BOAST LATER, YOU RAW FUCKING CHICKEN!
VROOOOM

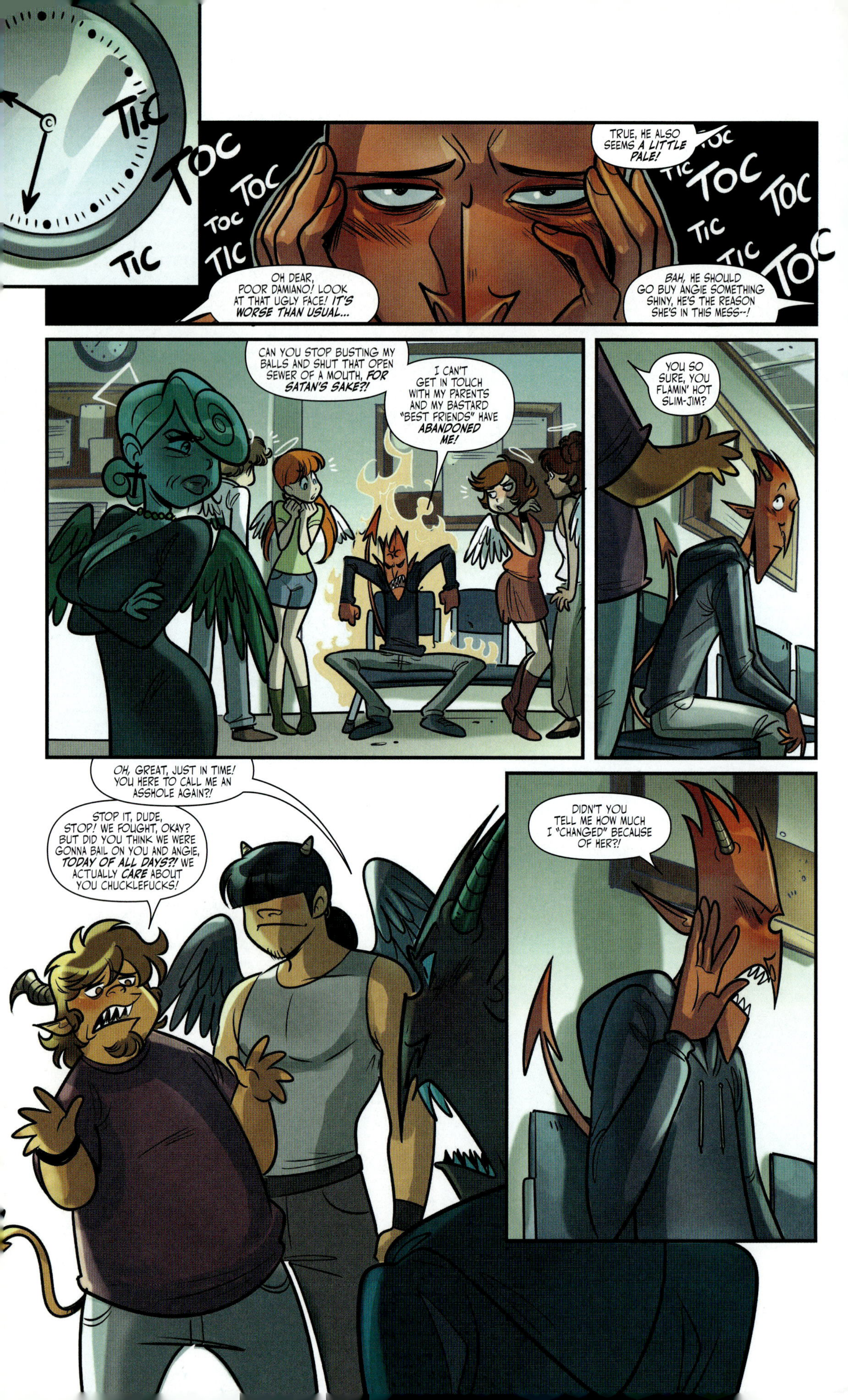
TIC
TOC
TIC
TOC
TOC
TIC
OH DEAR, POOR DAMIANO! LOOK AT THAT UGLY FACE! IT'S WORSE THAN USUAL...
TRUE, HE ALSO SEEMS A LITTLE PALE!
BAH, HE SHOULD GO BUY ANGIE SOMETHING SHINY, HE'S THE REASON SHE'S IN THIS MESS--!
CAN YOU STOP BUSTING MY BALLS AND SHUT THAT OPEN SEWER OF A MOUTH, FOR SATAN'S SAKE?!
I CAN'T GET IN TOUCH WITH MY PARENTS AND MY BASTARD "BEST FRIENDS" HAVE ABANDONED ME!
YOU SO SURE, YOU FLAMIN' HOT SLIM-JIM?
OH, GREAT, JUST IN TIME! YOU HERE TO CALL ME AN ASSHOLE AGAIN?!
STOP IT, DUDE, STOP! WE FOUGHT, OKAY? BUT DID YOU THINK WE WERE GONNA BAIL ON YOU AND ANGIE, TODAY OF ALL DAYS?! WE ACTUALLY CARE ABOUT YOU CHUCKLEFUCKS!
DIDN'T YOU TELL ME HOW MUCH I "CHANGED" BECAUSE OF HER?!

SINCE TODAY I S A SPECIAL DAY, I'M GONNA BE HONEST. YEAH, GRUGNO AND I WERE PISSED WHEN YOU LEFT. BUT WE UNDERSTAND.
WHO THE HELL DID WE THINK WE WERE FOOLING? THE BAND WAS A FAILURE, MAN! WE'RE NOT KIDS ANYMORE, AND IT'S TIME TO TURN THE PAGE. IT WAS JUST A STUPID IDLE-HANDED DEVILS' DAYDREAM...
THAT'S NOT TRUE! I ALWAYS BELIEVED IN IT--IT WASN'T JUST SOME DUMB FANTASY!
YOU DIDN'T SEEM TO THINK SO THEN...
PLEASE, GUIDA... I LOVED WHAT WE DID. I DON'T WANT TO THROW IT ALL AWAY. I WAS JUST... WELL, YOU DO KNOW THAT EVERYTHING IS ABOUT TO CHANGE?
WE KNOW!
BUT THAT DOESN'T MEAN I'M GONNA LEAVE "THE BREAKING BALLS"! IT'LL TAKE SOME TIME, ESPECIALLY WITH THE NEW BABY, BUT WE CAN STILL GO ON--TOGETHER!
AND WE'LL BECOME SO FUCKING FAMOUS! AND IF THAT DOESN'T HAPPEN, WELL--I STILL WANT TO TRY! WE DESERVE IT-- IT'S OUR DREAM!

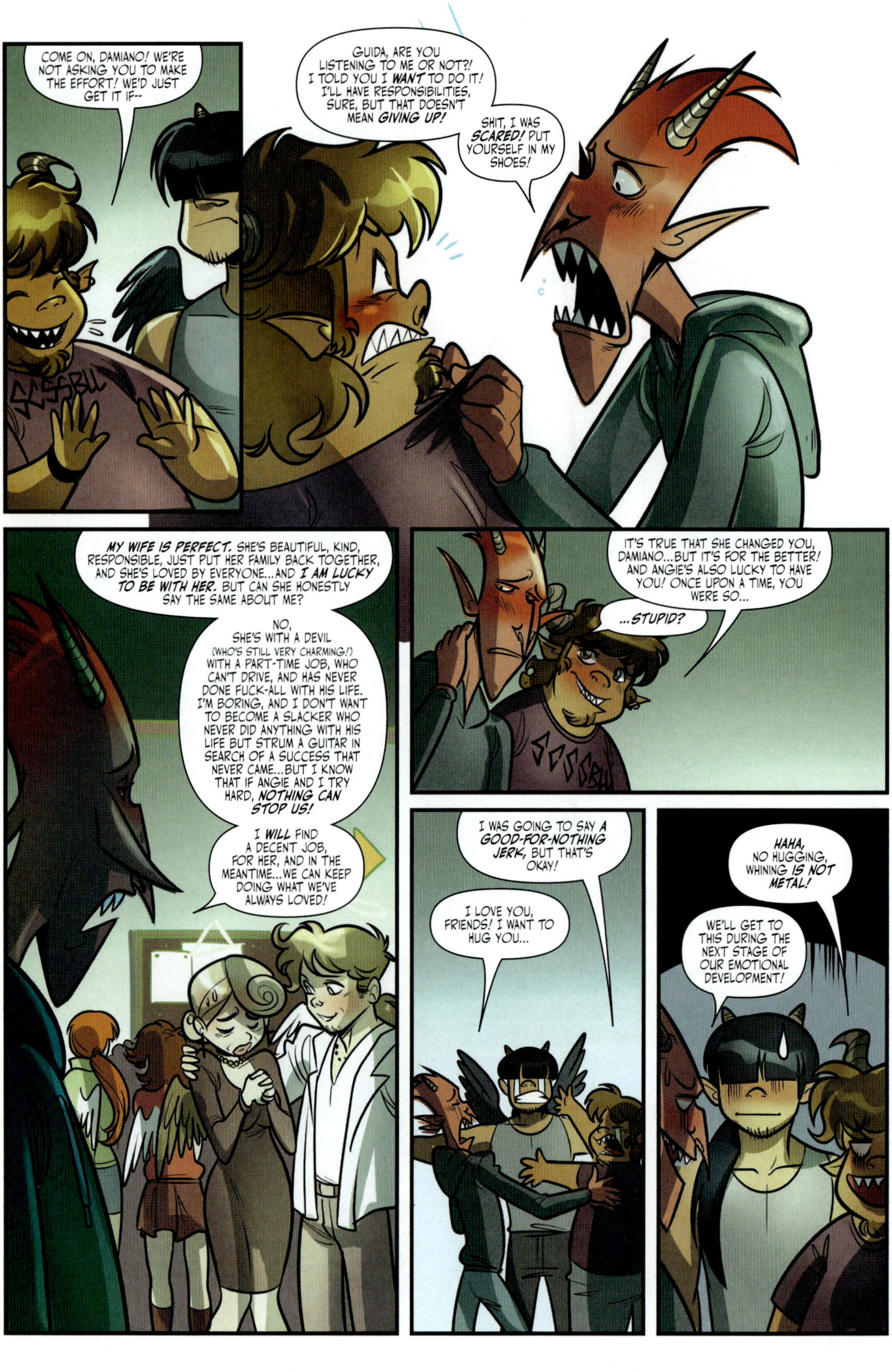
COME ON, DAMIANO! WE'RE NOT ASKING YOU TO MAKE THE EFFORT! WE'D JUST GET IT IF--
GUIDA, ARE YOU LISTENING TO ME OR NOT?! I TOLD YOU I WANT TO DO IT! I'LL HAVE RESPONSIBILITIES, SURE, BUT THAT DOESN'T MEAN GIVING UP!
SHIT, I WAS SCARED! PUT YOURSELF IN MY SHOES!
SCSSBU
MY WIFE IS PERFECT. SHE'S BEAUTIFUL, KIND, RESPONSIBLE, JUST PUT HER FAMILY BACK TOGETHER, AND SHE'S LOVED BY EVERYONE...AND I AM LUCKY TO BE WITH HER. BUT CAN SHE HONESTLY SAY THE SAME ABOUT ME?
NO, SHE'S WITH A DEVIL (WHO'S STILL VERY CHARMING!) WITH A PART-TIME JOB, WHO CAN'T DRIVE, AND HAS NEVER DONE FUCK-ALL WITH HIS LIFE. I'M BORING, AND I DON'T WANT TO BECOME A SLACKER WHO NEVER DID ANYTHING WITH HIS LIFE BUT STRUM A GUITAR IN SEARCH OF A SUCCESS THAT NEVER CAME...BUT I KNOW THAT IF ANGIE AND I TRY HARD, NOTHING CAN STOP US!
I WILL FIND A DECENT JOB, FOR HER, AND IN THE MEANTIME...WE CAN KEEP DOING WHAT WE'VE ALWAYS LOVED!
IT'S TRUE THAT SHE CHANGED YOU, DAMIANO...BUT IT'S FOR THE BETTER! AND ANGIE'S ALSO LUCKY TO HAVE YOU! ONCE UPON A TIME, YOU WERE SO...
...STUPID?
I WAS GOING TO SAY A GOOD-FOR-NOTHING JERK, BUT THAT'S OKAY!
I LOVE YOU, FRIENDS! I WANT TO HUG YOU...
HAHA, NO HUGGING, WHINING IS NOT METAL!
WE'LL GET TO THIS DURING THE NEXT STAGE OF OUR EMOTIONAL DEVELOPMENT!

WAIT, WAS THAT SMOKE?!
YO, DUDE-- I THINK IT'S YOUR DAD!
SCSSBU
WHAT ARE YOU DOING HERE?
ANGIE IS IN LABOR! WHERE WERE YOU AND MOM?! I COULDN'T GET EITHER ONE OF YOU ON THE PHONE!
HOW DID YOU KNOW TO COME?! AND WHY ARE YOU SMOKING IN A HOSPITAL?!
BUT THEY ARE ELECTRONIC! AND ANYWAY, I'VE MY GOOD REASONS!
AHH, LET'S PUT A CIGARETTE-- ER, PIN IN THAT, THERE'S SOMETHING YOUR MOTHER AND I WANTED TO TELL YOU--
THE LITTLE DEVIL IS FINALLY HERE!
HOORAY!
ER...EXCUSE ME, I WAS TALKING TO THE GENTLEDEVIL WITH THE BOW TIE AND THE BIG HORNS!
ER...I...
DAVIDE

COME... MEET YOUR BROTHER LUCIO, DAMIANO!
ZZZZ
BUT... HOWWHENWHAT? I DIDN'T NOTICE ANYTHING...MOM'S BELLY...
MY, ER, GENEROUS CURVES HID IT, AND WE DIDN'T WANT TO TELL YOU WHEN YOU WERE SO BUSY AND STRESSED ABOUT YOUR FRIENDS AND ANGIE--WE DIDN'T WANT TO BE A BURDEN!
OU'RE SO OL--ER, AGED LIKE FINE WINE!
HEY, WE'RE NOT OLD! AND IT WASN'T LIKE WE WERE TRYING!
AND WHO SUSPECTED YOUR FATHER WAS STILL FIRING LIVE ROUNDS! STILL, IF YOU PLAY THE LOTTO ENOUGH, SOONER OR LATER, YOU'RE GONNA HIT THE JACK-OFF-POT, AND THAT HORNY HOG POSITION DEFINITELY HELPED--
BLUARGH
BLUARGH
BUT IT'S WEIRD! THEY'LL HAVE A KID AND A GRANDKID THE SAME AGE!
WEIRDER THAN ME, WHO ACCIDENTALLY TRIED TO BANG HIS OWN SISTER?!
AHHH...IT SEEMS THAT OUR LIVES ARE WRITTEN BY AN UNSTABLE AND PERVERSE MIND...
HEY!
SIR...IT'S YOUR TURN NOW!
GABRIELE
...

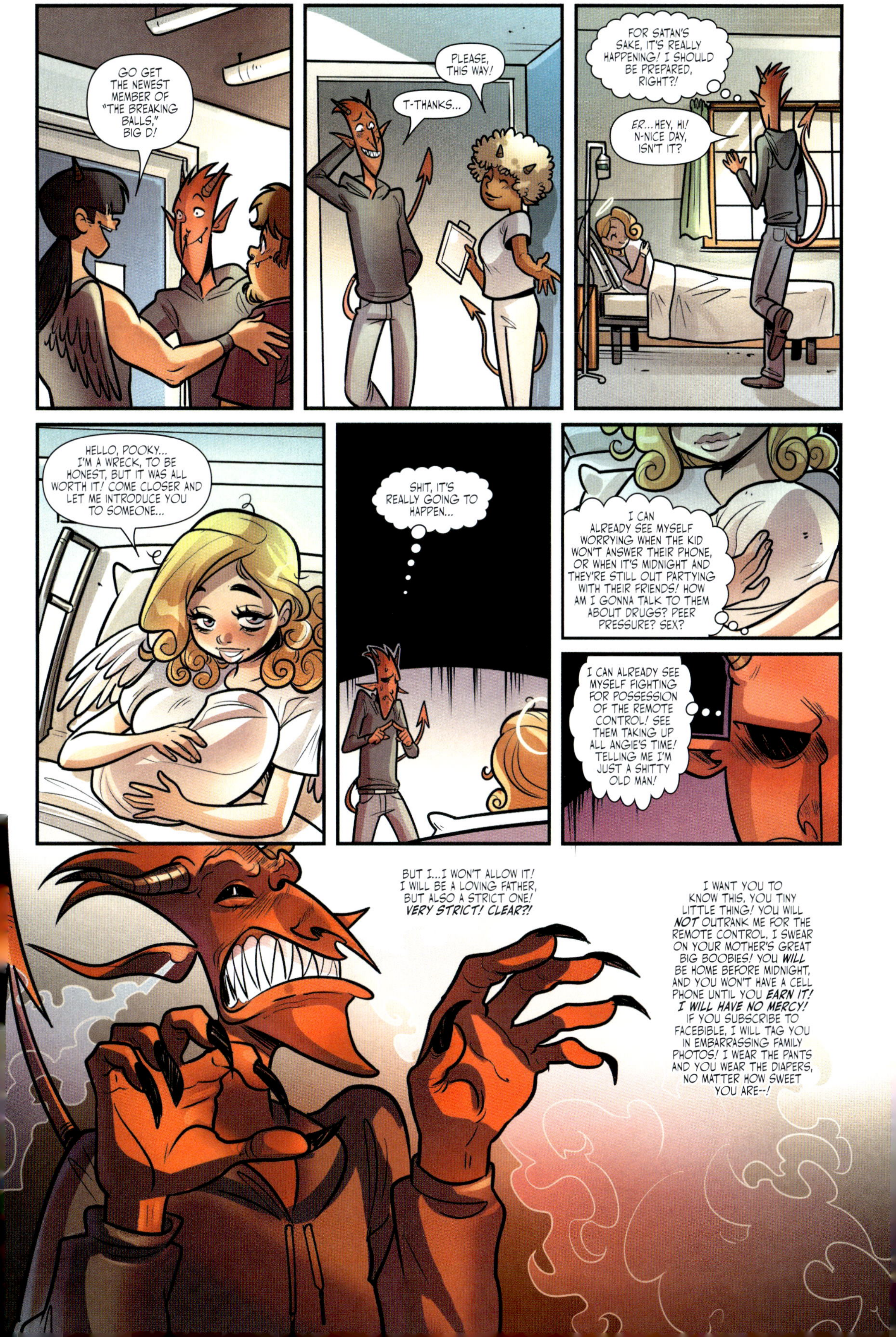
GO GET THE NEWEST MEMBER OF "THE BREAKING BALLS," BIG D!
PLEASE, THIS WAY!
T-THANKS...
FOR SATAN'S SAKE, IT'S REALLY HAPPENING! I SHOULD BE PREPARED, RIGHT?!
ER... HEY, HI! N-NICE DAY, ISN'T IT?
HELLO, POOKY... I'M A WRECK, TO BE HONEST, BUT IT WAS ALL WORTH IT! COME CLOSER AND LET ME INTRODUCE YOU TO SOMEONE...
SHIT, IT'S REALLY GOING TO HAPPEN...
I CAN ALREADY SEE MYSELF WORRYING WHEN THE KID WON'T ANSWER THEIR PHONE, OR WHEN IT'S MIDNIGHT AND THEY'RE STILL OUT PARTYING WITH THEIR FRIENDS! HOW AM I GONNA TALK TO THEM ABOUT DRUGS? PEER PRESSURE? SEX?
I CAN ALREADY SEE MYSELF FIGHTING FOR POSSESSION OF THE REMOTE CONTROL! SEE THEM TAKING UP ALL ANGIE'S TIME! TELLING ME I'M JUST A SHITTY OLD MAN!
BUT I...I WON'T ALLOW IT! I WILL BE A LOVING FATHER, BUT ALSO A STRICT ONE! VERY STRICT! CLEAR?!
I WANT YOU TO KNOW THIS, YOU TINY LITTLE THING! YOU WILL NOT OUTRANK ME FOR THE REMOTE CONTROL, I SWEAR ON YOUR MOTHER'S GREAT BIG BOOBIES! YOU WILL BE HOME BEFORE MIDNIGHT, AND YOU WON'T HAVE A CELL PHONE UNTIL YOU EARN IT! I WILL HAVE NO MERCY! IF YOU SUBSCRIBE TO FACEBIBLE, I WILL TAG YOU IN EMBARRASSING FAMILY PHOTOS! I WEAR THE PANTS AND YOU WEAR THE DIAPERS, NO MATTER HOW SWEET YOU ARE--!

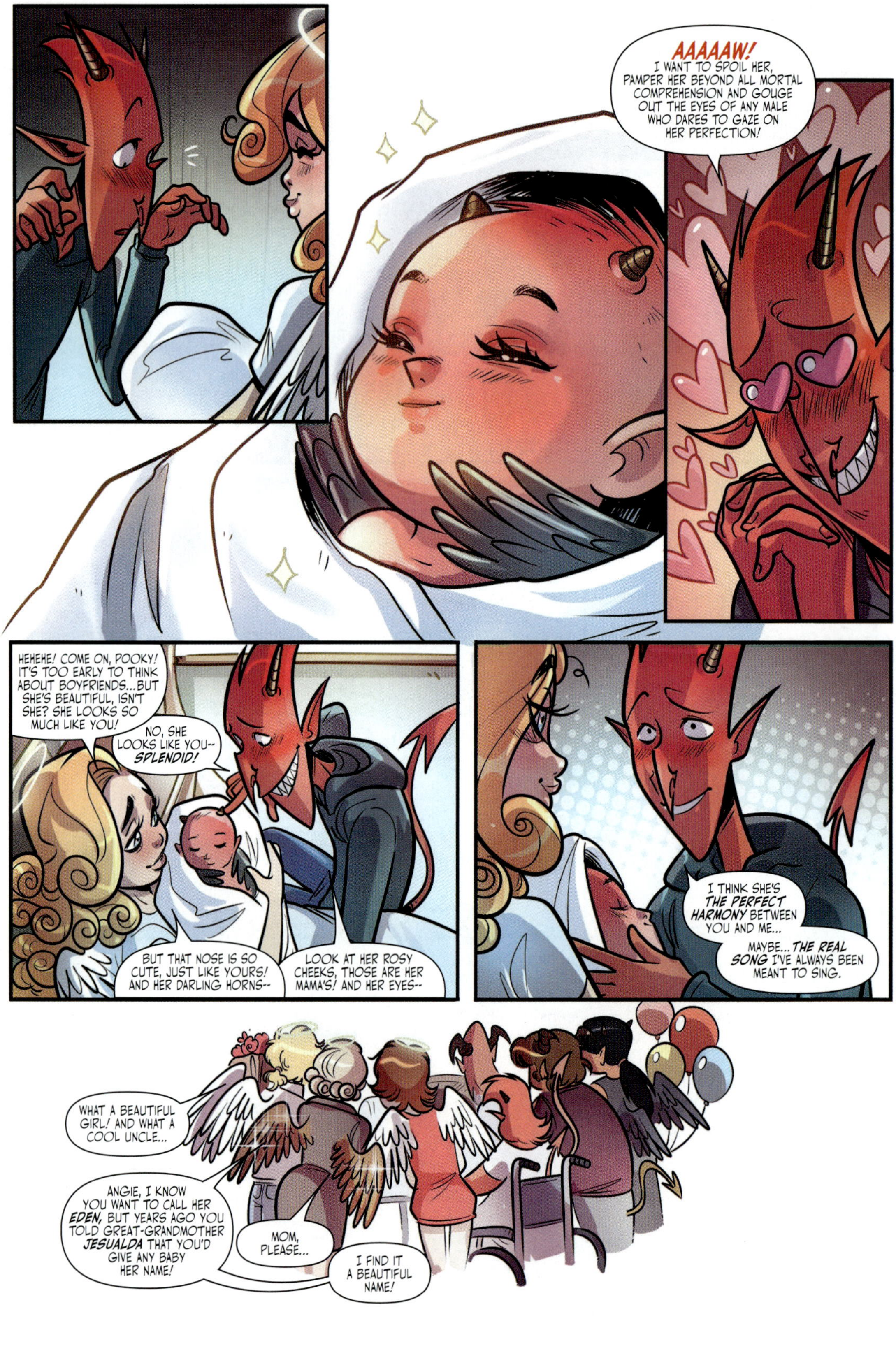
AAAAAW! I WANT TO SPOIL HER, PAMPER HER BEYOND ALL MORTAL COMPREHENSION AND GOUGE OUT THE EYES OF ANY MALE WHO DARES TO GAZE ON HER PERFECTION!
HEHEHE! COME ON, POOKY! IT'S TOO EARLY TO THINK ABOUT BOYFRIENDS...BUT SHE'S BEAUTIFUL, ISN'T SHE? SHE LOOKS SO MUCH LIKE YOU!
NO, SHE LOOKS LIKE YOU-- SPLENDID!
BUT THAT NOSE IS SO CUTE, JUST LIKE YOURS! AND HER DARLING HORNS--
LOOK AT HER ROSY CHEEKS, THOSE ARE HER MAMA'S! AND HER EYES--
I THINK SHE'S THE PERFECT HARMONY BETWEEN YOU AND ME...
MAYBE... THE REAL SONG I'VE ALWAYS BEEN MEANT TO SING.
WHAT A BEAUTIFUL GIRL! AND WHAT A COOL UNCLE...
ANGIE, I KNOW YOU WANT TO CALL HER EDEN, BUT YEARS AGO YOU TOLD GREAT-GRANDMOTHER JESUALDA THAT YOU'D GIVE ANY BABY HER NAME!
MOM, PLEASE...
I FIND IT A BEAUTIFUL NAME!

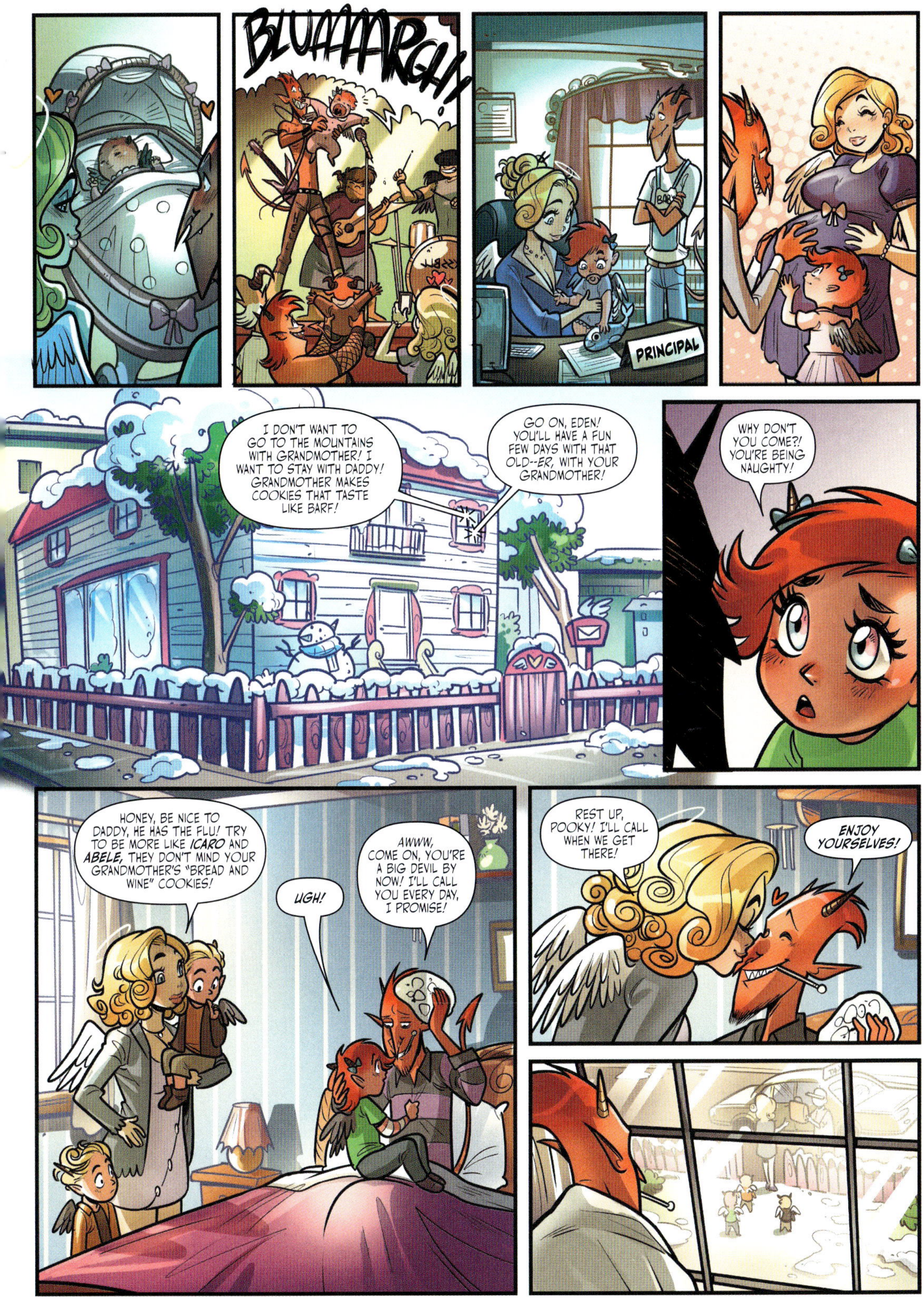
BLUAAARGH!!
PRINCIPAL
I DON'T WANT TO GO TO THE MOUNTAINS WITH GRANDMOTHER! I WANT TO STAY WITH DADDY! GRANDMOTHER MAKES COOKIES THAT TASTE LIKE BARF!
GO ON, EDEN! YOU'LL HAVE A FUN FEW DAYS WITH THAT OLD--ER, WITH YOUR GRANDMOTHER!
WHY DON'T YOU COME?! YOU'RE BEING NAUGHTY!
HONEY, BE NICE TO DADDY, HE HAS THE FLU! TRY TO BE MORE LIKE ICARO AND ABELE, THEY DON'T MIND YOUR GRANDMOTHER'S "BREAD AND WINE" COOKIES!
UGH!
AWWW, COME ON, YOU'RE A BIG DEVIL BY NOW! I'LL CALL YOU EVERY DAY, I PROMISE!
REST UP, POOKY! I'LL CALL WHEN WE GET THERE!
ENJOY YOURSELVES!

WHOO-HOO! THE SECRET "THERMOMETER IN HOT TEA" ALWAYS WORKS!
AND NOW, FOR A FEW DAYS WITHOUT TOYS, BOOGERS, SCREAMS, OR STRESS!
I CAN GAME UNTIL FOUR IN THE MORNING IF I WANT!
NO MORE LAUNDRY TO WASH FIVE TIMES A DAY!
NO MORE STUPID CARTOONS-- OKAY, SOME ACTUALLY AREN'T STUPID, SOME ARE PRETTY GREAT--
I WON'T HAVE TO BREAK MY BRAIN COMING UP WITH TEN NEW MAKE-BELIEVE STORIES A DAY!
...EVEN IF IT'S ACTUALLY A LOT OF FUN!
NO MORE FINGERS GLUED IN WHATEVER STICKY THINGS THE KIDS MAKE AT SCHOOL...
EVEN THOUGH THE VERY UGLIEST OF THEM MAKES MY WHOLE DAY...
NO MORE EXHAUSTION SO DEEP THAT ANGIE AND I CAN NEVER FIND SOME "US" TIME...
THOUGH SOMETIMES WE STILL GET LUCKY, HEHE...
PLIIIIN!
I'LL JUST HAVE A FEW... RELAXING... DAYS... YEAH...

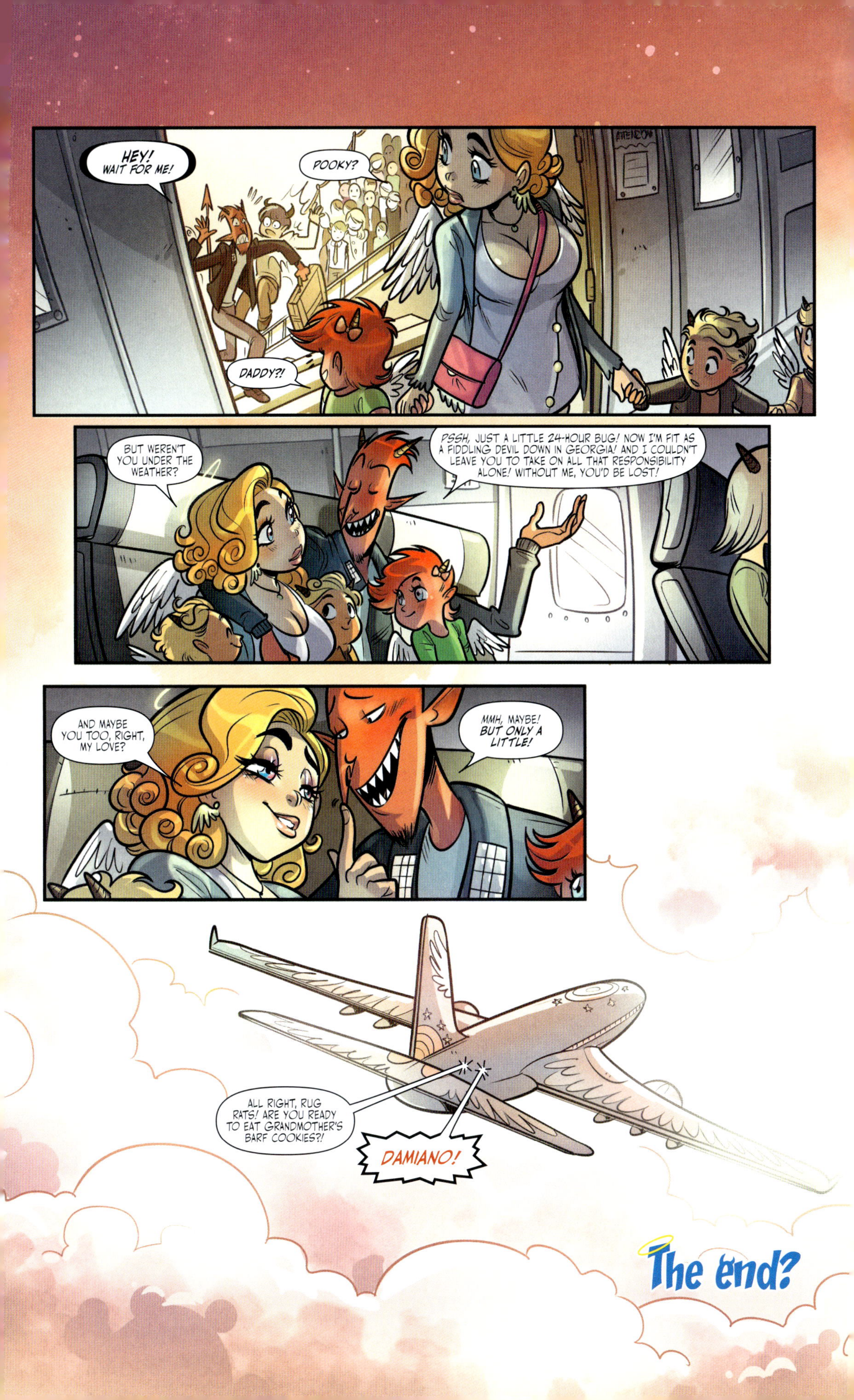
HEY! WAIT FOR ME!
POOKY?
DADDY?!
BUT WEREN'T YOU UNDER THE WEATHER?
PSSH, JUST A LITTLE 24-HOUR BUG! NOW I'M FIT AS A FIDDLING DEVIL DOWN IN GEORGIA! AND I COULDN'T LEAVE YOU TO TAKE ON ALL THAT RESPONSIBILITY ALONE! WITHOUT ME, YOU'D BE LOST!
AND MAYBE YOU TOO, RIGHT, MY LOVE?
MMH, MAYBE! BUT ONLY A LITTLE!
ALL RIGHT, RUG RATS! ARE YOU READY TO EAT GRANDMOTHER'S BARF COOKIES?!
DAMIANO!
The end?

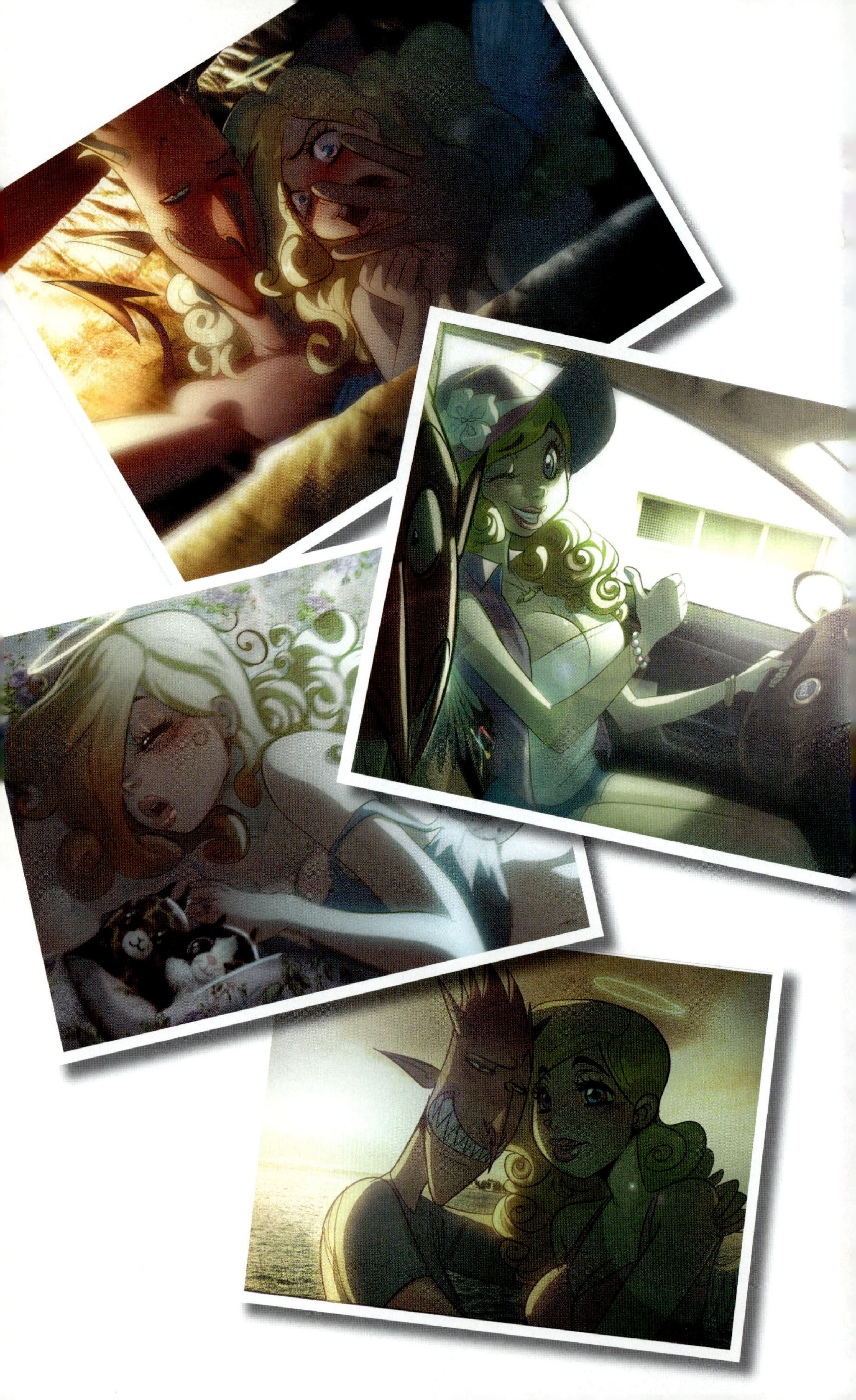

UHAAAAA!
OH, POOR EDEN... POOKY, DO YOU MIND...?
NOT AT ALL! YOU JUST TRY TO REST UP, YOU'VE BEEN THROUGH AN ORDEAL!
UHAAAAA!
UHAAAAA!
I-I CAN DO IT!
OH, GROSS!
UHAAAAA!
DO YOU WANT YOUR BOTTLE? YOUR PACIFIER? DO YOU NEED BURP'UMS?
UHAAAAA!
AHHHH...FINALLY, SHE'S SLEEPING!
ZZZ
UHAAAAA!
OH, POOR EDEN... POOKY, DO YOU MIND...?
?!
UHAAAAA!
UHAAAAA!
UHAAAAA,
ARGH!
AND SO, THE DEVIL'S PERSONAL CIRCLE OF HELL BEGAN.
AGAIN, AND AGAIN.

COVER GALLERY

ISSUE #1 MAIN COVER
BY MIRKA ANDOLFO

ISSUE #2 MAIN COVER
BY MIRKA ANDOLFO

ISSUE #3 MAIN COVER
BY MIRKA ANDOLFO

ISSUE #4 MAIN COVER
BY MIRKA ANDOLFO

ISSUE #5 MAIN COVER
BY MIRKA ANDOLFO

ISSUE #6 MAIN COVER
BY MIRKA ANDOLFO

ISSUE #7 MAIN COVER
BY MIRKA ANDOLFO

ISSUE #1 VARIANT
BY ELIAS CHATZOUDIS

ISSUE #1 VARIANT
BY LORENZO DE FELICI

ISSUE #1 SEXY B&W ANGELINA VARIANT
BY MIRKA ANDOLFO

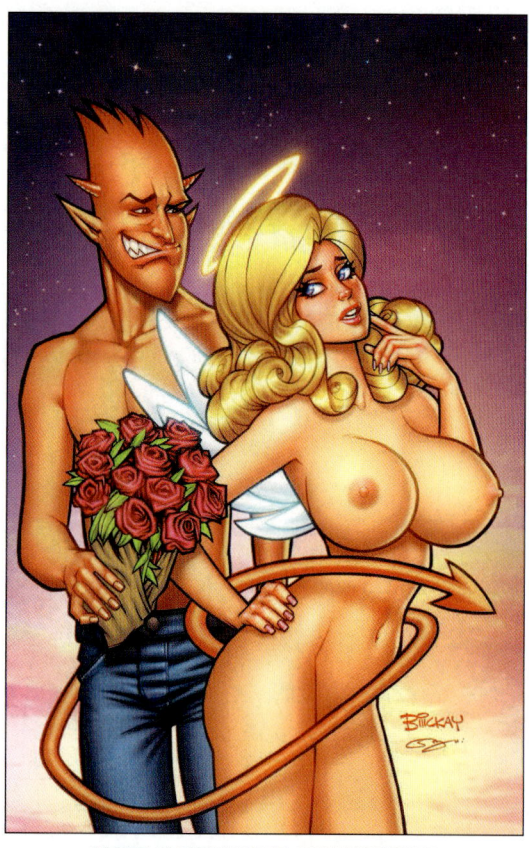

ISSUE #1 PRIMETIME COLLECTIBLES EXCLUSIVE VARIANT
BY BILL MCKAY

ISSUE #1 SAD LEMON COMICS EXCLUSIVE VARIANT
BY MIRKA ANDOLFO

ISSUE #1 SAD LEMON COMICS EXCLUSIVE VARIANT
BY LAURA BRAGA

ISSUE #1 UNKNOWN COMICS EXCLUSIVE VARIANT
BY RYAN KINCAID

ISSUE #1 RYAN KINCAID EXCLUSIVE VARIANT
BY RYAN KINCAID

ISSUE #1 ANNA ZHUO EXCLUSIVE VARIANT
BY ANNA ZHUO

ISSUE #1 COMIC KINGDOM OF CANADA EXCLUSIVE VARIANT
BY CARLA COHEN

ISSUE #1 PASTIME COMICS EXCLUSIVE VARIANT
BY SABINE RICH

ISSUE #2 VARIANT
BY LINDA LUKSIC SEJIC

ISSUE #2 VARIANT
BY SABINE RICH

ISSUE #2 VARIANT
BY MIRKA ANDOLFO

**ISSUE #2 COMIC KINGDOM OF CANADA
EXCLUSIVE VARIANT**
BY CARLA COHEN

ISSUE #3 VARIANT
BY EJIKURE

ISSUE #3 VARIANT
BY ALESSANDRO VITTI

ISSUE #3 GUSTAV KLIMT HOMAGE VARIANT
BY MIRKA ANDOLFO

ISSUE #4 VARIANT
BY ELIAS CHATZOUDIS

ISSUE #4 VARIANT
BY JON LAM

**ISSUE #4 "LOCANDINA" HOMAGE—
MOVIE POSTER VARIANT**
BY MIRKA ANDOLFO

ISSUE #5 VARIANT
BY STEVE MORRIS

ISSUE #5 VARIANT
BY JON LAM

ISSUE #5 CAT ANGELINA
PURRRR-FECT VARIANT
BY MIRKA ANDOLFO

ISSUE #6 VARIANT
BY CIRO CANGIALOSI

ISSUE #6 VARIANT
BY GABRIELE BAGNOLI

ISSUE #7 ANGELINA & DAMIANO IN LOVE VARIANT
BY MIRKA ANDOLFO

ISSUE #7 PENCIL SKETCH VARIANT W/ DAMIANO, ANGELINA & CHILD VARIANT
BY MIRKA ANDOLFO

SKETCHBOOK

·BY MIRKA ANDOLFO·

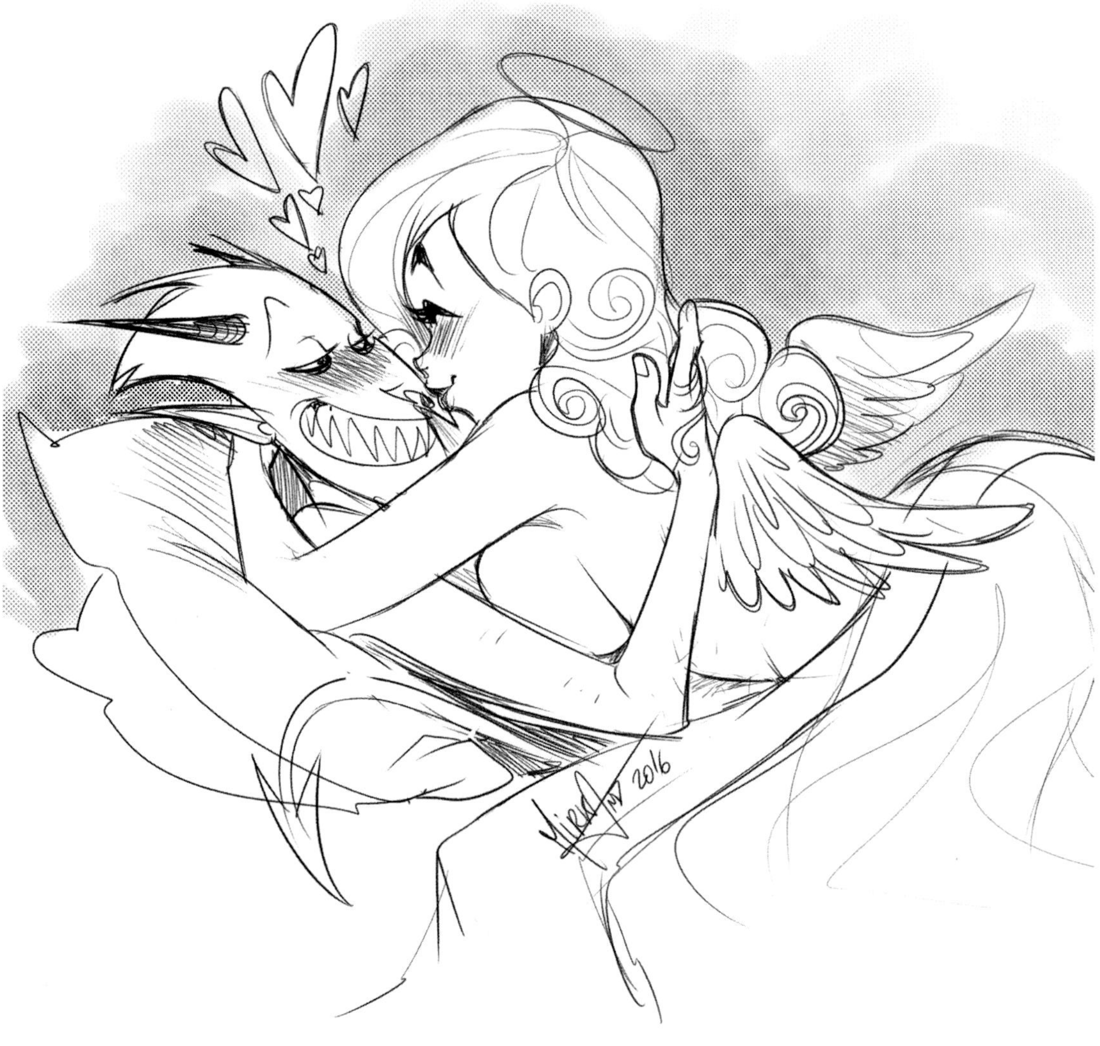

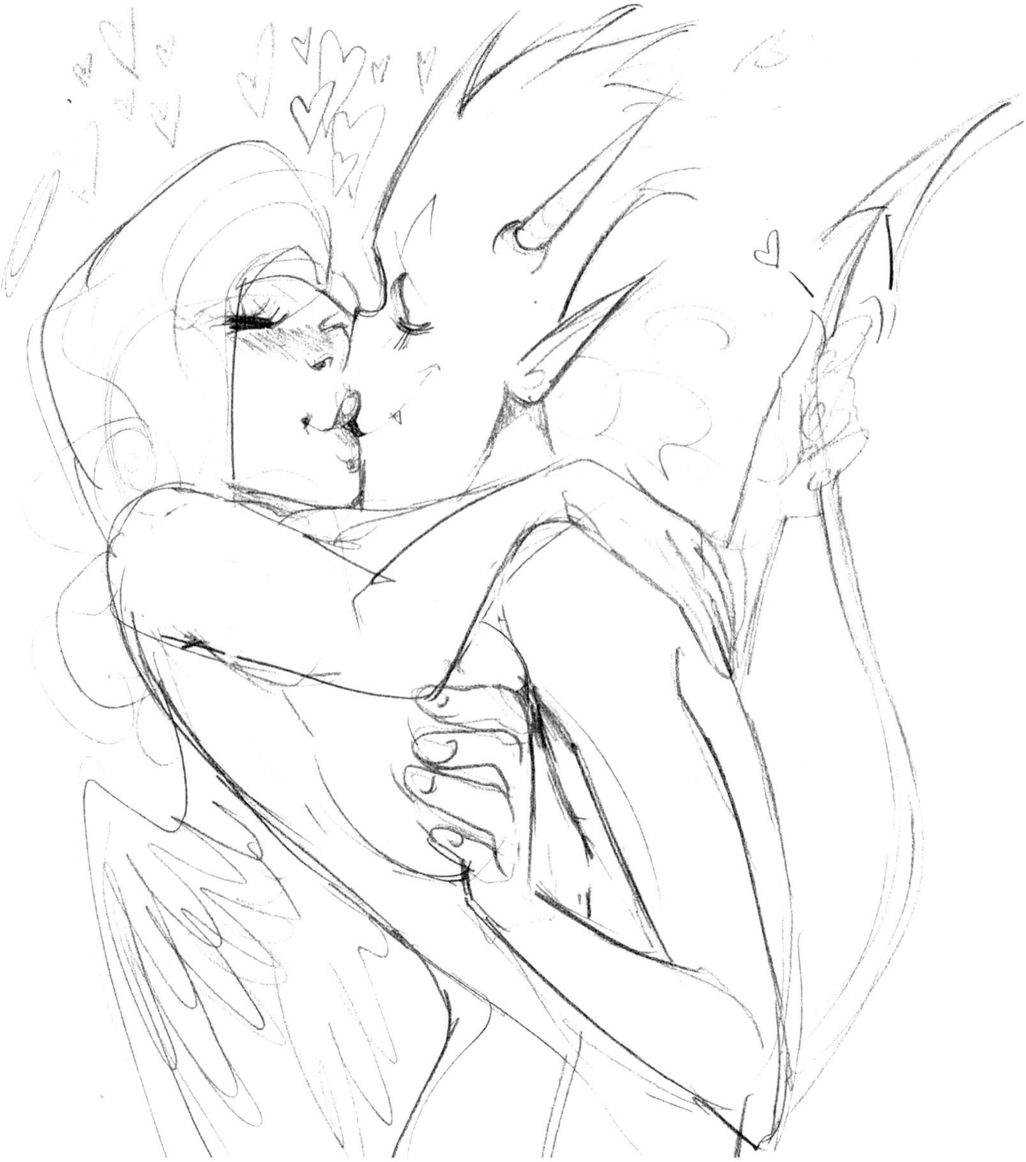

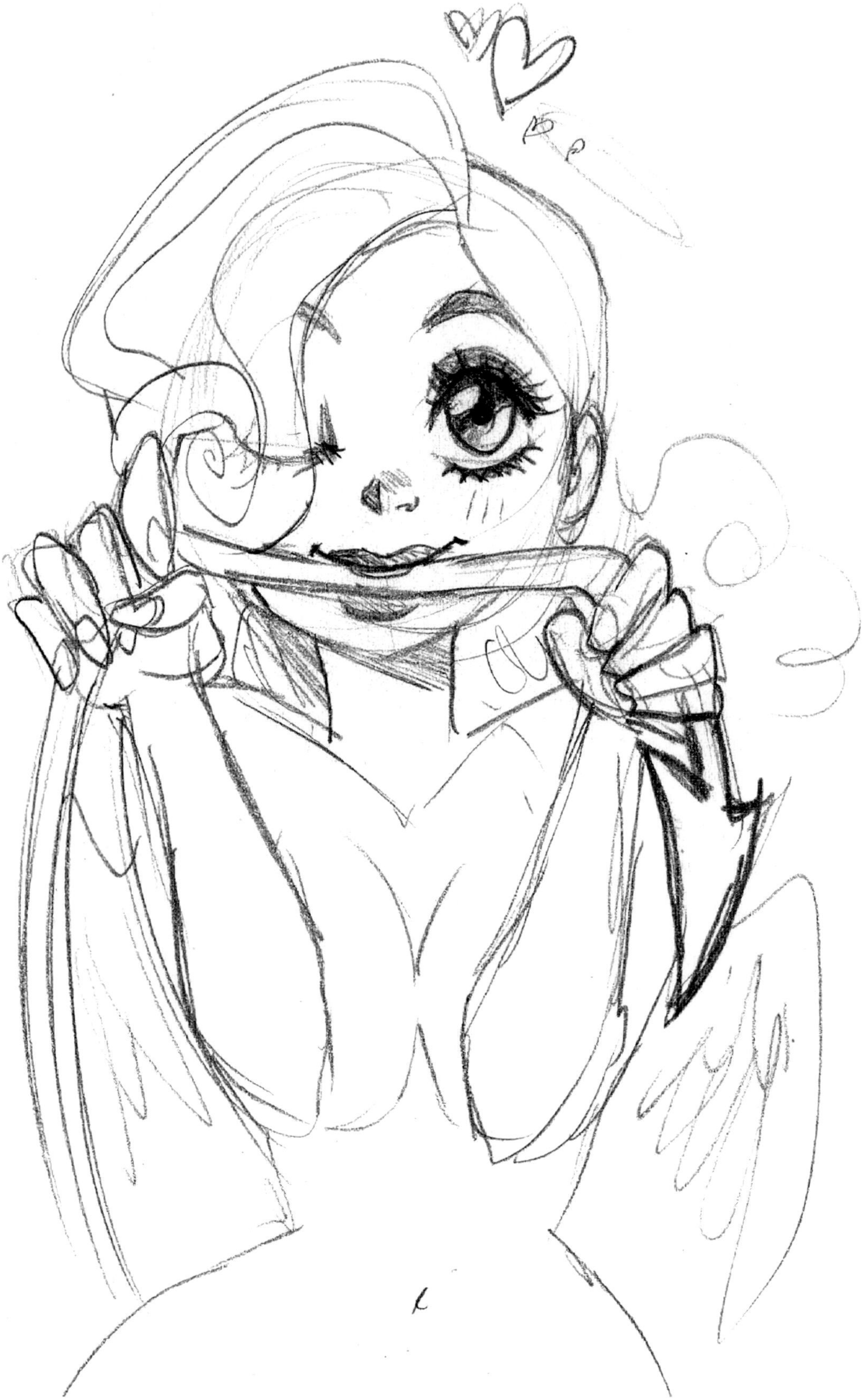

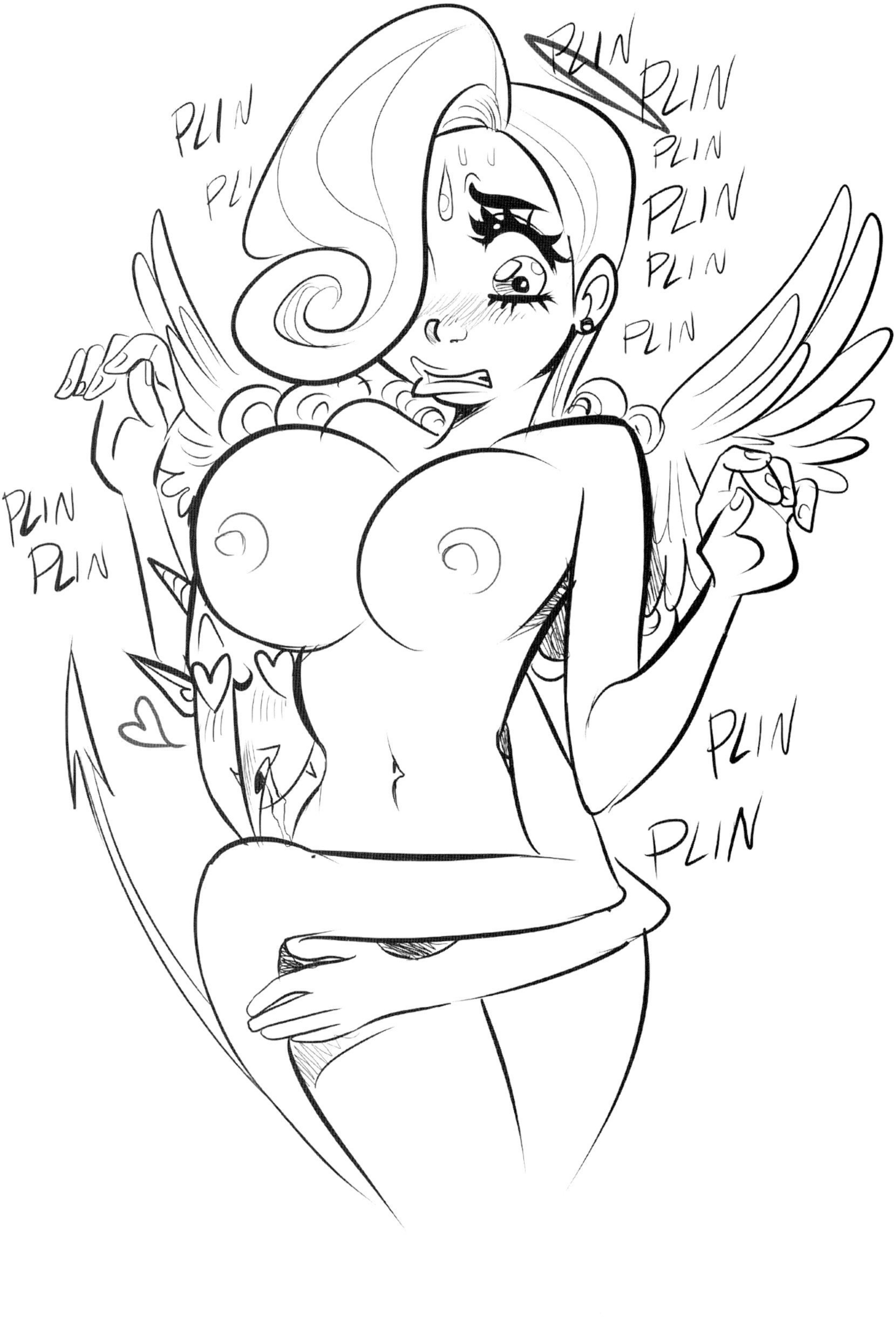
PLIN
PLIN
PLIN
PLIN
PLIN
PLIN
PLIN
PLIN
PLIN
PLIN
PLIN
PLIN

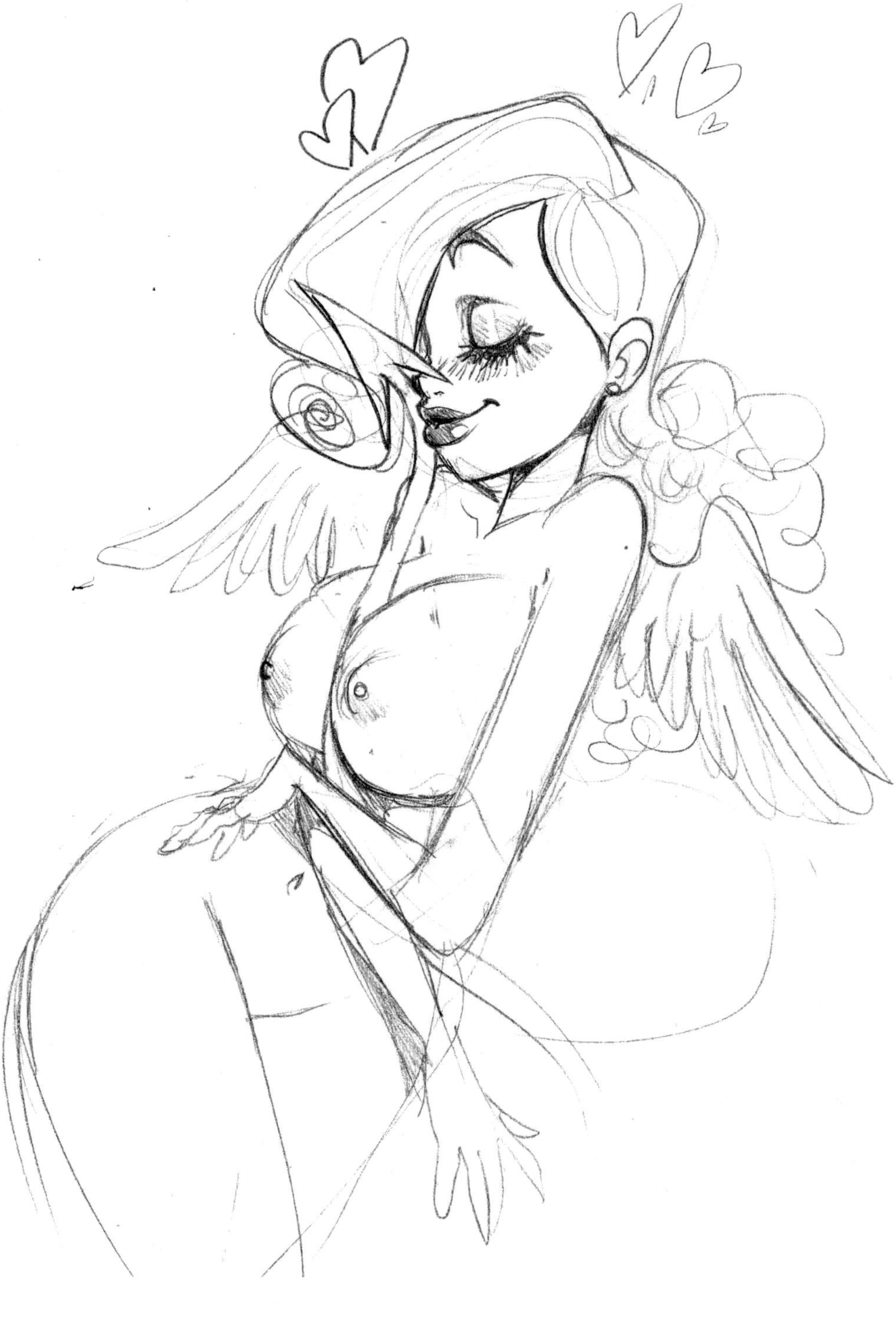

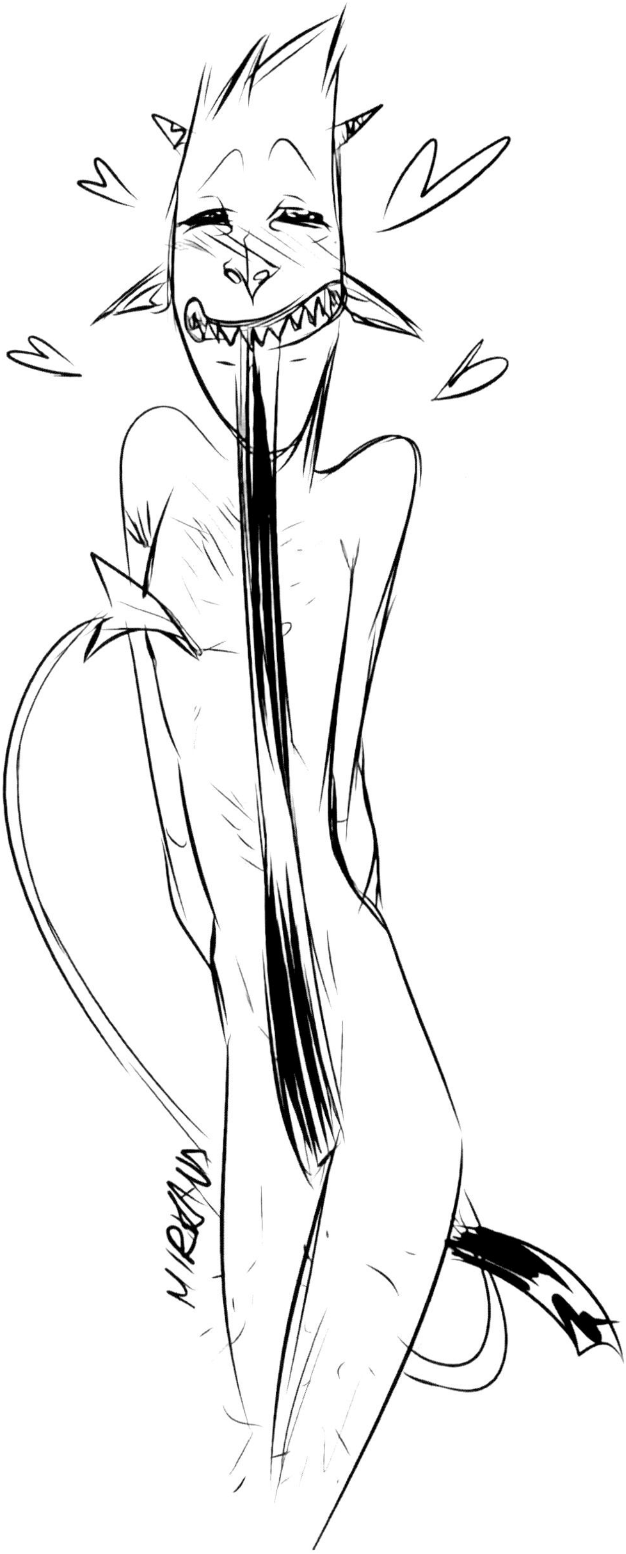

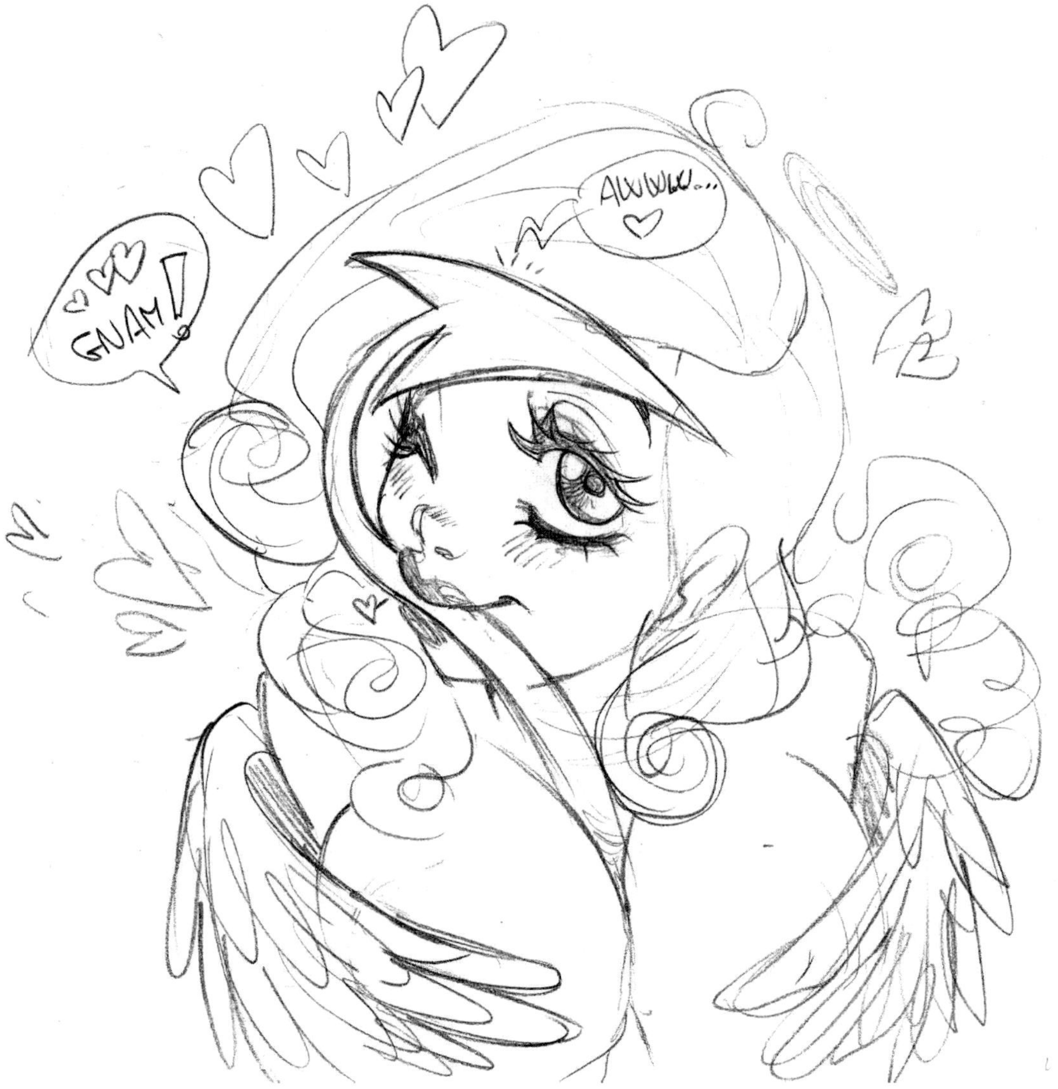
GNAM!
AWWW...